STAY

Allie Larkin

DUTTON

DUTTON
Published by Penguin Group (USA) Inc.
375 Hudson Street, New York, New York 10014, U.S.A.
Penguin Group (Canada), 90 Eglinton Avenue East, Suite 700, Toronto, Ontario M4P 2Y3, Canada (a division of Pearson Penguin Canada Inc.); Penguin Books Ltd, 80 Strand, London WC2R 0RL, England; Penguin Ireland, 25 St Stephen's Green, Dublin 2, Ireland (a division of Penguin Books Ltd); Penguin Group (Australia), 250 Camberwell Road, Camberwell, Victoria 3124, Australia (a division of Pearson Australia Group Pty Ltd); Penguin Books India Pvt Ltd, 11 Community Centre, Panchsheel Park, New Delhi–110 017, India; Penguin Group (NZ), 67 Apollo Drive, Rosedale, North Shore 0632, New Zealand (a division of Pearson New Zealand Ltd); Penguin Books (South Africa) (Pty) Ltd, 24 Sturdee Avenue, Rosebank, Johannesburg 2196, South Africa

Penguin Books Ltd, Registered Offices: 80 Strand, London WC2R 0RL, England

Published by Dutton, a member of Penguin Group (USA) Inc.

First printing, June 2010
10 9 8 7 6 5 4 3 2 1

LIBRARY OF CONGRESS CATALOGING-IN-PUBLICATION DATA

Larkin, Allie.
Stay/Allie Larkin.
p. cm.
ISBN 978-0-525-95171-1 (hardcover)
1. Young women—Fiction. 2. Separation (Psychology)—Fiction. 3. German shepherd dog—Fiction. 4. Human-animal relationships—Fiction. I. Title.
PS3612.A6485S73 2010
813'.6—dc22 2009041437

Printed in the United States of America
Set in Goudy Old Style
Designed by Eve L. Kirch

For Jeremy, Joan, and Argo.
I couldn't have done this without you.

Stay

Prologue

Six years ago, Peter and I were having one of our weekly dinners at this little Italian restaurant just off campus. The food wasn't good and the service was awful, but they served us without asking for ID if we ordered by the bottle instead of the glass.

We were halfway through our second bottle, because, hell, we'd walked, finals were over, and it was all on his dad's credit card.

We talked and laughed and the room got hot. Pete's face was flushed and his hair was messy because he kept running his hands through it. "So, I think I got at least an A-minus in Poly Sci. Maybe an A," he said, his hair falling back into his eyes again. He rambled on and on about his estimated grades for each course, and how they all fit into the greater plan of his law school application, even though we'd only just finished our freshman year. Peter liked to have every detail of his life planned out well in advance.

I wanted to absorb his every word, but I was too busy studying the angle of his perfect square jaw and thinking about what it would feel like to press my lips against his slightly stubbly chin and work my way down his neck. I thought about his hands, strong from years of tennis, and how they'd feel against my bare back after he'd ripped my clothes off.

"How do you think you did on the Rhetoric final?" Peter said, interrupting my pornographic daydream before I could even get to the part where he knocked our plates off the table and took me right there in the middle of the restaurant.

"Okay," I said, avoiding eye contact, like if I looked into his eyes he would somehow know what I'd been thinking. "It wasn't too— It was fine."

"I was expecting worse," Peter said, nodding, before he launched into a full description of his summer internship at his dad's firm, and I went back to thinking about hands and chins and mouths and that perfect, perfect jaw.

We finished our meal; we both ordered dessert and ate off each other's plates until there wasn't a crumb left. The other customers were long gone and the waitress kept clearing things off our table to get us to go. Even the sugar packets were gone. All we had left was our bottle and the glasses on the white tablecloth we'd splattered with wine and red sauce.

"I always have such a great time with you," Peter said, splitting the rest of the wine between our glasses.

"I am a hell of a lot of fun," I deadpanned, finally getting the courage to look him in the eye again.

"I'd like to propose something, Van," he said, raising his glass and pulling his chin in to his chest in an attempt to look formal.

My heart thumped a loose drunken beat. I raised my glass. My hand wobbled.

He smiled wide. His bottom lip was stained purple from the wine, but his teeth were as perfect as Chiclets. "Will you marry me," he asked, clinking his glass against mine, "if we're not married by the time we're thirty?"

My pulse spiked as elation crashed into the insult of being his backup plan. From fiancée to consolation prize in a matter of seconds.

"Make it thirty-two," I said, clenching my teeth into a smile. "At least give me a fighting chance."

Chapter One

The wedding was more than I ever could have wished for. The church was dark and simple. White candles in glass sconces lined the gray stone walls, and a gigantic candelabra cast a golden glow on the altar. The pews were trimmed with sprigs of bittersweet and branches of Chinese lantern plant tied with brown and orange gauzy ribbons.

The wedding was perfect, except for two things. The satin bridesmaids' gowns that were ordered in deep, rich cinnamon showed up two days before the wedding and were bright Halloween pumpkin. And instead of standing across from the groom, beaming, I was standing across from his first cousin, Norman, smiling a hollow smile like a jack-o'-lantern.

That, and I probably wouldn't have gone with *brown* roses. I tried to talk Janie out of them.

"Brown is the color of dead flowers, Janie."

"But they don't look like dead flowers, Van. They're elegant."

It was a lost cause. *Martha Stewart Weddings* had a spread of fall bouquets, and Janie's mom made a ton of trips out to Connecticut to exactly the same florist to have exactly the same bouquets made for Janie's wedding.

Out of the corner of my eye I saw Janie's cousin Libby standing next to me, dabbing at her eyes with a lace-trimmed handkerchief. Not only did she have the teary smile down, but she somehow managed to look fabulous in bright orange. I couldn't see Bethany, Janie's college friend, from where I was standing, but I was sure she was crying appropriately as well. She seemed like the type. At least she looked awful in her dress too.

I spent the whole ceremony with my hands wrapped around my bouquet of bittersweet and Janie's brown roses, digging my nails through my orange satin gloves into the back of my other hand.

I missed the part about anyone having any reasons as to why these two blah blah blah blah blah . . . I missed the "I do's" and all that crap. I just stood there and concentrated on pressing hard enough to feel pain through two layers of thick satin.

I tried not to look at Peter, in his slate gray tuxedo and shiny shoes, as perfect as the porcelain groom Janie ordered for the top of their wedding cake. And I tried not to look at Janie, glowing in the reflection of candlelight sparkling off of the crystals hand-sewn along the neckline of her dress. I stared at the brown roses and tried to make it look like I was solemnly meditating on the meaning of marriage and the serious commitment being made before my very eyes.

Then they were kissing and the whole deal was done. Janie pressed her hand against Peter's chest to keep him from kissing her too long or too hard or in a way that might be inappropriate for the photographer to capture. I would have held him as close as I could for as long as I could, but I tried not to let myself think about it. I put the jack-o'-lantern smile back on my face and handed Janie her brown flowers.

Norman and I followed them down the aisle, my hand positioned just above the crook of his elbow the way Vanessa, the wedding planner, showed me. We walked in "step-pause" time. Norman reached across with his other arm and put his hand over mine. I kicked him in his calf during the pause part of our procession walk, and hissed, "Don't get ideas, Normy," through my smile. He dropped his hand back to his side.

At the reception at the Kittle House, Norman rambled through a long and painful toast that started with how he and Peter used to think girls had cooties and ended with a diatribe about his divorce and how he couldn't have gotten through it without Peter. We raised our glasses of champagne before switching over to spiced wine for the traditional Thanksgiving feast, spread out across the tables like a picture of gluttony from the time of kings and knights.

I was thankful that Janie's father decided it was tacky for the maid of honor to toast the couple. This was a rule he probably made once he realized I was going to be Janie's maid of honor, no matter what he had to say about it. Charles Driscoll hated me ever since I taught Janie the f-bomb in fourth grade. Janie got sent home from school for saying it in front of her teacher, leaving a permanent mark on her pristine school record.

Charles will always blame me for Janie not getting into Harvard and having to go to Brown instead. He will forever be convinced that the f-bomb blemish on Janie's permanent grade school record had kept her out. In reality, she stuffed her application in my book bag instead of the mailbox. Every time I see him now, I want to scream, "It's not because I taught your daughter to say *fuck*, it's because she didn't want to go to Harvard, you dumb ass!" but in honor of the wedding, I resigned myself to, "Mr. Driscoll, you must be so proud."

After the first course, Peter stood up to say a few words about his lovely bride and the joyous occasion. He described Janie as *angelic*. He kept calling her Jane. He used the word *joyous* more than once, and quite frankly, it was overkill.

Just when I thought he was finally done, he said, "I also want to thank Savannah Leone for being such a wonderful friend to me and my wife." He laughed softly and looked into his champagne flute. "Wow, my wife. It's so strange and amazing to say that word." He reached over and kissed Janie on the cheek. The wedding photographer had a field day. "Anyway," Peter continued, "as I was saying, Van is the real deal. She's a true friend, and

I would have stolen her for my best man, if Jane had let me—no offense, Normy—but I think Van would look far more stunning in that tux, don't you?" He laughed again and waited for the crowd to laugh too. "The truth is, if it weren't for Van, Jane and I never would have met. So if we're going to raise our glasses to toast to this union, let's also raise our glasses to Van for starting it all."

The room filled with clinks and the murmur of three hundred of their closest friends saying, "Cheers." Janie clinked her glass against Peter's and then turned to tap mine, but hugged me instead. "I love you," she whispered into my ear. "I don't know what I'd do without you." Her ribs pulsed against mine and her breath quickened.

"I love you too, but nobody likes a weepy bride," I said, pulling away, trying my best to smile. "Pull yourself together, lady!" I picked up my napkin. "Look up." Janie looked to the ceiling and I used a corner of the white linen to soak up a tear that was balanced on her lashes before it could make a mess of her makeup. "We can be sappy another day."

I wished I could vanish, just melt into the floor, leaving behind nothing but a puddle of orange satin and shoes dyed to match.

When Janie and Pete got up to get ready for their first dance, I started seriously contemplating hiding in the coat closet with a bottle of champagne and an armload of Jordan almonds wrapped up in that stupid white netting. I was supposed to be happy for them. I was supposed to be cheering them on. That's what it means to be a maid of honor—it's about being eternally excited and supportive for every single little second of the wedding, and I couldn't even bear to watch them dance.

"Well, Vannie, I haven't seen you in ages." Peter's aunt Agnes sat down next to me. She never had her own children, and as far as she was concerned, the sun rose and set around Peter. Peter worshiped her, but I called her Aunt Agony. She took us out to dinner a few times up at school, but a good meal was never worth listening to her talk. "We have to catch up. Tell me everything about everything, dear."

"First dance." I pointed to the dance floor as Peter and Janie walked toward each other and met in the middle. "I'd better go. Maid of honor."

I gave her a big closed-mouth smile and got up to stand at the edge of the dance floor. I wasn't sure which form of torture was worse.

While I stood with the crowd, watching the happy couple dance to "The Way You Look Tonight," Diane Driscoll came over and put her arm around my waist. She leaned against me and rested her head on my shoulder.

"We did a good job with our little girl, don't you think, Vannie?" she said.

I didn't know if she meant tonight, or in general. And I couldn't tell if I was included in the "we" or if she just meant her and Charles.

But then she said, "I wish Natalie could see this," and I knew the "we" meant her and my mom. "You know, you look just like she did the first time I met her," she said, and lifted her head to kiss my cheek. She put her head back on my shoulder, and I felt her tears run down my arm while we watched Janie and Peter finish their dance with the complicated turn Vanessa taught them.

She wiped at her eyes quickly and turned toward me, grabbing both my arms. "You're coming back to stay at the house tonight, right?" she said. "I set up the carriage house with junk food and movies. I thought we could celebrate like old times."

My mom and I used to live in the Driscolls' carriage house, which was two hundred and eighty-two steps from the front door of the main house (Janie and I counted the summer before we started fourth grade) on their sprawling property in Chappaqua. It was weird to think of Diane commandeering it for her own celebration. Even though it was technically her carriage house, I always thought of it as mine and my mom's.

You can't substitute me for my mom, I wanted to tell Diane. But I didn't. "I have to go back up to Rochester tonight," I said. "I've got a big grant due next week, and I didn't bring my laptop."

"Oh no you don't. No one works on Thanksgiving weekend, Savannah Leone. Not even you." She patted my arm, and then squinted up her eyes like she was staring into the sun. "That dress is unfortunate," she said, grabbing a handful of the skirt of my satin dress and letting it fall again. "I can't believe those idiots at the bridal store got the color so wrong! Why would there even be an option for bright orange? Who would choose this on purpose?"

"It's not that bad," I said, trying to downplay the error. We'd already been through hours of dress drama prior to the ceremony. Diane was livid. Phone calls were made, threats were screamed. There were tears. There was cursing. And none of it made the dresses any less orange.

Diane let out a disgusted sigh and shook her head. "You look like a pumpkin, dear," she said, flatly. Then she kissed me on the cheek. "I'll see you back at the carriage house. We'll have fun." She gave me a broad smile and a nod like it was decided, and ran off to hug Janie.

I missed the way Diane's eyes used to crinkle at the sides when she smiled. My mom nursed her through her face-lift and a few months later Diane nursed my mom through all the chemo.

I stood there, watching Diane brush a curl of hair off of Janie's cheek. I wished for a way to clean out my head so I could just be happy for Janie instead of thinking about Peter, or about how even if I did get over Peter and found someone else to fall in love with, my mother would never be there to fix my hair at my wedding.

I felt a cold hand on my shoulder.

"Van?" Peter said. "I need a favor."

I turned around and looked at him. His tie was loose and the top button of his shirt was undone. His cheeks and his nose were flushed bright red, and I couldn't help but wonder what it would feel like to have all that breathless excitement be about me instead of Janie.

"Sure," I said, trying not to make eye contact. I was certain that looking into Peter's blue-gray eyes would break my heart.

"I know you're enjoying the wedding, but . . ." He stopped and looked at Norman, who was slumped over the bar getting yelled at by the woman bartending. "Norman was supposed to go over and set up the room. But he's not—" He tilted his head in Norm's direction and raised his eyebrows. "Can you?"

"No problem," I said, hoping the relief at having an excuse to leave wasn't oozing down my face.

"You're the best, Van." He grinned from ear to ear and slapped my back like we were locker room buddies. "I don't know what I'd do without you." He handed me a set of keys attached to a silver Playboy bunny with a diamond eye. "Norman's car," he said, rolling his eyes. "The box is on the front seat. It should be self-explanatory." He hugged me and rested his chin on my bare shoulder for a second. "You're okay to drive, right?" His breath was hot. He pulled away to give me a good look, like he was making sure.

"Okay," I said, staring at his shiny new platinum wedding band.

"Thanks, Van. I owe you one." He gave me a quick peck on the cheek before running off. I felt the pressure of his lips on my face even after he'd disappeared into the crowd.

Janie and her dad had just started dancing to "Thank Heaven for Little Girls." Creepy. I took it as my cue to go. I ducked into the coatroom to grab the brown faux fur wrap Janie gave me as a bridesmaid's gift, and made my escape to the parking lot.

I walked around the lot, clicking the door opener until the lights on a silver BMW lit up. The license plate read LADEZMAN.

When I put the key in the ignition, Michael Bolton blared from the speakers. I took out the CD and threw it on the backseat. Flipping through the CDs in the console, I found Boston. I slid it into the CD player and backed out of the parking space to the opening chords of "More Than a Feeling."

My mom and I were closet Boston fans. We kept all of our Boston records under her sweaters on the top shelf of her closet and listened to them only when we knew there was no chance of anyone coming over.

I tore down the gravel road away from the Kittle House and made the tires squeal when I turned onto paved road. Normy's car hugged the turns of the Saw Mill River Parkway as I made it from Chappaqua to Tarrytown in record time.

I drove down to Westchester early, and Janie and I spent the two nights before the wedding in the bridal suite at a hotel called the Castle on the

Hudson in Tarrytown. It was awful. I had to sit next to her in the spa getting my nails painted some color called Raisin Sunset, listening to her go on and on about every little detail, and every last thing she and Peter had said to each other about the wedding. I tried my best to act like the friend I was supposed to be. Thankfully, Janie was too wrapped up in everything to notice how miserably I was failing.

"Oh, Van," she gushed, waving her unpainted hand at me, while the woman doing her nails struggled to keep her other hand still. "I can't wait until you fall in love!"

My stomach lurched forward. I felt like the truth would spill out of my mouth if I didn't fight to keep it down. I pictured the words coming out of my mouth like those shadow people on *The Electric Company*, syllables at a time, hanging in midair until they spelled out *I am in love with your fiancé*, while Janie watched in horror.

"I want you to feel like this," Janie said, "like there is one person for you and you've got him. The first time I saw him, that night in your dorm, I just knew. You know it when you find it, Van."

But what happens when you find it and it doesn't find you back? I thought about all the substitutes, the guys I dated in secret so I wouldn't discourage Peter from picking me if he had the chance to again—the one with the contraband iguana in his dorm room and the Mr. Spock costume in his closet, the one who could burp the periodic table of elements, the one who plucked his eyebrows and swore he didn't, the sweet one after college who wanted me to move in, right when Janie and Peter were going through their rough patch and I thought maybe, just maybe, I'd finally have a chance. All of them paled in comparison to Peter. It was like they weren't even men. They weren't the same species or something. They didn't make me feel anything, but with Peter, all he had to do was look at me and I felt everything. I felt pretty and special and important and smart. When he looked at me, I felt like we were the only two people who mattered.

I looked over at Janie, who was chattering on about her honeymoon plans, and felt like the worst maid of honor in the history of maids of honor. I silently vowed to stop thinking about her future husband completely, even though I knew it was a false promise. The manicurist coated each of my nails in three quick strokes. I tried to focus on that and clear my head of everything else. One. Two. Three. My thumbnail was brown. One. Two. Three. Index. One. Two. Three. Middle finger.

"When we plan your wedding," Janie said, breaking my focus, "we can do everything we didn't get to do for mine."

I couldn't think of anything that hadn't been done for her wedding. From the Rube Goldberg ice sculpture for chilling shots to the potted orchid centerpieces on each table, every element of the wedding had been planned with lavish precision. Janie had yet again forgotten that there was a very big difference between being the daughter of Charles and Diane Driscoll, and being the daughter of Charles and Diane Driscoll's housekeeper.

If I ever did fall in love with someone other than Janie's husband, my wedding would probably be more of a city hall and Best Western affair. Maybe there'd be trays of baked ziti congealing over Sterno candles or desiccated stuffed cod swimming in lumpy cream sauce, but certainly not three separate dessert courses and a ten-piece jazz band.

After we got our nails done, I had to go with Janie to pick out lingerie for the wedding night.

"I'm so glad you're here," she said, breathlessly, handing me hangers as she pulled gowns off the rack to take to the dressing room. "Mom wanted to come, but this just isn't something you do with your mother! And I've been dreaming about shopping for my wedding with you since we were like seven at least." She looked up at me. I thought she might get teary for a second, but then she bounced over to the next rack. "Ooh, we haven't seen those yet!"

She was so happy. I felt awful about feeling awful.

"Why don't you start trying these on." I ushered her into a dressing room. "I'll scope out the rest and bring over the good ones."

I grabbed every nightgown in the size-four section in one scoop and fed them to her one at a time over the door. The nightgowns were so tiny. I held one up to myself in front of the mirror. It looked like a doll dress. But then, Janie's waist was like the size of my thigh. We were cut from very different molds. Next to a normal-size person, I was average—a little on the tall side, and maybe I could stand to lose a few pounds—but next to Janie, I was an Amazon woman. Where she was angled, I was rounded. Where she was diminutive, I was bulky. I had a full seven inches on her five-foot-two frame. And to make it worse, she had this annoying habit of wearing ballet flats all the time. She didn't feel the need to compensate for her height at all. She liked to emphasize it, like she was basking in the simplicity of her stature and figure. Janie was the type of person who could wear a potato sack and make it look like haute couture. On me, it would look like a potato sack. Plus, it would be way too short, and so tight across my boobs and butt that it would be completely indecent.

There was a brief little span of time when it didn't bother me much. Janie was built like a twelve-year-old boy, and I was an early bloomer. In high school, most guys who wouldn't give her a second look would follow me with their tongues wagging. But now, she wasn't underdeveloped as much as refined. Everything about her was delicate, and everything about me felt overdone. Her hair was the perfect shade of chestnut. Mine was the kind of jet-black that almost looked blue in the wrong light. In the summer, even after hours in the sun, Janie would walk away a little golden, with perfectly pink cheeks. I'd turn a brash bronze instantly. Away from Janie, I felt like a normal person. Sometimes, I even felt beautiful. But next to her, my ears were too big, my nose was too round, my hands were too manly, and I couldn't help but notice the way my thighs slapped together when I walked. And it was worse now that Peter was giving Janie so much more than a second look.

Janie was partial to a white satin gown with a high neck and a crisscross back, but then I handed her a red satin slip trimmed in black lace.

"Van! This is so un-wedding-y," she said, trying to cover herself with her arms while I peeked in the dressing room. But she looked incredible and she knew it. With her dark hair piled up on her head in a sloppy bun, and the contrast of the red and black against her pale white skin, she looked regal and a little slutty at the same time. And she gave in, using me as her excuse to be wild.

"I guess you're not going to stop pestering me until I get it, so I might as well," she said, sighing and shaking her head like she was annoyed with me, even though she was grinning.

I wondered if there's a special place in hell for jealous bridesmaids.

I was singing "Rock and Roll Band" at the top of my lungs when I got to the Castle on the Hudson, but I stopped singing before I pulled up to the front door. I turned the stereo off and gave Normy's keys to the valet. I lugged the brown cardboard box out of the backseat. No one offered to help me with the box as I walked through the lobby to the elevator. My heels clicked on the marble and one of the orange gloves fell out of my purse. A bellhop rushed over frantically to hand it back to me. The concierge gave me a dirty look. I must have looked like a cheap hooker in my bright orange satin and fake fur. I couldn't get to the elevator fast enough.

When I got to the room, I pulled the box apart quickly. I didn't want to drag it out any longer than I had to. There was a big box of red rose petals, vanilla-scented votive candles in crystal holders, a book of matches, and a satin JUST MARRIED banner.

I threw big handfuls of rose petals on the bed, the floor, and the armchair, and tied the banner to the end posts of the bed. Peter could have had the concierge do this.

I couldn't decide if I was supposed to light the candles. It was probably the point of having someone come get the room ready: so Peter could carry Janie over the threshold into a perfect, candlelit room. But I didn't think burning down their honeymoon suite was the way to go, so I arranged them in a circle on the dresser and left the matches next to them.

In the bottom of the box was a white satin nightgown with a strappy crisscross back. I pulled the tags off and laid it out on the bed. I went into the bathroom and found Janie's red slip hanging on a padded hanger. I took it down and tucked it in the bottom of her suitcase.

Chapter Two

I'd ridden in the limo with Janie on the way to the church, so my car was still at the Castle. It was the only economy car in the lot. The valet handed me my keys and rushed off before I could even say thank you. He gave me a better reception when I showed up in Norman's car, but then, on top of being four times more expensive than mine, Norman's car didn't smell like stale French fries and old coffee.

I took a long time driving back. I really had intended to be there for the end of the reception, but I took back roads instead of the parkway. I drove by the high school where three new buildings had sprung up since I graduated.

Past the high school was the dead-end road where Kevin Ritter and I used to park. When we were in high school, developers cleared the road to build houses there. On warm nights, we would get out of the car and explore the house skeletons. Now, they were real houses with mailboxes and brass knockers on the doors. I drove slowly past the house that had *15* painted on the mailbox in curly numbers with reflective paint. The blue light of a TV flickered in the living room.

I wanted to drive up the driveway, rap the brass knocker on the red front door, and tell the family inside, "The first time I had sex was on your living room floor." I pictured a horrified woman in pearls covering her little boy's ears while her husband slammed the door in my face. I turned my car around in the cul-de-sac and kept driving.

I drove to Gedney Park, where my mom and I used to go with fold-up beach chairs and a canvas bag full of romance novels to sit by the pond and "get away." I parked in the lot and walked around the man-made pond, my heels sinking in the not-quite-frozen ground, until I found our spot—the place where the land curved into the kidney-shaped pond. It was a few yards away from the pavilion we pretended was our house.

Diane could never understand why we wouldn't rather lounge by the pool. But when we lounged by the Driscolls' pool, my mom was still working. Even if she was supposed to be off duty, something always came up. Gedney Park was away from all things Driscoll, and that felt good. It felt so good that we didn't care if we looked silly in our baseball hats, cut-off sweatpants, and dollar store flip-flops. We sat by the pond, throwing stale cereal to the ducks, while we questioned who had already read which book before we settled in.

My mom always read a few chapters and then turned to me to say, "So what's new, kiddo?" She'd sit sideways, hook her feet around the legs of my chair, and listen like I was the only person in the world.

At home, my mom was always on edge. Anything I tried to tell her could be interrupted by the cook quitting again, or the gardener planting the wrong kind of roses, or Janie calling to say she needed a ride home from a friend's house; but at Gedney Park, there was no phone, no cook, no Janie. She was all mine, and I didn't have to share her with anyone.

When we first started going to the park, I told her things like how Karen's mom was letting her get highlights, and that Missy Gribaldi's parents bought her a horse for getting straight As. The last time we were there, we talked about Peter. It was late summer, right before the beginning of my last year of college. It wasn't sunny or particularly warm. It was threatening to rain, but my mom insisted we go.

"It's our last chance before you go back to school," she said. "I have to help Janie pack tomorrow."

So we loaded up the tote bag with books and hauled the beach chairs out to our spot. My mom didn't even bother with the pretense of picking a book. She planted her feet on the side of my chair and dove right in.

"Can we talk about it?" Her voice was soft but not tentative. It was a demand, not a question.

I didn't look at her, but I could feel her studying my face.

"Talk about what?" I asked, trying to keep my expression as neutral as possible.

"Well, what I can't figure out," she said, "is what hurts worse." She tucked a piece of my hair behind my ear. "Pete in love with your best friend, or Janie in love with the man you've been worshiping for three years."

I raised my eyebrows and tried to pull off an "I don't know what you're talking about" look, but she didn't fall for it.

"Come on."

"I didn't worship him," I said. "It's not like I was some sort of stupid puppy dog or anything." I wrapped my feet around the bar at the end of my chair. "I'm just not Janie."

"You look at me," she said, planting her feet on the ground and resting her elbows on her knees. "Janie is a lot of things, but she'll never be you." She grabbed my hand. Her eyes watered up. "You really are something." She dabbed at her eyes with her index finger, and wiped tears across her cheek into her hair. "It's short, you know. It's really short, Van. And you can't—you can't let him go. You can't let him go just because it's Janie."

Standing in our spot in the cold, by myself, I realized she must have known then that she was terminal. And I couldn't help but think that maybe it's a lot easier to give advice like that when you know you won't be around to see how it all pans out.

I stared at the water in the orange haze of light pollution creeping up from the city. My toes hurt and my fingers felt stiff. I tried to pull my arms up into the wrap Janie gave me so I could stay for a few minutes longer, but it was just too cold. I made my way back to the car. Step, sink, step, sink.

Back in the car, I turned the heat on full blast, but it hurt more to thaw out than to be cold.

By the time I got back to the reception, it was after midnight. I drove down the dirt road to the Kittle House just in time to see Peter and Janie climbing into the limo, while everyone waved and blew bubbles at them. I parked the car and turned the lights off so they wouldn't see me when the limo drove past.

Norman wandered up and down the rows of cars. He kept stumbling and steadying himself on the nearest car, setting off alarms as he went. His jacket was off, his shirt was unbuttoned, and his shirtsleeves were rolled up. I could see when he walked past my car, hitting the hood with his palm, that he wasn't wearing an undershirt and his chest was red and hairless. I thought about getting out to tell him where his car was, but then he vomited down the side of a black Mercedes. I started up my car and headed over to the carriage house.

Chapter Three

My key still fit in the lock, but the doorknob was polished free of all of our scratches. When I opened the door, the rest of the carriage house apartment was like that too. Everything was still there, but it was shinier and arranged like someone had dressed a television set to look like the carriage house. My mom's worn-out romance novels were out of their beach bag, lined up on their own shelf in the big white built-in bookcase. The floors had been refinished and none of our shoe scuffs were left. The living room rug had either been steam-cleaned by a master, or replaced with the exact same one, only new.

Under the coffee table were three whitewashed wicker baskets filled with back issues of my mom's *People* magazine subscription. They weren't our wicker baskets. Diane must have bought them. More magazines were fanned out on the coffee table we'd made out of an old whitewashed half door. The one on top had a headline about the sexiest man of the year and a picture of Hugh Jackman. I picked up the magazine and looked at the address. It was still addressed to Natalie Lion.

"Natalie Lion," I'd yell to my mom when I brought the mail in. "Your magazine is here."

"Grrrrroar!" she'd yell back, and grab it away from me.

Her issues of *People* were usually puckered up from getting wet while she read in the bathtub. And she always threw them out when we were done reading them.

In the kitchen, there were plastic oranges and bananas in the hanging fruit basket where our bruised bananas used to live.

"Geez, Diane!" I said out loud. "What's up with all the fake fruit?" It was weird to hear my voice. I almost expected someone to come out of one of the bedrooms and say hello—a made-for-TV movie actress playing me, or maybe I expected to see my mom.

I walked over and opened up the fridge. Diane had indeed stocked it with our favorite junk foods. Potato salad and cannolis from Bueti's Deli. A pizza box took up the second shelf. I slid it out and took a peek. It was a whole large black-olive pizza. I wondered if cold pizza still tasted good when it wasn't left over. Who buys a whole pizza and just sticks it in the fridge? It was weird, the way she'd gone out of her way to make everything the way it used to be—like my mom was still alive, like nothing had ever happened, like cold pizza and cannolis could make everything okay again. Diane wasn't usually one to be overly sentimental. I wondered what she was up to.

There were no toothpaste spit splatters on the mirror in the bathroom. The end of the toilet paper was folded in a triangle, and there was a stack of fluffy towels—bath towel, hand towel, face towel—waiting for me on the counter by the sink. They weren't our towels. They were white and fluffy and didn't have frayed strings tangled with hair hanging from the ends. There was a basket full of beauty products on the counter.

"What's with all the baskets?" I said, out loud again, as I riffled through bottles of the hair spray I used to use, Love's Baby Soft, and my mom's Oil of Olay.

Toward the back of the basket was a bottle of 5th Avenue. I pulled the cap off and smelled the sprayer. I sprayed it into the air and everything smelled like her. I could almost feel her warm, bony hand on the side of my cheek. I could almost see the pinwheels in her blue eyes and the spot on her nose where two freckles overlapped. It was the only thing my mother ever splurged on. She used to buy it for me to give her every Christmas, because she felt guilty about spending that kind of money on herself.

She always found my hiding spot for Christmas presents, and she'd tuck the bottle in along with them. Every year, I'd wrap the long gold box in cheap paper and wait to see her fake surprise as she unwrapped it. It was my favorite Christmas tradition. "Van! You shouldn't have," she'd say, and wink at me. She'd make four ounces last all year. This bottle was only about a quarter gone. She died three months before my college graduation.

I heard someone fumbling with the front door. The knob turned and I could hear the bottom of the door brush up against the rug. The long eerie squeak my mom and I had gotten used to was gone.

"Diane, this is creepy," I yelled from the bathroom.

"What?" It wasn't Diane. The voice was deep and had grit.

"Peter?" I walked into the living room. He stood in front of the couch with his hair in every direction and his tie stuffed in his jacket pocket. His jacket and shirt were unbuttoned and a red wine stain bled down the front of his undershirt.

"Peter, what the fuck are you doing?"

He didn't say anything. He just stared at me with his mouth open like I was a horror movie or a train wreck and he couldn't look away.

Looking at him, I could picture in my head so clearly what it would be like to have him grab and kiss me and tell me that it was all a mistake and he really wanted me all along. I took a deep breath, promising myself that even if I was in the middle of that kind of bizarro reality, I wouldn't allow anything of the sort to happen.

"You don't have to look at me like that, Pete," I said, grabbing at my orange satin. "I didn't pick the color of this dress."

I was expecting a smile or at least a hint of amusement in his eyes, but there was none. He shut his mouth and pressed his lips together in a thin, hard line.

I walked over to him. As I got closer, I saw how glassy his eyes were, and realized he was fighting back tears.

"Peter! Sit." I plunked down on the couch and leaned over so the place I patted for him to sit was far enough away from me. He stumbled over to the couch. He smelled like a communion chalice.

"You didn't come back," he said. "I thought you were going to come back, Van." He looked at me, and I could see what he must have looked like as a seven-year-old. His eyes were big and sad, his dark eyebrows raised and wrinkled. "I didn't get to say good-bye."

"You can't be here," I said, thinking that Diane was probably in a limo on the way back from the wedding already. "Where's Janie?"

"She's at the Castle," he said, running his hand across his chin like he was feeling for stubble.

"Why are you here, Pete?" I looked at his shoes, searching for scuffs. There weren't any. "You have to go."

"You didn't come back," he said. "You didn't say good-bye. I'm leaving for two weeks and you didn't even say good-bye." He leaned over and put his arms out for me to hug him.

I wanted to lean across the couch and hug myself as close to him as possible, but I pressed my ribs into the arm of the couch to get as much distance as I could. It took everything I had not to dive into him. I could almost feel how it would be to hold him. I knew he would be warm, and his neck would still smell like aftershave. I knew if I rubbed my cheek against his, I would feel the beginnings of tomorrow's stubble scratch my skin. And I knew, this time, if I let myself hug him it would be different from all the other times. It wouldn't be a friendly hug.

"It took a long time," I said, pulling at the fingers on my left hand, "all the rose petals and candles and everything."

He leaned his elbows on his knees and dropped his face in his hands. He didn't seem at all like Peter. His whole body vibrated. He let out big, hoarse sobs. "You're my best friend and you didn't even say good-bye." He looked at me through the spaces between his fingers, and then closed his hands.

"Janie was there. I'm pretty sure that's the important part, Pete." I put my hand on his back, lightly, ready to pull it off should Diane come storming in, or lightning strike me.

He lunged over and buried his head in my lap.

"How drunk are you?" I asked, letting my hand stroke his hair, just once.

"Very, very," he said into my leg. His breath was warm and damp.

Crap.

"You're okay." I let myself stroke his hair again. It was soft and fine, and bristled slightly at his neck. "You've got to get back to her," I said, pulling my hand away. His tears soaked through my dress and made it stick to my thigh. It was too close.

My head was rushing around in this circle of wanting to know why he had come, and not wanting to know at all. If he told me he realized he loved me and wanted to be with me, what the hell could I do about it anyway? It's not like I could say, "Hey, I feel the same way. Let's ditch Janie and go on your honeymoon."

I leaned forward, and pushed up on my toes to get Peter to move. He didn't budge. I started thinking about how easy it would be to reach down and kiss him, and how once I started kissing him, I wouldn't be able to stop. I shifted my weight, took a deep breath, and let it hiss out between my teeth. "You have to go back!"

I stood up, and he fell off the couch, knocking his head on the coffee table. He sat up on his knees and rubbed his head.

"Jesus, Van! What the hell—"

"I'm calling you a cab," I said firmly. I walked into the kitchen and picked up the wall phone. Through the window, I could see the limo waiting outside. "You took the limo? What did you do, drop her off and leave?" Pete nodded. "Where does she think you are?"

"I told her I left something at the reception," he said. "I needed to think. I couldn't breathe." He was crying, hard. His face crinkled up, and his shoulders slumped. I wanted to hold him and stroke his hair again. I wanted to tell him it was all going to be okay. I wanted to tell him I loved him, but I couldn't stop thinking of Janie, alone in a roomful of rose petals, wearing that white satin nightgown, waiting for her husband.

"You can't just leave her waiting for you on your wedding night," I said, biting the inside of my cheek to hold back tears. I shook my head at him, hoping that even if he wasn't listening to my words, he'd still get it. "You can think later." My tears started to overflow. I wiped them away quickly, hoping Peter was too drunk to notice. "It's just wedding jitters. Too many drinks. It'll pass."

He stared at me, still on his knees. "Van—" He stood up. "Savannah, I—"

"Shut up, Pete," I yelled. "You shut the hell up." I slapped my hand on the kitchen counter hard enough to make it sting.

Peter grabbed my hand and held it, his fingers squeezing mine hard. He leaned forward, so close that I could feel the heat of his cheek against mine. I knew I should pull my hand back and walk away, but I couldn't. I couldn't move at all. I closed my eyes.

"Savannah," he whispered. "I need to—"

The doorknob clicked. Peter dropped my hand. The door opened, and my heart took a flying leap. We stepped away from each other quickly.

Diane walked in. Had she seen us? Had there been anything to see? I opened one of the kitchen drawers like I was looking for something.

"Pete?" Diane said. "Wha— Where's Jane?" She looked tired.

Pete looked at me like a lost kid in the grocery store. He sniffed and wiped at his eyes with the back of his hand.

"Pete sent me to decorate the room," I said, closing the drawer. "And he had this bracelet that I was supposed to leave—" I waited, hoping Diane would just say something and I wouldn't have to finish, but she didn't. She stared at Peter with her eyebrows raised. "I was supposed to leave it in a champagne glass, but I—I forgot."

"Oh," Diane said, pulling her arms out of her coat, one sleeve and then the other. She draped it over the back of the armchair. I don't know if she believed me. She always had a good poker face.

"So, it was in my purse, but now I can't find it." I walked over to the back of the couch like I was retracing my steps. "I threw my purse on the couch when I came in—"

"Pete," Diane said, "Janie won't care about the bracelet." She walked over behind Peter and put her hands on his shoulders. "It's not worth getting upset over." Her voice was hard and brisk.

Diane looked up at me. I made a face and gestured drinking with my hands. Diane smiled a sad, tired smile, patted Peter's shoulders twice, and said, "Get up, buddy."

Pete leaned on the coffee table to pull himself up.

"Okay," Diane said. "You take that flat little tush of yours back to your wife."

Peter looked at his shoes. Damnit, Pete, I thought, look at her. Don't look so guilty.

"Van and I will look for this bracelet of yours," Diane said, "and you can give it to Jane when you get back."

I knew that tone. Shit, I thought. She knows there is no bracelet.

Pete nodded at Diane. He walked to the door, with his head hanging, mumbling, "Thanks."

When the door clicked shut behind him, I expected Diane to start in on me, ranting or questioning or something. But she plopped on the couch, used the side of the coffee table to pull off her heels, and said, "Get me a drink, Van, will you?"

I grabbed a tumbler from the cabinet, plunked two pieces of ice in it, filled it with bourbon from the bottle under the sink, and walked it over to her. I set it on the coffee table, using one of the magazines as a coaster.

"Thanks, sweetie," she said. She stirred the ice around with her pinkie for a minute and took a sip. She looked up at me, searching my face for a reaction; I looked straight into her eyes and tried not to flinch. When Janie and I were in high school, I got Janie drunk and tried to convince Diane it was food poisoning. She'd studied my face until I cracked.

She patted the couch next to her, and even though all I wanted to do was run out to my car and speed away, I sat down.

"They'll be fine." I said, hoping I sounded convincing. "I'm sure the bracelet will turn up."

"We'll all be fine," Diane said. She stared into her drink like she was having a conversation with it.

"Okay, you know what, Diane? I don't know why he was here. I don't know what this was all about."

Diane put her drink on the table and reached into one of the magazine baskets. Slowly and methodically, she pulled out a glass ashtray, a silver lighter, and a pack of unfiltered Camels. She lit two cigarettes at once and handed one to me. "Don't you, though?" she said, smiling.

"What?" I took a drag and scrambled for something to say. "Diane, I–"

"Oh, Vannie." She put her arm around me and passed me her drink. "Drink with me, okay? Let's just get really drunk."

Chapter Four

I woke up with my face smushed up against the arm of the couch and my head throbbing. Diane was passed out in the oversize chair, her head resting on one arm and her feet hanging off the other. With her head tipped back and her mouth wide open, she snored like she had an old man trapped in the back of her throat.

I slid off the couch onto the floor and leaned on the coffee table to stand up. My last glass of bourbon was still on the table, swimming in a puddle of condensation. It was full. Diane's glass was empty. She'd been about three drinks ahead of me all night.

I tried to walk into the bathroom quietly, but I tripped over one of my shoes and steadied myself with a loud thunk. Diane didn't budge.

I pushed the bathroom door closed behind me. It clicked softly, but I figured if my stumbling around didn't wake Diane up, that wouldn't either.

There was a red stripe down my cheek from the piping on the couch seam. My mascara had shifted and soaked into the creases under my eyes.

I'd never finished taking my bridesmaid updo down, and there were half a million bobby pins sticking out of my head. I tried to pull one out, but it was hopelessly stuck. My hair had been sprayed and teased into the consistency of a Brillo pad.

I was still in my orange dress. I'd unzipped the back after my second drink. My strapless bra had slipped down almost to my waist. I unhooked it and pulled it out of my dress.

I used to be able to pass out drunk on a couch and wake up looking vampy and metropolitan. Somewhere around twenty-three it became necessary to wash and tone and moisturize so I didn't look like a freak show when I woke up.

When Janie and I slept at the Castle, she fell asleep without even washing her face, and woke up looking like an angel and smelling like a flower garden. Her dark hair wasn't knotted or tangled; it rippled in soft waves, and the tiny smudges of mascara under her eyes looked like they'd been drawn by a makeup artist.

It didn't seem real that Peter had been stumbling around the living room the night before. Diane hadn't said anything more about it. I waited all night, steeling myself for a big argument. She kept hinting that one was coming—tiny land mines she would set up but not detonate. And she would give me knowing looks between gulps of bourbon, while she chattered on and on about Janie and Peter touring through Europe for the next two weeks on their honeymoon. Diane had apparently played travel agent, planning every last detail down to restaurant reservations.

"And when they're in the Loire Valley, I set them up in the best room at the Château de Coligny in the rue Condé," she said, hitting the accents too hard, like a French whore in a bad movie. "That should put them in honeymoon mode for a very long time. They won't have to lift a finger"—she took another gulp of her drink— "or get out of bed." She snorted and stared at me, cold and hard, over her glass.

I ran the water in the sink; it got hot much quicker than it did in my condo. I washed my face with one of the fluffy washcloths and the milled French soap from the soap dish. It was Diane's brand, not ours. It smelled like lemongrass. She'd always hated the smell of our pink Dove soap. It was funny the way she'd kept some things exactly the same but changed others. It was an inexact replica. Everything was just a little off. I dried my face on the hand towel. I used it to wipe under my eyes, leaving moon-shaped black streaks on the bright white towel. I slathered on some of my mom's Oil of Olay from the toiletry basket.

Diane hadn't always lived to push my buttons. We used to be friends, partners in crime, but now, since my mom died, we didn't know how to act around each other.

When we were younger, Janie didn't care about clothes or shoes or fancy restaurants, so Diane would take me with her to buy dresses for all of the fund-raising galas she had to go to. She hated going to galas, but events like those were par for the course. The Driscolls were a dusty old family with dusty old money. It was railroad money, originally, but the bulk of the business Charles Driscoll did involved using Driscoll money to make money. He took a car into the city every morning and came home to retreat to his study, where he yelled into the phone about things like futures, crude oil, and lean hogs. When he was done yelling about work, he yelled at Diane about how he didn't like the way the hedges had been trimmed, and the new shirts she bought him were scratchy, and he wanted meat for dinner instead of that goddamned spa food the cook made.

As a Driscoll wife, Diane had to go to every fund-raiser for every cause under the sun, and at those events, it was important for her to dress appropriately and make appropriate small talk with people she found supremely boring. She dreaded every event, and couldn't wait to come home, collapse on our sofa, and give us the dirt on Claudia Von Hoeffing's eye work and how Richard Wertlinger was getting handsy with a cocktail waitress in the coat closet. But as much as Diane hated going to galas, she loved buying dresses for them. She'd sign me out of school and we'd spend the day hopping from Neiman Marcus to little boutiques. We'd wrap up the day with massages and facials.

We never told my mom or Janie. We never talked about not telling them, but it was understood. One of the first times we went, my mom pulled into the driveway at the same time we did. Diane told my mom I was sick and the school called her to come pick me up after they couldn't get through at the carriage house.

My mom smoothed my hair and looked concerned.

Diane said, "I have some tea that will make her feel better. Van, you go get yourself in bed, missy." She pouted at my mom like she felt bad for me. "Come on, Nat. I'll get it for you." As they walked away, she looked over her shoulder and winked at me.

I ran up to the carriage house and pulled the tape out of the cassette in our answering machine so it looked like it had broken.

But then there was the secret Diane kept from me. For almost a year she didn't tell me. And neither did my mom. And when they finally told me, and I came home from college to be there, my mother was small and frail and bald under her red designer knit cap.

I walked into the carriage house and they were both in my mom's bedroom. They didn't hear me, and I watched in horror as my mom and Diane had a serious discussion over the fabric swatches for her casket.

"Satin is too flashy, Diane," my mom said. "It's not me." She held up a rectangle of gray wool.

Diane made a face like she'd just sucked a lemon and shook her head. She grabbed for another swatch and held it up, smiling.

"It's classic, Nat," she said, "and the dark pink is just so—" and then she saw me and stopped like she was caught in the headlights.

They had their own language about it. They had their own routines. Diane knew all the names of all the pills in the orange bottles that lined the bathroom counter. She could identify them by color and shape and she knew the dosage by heart. And until I saw them picking out options on the casket like it was a new car, all I had heard were phrases like *lump removed* and *routine procedure*. And I'd believed my mother when she'd said, "Everything will be fine, sweetie."

The funeral was awful. Diane talked my mother into every lavish accommodation Driscoll money could buy. It was their pet project. They'd planned every detail from the moment they heard the word *terminal*. And it all upset me—from the ornate urns of yellow roses to the gray raw silk cover on the guest book at the funeral parlor (to match the casket fabric they finally agreed on) to the fact that they acted like it was normal to plan your own funeral. The details made me feel so far away—like I didn't know either of them. And I wasn't sure if it was the distance from my mother or the distance from Diane that bothered me more, but Diane was the only one around to take the heat for it.

I screamed at her. I cried. I called her every version of every name for the Devil I could think of. I threw things. And then I drove back up to Rochester and stopped answering the phone.

Janie told me that Diane went to my college graduation, and sat in the stands with a huge bouquet of flowers, looking for me in the sea of black robes. I spent that weekend in Ithaca at the Holiday Inn watching bad movies on the free cable. And after that, when Diane came to visit Janie, I was always out of town. It was easier to avoid Diane than it was to see her, because no matter how hard I tried, I couldn't forgive her for not telling me how sick my mom really was. I would have dropped out of college. I would have taken care of my mother. I would have known which pill was for what, and I would have held her hand through chemo and brought her Popsicles and made her laugh. I could have had a few more memories of my mom, and I would have held on to every single one as tightly as I could.

For a while, Diane kept trying. She called every Sunday. She left overly chirpy messages on my answering machine, saying things like, "I hope you had a great week," even though it had been months since we talked. She sent me the kind of "Thinking of You" cards old ladies send each other in Hallmark commercials. She even had flowers delivered on the first anniversary of my mother's death. I ignored all of it, and eventually, the phone messages became holiday-only events, and her voice sounded more clipped than chirpy. I got a card on my birthday, and another one at Christmas. The anniversary of my mother's death came and went several times over without any fanfare.

Throughout the wedding events, I kept my distance as much as I could. I had a fake smile I wore just for Diane, and until she'd invited me back to the carriage house, she'd acted cool and polite, like I was just another one of Janie's college friends, like we had no real history.

I slipped off my dress, dropped it in a big orange puddle on the floor, and sat on the side of the tub. I plugged the drain, turned the faucet on, and squirted a generous helping of lilac-scented bubble bath into the stream of water. I left the water to run while I peeled off my black panty hose. The mean red mark they left around my waist made it look like I'd slept with a tourniquet binding me.

Diane knocked on the door and opened it at the same time.

"I have to pee like a demon, Van." She did a nervous jig into the bathroom, lifted up the toilet lid, scooched up her dress, and sat down. "Hope you don't mind," she said, smiling at me. "God, Van, I would kill for your boobs. I didn't know nature made them that way."

I felt so self-conscious. Diane took me to buy my first push-up bra, peeking over the door while I modeled each one, but I knew her then.

"When you go to get yours replaced, I'll give you a picture," I said, and then felt awful immediately. We used to have the sarcastic banter thing down. We said things like that to each other all the time and it was funny, but now, it just came out mean. I didn't want it to be, but I didn't know how to stop it. Maybe Diane felt the same way. I wondered if there was some way to suck the venom out. I ran my hand under the faucet to make sure the water was okay.

Diane flushed, but didn't leave. She closed the toilet lid and sat back down. I turned away from her and slipped my underwear off quickly.

"Nice underwear, Vannie. Were you thinking someone might see them?" Her voice was supersmooth.

"Aw, Diane, thanks for noticing," I said, trying to make my voice equally smooth. I stepped into the tub and pulled the shower curtain closed.

The backside of the shower curtain, blurred by the clear plastic liner, was familiar and safe. My mom and I bought it at a closeout sale. It was hideous and comforting at the same time. Fat purple fish blowing orange bubbles swam along in a green sea. The fish had eyelashes and bright pink lips like they were wearing lipstick.

I sat down and pushed my feet up against the end of the tub so I wouldn't slip down too far.

"Good," Diane said. "Now we can talk."

"Crap, Diane. I don't want to talk. I've got to take a bath and get my ass in the car. I have to work tomorrow."

"Well then, you clean, I'll talk." Her voice was suddenly stern. She peeked her head around the side of the shower curtain. "Multitasking, Savannah."

I snapped the curtain closed, scooped up a handful of bubbles, and clapped my hands together. A clump of foam landed on my nose. It was hard to focus on and harder to look past.

"You've lived in Rochester for a long time now, huh?" Diane tapped the tips of her fake fingernails against the marble.

I strained my eyes to watch the tiny bubbles popping on my nose.

"So?" I wiped the rest of the foam away.

"I just never saw you as an upstate person. I thought you'd be somewhere more exciting—living in London or Paris. At least getting a loft in SoHo. Not Rochester."

"Diane—"

"What are you staying for, anyway? I mean, you don't have to stay. It's not like you have family up there. Peter and Janie—they have Peter's family. Peter has his dad's firm. They have a reason to be up there. You don't."

"I have my job, and it's not like I have family here either."

"It's not like you have a real job," Diane snapped. She didn't understand what I did at all. Working from home and wearing sweats instead of suits took all the legitimacy out of it for her. When Janie told her I started freelancing as a grant writer, Diane left me a twenty-minute message about the merits of getting a good, solid office job with good, solid benefits. Hysterical, really, since she'd never done it. She met Charles when she waited tables at the Larchmont Yacht Club, the summer between her sophomore and junior years at Manhattanville. She got pregnant with Janie halfway through her junior year and quit school. They got married, despite the protests from Charles's parents, and Diane never worked another day.

"I do too have a real job," I said, feeling like a child, tempted to add *you big meanie.*

"You don't have an office."

"I have clients. I have connections in Rochester, Diane. I'm established."

Diane's nails stopped clicking. "But you've got to be *lonely.*" She lingered on the word *lonely*, drawing it out like a song lyric. "I mean, you don't really know anyone up there anymore, do you? Everyone from school must have left by now." The clicking started again. "Janie and Pete will be busy with the house and all. Babies. Married people don't keep single friends around, Van. You just won't have anything in common, and I know you don't want to be a third wheel."

I flipped the bird in her direction, shielded by the shower curtain. I pedaled my feet, making small waves that hit the walls of the tub.

"What are you doing in there?" she asked.

I didn't answer. She didn't say anything either. It was quiet except for the sound of my waves. I broke before she did.

"I'm trying to take a bath, so I don't get stuck in the car for eight hours smelling like a booze hound." I coughed lightly. "No offense." It was one of those things we would have laughed at together before, but now Diane stayed silent. "So, what do you want from me?" I said, quickly.

"I just don't want to see you get left behind, Van. Maybe it's time you did something new, took a chance at something. Or someone. Start over somewhere else."

"What do you mean?"

"We haven't really talked since the funeral," she said.

"Well, I've been busy," I said, praying she'd pick a different subject. I couldn't get into it with her. I just couldn't.

"Your mother left you some money, you know."

"My mother didn't have any money." The water in the tub was starting to get cold, but I didn't want to get out and lose the protection of the shower curtain.

"She had fifteen thousand in savings. And then there was the life insurance. That was in your name."

"What life insurance? She didn't have life insurance."

"How would you know? You don't know these things, Van," she said, like I was still some silly kid.

"What are you pulling?" I asked. The bubbles in the tub were mostly popped now, but the bubble bath had left the water an awful green-gray color. My legs looked swollen and too white. "Am I supposed to be grateful?" I hugged my knees up to my chest so I wouldn't have to look at them anymore.

"You don't have to be grateful, Savannah. It was one of your mother's employee benefits." There was the slightest hesitation in her voice—this extra breath before she said *employee benefits*.

"So why haven't I heard about this before?"

"You refuse to take my calls. You won't meet me for lunch when I come to see Jane."

"Why not have Janie tell me?"

Diane took an audible breath and forced the air out through her nose. "You know how she is. This isn't between you and her. This is between you and me."

"I just—" I stood up. The water dripped off me and sounded like a rainstorm. "Isn't some man in a bad suit supposed to come and tell me this?"

"You watch too many movies."

"Call it what it is, Diane." I pulled the shower curtain open, and stepped out onto the bath mat.

Diane was leaning her butt against the counter, with both hands stretched behind her. Her right hand curled into the sink, still tapping. Her legs were crossed, and she was resting on the balls of her feet. Diane's feet were like Barbie's. She'd worn heels for so long that she couldn't stand flat-footed. I scanned her face for hints of unease, but she was hiding behind her surly smile.

"Call it what it is? Insurance money. Is that what you wanted to hear?"

I got up close to her; close enough to drip water on her dark red satin dress, leaving black splotches across her chest. I reached around her to grab a towel.

We locked eyes while I wrapped the towel around me. I was hoping for some speck of light, but her eyes were set and dark.

I walked away, my wet feet slapping loudly against the floor.

"I know a payoff from you when I see one, Diane," I said.

"You might want to get your eyes checked, missy," Diane said. "You don't know—"

I shut the door behind me, leaving her in the bathroom so I wouldn't have to hear the rest of her excuses. I shut myself in my old bedroom, and opened drawers to scavenge for left-behind clothes so I wouldn't have to wear my orange gown again.

I opened and closed the top drawer of my dresser three times, like maybe if I looked one more time it wouldn't be empty. My hands were shaking. This was not the first time I'd seen Diane throw money at a problem to make it go away. It was just the first time I'd ever been the problem.

Janie had a crush on the pool boy the summer she turned seventeen. Every time he showed up to clean the filters, Janie made it her business to be outside at the pool sunning herself in her classy black one-piece and movie star sunglasses. When the pool boy started flirting back, Diane was furious. "I don't pay that boy to make attempts at impregnating my teenage daughter," she'd whispered sharply to my mother when she thought I was out of earshot. Even though the poor boy had done nothing more than smile and make small talk with Janie, Diane decided he had to go. On his next visit, Diane sent me down to the pool with an envelope for him, while Janie was in the bathroom applying sunscreen. I peeked in the envelope before I delivered it. There was a bank check for two hundred dollars, and a note written in Diane's curvy script telling him that his services were no longer needed and any attempt to contact Jane would not be met kindly. We never heard from him again.

And, when my mother graduated from college with a degree in art education after years of night school, Diane gave her a congratulations card and a check that turned all the studying and homework she'd done into an exercise in futility. The bonus and the raise Diane gave her paid much more than teaching ever would.

"It doesn't matter, Mom," I told her. "Teachers make good money, right? We'll be fine. We don't need a big apartment."

My mom looked broken. She sat there, tracing the letters as they went from blue to purple to red, spelling out *Natalie Mavis Leone.*

"You can't buy her, Diane!" I'd yelled, thinking about all the times I'd watched my mother run out the door frantically, to try to make it to class on time after a full day of work, textbooks in one hand and the peanut butter sandwich she'd call dinner in the other. She'd been working to be an art teacher so hard for so long, and I hated that Diane was taking it away from her. "You can't buy us."

Diane was sitting at her makeup table, taking a drag of her cigarette. She talked without air. "Oh, I know, I'm such a horrible person, giving my head housekeeper a bonus and a raise like that." She blew the smoke out after her words, and waved it away like I was just being silly.

"You can't buy us," I said again, since I couldn't find a better argument.

"You don't come cheap, Vannie," Diane said, laughing. "No kid does." She used the mirror to make eye contact with me while she pinned her hair up in a French twist. "You need food and clothes. Eventually, you'll need to go out in the world and get a good job, and you can't do that without going to college. Your mother can't do all of that herself on an assistant art teacher's salary." She tucked a stray hair up and pinned it. "This is a good thing," she said, smiling, like it was absurd for me to think otherwise. "This is a nice thing I'm doing."

So my mother turned down her dream job at Rye Country Day School, and I went to the University of Rochester on a partial scholarship and a grant from the Driscoll Housekeeping Society.

I rounded up some grandma-cut cotton undies with yellowed elastic, a tattered gray sports bra, and a pair of brown-and-beige-striped socks with matching holes at the big toes. The closet was pretty much empty, with the exception of a pair of black stirrup pants hanging up, and a pair of jeans folded on the top shelf. I grabbed the jeans. They were from my short-lived, but memorable, badass phase in high school. They had a hole below the knee and another one under the butt that was loosely stitched with a black shoelace. I pulled them on. They were cold, and the seams creaked. They still fit, but they were much tighter across the hips than they used to be.

I left my bedroom out of necessity. I couldn't find a shirt. The bathroom door was open. "Diane?"

No answer. Her coat wasn't draped over the back of the couch anymore.

I went over to the kitchen window and saw Diane walking briskly toward the main house. Her camel-hair coat was open and billowing out behind her.

There was an envelope on the kitchen counter with *Savannah Leone* scrawled across it in Diane's bold, curvy script. The back was sealed with a silver diamond-shaped sticker—an ornate *D.* I slid my finger along the envelope flap. The seal lifted but didn't tear. Inside was a bank check for one hundred and seventy-five thousand dollars.

I pulled the check out and looked at it. It was powder blue and watermarked, Manhattan Savings Bank printed in the upper left-hand corner like the framework of an old Roman palace. The check was made out to me, Savannah Marie Leone, in plain block carbon-transferred letters that went from blue to purple to red. There was no other name attached—no insurance company title, no trace of the Driscoll name.

I started to crumple the envelope up in my hand when I realized there was something else in it: a strip of paper folded up like an accordion. It was a photo booth strip of me at thirteen with big puffy bangs that had taken many turns around the curling iron and clouds of L.A. Looks hair spray to perfect. I had a mouthful of metal I was trying to hide. The first two pictures had my forced attempt at a mature and sexy nonsmile. The third was blurred. I was moving my head to look toward the curtain. In the fourth, my mouth was wide open, braces gleaming in the flash, eyes squinted shut with hysterical laughter.

"You better not be flashing your boobs in there, young lady!" Diane had yelled.

It was one of our first hooky-day shopping trips. Diane had never been in a photo booth before and there was one in the food court on the way to the ladies' room.

She had been bitching that my insistence on drinking a large strawberry smoothie from Fruit & Co. and my greater insistence on not wetting my pants in the middle of the mall were making us late for meeting her personal shopper at Neiman Marcus.

"Van, I told you that a small was enough," she said, from the stall next to me in the bathroom, where I heard her pee a long steady stream too. "We don't have a lot of time, and I need a dress for the Neuberger gala this weekend," she lectured, like I didn't know why we were there or that we needed to get home before my mom noticed.

As we washed our hands, she shook her head and said, "You're just like your mother. Drink and pee. Drink and pee." She sighed and yanked paper towels out of the dispenser.

And I felt so awful, like I was ruining something that hadn't even taken off yet. I'd annoyed her. I was some baby with a tiny bladder who was turning into an inconvenience. Maybe she wouldn't take me again.

But as we walked back, she stopped for a second at the photo booth. She ran her hand along the curtain.

"I always wanted to do this when I was a kid," she said.

"You've never been in a photo booth?" I asked. I loved the fact that I had and for that second it made me superior.

I pulled a wadded one-dollar bill out of my pocket, held it tightly from either end, and rubbed it up against the corner of the machine to straighten it out.

"Get in," I said, feeding the bill into the slot. "Here's your chance."

She looked like she wasn't going to go. The first shot clicked. I grabbed her purse and gave her a little shove.

The first picture on Diane's strip was just the curtain. The second one was blurry, her hair falling in her face as she sat down. The third caught her trying to smooth her hair, but by the fourth, she was smiling wide and crossing her eyes. I loved that last picture of her, and I loved that I was the only person who knew it existed.

We'd traded strips. She made me pinkie-swear not to show the pictures to anyone. I got the feeling that she'd never made a pinkie swear before either.

I couldn't believe she'd kept my strip all this time, maybe folded up in her purse the same way I kept hers.

I pulled the ends of the strip of me and straightened them out to see the whole series all at once.

My knees wobbled. I slid down and sat on the kitchen floor. She paid to keep us, back when my mom wanted to be a teacher. She paid us to stay and now she was paying me to leave. This was "stay away from my daughter's husband" money. This was "start a new life for yourself and forget about Peter" money. This was "I'm done with you" money. She didn't even want to keep my picture anymore.

The check with my name on it was thin, like onionskin. I closed my eyes and thought about how it would feel to rip it in tiny pieces and feed it to the garbage disposal, but I didn't. I folded it up and tucked it in my purse. I fished through my purse and found the strip of Diane, folded up like an accordion, shoved in one of the credit card compartments of my wallet. I left it on the counter without taking one last peek of Diane crossing her eyes.

The car ride back was awful. I hit every Dunkin' Donuts drive-thru between Newburgh and Binghamton, and by the time I got to Syracuse, my bladder was bursting. I drove with my thighs pressed together, sweating and praying and cursing all at once.

When I got to the Chittenango rest stop, the only spot I could find was way over with the trucks. I ran across the parking lot in my orange satin heels, brown striped socks, holey jeans, and my mother's black Boston sweatshirt with the neon pink and orange spaceship on it. Cold air lapped in through the hole under my left butt cheek. Someone whistled and I flinched, knowing that they could probably not only see my ass through the black lacing, but they could see my ass constricted by the cracking band of my granny panties, hanging out there like a big white bratwurst. It had seemed like too much of a hassle to get my bag out of the trunk and drag it up to the carriage house to change before I left, but really, it wouldn't have been.

"Oh God, oh God, ohGodohGodohGod," I said, breathing in deeply. I unbuttoned my jeans the second I walked around the bend into the ladies' room. "OhGodohGodohGod!" I burst into an empty stall, pulled my pants down, and peed. It was nonstop, and I couldn't keep my balance in those stupid heels on the tile floor, so I ended up sitting full on a wet seat. And somehow, I felt like it was all Diane's fault.

I got back to the car and turned the radio on full blast. All the New York City stations had faded into crackly fuzz hours ago, and I wasn't close enough to get my Rochester stations, so I put the radio on scan and waited for something good. There was nothing. I settled on country music because it came in clear enough to play loud. But even with some guy bemoaning his empty refrigerator and the lost love who stole his cat in full twang at high volume, I couldn't drown out the voice in my head saying, *No fair, he was mine first.*

Chapter Five

The first thing I noticed about Peter was the soles of his shoes.

Not only was I late to my very first class on my very first day at the University of Rochester, but when I walked in the room, the heel of the Steve Madden Mary Janes Diane bought me as a going-away present caught on the lip of the door frame.

I flew forward, throwing my books across the room, landing on my stomach in a dry-land belly flop. When I looked up, I was face-to-sole with a pair of boat shoes—the tan leather kind with laces twisted into funny little knots instead of tied.

Oh, God! I thought. How embarrassing for him, wearing shoes like that. I pretended in my head that it was far worse for him to wear old-man shoes than it was for me to make my first impression on a lecture hall full of students by getting rug burn on my belly. It wasn't an illusion I could keep up for long, because it was impossible to drown out the laughter that poured from the stadium seating like surround sound.

The boat-shoe soles hit the ground as the wearer of them stood up and offered his hand to me. His fingers were thin but strong: piano hands, as my mom always said. He grasped my hand like he was giving me a firm handshake and helped me to my feet.

"Don't worry," he said. "No one noticed." His voice was deep and amused, his soft lips pursed in a kind smile. His eyes were a dark grayish blue, and they sparkled from the shade of his heavy brows. He had a cleft in his chin like Cary Grant, and his pale skin was shadowed with the slightest hint of dark stubble.

"Well, we can pretend no one noticed, at least," he said. "Can't we?" He moved his bag off of the seat next to him and said, "Sit. I'll get your books."

I sat down, tucked my purse under my chair, and crossed my legs.

Just as I thought I'd gotten my bearings, I looked up and caught the glare of Dr. Gurttle.

"Well, well, you certainly know how to make an entrance." He pulled his glasses down his bulbous nose and raised his eyebrows as the class erupted into giggles again. "Miss—"

"Leone," I said, glad I hadn't had time for breakfast because I surely would have lost it.

"Miss Leone." Dr. Gurttle pushed his glasses back up the slope of his nose. He made a noise that sounded like *tah tah tah* as he thumbed through the pages on his lectern. When he got to the page he was looking for, he scribbled something and then looked back at me. "Miss Leone, I'll be looking for you to make up for this first impression."

Boat-shoe guy sat down next to me and handed me my books. "Don't worry about it," he whispered. His breath was hot and smelled like cinnamon. "I hear this guy is a real wanker."

He settled into his chair and leaned on the armrest. Our arms were touching. And with that, before I even knew his name, I was madly in love.

He bought me coffee after class. I remember every moment of that day, because it seemed like the most perfect thing that had ever happened to me.

He paid like a grown-up, unfolding his leather wallet on its way out of his back pocket, sliding a folded ten to the barista with his index and middle fingers, instead of digging crumpled ones out of his front pocket the way I still do. I didn't offer to pay for mine. I knew it would make me look like an amateur, but I was beet red the whole time anyway.

I suggested walking along the canal path by the chapel, because I didn't think I could deal with sitting across from him while I got all sweaty and splotched up. But it was Indian summer weather, and way too hot for my black turtleneck sweater. At least there were leaves and the canal and the clouds for him to look at instead of my splotches and sweaty hair sticking to my face.

I couldn't think of anything to say. He didn't say anything either, and I felt like I was disappointing him—like I hadn't earned the cost of my coffee.

The leaves were falling and the clouds parted for a split second before going back to the Rochester gray I wasn't used to back then. "Rochester has more rainy days than Seattle," my mom had said when she tried to get me to apply to Sarah Lawrence.

"We've never been to Seattle," I said, waving my yogurt spoon at her, dripping pink all over the place mat, "so we can't compare it appropriately."

"We watch *Frasier*," she said, sticking her tongue out at me and swatting my arm with the Sarah Lawrence catalog. "Clean up after yourself. What do you think, you have a maid or something?" She laughed freely, enjoying her own joke.

I thought about telling Peter that I was homesick, but it seemed too needy. I thought about asking him if he knew of any good parties coming up, but he didn't seem like the type to go to a kegger.

"You know, Rochester has more rainy days than Seattle," I said to Peter, settling on something safe and mature.

"You don't say," Peter said, smirking. Even his smirk was charming; it showed off the dimple in his right cheek.

"What?"

"Well, I'm from Mendon. It's like fifteen minutes from here." He gestured to his right like it was just across the canal.

"Do you live at home?"

"No." He laughed, and it was easy and warm. "My father wanted me to get the college experience, but my mother didn't have faith in me doing my own laundry."

I thought about the Sarah Lawrence brochures and how my mom said if I went there I could live at home and we'd save money.

"I'm not from here," I said.

"I can tell," he said. I must have looked confused. "The accent. New York City?"

It was funny to hear him call it New York City. In Westchester, we just called it *the city*. Here, that meant downtown Rochester, and everyone's voices sounded slightly sour when they said it. And it was funny that he thought I had an accent. I didn't have an accent. People from the boroughs had accents. My mom had an accent from growing up on Long Island, which she said like it should have been spelled *Lon Guyland*. People from Rochester had accents too—sharp *As* and weird ways of pronouncing things. My roommate told me she was from a town that sounded like Chai-lie when she said it, but when I saw her high school yearbook on her bookshelf, it was spelled Chili.

"I'm from Westchester," I said.

"Ah." He smiled at me like that told the whole story. Even though I knew he had the story wrong, I let him think he was right. "So you're a long way from home, huh?"

"Yeah," I said, making sure my voice didn't tremble.

I think it did anyway, and I think he noticed, because he gave me a long, sympathetic look and said, "You'll get used to it. It'll get easier."

"Yeah," I said, looking deep into his eyes. My heart was thumping up in my throat. The collar on my sweater felt tight.

We walked under an overpass into a park and stood on a footbridge that arched over the canal. The water was littered with yellow leaves and their reflections, sprinkled at the sides of the canal like confetti. Back toward the school, the crew team was just leaving the dock.

"This is beautiful," I said, looking down at the water.

"Don't come here by yourself," he said, resting his coffee on the concrete railing and leaning up against it.

"Oh." I leaned next to him.

"There's an element here that's not safe." He shook his head and moved a little closer to me.

"What kind of element?" I said, trying not to smile at his stodgy choice of words. As I pushed my bangs out of my face, my elbow knocked up against his coffee cup and it fell into the canal. "Shit!" I reached for it after it was already gone and felt ridiculous. It bobbed in the water and got caught in the current.

"Don't worry about it. I was almost done anyway." He looked for my eyes when he talked and smiled when they met his.

"I didn't mean to litter." After I said it, I cringed. It seemed like such a junior high school do-gooder thing to say. I didn't want him to think of me like that—some Goody Two-shoes from Westchester, impeccably groomed for a life of dinner parties and reading the society pages. I wanted to be my interesting and alluring college self.

"I don't either, but I'm not about to jump in after it. Are you?" A perfect chunk of his shiny dark hair fell across his forehead. It was just short enough to avoid getting in his eyes. "What can you do?"

We walked to the other side of the bridge to watch the cup float down the river.

I pictured myself, perched on the railing, stripping off my plaid skirt and sweater to dive in after his coffee cup. It would be wild and rebellious and faintly reminiscent of an Aerosmith video.

"You're not, right?" He laughed.

"What?"

"You looked like you were considering going after it."

"We used to go bridge jumping in high school," I said, pretending I'd been reminiscing. "In the reservoirs. Off these old train trusses."

"I didn't think you were allowed to swim in reservoirs."

"You're not," I said.

"You didn't get arrested?"

"Nah." I waved it off. He looked at me in awe, and I liked feeling dangerous.

I'd really only gone once, with my public school friends. Diane was out in the driveway, smoking in her nightgown, when I got home. She'd probably just had another fight with Charles. She gave my wet jeans and dirty bare feet the once-over and said, "Don't embarrass us, coming home in a police car with flashing lights and that whole mess, Savannah Leone." She slurred her words, and dragged out my name until it was ridiculous. The next day, she didn't show any signs of remembering, but I never went bridge jumping again. So much for wild, dangerous rebellion.

"My dad would kill me if I ever did anything like that," Pete said, stepping away from the railing and putting his hand out in an "after you" gesture. "We should go. I have class."

On the walk back, he told me about how his dad was grooming him to join his firm, and that he expected to be a partner by the time he was thirty.

"So no bridge jumping for you, huh?"

"Nope. I've got to keep my nose clean. But it's a small price to pay for a killer job and a brand-new Audi when I graduate." He flashed me his perfect white smile.

When we got back to the chapel, Peter stopped and shuffled his feet around. "Well, this is me," he said, pointing across the street.

"So, Friday," he said, "there's this party in my dorm. You game?"

"Yeah," I said, trying really hard to stifle my smile and play it cool. "I could be game."

He ran his hand through his hair. "I'll get your number in class on Wednesday." He was so obviously dropping me off. This was the end of our coffee time. So even though I had to go back to the center of campus too, I pretended that I had to stick around the chapel. He turned and started walking toward campus.

"Thanks for the coffee," I yelled after him.

He turned around and walked backward so he could look at me. "Anytime."

I went into the chapel and stared at the stained-glass windows for a few minutes to give him some lead time.

Chapter Six

The first five hours of my trip back to Rochester were fueled by rage and coffee. The two and a half hours from Chittenango to my condo were excruciating. I was so angry and I didn't know where to put it. The caffeine buzz wore down to jitters. I was lonely. I picked up my cell phone, balanced it against the steering wheel, and scrolled through my address book. It was full of people I didn't know anymore—college friends who left Rochester after school, who'd stayed in my cell phone to fill up space so I felt like I still knew people. Thirty-seven people in my phone, and I only ever called two. And even if Peter and Janie weren't on their honeymoon, I couldn't call either of them about this.

I felt gross—repulsive—obvious. Even though I'd never taken my mom's advice—I'd never said anything to Peter—everyone knew. Everyone knew I was such a pathetic loser that I went dateless to watch the love of my life marry my best friend.

I threw the cell phone down on the passenger seat. I bit my nails until my fingers bled, spitting chips of Raisin Sunset polish into the console. I drove with my knee while I put my hair in a ponytail and then used one hand to rip the elastic out of my hair two minutes later.

I ate the gumdrops I picked up in the rest stop gift shop. They stuck in my teeth, and just as I'd free the remains of one, I'd pop another one in my mouth like I couldn't control it. I grabbed a green one after I swore I was done, so I rolled down the window, chucked it out, and watched it bounce down the road in my rearview mirror like a frog jumping. I grabbed two more and threw them out at the same time. They bounced into each other and disappeared. I threw gumdrops out the window until I had one left. I ate it, and spent the last twenty minutes of my drive picking orange goo out of my teeth.

I wasn't comforted by the bump at the end of the driveway, or the sound of the garage door opening. Coming home wasn't the refuge that it usually was. I felt like Diane's check was working to evict me already. I tapped the garbage can with my bumper, so I knew I was in far enough, and closed the garage door. I grabbed my purse but didn't bother taking my overnight bag out of the trunk.

My condo was stale. It was cold and I could smell the carpet pad. It wasn't a home. It was just a place to crash. I had tried to make it a home. I spent a week taping paint chips to the walls and studying them at different times of day like I'd read you were supposed to do. I went to Home Depot and bought every little roller, corner brush, and width of blue tape I could find. I got a different color of paint for every room, and a big orange book on home repair that had a chapter on painting. I read the chapter over and over until I was sure I knew the drill. I started in the living room. I taped and put down drop cloths and cut in like the book said. I got the wall behind the couch painted bright blue. But the blue didn't have that midnight-in-Venice kind of quality the little chip had. It looked like Superman's tights, so I stopped with that one wall, thinking I'd fix it eventually. I told Janie and Pete I'd picked it on purpose, and painting one wall was the newest style on the design shows that plagued the cable channels late at night.

Except for the blue wall, the whole condo was department store white and neutral. Even the things I'd bought for the condo were neutral. I was going to buy a red toaster, but Janie talked me out of it.

"That's awful, Van. Who buys a red toaster?"

Every time I saw that eggshell-colored toaster I wanted to scream.

I kicked off my shoes, pulled a plastic pitcher out of the cabinet under the counter, and made some grape Kool-Aid. I grabbed one of the twenty-four-ounce plastic cups the pizza place gives you when you get delivery, and filled it halfway with ice. I filled it up another quarter with Kool-Aid, and topped it off with vodka. I stuck a bendy straw in it, and walked around to check on the rest of the house. No phone messages. I didn't bother going out to check the mail. I never got anything other than utility bills and credit card offers. The bathroom smelled like mildew, because I hadn't cleaned up my wet towels before I left. The spider plant I never watered was more brown than green now. Other than that, nothing changed. Everything was right where I left it. No surprises.

I slurped my Kool-Aid down to the ice and went back to the kitchen to make myself another drink. The toaster was sitting on the counter, mocking me. I unplugged it and threw it in the garbage. It was almost as satisfying as it would have been to chuck it out my car window like a gumdrop.

I was still wearing my awful laced-up high school jeans, so I took my new drink upstairs with me to change. The stairs felt longer and steeper than usual.

It had been a few weeks since I'd done laundry, and I'd packed all the clothes that were both decent and clean. The only clean PJs I had left were the ones I absolutely hated. They were infamous. Old and worn; pale blue and red plaid; big, boxy, and, like most of my clothes, they had pale yellow coffee stains everywhere.

When it first happened—when they met and it was love at first sight—I blamed it on those pajamas. As much as I hated them, I couldn't bring myself to throw them out because they gave me something substantial to blame.

Janie came to visit me at the U of R over her spring break, junior year.

She drove up on a Friday afternoon. I told Peter I couldn't make our dinner because I thought I was going to fail my psych midterm.

"In fact," I told him, while we were walking to the dining hall for breakfast, "I'm just going to put myself in seclusion this weekend."

Peter met me at my dorm every morning and we walked over together. It was his solution to the fact that I was chronically late for my first class. He thought if I was up and out, I was more likely to make it on time—so, he came to get me every single morning. It was the best part of my day.

"Come on," he said. "I found this Indian place." He raised his eyebrows up and down at me and smiled. "Apparently, it's a total dive, but Connor from my lit class says it's really good, and he's a total food snob. He says you'll actually see Indian people eating there. That's how good it is."

"You don't like Indian food," I reminded him, fighting the urge to touch his face. Every time I was around Peter, no matter how much time we spent together, I had to make a concentrated effort to keep my hands off of him. Something about the line of his jaw, and the smoothness of his skin, just made me want to grab him, smell his neck, hold his body against mine. I'd never felt that way about anyone before. It was hard to focus on anything else.

"You like Indian food. You were just talking about it. And I always make you eat Chinese."

"You're always the one buying," I said, calling out something we never talked about.

"I'm a gentleman." He scrunched up his nose and shook his head at me like I was being ridiculous. "Come on, Van. Indian. We'll order in if you want. You can smell up my room with curry and I won't even complain. Friday. It's our thing. Come on!"

"Pete, I want to, but I can't," I said. It was killing me to turn him down. "I really have to study."

"It's just dinner. I'll leave you to study for the rest of the weekend."

I made a fist and pushed it into his shoulder. "Next week. I promise."

"Yeah," he said. "Okay." He looked hurt, but I thought my absence might make his heart grow fonder. And I knew that I didn't want him to meet Janie.

When Janie came up to visit me at the U of R, she brought charcoal masks and nail polish. We painted our toenails and hobbled around with toe separators stuck to our feet, and it was so nice to just hang out with her again. It was familiar and fun, and in my head I rationalized that this was why I didn't want Pete around. I didn't want him getting in the way of me spending time with my best friend. I wanted a weekend with Janie that was just like old times.

I'd swept the video store clean of Matt Dillon movies. We were all settled in with pizza and Pop Rocks, watching *The Outsiders*, when Pete knocked on the door.

I opened it without thinking. Peter didn't live in my dorm, so he usually had to buzz me to get in. It didn't occur to me that it could be Peter, but it was. He'd snuck in with some other girl's boyfriend.

"Wow," he said, surveying the scene. It must have been drizzling outside. Droplets of water sparkled on the fuzz of his black Patagonia fleece. "Seclusion usually means staying by one's self. And studying means actually looking at bo—"

"What are you doing here?" I felt for leftover globs of mud mask around my hairline and tried to hold my arm across my chest to hide the coffee stain over my left boob.

He looked right in my eyes, wrinkled up his forehead, and let out a quick sigh. "Thought you might want my psych notes from last semester. I thought if I helped you study, we could grab dinner tomorrow. Silly me," he said flatly, handing me a maroon notebook, and walking past me into my room.

Janie was sitting cross-legged on my floor in front of the TV. She had her hair pulled back with a thick black headband. When we'd washed our masks off, she'd carefully wiped away every trace of hers, and smoothed pale pink gloss over her lips.

He stretched his hand out to her. "Peter, and you are?"

"Janie," she said, standing up. Her pajamas were adorable: pink satin pants with rosebuds on them and a matching tank top with a big beautiful rose blooming across her chest.

And that was it. That was the beginning of the end. I could see it in the way they looked at each other. Not only did I lose him to Janie, but I couldn't continue on with my theory that maybe he was gay and that's why he'd never made a move on me.

A few weeks later, Peter canceled our Friday night dinner.

"I'm going into seclusion for the weekend," he said, flashing me his movie star smile.

Seclusion meant Rhode Island.

He visited Janie at Brown and brought me back an *I'd Rather Be in Rhode Island* T-shirt.

"I guess we both would," he said. "Right? She is your best friend and all."

I had no problem throwing the shirt out. I wadded it up in a ball and threw it off the second-floor balcony into the Dumpster after Peter went back to his dorm to call Janie.

I couldn't blame the shirt, but the pajamas I could blame. If only I'd had cuter pajamas, maybe Janie wouldn't have looked so freaking spectacular in comparison. I knew it was ridiculous, but it was all I had.

I left the evil pajamas in my dresser drawer and dug through the pile of clothes in the bottom of my closet until I found a pair of black capri leggings. I pulled the jeans off. They stuck on my calves, and I pulled so hard that they turned inside out. I left my mom's Boston sweatshirt on. The inside was worn down to soft, nubby pills, and the rubbery decal of the spaceship was cracked and peeling off. Pulling up the collar and tucking my nose under, I breathed in deeply, convincing myself that I could still smell my mom's perfume on it.

Three more drinks put me on the couch with my laptop, checking my e-mail and watching TV. I had forty-seven new messages, but they were almost all spam. The only real new message I had was a long e-mail from a client updating me on a project so I wouldn't have to "waste time" getting caught up Monday morning. I didn't write back.

I got up to make myself another drink, sucking down half of it in the kitchen and filling up again, before I stumbled back to the living room, narrowly avoiding a collision with the coffee table. I flopped down with my legs over the back of the couch and grabbed the remote.

There was a show on about a wedding. The wedding party was standing at the edge of a cliff overlooking the ocean in perfect wedding attire. It was on Lifetime, so most likely, the bride was going to find out her husband was really married to women all over the country, or her maid of honor was trying to kill her, or she and her new husband would have a kid and the babysitter would try to move in on her territory and start wearing her clothes. But right at that moment in the movie, everyone was all smug and delighted with themselves, and it made me sick.

"He doesn't really love you," I yelled at the television as I changed the channel. "He doesn't really love you," I whispered, slowly, feeling the sting in my eyes as I said the words. I sat up, took a long sip of my drink, and wiped my teary eyes with the back of my hand. "Fuck him," I said, getting up to make another drink. "Fuck." I dropped a few more ice cubes into my cup, splashing myself. "Him."

I walked back into the living room, tripping a little when my sock caught on the carpet. I grabbed the remote and flipped through couples kissing, a sale on manufactured diamonds on the Home Shopping Network, and some design show where a couple celebrating their twenty-fifth wedding anniversary was getting a makeover for their big celebration. Everything reminded me of Peter.

Finally, I settled on an old black-and-white episode of *Rin Tin Tin*. The dog dwarfed the child actor who played his sidekick, and a bunch of men in uniforms wearing toy guns on low-slung holsters delivered wooden lines like, "I'm the fastest shot in this town, sir!"

I got comfortable on the couch with my laptop, and started deleting my junk e-mail with the TV on in the background, but the dog was incredible, and I couldn't stop watching. He saved people and warned of certain danger. He was always there when needed. He never let anyone down.

I typed *Rin Tin Tin* into my search engine, and got the official Rin Tin Tin website. Apparently, it wasn't just one dog. There had been a long line of Rin Tin Tins. German Shepherds. I read the history of the first one, slurping through my fourth Kool-Aid. I got to the end, and was putting my laptop aside to get a refill, when I noticed a heading on the sidebar: PUPPIES. I poured another drink and raced back to the computer, only to learn that the next litter of puppies was all sold before they were even born.

I looked for German Shepherd puppies in Rochester, but all I could find was a breeder in Canada who specialized in police and cadaver-recovery dogs. There was a detailed explanation of training the dogs with a coffee can punched with holes and filled with human remains. I snapped my computer shut, but then Rin Tin Tin jumped over a burning hay bale to save his master.

That's what was missing. That's what I needed. Rin Tin Tin wouldn't leave me for thin thighs and an aristocratic nose. Rin Tin Tin would be a loyal friend.

I went back to looking for a puppy. The words on the screen were starting to blur, but I didn't care. I needed a dog, and I wasn't going to stop until I found one. I clicked from one site to another, and then, I saw him.

He was a shaggy ball of fur. Jet-black, except for a small pink tongue hanging out of his mouth. His head was tipped to one side like he was listening to something intently. One of his ears flopped over. The breeder was in Bratislava, Slovakia, and the site wasn't in English, with the exception of a few shaky translations. At the top of the picture of the puppy, it said something I couldn't read, and then MALE 11/5. The puppy was only a few weeks old. He was just a baby. Under his picture, there was a link that said ORDER FORM. I moused over it, ready to click.

I took another long slurp of my Kool-Aid. I couldn't just decide I wanted a dog and order one off the Internet. It was crazy. Crazy! I tried to go back to watching *Rin Tin Tin*, but I couldn't stop staring at the picture of the puppy. It was like one of those paintings where the eyes follow you everywhere. From every angle, I felt like that dog was looking at me. He was going to be taken away from his mother. He was going to be given to some random family and he was going to get lonely and miss his mom and they wouldn't understand. Not like I would.

"You need me, don't you?" I asked him. I felt like his eyes looked more and more sad and lonely every time I looked at the picture.

I clicked on the link. The order form said that the cost for the dog was one hundred and forty thousand koruny, which, seven drinks in, I figured was like pesos or lira or something like that, where a thousand of them equaled a dollar. I thought about looking it up, but my vision was starting to blur, and I wanted a dog. Now. I didn't want to wait any longer than I had to. What if someone else was sitting around in their pajamas watching the *Rin Tin Tin* marathon, realizing they needed a dog too? What if, in the time I took to look up the conversion rate, someone else bought my puppy? Someone else would get to cuddle up with that little ball of fuzz. Someone else would get sloppy dog kisses on their cheek. Someone else would have a true and loyal friend who would hop over burning hay bales for them, and I'd still be alone. It was probably really cheap. Cheaper than buying a dog from the United States even, I was sure. I grabbed my purse off the coffee table and riffled through the mess of business cards and discount cards, dropping them all over the couch, until I found my credit card.

Ha, Diane, I thought, remembering the time my mom asked her if we could get a dog. I was eleven and had just read *The Call of the Wild* in school. I spent an entire weekend planning for my puppy: where he would sleep, how I could pay for his food with my allowance. I made a chart of how I could squeeze in homework and take him on long walks, and Diane stuck a pin in it in two seconds. "Dogs are filthy. They lick their assholes. You can't be serious, Nat," she said when my mom asked her.

Well, this was my house and my dog, and Diane was done with me anyway.

I had to type my credit card number into the website four times before I got it right and it went through, but finally, it worked. The site said to expect a confirmation e-mail shortly.

Holy shit, I thought, as I flipped my credit card onto the coffee table. I just bought a dog. I felt like I should be panicking, but on TV, another *Rin Tin Tin* episode was starting. A tinny horn played a revelry while soldiers scrambled to attention, and a noble-looking Rin Tin Tin stood high on a rock watching them all, the breeze blowing his fur ever so slightly, a flag waving in the background. I could feel the excitement building. I was going to watch this episode carefully. I had to learn about German Shepherds.

I made myself another drink. I was almost out of Kool-Aid, so this one was mostly vodka. I sat down again, clicking the refresh button on my e-mail compulsively, waiting for information on when I could pick up my dog. But ten minutes later, there was still no e-mail. Fifteen minutes later, nothing. Twenty minutes, twenty-five minutes, then a half an hour and still nothing.

What if there is no dog? I thought. What if this was some kind of scam like those Nigerian prince e-mails? What if some Slovakian pervert was using my credit card number to buy porn and crack? I could picture him, in a dirty white undershirt, drooling over disgusting pictures in a dimly lit room. Maybe he wasn't even Slovakian. Maybe there was some kind of messed-up crime ring that preyed on lonely women watching dog movie marathons by pretending to be dog breeders in post-Communist countries.

I took another chug of my drink. Even though it was light on the Kool-Aid, it was starting to taste like cough syrup. As soon as I got it down, it started to come back up. I tasted it in the back of my mouth, and ran to the bathroom.

I heaved and heaved. Toilet water splashed up in my face. My hair got in the way and ended up covered in purple puke. Finally, I felt like I came to the end of everything that was left in me. I spit into the toilet and started crying.

I cried about everything from way back when Diane told my mom I couldn't have a dog, to Peter and the wedding and the check, my mom dying, the photo booth picture, and the Slovakian pervert. I cried because I really had no one. There was no one on my side. No one rooting for me above everyone else. There wasn't even anyone rooting for me to come in second place. There was no one to hold my hair back, or wipe my forehead with a wet washcloth. All I had was me, and it wasn't enough.

I curled up on the smelly bath mat and cried until I couldn't squeeze tears out of my eyes anymore. Then I just lay there and clenched my teeth, listening to my breath whistle through my nose until I fell asleep.

I woke up on the bath mat, smelling like wet towel mildew and vomit. I leaned up on my elbow. My heart was beating in my forehead and my stomach lurched forward again. I pulled myself up to the toilet and heaved, but nothing came up. My stomach felt like an empty tube of toothpaste squeezed against the side of the sink to get the very last bit out. My eyes were so puffy that I could barely keep them open.

I stumbled downstairs, started a pot of coffee, and downed some aspirin. The living room was a mess. An empty ice cream carton leaked sticky chocolate goo all over the coffee table. My laptop was open on the couch. The TV was on, blaring an infomercial for some carpet sweeper that could pick up lug nuts.

I couldn't remember much more from the night before, other than coming home and making myself a drink. I went back into the kitchen to grab a wad of paper towels to wipe up the ice cream. All of a sudden, I had a horrible thought and my heartbeat spiked: What if I'd called Diane and told her off? What if I'd called Janie and confessed or called Peter and told him I loved him?

It wouldn't be the first time I'd drunk-dialed. In college, I had a horrible habit of calling my mom to tell her embarrassing details of my life while under the influence. And like a good mother, she never let me live it down. "Hi, drunkie," she'd say when I called the next day, hungover, oblivious to my prior indiscretions, "I hear you flashed your RA last night." She never got mad. She always chalked it up to normal college behavior, something she knew nothing about. I wished she'd put the fear of God in me and made me join a convent where they were so straight that they substituted grape juice for communion wine, or at the very least, I wish she'd trained me to never make phone calls while intoxicated.

I scrambled around looking for my cell phone and held my breath while I checked my recent calls.

Nothing. No calls. I let the air out of my lungs slowly, feeling the blood return to my extremities. Then I realized that drunk e-mailing could be just as dangerous.

I sat on the couch yelling, "Come on, come on, come on!" while my laptop wheezed its way out of sleep mode. "Sent mail. Sent mail," I hissed through my teeth, waiting for the site to load. I typed in my user name and password, but before I even hit the SIGN IN button, I had a sudden flashback: sitting on the couch with my laptop, clicking REFRESH over and over and over again, waiting for a purchase confirmation. What did I purchase? Did I break down and buy that absurdly expensive laptop I'd been eying for months? My heart pounded while I waited for my stupid slow Internet access to take me to my e-mail. And then there it was, an e-mail with the subject line *Potvrdiť pes*. It all started coming back to me. The fuzzy black puppy. Rin Tin Tin. German Shepherd. Burning hay bales. A deep voice with a heavy accent. I pasted the subject line into Google translate. *Confirm Dog.*

"Fuck!" I yelled. "Fuck, fuck, fuck!" I bought a puppy. I bought a puppy off a fucking website like some kind of moron who doesn't even understand that you don't buy a freaking living being off the Internet.

I translated the e-mail sentence by sentence. The dog would be at the Rochester International Airport on a flight from Bratislava arriving at two thirty in the morning on Thursday. At the end of the receipt it said, *Mastercard*, and then *one hundred and forty thousand koruny*. I looked up an online exchange rate calculator and held my breath, feeling my pulse pounding in my temples. I entered the numbers, hit GO, and closed my eyes before I could see the results.

It's probably not that bad, I told myself. I remembered a girl from college who adopted a dog from the local animal shelter when she got her own apartment. It cost her two hundred and fifty dollars. Add to that shipping costs, and it would maybe double. I mean, how much could it cost to ship a teeny-tiny puppy? Five hundred dollars, I could handle, I told myself. I'd eat ramen noodles for dinner. I'd pay it off over a few months. Or I'd take on an extra freelance job or two. I'd barely feel the pinch.

I took a deep breath, opened my eyes, and looked at the screen. It said I'd spent six thousand and one dollars on a dog.

I ran back to the bathroom to throw up again.

When I was done, I got in the shower and winced as the hot water magnified my stench. Stomach acid, grape Kool-Aid, and mildew wafted around in the shower steam until I reached for the shampoo and started washing it all away. The hot and cold dials squeaked loudly as I turned the water off. The slapping sound of my bare feet hitting the tile floor echoed, and it was so quiet that I could hear the hum of the refrigerator from all the way downstairs, like a constant reminder that there was no one else here to make noise. I'd felt lonely before the wedding and the check, but I hadn't realized how far it could go, or how quiet it could get.

I could have called the kennel in Slovakia to cancel my order, or called the credit card company to see if they could stop the payment, but I didn't. I wanted to have someone on my team, even if that someone was only a dog. I wanted that kind of constant companionship and intense loyalty. I wanted someone to sleep at the foot of my bed, and keep me company while I was working. And it's not like my dog was going to be bigger than a child actor when he showed up. I was getting a tiny puppy. I could handle that.

Chapter Seven

I slept off my hangover through the weekend and by Monday, all I could do was think about my puppy. I didn't know anything about owning a dog, so I went to the library and pored over books on dog intelligence, an "idiots" guide specifically for German Shepherd owners, and a book about being a pack leader. One book was about how to be your dog's best friend. It was written in the seventies by a bunch of monks who bred German Shepherds at some monastery in the Catskills. It smelled kind of musty, like a basement in an old house, and the pages were water-stained and dog-eared, but the black-and-white pictures of German Shepherds playing with the monks kept me reading. The book talked about letting your dog share every aspect of your life, sleeping on your floor at night, lying down at your feet while you ate dinner.

I read that a German Shepherd is capable of understanding as many words as a three-year-old child if challenged appropriately. When I got home from the library, I ordered more books on training and discovered a line of puppy toys designed to encourage creative play. The beginning of the week was a blur of credit card orders and trips to the pet store to get supplies. It helped me get my mind off of Peter. Or in the very least, it gave me something productive to do when I couldn't stop thinking about Peter.

What was Peter doing, coming to see me on his wedding night? What had he been about to say when I cut him off? I imagined it over and over again.

In my mind, Peter says, "Van— Savannah, I—" but this time, I don't cut him off. Peter says, "Savannah, I love you. I've always loved you and I can't hide it anymore. I need to be with you." Only it doesn't sound like some bad movie, it sounds amazing, because Peter is saying it and he means it and he puts his arms around me and kisses me and we make love on my old bed in the carriage house. Later, when Janie finds out, she's not upset, because she's secretly in love with the heir to some great shipping fortune, who looks like a Greek god and has a name like Balthazar or Adonis, and the four of us end up being dear friends and we have these amazing dinners on Janie's patio overlooking the Aegean Sea at sunset. We laugh about how we almost got everything so horribly wrong and toast to getting it right with globe-shaped glasses of red wine. We eat crusty bread dipped in olive oil, and Peter wraps his arm around my sun-kissed shoulder. "What was I thinking?" he says, gesturing to Janie, and we all laugh, because it's so obvious that what Pete and I have is true love, and Janie's happy too.

When I'd snap out of it, and my face didn't feel flushed from getting too much sun, and all there was outside was cold and gray and I was still alone, and Peter was still off in Europe with Janie, I'd make another run to the pet store to buy Nylabones or treats, and think about cuddling up with my puppy and watching movies, or taking him for long walks, because that was a dream that could actually come true.

On Wednesday night, I set up everything. I put food bowls on the kitchen floor on a little bone-shaped place mat, but then I worried about my puppy dropping food out of his bowl and eating off the dirty floor. I didn't even own a mop, so I got down on my hands and knees with a bottle of Windex and a roll of paper towels and scrubbed a floor that hadn't been more than spot-cleaned in the two years since I moved in. I pulled out dried-up ziti from under the stove, and a baker's dozen of dehydrated peas from under the refrigerator. The scary thing was that I hadn't even eaten peas since I moved into the condo, so I'd actually pulled someone else's dehydrated peas out from under my refrigerator. I scrubbed the toilet because dogs drink out of toilets, but I worried that he might drink some lingering cleaner, so I flushed fifty times. I hid candles and stashed shoes. I scooted around the house on my knees looking for sharp edges and objects that could obstruct airways. Before I knew it, it was two in the morning, and it was time to go get my puppy.

It's weird to claim baggage when you haven't flown anywhere. I didn't quite know what to do with myself. I felt like I should be holding up a sign saying LEONE or GERMAN SHEPHERD or something.

When I got to the baggage claim section, there was an enormous green plastic crate on the floor in the corner.

I walked over and peeked in the crate. It was dark. There were shadows of a dog shape—sharp ears and a snout the length of my forearm—but I couldn't see much until a pink tongue the size of a strip steak dropped out of nowhere. Geez, that's weird, I thought. Someone else is picking up a dog too.

I backed away from the crate and walked over to the freight pickup window, slapping my driver's license down on the counter.

"Ms. Leone, you're here for the dog, aren't you?" The clerk behind the counter was a nice-looking man with dark brown hair slicked back with copious amounts of hair grease. He had a brilliant white smile, orange-tanned skin, and dimples. The airport ID tag hanging around his neck read PETER MARINO and showed a picture of him giving the camera a sly smile, like he was posing for a magazine cover. He was a completely different kind of Peter. He wasn't even a Pete. I bet his friends called him Petey.

"I'm here for the puppy," I corrected.

"That is one big puppy, ma'am," Petey said, pointing to the pink tongue in the gigantic crate. "Real sweet, though. Hasn't barked once." He shoved a paper across the counter at me. "Sign here," he said, making a big sloppy X with his pen. My heart plunged into my toes.

"I'm sorry," I said, taking the pen from him. My hand was shaking. "There's got to be another crate. That big one, that's someone else's. I'm here for a puppy." I held up my hands, about two feet apart, to show him how big I thought the puppy was supposed to be.

He laughed. "We've only got one dog, here, ma'am, and your name is on the crate."

I could barely get my hand to work the pen. My signature was a long squiggly line. How was that beast in the big green crate my puppy?

Petey wasn't paying attention to me, he was staring longingly at the crate. "Okay, he's all yours."

I wanted to tell him he could have the dog, and the closer I got to the crate, the more I wished I had. The crate came up to my hip bone, and the dog, from what I could see of him, took up most of it. The muscles of my heart were working hard and skipping beats. I had a tiny black puppy collar with little silver stars on it tucked in my purse along with a skinny black leash. It didn't look like it would fit around this beast's leg. I pictured myself leading a big black wolf through the airport with a collar on his leg.

Petey came out of a door labeled EMPLOYEES ONLY. I tried to keep my eyes averted so he wouldn't see the panic on my face.

"Miss?" He walked over to the crate and tapped on it. "Miss Leone? I'm on break. I can help you get him to your car if you want."

"Oh. Uh." I didn't want to take up this poor man's break, but there was no way I was getting the dog and the crate to my car alone. I looked up at him and nodded.

He snagged a big metal baggage cart and pulled the crate onto it, grunting loudly and straining himself until the veins in his neck popped out. I felt so guilty. I should have brought someone with me to help. But really, even if I'd been willing to openly admit that I gave my credit card number to a Slovakian website and prayed for a dog in return, I didn't have anyone to help me.

We got out to the parking lot. Petey huffed and puffed and his breath made a cloud that circled his head and trailed behind him. I worried he might explode. I wanted to help him, but I didn't know what to do. I walked fast next to him and put my hand on top of the crate like I was helping to steady it.

"Where's your car?" he asked, grunting.

"Over there." I pointed to my little silver Corolla.

Petey stopped and looked at me, then he threw back his head and laughed up at the sky, "Ha! Ha! Ha!" He vibrated. His sides heaved in and out under his thin shirt. "You think you're going to get this guy in there?" he said. Tears welled up in his eyes from laughing so hard.

"Well, I thought he'd be—" Tears welled up in my eyes too. "I thought he'd be smaller," I said. I was laughing and crying at the same time. Tears ran down my face and dripped off my chin.

"Well, then we'll just have to see what we can do here, right?" Petey pulled a tape measure out of his pocket and measured the crate and then the car door and then the crate again.

"He's gonna have to come out." He pushed the button on his tape measure and the tape snapped back in.

The beast stirred in his crate.

"What do you mean, come out?"

A car drove by us and the headlights shone into the crate. Teeth gleamed.

"Well, you gotta take him out of there sometime, lady. If you want me to help you, we're gonna have to take him out now."

Petey had me back the car out into the aisle. After a lot of maneuvering, he got the crate lined up pretty closely with my car door. From the front seat, I reached around and unlatched the crate door. The dog jumped onto the backseat. I hopped out of the front seat and slammed the door.

The dog was huge. The size of a person. He took up the whole backseat. All I could see was black. His fur was long, and so black it looked blue at the tips, even in the orange parking lot light. I was terrified.

"Whoa," Petey said. "What kind of dog is that?"

"German Shepherd," I said, running around the crate.

"That's not a German Shepherd. He's black. He has long hair."

"He's supposed to be a German Shepherd," I said.

The dog stared at us with his mouth open. His biggest teeth were the length of my little finger. A long string of drool dripped from his tongue, landing on the car seat.

Petey grabbed the crate.

"I'm gonna pull away. You shut the door."

I nodded and took a deep breath.

Petey pulled the crate away, but I hesitated a split second and the dog's head got in the way.

The dog pushed past us.

"Fuck!" I yelled. I didn't know if I should run after him. I didn't know if he'd bite me.

"Don't panic!" Petey said. "You can't panic."

"What am I supposed to do?" I asked.

"Let's just see what he's going to do."

The dog was about twenty feet away from us, sniffing around a lamppost.

"No! You don't understand! He's– I paid– He's–"

The dog lifted his leg and started peeing.

Petey chuckled. "When you gotta go . . ."

"What are we going to do? How are we going to get him in the car?"

"Calm down," Petey said, wagging his finger at me. "You're forgetting something very important."

"What?"

"Dogs like riding in cars." He pulled his bottom lip up, and raised his eyebrows like he'd just told me the great secret of the ages.

"That's it? That's all you've–"

The dog stopped peeing and put his leg down.

Petey made a clicking sound in the side of his mouth. "Come 'ere. Come 'ere, boy." He leaned in and smacked the backseat.

The dog ran over at full speed and jumped on the seat. Petey slammed the door shut behind him.

"See," Petey said. "Dogs like riding in cars."

I didn't think of Slovakia as a place that had cars. I pictured a little gnome man taking the dog to the airport in a hay cart pulled by a donkey, but the dog looked comfortable in my car. He sat on the seat and stared at us through the window, his breath fogging up the glass.

"He's a good-looking dog, whatever kind he is." Petey hit his palm on the roof of the car. "Okay, next order of business. You know you're not going to get this crate in your car without breaking it down, right?" He went over to the crate and turned the locks along the side to release them.

I walked around to the other side and did the same. My fingers were freezing, and it hurt to push the plastic dials to unlatch the top from the bottom. Petey got all the latches around the back of the crate before I'd finished two. We took the front grate off and nested the top of the crate in the bottom.

"Here," he said, pulling a white envelope covered in packing tape out of his back pocket. "This was taped to the other side."

I didn't know what it was and I didn't want to find out with Petey looking on, so I shoved it in my coat pocket.

"Do you have any rope in your car?" Petey asked, and I knew he doubted that I did.

"No." I opened the trunk. There was a mass of old Tupperware containers and travel mugs that hadn't made it back home and into the dishwasher after being used. In the mess was an old ripped pair of panty hose.

"We can use these," I said, pulling the panty hose out of my trunk and wadding them up in my fist. Petey grabbed for them. I yanked them out of his reach. "I'll do it."

Petey lowered the crate pieces into my tiny trunk and shifted them around until he seemed assured that they were as stable as they were going to get. I tied the panty hose from the loop at the top of my trunk through the holes in the crate and into the loop at the bottom of the trunk. I pulled tight until the panty hose were out of stretch. I tried to tuck the crotch of the panty hose into the trunk, but it sprang back up.

"Well, there you go," he said. "All set."

"Here." I tried to hand him a ten.

He put his hand up and shrugged away from me. "No. No. That's fine." He shoved his hands in his pockets and walked away, yelling over his shoulder, "Good luck to you, Miss Leone."

I stared into the car window. The dog lay across the backseat with his head up like a sphinx, watching me.

Don't show fear, I thought. That's what people always say about dogs and bullfighting and bees. It's important not to show fear. I took deep breaths, but the cold air was stinging my lungs. I cheated and took shallow breaths, and before I knew it I was hyperventilating. I leaned up against the car at the driver's side and put my head down, breathing into my armpit to try to catch warm air.

The car rocked. I looked up, and the dog was in the front seat, staring at me through the window. I leaned in closer. His eyes were warm and brown. He cocked his head to the side and I felt better. I slowed my breathing back to normal.

"Okay, you have to get in the backseat," I said. He tipped his head to the other side. "Backseat," I said louder. "Backseat." I tapped on the back window. The dog jumped into the backseat and sat down.

I opened the car door and got in. He leaned forward, nudged my arm, and rested his head on the console. I reached over and patted his head. My hand shook. His fur was softer than I thought it would be.

I wiped the condensation off the windshield with my fist, and started the car.

The dog was quiet for the whole car ride. He sat in the backseat and looked out the window. I watched him in the mirror and wondered if the view from the car looked different to him here.

Chapter Eight

When we got to the house, the dog circled upstairs and downstairs, in and out of every room. He repeated the cycle, in the same order, several times. I followed him, hoping I hadn't left anything out in my dog proofing. He kept his nose to the ground the whole time. Finally, he got back to the kitchen, walked over to me, and sat down. The condo passed his inspection.

"Water? Do you want water?"

He stared at me.

I walked over to the water bowl, and pointed to it. He didn't budge. I kicked the bowl with my foot and the water lapped against the sides. He came over, sniffed it, and started drinking. He drank until the bowl was empty. Then he sat in front of me again and stared. I wasn't scared, but I felt uneasy, like he was expecting me to do a song-and-dance number for him or something.

I still had my coat on. I remembered the envelope. The packing tape on the envelope stuck to the inside of my pocket and collected red fuzz.

On the front of the envelope *Regalhaus vom Stoffelgrund* was spelled out in funny little squared-off letters.

"Is that you?" I asked, pointing to the paper like he could read it. "Regalhaus?" He stood up and walked closer to me, sat down, and pressed his head against my leg. "Regalhaus vom Stoffelgrund? You have a last name?" I scratched his head. "You don't look like a Regalhaus. What should we call you?" The hair behind his ears was soft and wispy like duck down.

"Bill?" I said. He pulled his head away from my leg and looked at me. "Bill?" I said, again. He cocked his head to the side. "Carl?" He tipped his head to the other side. I got the giggles. As much as I'd always wanted a dog, I hadn't been around them much. It was weird the way he hung on my every word like he was waiting for one that applied to him. "Denny? Eric?" I asked, going through the alphabet. He looked me straight in the eyes, and his head tipped from one side to the other with every name, like he was considering it. My giggles turned to hiccups. "Fritz? George? Harold?" He yawned. "Yeah, you don't look like a Harold. Ichabod? How about Joe?" I hiccupped loudly. He pawed at my leg. "Joe?" I put my hand out and he slapped his big fat paw into my palm. "Nice to meet you, Joe." I gave his paw a good shake, and crouched down next to him. He nuzzled his head under my chin, and it was like the good strong hug I'd needed for such a long time. Joe rested his head on my shoulder and I wrapped my arms around him and hugged back.

I pushed his head aside so I could open the envelope. Inside were what looked like medical forms and a piece of yellow paper with blue-ruled lines. The yellow paper was filled with more squared-off lettering in pencil. The first line of the page read *Befehl* with *Command* written next to it.

The rest of the page had words written without English translation.

I read the first one.

"L'ahni."

Joe hit the ground, pressing his chin to the floor.

"Sadni."

Joe sat up at attention.

"K Nohe."

Joe circled me and sat down at my left side.

"Are you serious, Joe? There's a command for that?"

I said it again. "K Nohe." Joe circled around again and sat.

"Good boy, buddy."

I read the next one. "Štekat'."

Joe let out a bark that made my eardrums itch.

"What?"

He looked at me.

"Štekat'."

Joe barked again, even louder this time. I stepped back.

"Okay, Joe. Should we stop with this until I know what they mean?"

We went to the garage to get his crate out of the car. I untied the panty hose and pulled the crate pieces out of the trunk. Joe ran ahead of me while I dragged it all up to my bedroom. He sat next to me, watching intently while I put it together. Even with warm fingers it took me a long time to get all the dials turned.

Joe's eyelids closed into little slits and his head drooped.

"Here, buddy." I walked over to the bed and patted the mattress. He jumped up. "Lie down." Joe looked at me blankly. "L'ahni." He plunked down on the bed. I rubbed his head lightly, and he closed his eyes. By the time I finished putting his crate together, he was passed out with his head on my pillow, snoring.

I changed into sweatpants and a T-shirt and turned off the light. Joe was asleep on the side of the bed I usually slept on, so I climbed in next to him. The bed was already warm. Joe rolled over and pressed his nose up against my forearm, and he sighed like he was letting go of the weight of the world. Something about that sigh and the breath whistling out of his nose made me feel safe. I tried to reach for the remote, but I couldn't get it without taking my arm away from him, so I just lay there, listening to him breathe until I fell asleep, and for the first time since the wedding, I didn't dream of Peter, sunsets, or Greek gods for Janie.

Chapter Nine

Joe woke me up around eleven thirty by whimpering and pawing at me.

"Do you have to go out?"

Joe cocked his head to the side.

"Out? Outside?"

He whined.

"Okay, just give me a minute." I got up and went to the bathroom to pee and run a brush through my hair. Joe followed me and waited at the door, whining. I pulled some wrinkled jeans and an old sweatshirt out of the clothes hamper. Joe scratched at the bathroom door. "One sec!" I pulled my hair into a ponytail, and opened the door to the most awful stench. Joe's ears were flat against his head, and his eyes looked big and sad. At the end of the hallway, by my bedroom door, was an enormous pile of poop, right there on the beige carpet.

"Oh, God!" I yelled. "What did you do?"

Joe whimpered and got as low to the floor as possible, like he was trying to be invisible. It was like he was completely humiliated, which was understandable. In the same situation, I'd be humiliated too. I should have taken him out before we went to bed.

I covered my nose with my sleeve and ran down to the kitchen to grab some spray cleaner. I scrambled through the kitchen, looking for something to use to scoop up the poop, but all I could find was a paper plate. I ran back upstairs, held my breath, and used the plate to scrape the pile off the carpet, but as I was doing that, Joe came over and gave the arm I was leaning on a good nudge with his nose. I lost my balance and slid into the pile, smearing the poop into the carpet with my sleeve.

"Fuck!" I yelled. Joe was completely unfazed. He sat down so close to me that his side was touching my leg, like nothing much had happened, and we were just being chummy in the hallway. My blood was boiling. I was covered in shit from my hand to my elbow. Actual shit. It was the grossest thing that had ever happened to me. I wanted to open the door and let him go. He could go poop on somebody else's shirt. But when I looked over at him, he cocked his head, and looked up at me with his big, sweet brown eyes, like I was the greatest being in the entire universe.

"You're lucky you're cute," I told him.

I took my shirt off, trying not to get the poop all over myself, and washed my hands, soaping up and rinsing three times. I scooped up the poop on the carpet with the paper plate and dumped it in the toilet. When I flushed, Joe came over. He watched the water in the toilet swirl around, wagging his tail like we were having a grand old time. I threw the paper plate and my shirt away in the bathroom garbage and tied up the liner. There was no way I was ever going to be able to wear that shirt again without thinking it smelled like poop, no matter how many times I washed it. I sprayed some carpet cleaner on the stain and left it to do its thing.

"Too bad we can't just teach you how to use the potty like a big boy," I told him as I ran into the bedroom to get a clean shirt. He gave me a solemn look and started whining again. He hadn't peed since we were in the airport parking lot, and I realized he probably had to go desperately.

"Okay. Okay. Let's go," I said, running for the door. Joe followed. I threw on my jacket, buttoning it all the way so no one could tell I wasn't wearing a shirt. I looped the leash around Joe's neck and held on to the tiny puppy collar. He whined and wagged his tail. As soon as I got the front door open, he pulled so hard that he almost ripped my arm off. Fresh air never smelled so good. But Joe wasn't going to let me stop to enjoy it.

"Slow down!" I yelled, but Joe strained against the leash like he would rather choke himself than stay still, so I picked up the pace. When I walked faster to try to get some slack on the leash, he walked faster too. But when I tried to slow down, he kept speeding along. The cold air stung my lungs and I was getting a stitch in my side. I wondered if somewhere on the yellow paper Joe came with there was a command for *stop being a jerk and walk like a normal dog.*

I was out of breath and exhausted before we'd even made it a quarter of the way around the block. Just when it seemed like Joe was starting to walk at a reasonable pace, a cat ran across the street about fifteen feet ahead of us, and Joe took off, pulling me along with him. He sprinted up the street.

"Joe! Stop! Stop! K Nohe! L'ahni!" I yelled, because they were the only commands I could remember. He didn't even hear me. He was practically dragging me down the street and I was running faster than I had since I was a kid playing tag on the playground.

Suddenly we hit a patch of ice, and my legs flew out in front of me. I fell on my ass right in the middle of the street, dropping his leash. As soon as I hit the ground, I could picture the big purple bruise I was going to get. Joe chased the cat until she ran up a tree, and then he came running back to me, tail wagging, like it was a job well done.

When I tried to get up, Joe put his big muddy paws on my shoulders and licked my face until I was covered with slime. "Damnit, Joe! Get off me!" I pushed him off and wiped my face with my sleeve. I got up and tried to brush the mud off my ass, but I only made it worse. I could tell I was going to be sporting a major bruise, and I was ready to go back to the condo.

I reached for Joe's leash but he ran, pulling it just out of range. He stood still and looked at me. I walked toward him and reached for the leash. Again he ran a few steps ahead. I stumbled, but kept going, trying to grab the leash. Every time I almost had it, he'd run. I felt like Charlie Brown trying to kick Lucy's football.

Joe grabbed the end of the leash in his mouth and shook his head violently like he was killing prey. Then he pranced around in the grass, mocking me.

"Stop being such a dick!" I said to him, feeling utterly ridiculous as soon as I said it. Joe raced ahead, the leash still in his mouth. He slowed down and walked a few paces in front of me, looking back every few steps to see where I was going. When he got the idea that I was going to make a turn, he turned too. He was following me, except he was in front of me.

When we got closer to the condo, he ran ahead, over to the mailboxes, lifted his leg, and peed on the Crosbys' mailbox post. And of course, at that very moment, Gail Crosby came out to get her mail. In the two years I'd lived in my condo, I had never seen Gail do anything other than get the mail and go for power walks. Her husband, Mitch, brought groceries home with him, and I had a hunch that he was the one cooking, and doing the dishes too. Mail was Gail's grand event. She curled and glossed and picked out a sweat suit that went well with the weather, and then she'd walk down the driveway like a runway model, sauntering back with her signature butt wiggle. The velour sweat suit of the day was flamingo pink. Joe finished his business and ran over to her, smelling the leg of her pants.

Gail tipped back her head and screamed.

"Oh, God, oh my God!" She hopped around and shook her hands. "He's attacking me!"

Joe ran around Gail, wagging his tail.

"I'm calling animal control," Gail yelled, scrambling for the door.

"Wait," I yelled, running to catch up with Joe. "He's my dog."

She was still moving frantically. It didn't even look like her feet were touching the ground, like when you're a kid and you're scared of monsters getting you at night so you don't want to touch the floor.

"That's not a dog." She pointed her finger at him. Her hand shook. "That's a wolf."

"No. He's not a wolf. He's my dog. This is Joe. See? Watch." I stepped in front of Joe, took a deep breath, and prayed he'd listen to me. "K Nohe!" He ran behind me and sat at my left side. "L'ahni!" His belly hit the pavement.

"Look, I'm sorry he scared you," I said. "He's a nice dog."

"That is not a dog. Mr. Buggles is a dog. That is a beast! How could you bring that thing here?"

"Gail, he's nice. I don't think he'd hurt anyone."

"You don't think? You don't think? You bring a lethal weapon—"

"He's a dog!"

"Mr. Buggles is a dog! That is a—"

"Mr. Buggles is a leash-trained rat!"

"Ah!" Gail clapped her hand to her cheek like I'd just slapped her. "You take that back, Savannah! You take that back!"

"Take it back? Are you twelve?" Joe was still lying at my feet. "Come on, Joe. Let's go." I walked back into the house, with Joe following me. I slammed the door loudly behind us.

Gail spent the rest of the afternoon crying in her kitchen, and I was pretty sure it was for my benefit. After I finished scrubbing the carpet in the upstairs hallway, opened every window in the condo even though it was freezing out, and lit every candle I owned to try to kill the smell, I dragged my comforter downstairs and spent the afternoon bundled up on the couch with Joe, watching TV with the volume up high enough to drown out Gail. My upper thigh was sporting the beginnings of a brutal bruise, so I sat on an ice pack.

Joe barked anytime there was a dog, doorbell, or car horn on the TV screen, but the rest of the time, he lay there with his front paws on my lap, nudging my hand whenever I stopped scratching behind his ears. And if I talked to him, he did a great job of pretending he was interested, tipping his head from one side to the other, or making his ears stand up at full attention.

We got up every hour on the hour to go outside, just in case. I wasn't taking any more chances.

Chapter Ten

The next day, Joe must have been good and rested, because after breakfast he ran around the condo at warp speed. He ran up the stairs, into the bedroom, jumped on the bed, jumped off the bed, sped down the stairs and into the kitchen, then turned on a dime and raced into the living room to jump on the couch. Then he pushed some of the cushions off the couch with his nose like he was throwing a temper tantrum, before tearing back up the stairs again to start the cycle all over again.

I didn't know what to do. I sat at the kitchen table, holding my mug of coffee protectively and watching in awe. When he raced by, he was a blur of black fur. He went through the entire cycle six or seven times before stopping in the kitchen. He was panting so hard I thought his heart might explode. He gave his empty water dish a good smack, and looked at me while it wobbled around on the floor, as if to say, "I demand water, damnit!"

"What, do you think you have a maid or something?" I asked, but I filled his water bowl anyway.

He spent the next few hours passed out in my office while I pulled my hair out over an arts-funding grant I was working on. I had only half the information the client promised and the deadline was fast approaching. I had this sneaking suspicion that if the grant didn't get turned in, my client wasn't going to pay for the work I'd done, even if it was their fault. With six thousand dollars' worth of dog sprawled out on his side on the floor, snoring, I really couldn't afford to work for free. After two hours of doing the best I could with the information I had to work with, I'd had enough and went online to translate the yellow paper of commands. Apparently, the command for *no* was *fuj*, which was pronounced "phooey." Great, I thought, as if it's not weird enough to walk around talking to your dog in a language you don't even speak, now I could sound like I was ninety years old. I might as well start saying things like "drat," "gosh darn it," and "golly gee willikers" too.

There were twenty-seven commands. The obvious useful commands came first: sit, stay, heel, bring, drop it, lie down. But then there were weird commands, things like "find narcotics" and "search the building." It was hard to think of Joe as the kind of dog who could sweep a building and bring down drug dealers, when he was busy drooling all over the carpet.

The writing on the back of the command sheet turned out to be a recipe for dog food made from boiled chicken, rice, celery, carrots, and olive oil. One of the dog books I'd seen at the library had a whole chapter about home-cooked dog food, and was adamant that feeding dogs people food was the best way to keep your dog healthy. I hadn't paid much attention to the book at the time, and I'd been feeding Joe fancy kibble that claimed to have "the perfect mix of proteins and antioxidants." But the recipe seemed simple enough. If that was what he was used to eating, it didn't seem fair to make him eat kibble. And I didn't have much food for me in the house either. Chicken, rice, and some veggies would be a major improvement on my steady diet of microwave meals and cereal.

I had to put Joe in his crate so I could go to Wegmans to get supplies.

"Poy-ed Sem," I told him, using the command for "Go inside," as I held open the door to the crate.

He stretched his neck and barked, his nose pointed at me, and his lips were tight around his mouth. It was a grumbling bark, like a complaint.

"Go," I said, pointing to the crate. "Poy-ed Sem." I felt like I was telling a teenager to go to his room.

He gave me a mournful look, then walked slowly into the crate like he was hoping I'd change my mind. I didn't, and he collapsed with a thud inside the crate.

"Good boy," I said, as I closed the door to the crate. He sighed heavily. I'd never realized how expressive dogs could be.

Wegmans wasn't crowded. I'd timed my trip perfectly: after the lunch rush and before the crush of people picking up dinner after work. It didn't take me long to round up all the ingredients and get through the checkout line. I couldn't have been gone for much more than half an hour.

When I got home, Joe met me at the door to the garage, wagging his tail and giving me a loud "hello" bark. At first I thought it was nice that he was greeting me at the door. It had been a long time since I'd had anyone to come home to. Then I remembered that I'd crated him.

"Oh no oh no oh no! What did you do?" I yelled, running upstairs to see how he'd gotten out of his crate. Joe followed as I walked down the hall and into the bedroom.

There was a huge hole in the corner of the crate at the air vents. Chewed bits of plastic were strewn around the room. Joe jumped around, picking up a big piece of plastic. He flung it across the room and then pounced on it. Then he brought it over to me, wagging his tail like it was a fun new game he'd just invented.

"You suck," I told him, bending down to pick up the pieces. The rough edges stuck in the carpet. I couldn't just sweep them into a pile with my hands, and my crappy old vacuum didn't get them all either, so I had to get down on my hands and knees to pick the little shards of plastic out of the carpet one by one. I tried to rationalize Joe's actions to get myself to calm down. I guess if I'd been shipped like cargo in an airplane, I wouldn't want to get back in my crate again either. But, as I was picking the plastic pieces out of the carpet, I noticed there were splintered pieces of wood in the carpet too. The dresser was fine, so was the TV stand. Then I saw it. Joe had chewed one of the legs of my bed like it was a big fat stick. There were big ugly teeth marks in the dark wood.

"Phooey," I yelled, even though I knew from my reading that it was after the fact and it wouldn't mean anything to him. I was frustrated that I didn't have a way to make him understand. Tears welled up in my eyes.

That bed was the only piece of honest-to-goodness, non-hand-me-down, non-secondhand, bought-from-a-furniture-store piece of furniture I owned. It was one of the few things I really took care of. I bought a special beeswax polish. I filled the little nicks and scratches. I did everything I could to keep it looking brand-new.

"Phooey!" I yelled. "Damnit! Damnit! Damnit!"

Joe dropped to his belly and pressed his chin to the floor. His ears went back against his head, and he whined.

I lay down on my back on the floor and touched the teeth marks in the bed. They were deep. Not so bad that the bed would collapse, but bad enough that no amount of polishing or wood filler would repair it. I could feel tears streaming down the sides of my face.

My mom ordered the bed for me when I moved into an off-campus apartment senior year of college. It was a total surprise. "Sorry I couldn't be there to help you move in," she said, when I called after the deliverymen left, "but I thought you needed something to mark your independence—your first apartment—a grown-up bed."

"It's not just my apartment." I'd moved in with two other girls from my department. It was a crappy apartment with stairs that creaked, and a perpetual keg party in the unit next door. "It's not that much independence," I'd said, worrying about what it cost. My mom's car was on its last legs, and I knew she should be saving for a new one.

"You can't sleep on a futon forever," she said.

It turned out to be the beginning of my independence. When I moved out of that apartment, I had to hire movers. Unlike all the other kids who discarded what didn't fit in the back of Mom and Dad's SUV, I had a big, heavy wood-framed bed and no one to help me move it. When I moved out of that apartment, I didn't have a mom anymore.

Practicality was never my mother's strong suit, but I think, maybe, she'd been trying to do what she could to get me settled in life. To make sure I was okay. To mark the milestones she could, because she wasn't going to be there for all the rest. I liked to think the bed was a "just because" kind of present, but I think it was much heavier than that. She probably already knew about the cancer when she bought it.

I could have asked Diane exactly when my mother found out she was dying. But maybe that was part of why I'd pushed Diane away. Sometimes, it's easier not to have the answers. Knowing wouldn't change anything. Either way, my mom had been trying to do something nice for me. Either way, Joe had just ruined my mother's gift. My mother was still dead, Peter was still married to Janie, and Diane was still done with me.

I lay there and watched my stomach shake, choking back sobs. And when I couldn't hold them back, it turned into that awful wailing, primal kind of cry that has a life of its own. I'd been doing everything I could to keep from getting that deep. I worked too much. I drank too much. I could let myself fall apart sometimes when I was good and numb, but it was scary, lying there, crying with every single part of my being.

Joe got up and plopped down again next to me. He let out a big sigh. I could feel his sides press into mine with every breath he took. He lifted his head and rested it on my chest. I wrapped my arms around his neck and cried that horrible cry, and it was much less scary because I wasn't alone.

Chapter Eleven

The next morning, Joe started up with the crazy running around again. His eyes looked wild as he ran past me, knocking a stack of junk mail off the coffee table as he went. I had no idea what was wrong with Joe, but I couldn't take it anymore. I went up to my office, turned on my computer, and did a search to see if there was anything I could do to stop Joe from going crazy all the time, but every site I read said to consult a vet before trying to treat any major behavioral problem, to rule out medical causes.

I grabbed the phone book and flipped through two pages of vet listings until I saw an ad for a Dr. Alexander Brandt. The ad had a sketch of a German Shepherd and said "Specializing in Large Dogs."

I dialed the number. Since it was Saturday, I wasn't actually expecting them to be open, but I figured I'd leave a message and get the ball rolling.

"Dr. Brandt's office, Mindy speaking." Her voice sounded like rainbows.

I told her I needed to make an appointment for my dog.

"Is he a patient here?" she asked.

"I just got him on Thursday," I said, warily. I really didn't want to tell her anything about how I got Joe. Luckily, she didn't ask.

"I have a cancellation this morning at eleven," she said. She was chewing gum. "Otherwise, looks like we can't get you in until December. Is the twelfth okay?"

"I can come in today," I said, despite the fact it was already ten thirty, and I was still in my pajamas.

"Okeydokey," she chirped. "See you soon!"

I hung up the phone and ran upstairs. By the time I showered and put on some mascara, I was already running late. I didn't even have time to brush my teeth. I threw on some jeans and a wrinkled T-shirt, and grabbed a pack of Doublemint gum off my desk. My hair made the back of my shirt damp.

When Joe got wind of the fact that we were going for a ride in the car, he acted like a kid at the gates of Disney World, jumping up and down, whining like crazy. I wished I could get that excited about riding in the car. Hell, I wished I could get that excited about anything.

Joe jumped in the car the second I opened the door. Then he sat in the driver's seat and licked the steering wheel. "Backseat," I told him. He jumped to the backseat immediately. There were some things he just seemed to understand naturally, like when he followed me into the bathroom and I didn't want company, I said, "Can I have a moment?" and he backed his way out so I could shut the door. There was no way he could have been trained to do that. I couldn't understand why sometimes he instinctively knew how to behave, but then he didn't know not to chew on my bed or eat his way out of his crate.

Joe bounced around on the backseat, checking out the view from every window. He barked at people waiting at the bus stop or crossing the street at stoplights.

When we got to the vet, I put Joe's puppy collar–leash combo on him. It looked like I didn't know what was supposed to go where. I wish I'd thought to buy him a real collar.

Dr. Brandt's waiting room was bright and smelled like pee. There was a huge fish tank in the middle of the floor and a lizard tank built into the reception desk. I watched the lizard eat lettuce while I waited for the woman sitting behind the counter to hang up the phone.

The woman waved at me and held her finger up to tell me she'd only be a moment. She was wearing a white turtleneck with little blue snowflakes and a baby blue cardigan. Her short blond hair was pulled into a springy little ponytail assisted by blue plastic daisy barrettes. There was a row of plastic angels on alphabet blocks that spelled out *Mindy* across the top of her computer monitor. "Okay now, we'll see you on the tenth. Well, you have a happy holiday season yourself!" She hung up the phone and grabbed the edge of the desk. "This must be Joe," she said, wrinkling up her little pug nose. She must have been over thirty, but she looked like she could still be bribed with a cookie.

"Yes," I said. "This is Joe." Joe sat next to me, leaning against my leg.

"Okay, I'm going to need you to fill out these forms." She handed me a clipboard with a pen dangling from a neon shoelace.

"I'm going to take him back and get him weighed."

She walked around the desk and took the leash from me. "Oh! This is cute," she said, holding up the collar handle.

"I—I thought he was going to be smaller."

"You're a big boy, there, Joey, aren't you," she said, scratching Joe's head. She walked away and he followed her the same way he followed me. I felt like crying.

I sat on a bench with my clipboard and tried to answer the questions as best I could. I knew Joe's birthday, and I did remember to bring the papers he came with, but they were all in Slovak. What if he wasn't really immunized? For all I knew, Joe could be horribly diseased. What if there was something really wrong with him and that's why he was so crazy?

"Okay, ma'am." The voice was soft and low with a slight twang. I hadn't even heard footsteps. "Mindy's got Joe in a room. You can come right on back." The man the voice belonged to was what my mother would have called a tall drink of milk. He was tall, thin, and wearing a red flannel shirt and blue jeans with layers and layers of paint stains.

I stood up. He took my clipboard from me with one hand and reached out to shake my hand with the other. His grip was firm and his hands were thick and calloused.

He took a peek at the clipboard and said, "Ms. Leone, I'm Dr. Brandt."

He looked like a farmhand or a stable boy, not a doctor. I thought vets were supposed to wear white jackets and green surgical masks. He had a mop of floppy sandy-blond hair.

"How's my dog?" I asked.

"Well, why don't you come with me and we'll take a look."

I followed him down a short hallway and into an exam room. He stepped back to let me in the exam room first. "After you," he said.

My arm brushed his as I walked past. "Sorry," I whispered, awkwardly.

Dr. Brandt smiled and pushed the hair out of his eyes.

Joe sat up on a big metal counter, and Mindy held his leash.

"This boy is such a good one!" Mindy said. She handed me his leash. "Why don't you stand here and hold this?"

I took the leash. Mindy cupped Joe's snout in her hands and kissed him on the nose. "Who's such a good boy?" she asked in a baby voice. "Who is such a good boy?" Joe licked Mindy's face. I felt like he was cheating on me.

Mindy stopped making out with my dog and shut the door behind her when she left.

"So," Dr. Brandt said, "Mindy said you just got this big fellow."

"Yes," I said, scratching Joe behind the ears.

"Where did you get him from?"

I thought about the papers from Slovakia shoved in my purse. I didn't want to explain the Rin Tin Tin movies and my vodka-fueled shopping spree. "ASPCA," I blurted out. "I got him at the pound."

"Okay, great. Do you have the papers?" He came up and patted Joe on the side.

"I forgot them at home," I said, scratching Joe's head hard.

"Okay, well next time you come in, we're going to have to go through shots and worm prevention. But at least we know he's had all the standard ASPCA care. That's a good baseline."

"Good," I said, feeling like I was lying to my teacher about my missing homework.

"So what seems to be the problem, buddy?" he asked like Joe might answer.

I told Dr. Brandt about the poop on the floor, the chewed crate, the couch cushions flying through the living room, and the temper tantrum on our walk.

"Okay," he said, absentmindedly as he felt Joe's belly. He looked in Joe's ears, checked his eyes, and pressed a stethoscope up to Joe's chest. Joe struggled a little when Dr. Brandt lifted his gums to check his teeth. "It's all right, buddy. It's just a quick look." Dr. Brandt stroked Joe's nose gently until Joe let him look in his mouth. Then he pried Joe's jaw open like a lion tamer.

Dr. Brandt patted Joe's side and went back to the counter. He scribbled in his file. "I think . . ." He trailed off and scribbled some more. "I think he . . ." He kept writing. "He . . ."

I was ready to scream for him to get on with it. Brain tumor? Some kind of rare Slovakian parasite?

Dr. Brandt put his finger up. "One sec." He flipped pages and checked off boxes. Finally, he closed Joe's chart. He looked at me and smiled. "You've got a healthy dog here, Ms. Leone. I don't see anything to be concerned about, and I don't think his behavior as you described indicates any underlying issues. Sometimes dogs coming from a shelter or another stressful situation have issues with being crated. Especially German Shepherds. They're very smart dogs, and they're very high maintenance. It's not uncommon to see issues when they're left alone. So, I guess my official diagnosis is that he's a German Shepherd puppy. Puppies are erratic. They have amazing fluctuations in energy, and—"

"A puppy?"

"Yes."

"How is he a puppy? He's huge!"

"Didn't the ASPCA tell you how old he is?"

"Um," I stammered, "I know he's not an old dog. I just . . . puppies are small."

"From looking at his teeth and overall development, I'd say he's five or six months old. Large dogs have a slow process to maturation. I think you'll see some puppy behavior well into two years. But I think that's all it is. I don't think there's anything to worry about."

I felt like he must have been missing something. No way was Joe a puppy. I was promised a puppy, but what I got was very much a dog. If Dr. Brandt was using that to explain Joe's behavior, he could be overlooking something big.

"So what would happen if we didn't have all the standard ASPCA care?" I asked.

"Well, there are a few other things I'd test for. Heartworm, parasites, things along those lines." He leaned back on the counter.

"Interesting," I said, trying to act casual. I couldn't cover up to save face if it meant Joe might not get the treatment he needed.

"It's rare, you know, someone dropping a dog like this at the pound, without a rescue group stepping in to take him." He smiled and raised an eyebrow. "Take a look at this snout. He's a purebred German Shepherd. Looks like he's from European lines. Beautiful. And a really nice temperament." I couldn't help but notice that Dr. Brandt had a really nice temperament too, and a really nice smile.

"I guess I lucked out," I said, shrugging.

"Down," he said to Joe.

Joe looked at him blankly.

"Platz!"

Joe just cocked his head to the side.

"L'ahni!"

Joe's belly hit the exam table. Traitor.

"Štekat'!" Dr. Brandt said, and Joe sat up and barked once. Dr. Brandt raised one eyebrow and looked at me.

"He's from Slovakia," I blurted out. "I accidentally bought him online." I wanted to hide under the exam table.

"Well, that would explain why he's trained in Slovak. My first guess was Germany." He turned away for a moment and scribbled something in Joe's file. I could see him smiling to himself, and when he turned back, his lips were firm and trembling slightly.

"Go ahead and laugh," I said.

"I wasn't going to laugh." He looked shocked.

"You know, I'd laugh if I were you," I said. My face got hot. Joe nudged his head into my armpit.

"Can I ask you something?"

"Sure."

"How do you accidentally buy a dog?" He smiled wide. He had nice teeth.

"Vodka," I said, "and a *Rin Tin Tin* marathon." I knew my cheeks were flaming.

"A dangerous combination, apparently," Dr. Brandt said, laughing openly.

I pulled Joe's paperwork out of my purse and handed it over.

Dr. Brandt smoothed the papers out on the counter and hunched over them, pointing to words on the page with his pen and muttering to himself.

"Is he okay?" I asked. "He has all the shots he needs, right?"

"Oh, of course! If you imported him, he had to have all the necessary injections before he got on the plane." He gestured to the page. "See here?"

I went over to stand next to him so I could see the paper. He smelled like soap and fresh laundry. Joe jumped off the table, pushed his way between us, and put his paws up on the counter.

Dr. Brandt and I laughed. "He knows we're talking about him," he said. He scratched Joe's head casually.

Dr. Brandt pointed to the top of the page where it said 11/5. "This is his birth date," he said.

"I think there was a mix-up. They sent the wrong dog—the wrong papers. There's no way Joe was born on November fifth." I worried about Dr. Brandt's abilities as a doctor. How could he think Joe could have gotten so big in just a few weeks? I didn't know a lot about dogs, but I knew Joe couldn't possibly have grown so huge so fast. Joe jumped down, and leaned against my legs.

"He was born in May," Dr. Brandt said.

Finally, it clicked. "European dates are backward," I said, smacking my forehead. "Eleventh day, fifth month. Oh, God! I thought they made a mistake and sent the wrong dog!"

"You got a much bigger dog than you bargained for, didn't you?" Dr. Brandt said.

"Yeah," I said.

"Were you scared?"

"A little."

"Are you going to keep him?" he asked.

"Of course," I said, shocked by the idea that I'd actually give him up. You can return a pair of jeans when they don't turn out to be as slimming as they looked in the dressing room. You can return milk that's gone sour before you even opened the carton. You can't just return a dog. And, as much as Joe was driving me crazy, I didn't want to send him back or give him up. I liked having him around.

"Well, he's healthy and stable. And he will calm down as he gets older. Just work with him. Make sure he gets enough exercise. Make sure he knows you're in charge. You'll be fine." He copied a few things from the papers into Joe's chart. I was still standing very close to him. My head buzzed like when your grade-school crush writes a note on your binder cover.

He folded up Joe's papers and gave them back to me, clicked his pen closed, and dropped it in his breast pocket. "So, looks like we'll need to see you in three months for some shots. Take care, Ms. Leone." He winked at me and walked out.

Three months. It was silly, but I felt a little slighted. Shouldn't he check back in with Joe sooner, just to make sure he was okay? By the time I thought to say "Thank you," or even just "Bye," he was gone.

Chapter Twelve

Joe had been with me for just under a week when I got the letter. I came home after a meeting to find a bright orange homeowners' association envelope tucked into the storm door. All of the condo notices came in color-coded envelopes, because Mr. Wright, the homeowners' association president, was the most anal-retentive person alive. Blue meant the water was being shut off for maintenance, green was always about lawn-related things—how many flamingos or gnomes or wind chimes you were allowed to display, or what color annuals you could plant—and yellow was all things electrical.

I got an orange envelope once before, when I didn't pay homeowners' dues for the first three months I lived in the condo. I didn't even know I had to, and then all of a sudden there was a bright orange envelope with an invoice for six hundred dollars and a handwritten letter from Mr. Wright explaining the importance of paying dues on time. After that, I paid two days ahead of the due date every single month, so by the time

I opened the letter, I was already fuming. I'd paid my fees. There was no excuse for this.

But I guess orange wasn't limited to homeowners' dues. Apparently Joe exceeded the weight limit for pets, which, according to the letter, was thirty-five pounds.

I marched down the street to the Wrights' unit and knocked on the door with my fist even though they had a shiny brass knocker. Mrs. Wright answered. Elizabeth Wright was a small, bony woman with sharp cheekbones and a weary, pinched expression that never went away. Mr. Wright called her Eliza, but when we first met, she introduced herself as Betsy. He pruned her name to his liking the same way he made the bushes in their front yard look like they were made of pom-poms.

"Oh, hi, Savannah. Come on in," Mrs. Wright said, eying the envelope in my hand. "I suppose you're looking for Harold." She pursed her lips like she was eating sour cherries. "I'll get him."

There was a framed watercolor of a duck wearing a kerchief and a big floppy hat in the entranceway. The condo smelled like meat loaf. I shoved the letter in my pocket, and took my leather gloves off. My hands were sweaty.

I heard whispers in the other room, and then Mr. Wright walked over. He was wearing a smoking jacket over a white undershirt, and his salt-and-pepper hair was slicked into a bouffant. I fixed my attention on the duck until I knew my smirk was under control.

"Ah, Savannah, I see you got my letter." He folded his arms in front of him and leaned against the wall.

"Yes. Yes, I did, and it's absurd!" I pulled the wadded-up letter out of my pocket and shook it in his direction. "Mrs. Mackenzie has six garden gnomes." I raised my hands to hold up six fingers to illustrate my point, but with holding gloves and the letter, I had no free fingers. I put my hands down. "Six. That's three over the allowed limit for lawn adornment."

"Well," Mr. Wright said, "Mrs. Mackenzie and I have an agreement about the gnomes. She—"

"Oh, I bet you have an agreement," I said, loosening my scarf. The thermostat must have been set to eighty-five at least. "The unit three doors down from me has so many wind chimes I feel like I'm in a creepy horror movie every time I walk outside. Do you have an agreement with them too?" I knew he knew about it. I'd seen him before, sitting in his living room window looking for rule book infractions through a pair of opera glasses.

"I have to stress, Ms. Leone, that this is quite a different matter. Residents have complained." He looked so smug. "And, if we let your dog stay"—he shook his finger at me—"the next thing you know we'd have pet lions roaming the cul-de-sac."

Pet lions. It made me think of Gail calling Joe a beast, and I realized where the witch hunt had started. It also meant I wasn't just fighting Mr. Wright. I was fighting Gail and probably most of my other neighbors too. When Gail got fired up, she made it her business to get everyone on her side.

If Peter were with me, he would know how to handle Mr. Wright. He had that lawyerly way of keeping his cool and acting appropriately. He would have looked down his nose at Mr. Wright and used words like *ergo* and *ilk*, speaking in quiet, reserved tones. I, on the other hand, wanted to pin Mr. Wright's head in my armpit and give him a noogie. Mess up his damn hair.

"So, because my dog is a little over the weight limit you think he should leave?" My voice wobbled. I knew I was chasing myself up a tree.

"From my best estimate, your dog is at least fifty pounds over the weight limit," Mr. Wright said. I could picture him in his window with his opera glasses, trying to get a good weight estimate when Joe and I walked past.

My mind raced for a counterargument. "You don't have a weight limit for people," I said. I knew I was grasping at straws.

"Weight limits for residents would be discrimination," he said.

"You're discriminating against my dog."

"He's not a resident," Mr. Wright said.

"He lives with me. He *resides* in my home."

Mr. Wright sighed. "He's not listed on your mortgage." He pulled at a thread on the sash of his jacket. "According to the homeowners' association rule book, you have thirty days to find him a new home."

"Are the Parkers' children listed on their mortgage? Because maybe they need to find their kids a new home too."

"Ms. Leone, you're being ridiculous. Now, I can get you a list of shelters that will take—"

"No, you're being ridiculous! He's my dog. I'm not going to take him to a shelter."

"We have these rules for a reason. We have these—" His face was getting red. He took off his glasses and rubbed the sides of his nose.

"Gail's dog yaps all day long, and you let her keep him."

"Gail's dog weighs seven pounds."

"Mr. Buggles wakes me up at five AM on Saturday morning, every goddamned weekend." I smacked my gloves in my hand.

Mr. Wright winced. "I understand that you're upset, but I ask that you not take the Lord's name in vain in my house."

"And I ask that you not tell me to find a new home for a member of my family." I wanted to smack my gloves across his face.

"It's not safe. A dog that size isn't safe. A bite from a dog like that could be lethal."

"But he doesn't bite. And did you see Mitch's hand when they first got Mr. Buggles? Mitch needed thirteen stitches."

"Exactly, and if a dog that size can do that kind of damage, think about the damage a dog the size of yours can do."

"That's not the point. The point is—there are dogs who bite and there are dogs who don't, and it's not about size. It's about being a good dog or being a barky, nippy piece of shit. Joe is a good dog. He's my family." I started crying. It wasn't just tearing up, it was full-out crying. "Fuck!" I wiped at my face with the back of my hand.

"Again, the language, I ask you to watch your language in my home." Mr. Wright's face looked like an overripe tomato.

"Holy fucking shit! Are you happy? Gee fucking whiz!" I was bawling.

The collar of my jacket was soaked. "FUCK FUCK FUCK FUCK FUCK FUCK FUCK!"

"Savannah, I'm going to have to ask you to leave."

"You don't even have to ask," I said. I walked out, and left the door open behind me.

Chapter Thirteen

I tried to put it out of my head when I got home, but it was impossible. Joe could tell something was wrong. He finished his dinner and then circled the kitchen three or four times, whining, before he collapsed on the floor with a big sigh. "You're telling me," I said. He rested his head on my thigh and looked up at me with his big brown eyes. I scratched his ears and fantasized about having a truckload of garden gnomes delivered to Mr. Wright's front yard.

After a failed attempt to focus on a made-for-TV movie about a cheerleader who gets murdered by the class nerd, I got up and started pacing. Joe followed. We walked around the coffee table and into the kitchen again and again. Joe lagged behind and then ran up ahead of me, looking back to see where I would go next.

I argued with Mr. Wright. First in my head, and then out loud.

"How dare you! How fucking dare you tell me I can't keep my dog in my home." I slapped my hand on the kitchen counter. "I pay the mortgage.

I clean the toilet. This is my house and he's my dog and he's not going anywhere!"

I ranted and raved through at least a dozen trips around the first floor before I noticed Joe had stopped following me. I called to him from the living room, but when he didn't come over to me, I walked into the kitchen to look for him. I found him hunched over by the door.

"Hey, buddy!" I said. "Whatcha do—"

He started heaving. It was a loud, hollow, gulping noise and his whole body lurched forward. When he finally puked, it hit the door and splashed back on him. He plunked down on the floor when he was done, looking defeated and humiliated.

"Joe!" I ran over to him and hugged him to me. The smell was obscene, like rancid meat, but I didn't care. I rubbed his temples like my mom used to do when I was sick. He whimpered and pushed his head into my lap. "It's okay, buddy. It's okay."

After a few minutes, he started heaving again. He stood up, and I ran to the phone to call Dr. Brandt's office.

After the first ring, I realized it was ten PM. The phone kept ringing and ringing, and I knew that no one was going to answer. Feeling hopeless and scared, I started to panic.

I was about to hang up, when someone picked up. "Hello?" answered a deep, scratchy voice. It wasn't Mindy's cheerful chirp. It was Dr. Brandt.

"My dog—my dog is throwing up everywhere. I—"

"Okay. It's okay. When he throws up, what's the consistency?"

"The consistency?"

"Does it look like what he just ate for dinner, or is it more of a bilelike substance?"

"It looks like dinner." Joe stopped heaving and collapsed on the floor again.

"It's probably just something he ate. Don't feed him for the next twelve hours or so, and see how he does. Okay?"

Another round of vomit splashed against the kitchen floor. "Oh, God! He's puking everywhere! I need help. I don't know what to do."

"Ma'am, I think he'll be fine. We're actually closed right now, but I'll give you the number of the emergency clinic, so if it gets worse you know who to call. Got a pen?"

"If you're closed—I just—I've never had a dog before and Joe is just—"

"Ms. Leone?"

"How did you know?"

"Well, who's gonna forget a dog named Joe? Look, I'm pulling an overnight with an emergency. Why don't you come down and I'll take a look at him, if it will make you feel better."

"Fifteen minutes?" I asked.

"I'll be here all night."

Chapter Fourteen

I buckled Joe in the car and backed down the driveway before I realized I hadn't changed my pukey clothes. I didn't even care; I just wanted Joe to be okay.

I had to knock on the door of the clinic for five minutes or so. The lights in the waiting room were off, but the heat lamp in the reception desk iguana tank gave off enough of a glow that I could see Dr. Brandt walking across the waiting room. He had a little hop in his step that made his hair flop in and out of his face. He came to the door and opened it with a key.

"Ms. Leone, good to see you," he said, with a big smile and no sense of urgency. "Come on in."

He held the door open for us. I walked in and Joe followed.

"No leash?" Dr. Brandt asked.

I rubbed Joe's head, and he leaned up against my leg. "He still pulls like crazy. It's easier without it."

"I would try for a leash when you take him out. If you work with him, he'll get better. Come on back; I'll take a look at him." He gestured grandly toward the hallway behind the reception desk. I felt like he was inviting me into his home.

"Exam four on the left," he said, and pointed in front of me. He didn't seem fazed by the fact that both Joe and I smelled like vomit.

"Why are you here so late?" I asked.

"I had an emergency call with a Golden. Car accident. She made it through okay, but—I like to make sure."

He pushed the pocket door on room four open, and smacked the exam table. Joe jumped up.

"Is he okay?"

"Let's take a look." He pulled open Joe's mouth. "Tongue's pink. That's good." He reached under Joe and pushed up on his stomach. Joe licked his face. "Well, that's good. If he had bloat, his tongue would be turning purple, and his stomach would be sore. He's fine." He patted Joe's rump. "Dogs get sick sometimes, and Shepherds have sensitive stomachs. They tend to be high strung. A lot of things can trigger it. Something he ate, something that threw off his routine."

Maybe my ranting and raving about Mr. Wright made Joe puke. I felt so guilty.

"I think he'll be just fine," Dr. Brandt said, smiling.

"Okay." I hadn't realized that I wasn't taking full breaths until I relaxed enough to breathe all the way again. But once I started breathing deeper, I started crying. Hard.

"Oh, oh, oh!" Dr. Brandt came running over to me. "Oh, Ms. Leone! He's going to be just fine." He put his hands on my shoulders. "Look at me. Joe is fine. He's okay." His eyes were clear, bright blue.

"Thank you," I said. My voice was tangled up in sobs. I was so embarrassed to be losing it in front of him. I just couldn't keep it together. I felt like everything in my life was balanced on the fine, fragile point of a pencil and it was way too easy to tip the wrong way when anything went wrong. I'd felt like this since my mom died and I was starting to wonder if it would ever go away. "Thank you. I just—"

"It's okay." Dr. Brandt kept one hand on my shoulder and reached over to the counter to get me a tissue.

"I'm sorry," I said. "I have a lot—a lot of—" I couldn't think of the word for it.

Dr. Brandt watched me patiently, waiting for me to finish what I was going to say. When I still couldn't find the right word, I started sobbing harder.

"It's okay. This happens. You were worried, and now you're relieved and—" He gave my shoulder a sympathetic squeeze. His hand was big and solid. Maybe from doing so many surgeries.

"I am relieved." I focused on his face. Dr. Brandt had beautiful eyes. "It's just that—" I took a deep breath and tried to calm myself down, but I burst into tears all over again. "I'm not going to give him up! I'm not."

Dr. Brandt wrapped his arms around me. "It's okay," he said, softly. "It'll be okay." He didn't seem to mind that I was covered with dog puke. I meant to pull away, but I needed it. I sank into him. His arms were strong and he was so warm. Joe jumped off the table and leaned into the backs of my legs.

I got the feeling Dr. Brandt was going to hug me as long as I cried. I felt silly standing there, letting Joe's vet hug me, but I liked the way I could feel his collarbone against my cheek, and I liked the way he smelled like pine needles and shampoo. His shirt was so soft.

Finally, he said, "Why would you have to give him up?" I pulled away and told him everything: Mr. Wright and Mr. Buggles, the garden gnomes, and the bright orange envelope.

"The thing is," I said, realizing I was ranting and not sure I could stop it, "he may be over thirty-five pounds, but he's not a yippy little shit."

Dr. Brandt's eyes sparkled. He pressed his lips together, the corners of his mouth turned up.

"Well, if you're not going to give him up, I guess you'll have to move," he said.

"Easier said than done," I said. "Can you even buy a house in thirty days?"

"Stranger things have happened," Dr. Brandt said, pulling himself up to sit on the counter Joe had just been on. "But I'm sure you can work something out. Maybe if you have a plan to move, they'll let you keep Joe in the condo a little longer. It would be unreasonable of them not to."

"Mr. Wright," I said, "is nothing if not unreasonable."

"But what is he really going to do if you don't have the dog out in thirty days? It's not like he can kick you out when you're already planning to leave, right?"

"Can he call animal control?" I had visions of Mr. Wright directing uniformed men with tranquilizer guns and big nets to come and capture Joe.

"Possible. Not likely, but possible. Tell you what," Dr. Brandt said. "If it takes more than thirty days, and you can't get an extension, you can leave Joe with me."

"Really? You'd do that?" I was starting to get drowsy. I yawned without covering my mouth.

Dr. Brandt didn't seem to notice. "Sure. Joe's a great dog." He tucked his hair behind his ear and it fell back in his face immediately. He had a laid-back, rugged thing going on, the shaggy hair, the faded clothes. I could imagine Diane having a field day with his scruffiness, but, really, it worked on him. He looked like he belonged in an ad for some super manly after-shave, maybe roping a steer or staring into a campfire.

"What do you do with your hair when you're in surgery?" I blurted out.

Dr. Brandt smiled and reached into the pocket of his lab coat. He pulled out a bright green terry cloth headband.

"No! Really?"

He nodded.

"Put it on!" I said, and he pulled it over his head and back up on his forehead.

"And then my scrub hat." He opened his arms posed with his palms out. "It's a nice picture, no?"

He had a good smile. It was big and toothy. One of his front teeth was slightly longer than the other. I thought about what it would be like to run my tongue along their edges to feel the difference. I blushed wildly.

I covered my mouth with my hand and faked a yawn, hoping the color in my cheeks would drain.

"You know," Dr. Brandt said, "I put a pot of coffee on before you got here. Come on." He jumped down from the table and gestured for me to follow him. Joe ran and pushed ahead of him. Dr. Brandt took us back to a small room with a coffeemaker and microwave on a counter next to a sink, and a sagging card table with two chairs in the corner. There was a refrigerator against the wall. It was avocado-colored and had a sign up that said FOR HUMAN FOOD ONLY.

"Milk and sugar?" Dr. Brandt asked, opening the fridge. He pulled out a carton of half-and-half and smelled it.

"Sure," I said.

He poured some half-and-half into two mugs and then followed with coffee.

"One packet or two?" he asked, holding up a packet of sugar.

"None, actually," I said, feeling silly that I'd agreed to sugar. "Just milk is fine."

He stirred my coffee for me with a spoon that had been sitting on a paper towel to blot. I tried not to think about how long the spoon had been there or who else had used it for what purpose.

He handed me the mug and then dumped three sugars into his coffee, opening the packets all together in one swipe.

"Thanks for the coffee, Dr. Brandt," I said, taking a sip. "And thanks again for seeing us so late. I know I worry too—"

"It's Alex," he said, giving me a sheepish smile, "Ms. Leone."

"Van," I said, automatically offering my hand to shake his.

He laughed and took my hand. He held it instead of shaking it.

"Nice to meet you, Van," he said.

Out of the corner of my eye, I saw Joe sniffing at the bottom of the fridge and before I realized what was happening, he had lifted his leg and peed on the corner of it.

"Phooey! Joe! Phooey!" I yelled, pulling my hand out of Alex's grasp and running over to shoo Joe away from the fridge. In the process, I spilled my coffee.

"Paper towels?" I asked, kneeling down by the puddle.

Alex pulled a wad of them from the holder over the sink. I put my hand out to take them.

"No, it's fine. I can do it." He didn't seem the least bit annoyed.

"I don't know what got into him," I said.

Joe flopped down on the floor and put his head in his paws.

"It's not his fault," Alex said, kneeling down next to me. "Mindy had her Jack Russell in the other day. Now, he's a yippy little shit. He marks everything." Alex rolled his eyes. "Joe was just following suit. Male dogs mark their territory. It's just what they do."

I thought about Peter's tearstains on my bridesmaid's dress.

Alex finished cleaning up the mess and slam-dunked the paper towels into the garbage can with a little hop. He lathered his hands up vigorously under the faucet, and dried them thoroughly, like he was about to walk into surgery.

"Let's get you a refill," he said, taking my cup from me.

He dumped what was left in the cup and poured me a new one with the same amount of cream as before. No sugar.

"Thanks," I said.

He pulled out a chair for me at the table.

"Have a seat," he said. "If you have the time. I don't want to keep you or anything."

"Sure," I said, staring into my coffee cup. "I mean, it's not like I had plans." I looked up and smiled at him.

"Do you play cards?" Alex asked, leaning back in his chair to grab a pack off the counter.

"Poker and Go Fish."

"Interesting." He plunked the cards down on the table. "Well, I don't have any chips here. We could play for kibble, but it smells pretty bad. Go Fish?"

"Sounds good," I said. I liked the way he looked right in my eyes when I said something, like every word I said was important to him.

We played three rounds, but the third round fell apart into giggles when Joe started snoring loudly under the table.

"He sounds like an old man," Alex said, snorting a little when he laughed. He didn't even cover his mouth or try to hide the fact that he snorted. He seemed so comfortable in his skin.

"That's quiet for him. You should hear him when we're sleeping. He wakes me up out of a dead sleep with that. Or when he's not snoring, he's pawing me in the back. Of course, it's still better than sleeping alone." As soon as the words came out of my mouth, I felt like I'd shared too much—a detail almost as personal as the fact that I danced around in my underwear singing "More Than a Feeling" at the top of my lungs every morning.

"I had a beagle when I was a kid," he said. "He did that every time he fell asleep." Alex put his cards down on the table. "The second he fell asleep, his legs would start moving"—he dropped his hands limp on his wrists and waved his arms around—"and he'd make these funny noises." Alex whimpered.

He was completely unaware of how ridiculous he looked, flailing around like that. I was embarrassed for him, but it made me feel less embarrassed for myself.

"My grandfather always said he was chasing rabbits," Alex said, giving me a big goofy smile.

"Oh," he said, looking at his watch. "I completely lost track of time. Can you stick around for about a half an hour and help me out with rounds?"

"Sure," I said. "But I don't really know what I'm doing or anything."

"You don't have to," Alex said, running around the table to pull my chair out of the way for me as I stood up.

When I turned around, I was face-to-face with him, close enough to feel the heat of his body. I could almost feel the fuzz of his flannel shirt against my cheek.

We visited a cat who'd had stitches after a brawl with a raccoon, a

Doberman recovering from being neutered, and a baby squirrel who'd lost her mother. Alex talked to all of them—things like "Hey kiddo, sorry about your balls," and "Aw, baby, you gotta stay away from those raccoons."

The Golden Retriever was groggy. Alex had amputated her front left leg because it was totally crushed by the accident. She was lying on her side and there was a big white bandage wrapped around where her leg used to be. Joe sat in the doorway where we told him to, while Alex took her vital signs.

"Okay, I'm going to give her another shot here. Do me a favor and rub her head. Give her the best head rub she's ever had."

I scratched her head, and she looked up at me. Her eyes were watery. When Alex gave her the shot, she closed her eyes and whimpered a little, but didn't move.

"You're a natural," he said. "That was great. Thank you." He touched my hand.

"How is she?" I asked. "Is she going to be okay?" I wanted to give him a sign, but touching his hand back seemed too obvious.

"Yeah, she looks good," Alex said, pulling his hand away and patting the dog on her side. "They adapt so well. She'll be up and running in a week or two."

"Really?"

"Yeah, you'd be surprised. Cut off a person's leg, and they're never quite the same, but this dog here—she won't even miss it."

He lifted the Golden off the table and rested her gently in a crate lined with worn pink towels.

"Wow. That's incredible."

"It really is. That's what I love about working with them. Dogs never feel sorry for themselves. They just keep plodding along."

We walked back to the doorway and Joe followed us down the hall.

"Thanks for staying with me," Alex said. He stopped and leaned against the wall. I leaned my back against the wall next to him. Joe came and sat next to me.

"Thanks for seeing us," I said. "I—I was so worried about him and—"

"Anytime, Van," he said, smiling. He leaned toward me and the space between us got smaller. "Do you think I could call you?" He pulled his knee up and rested his foot against the wall. "About Joe, and maybe not about Joe?"

"Yeah," I said, leaning toward him until our arms were just touching. "I think you could."

He nudged his arm against mine. It was gentle, but I almost lost my balance.

I was so tired. I closed my eyes for a second and thought about leaning into his arms and letting him hold me. I slid a little closer, so my shoulder was touching his.

I felt so comfortable. It was so easy to be with him. I closed my eyes.

"Are you sleeping?" he asked.

"No." I opened my eyes and looked at him. "Just resting my eyes."

"I've kept you here pretty late." Alex looked around me at his watch.

"I stayed on my own accord."

"It's two."

"Wow. I should go," I said, although I couldn't think of any reason why.

"Let me walk you to your car."

I pulled away from him and Joe followed us out. I used the remote to click the car open. Alex opened the back door and Joe jumped up on the seat.

"I'll call you later," he said, closing the door.

"You need my number."

"It's in Joe's file."

"Then you have my number." I reached for the door handle, but I didn't open my door.

"Well," he said.

"Well."

He leaned over and kissed me on the cheek. "Drive safely," he whispered.

I got in the car and he closed the door for me.

He walked backward away from the car and waved as we drove off.

I could still feel the pressure of his lips on my cheek. I concentrated on keeping that buzzing feeling in my face the whole way home.

Joe and I climbed into bed. I turned away from him once he started snoring and let my mind wander to Alex's uneven front teeth until I fell asleep.

Chapter Fifteen

I was just settling in to work, drinking coffee and reviewing the outline I'd made for the new grant I was working on when the phone rang. I ran for the living room to pick it up. Joe got excited and tried to push in front of me on the stairs, and I slipped and fell hard on my butt. I bounced up quickly and made it to the phone just before it went to voice mail.

"Hello?" I yelled into the phone, breathless.

"Van? It's Alex . . . Brandt."

"Hi, Alex Brandt."

He didn't say anything immediately, and I felt like I needed to fill the space. "Joe is feeling much better," I said.

"How are you doing?" Alex said.

"Well, I'm plotting a homeowners' association mutiny, so, you know, that's keeping me busy."

He laughed and I flopped down on the couch and pulled my knees up to my chest. Joe jumped up next to me and tried to lick the phone.

"Need any help?" Alex said.

"Well, I've never plotted a mutiny before, so I'll take all the help I can get. And, I think I need an eye patch, so there's that."

"Hook hand?"

"That might be going a little far," I said.

"Hey," Alex said, "if you can take a break from all the plotting, I was thinking we could take Joe for a walk at the park. I could help you work with him on walking on a leash. You game?"

"Yeah, I'm game."

"I have the afternoon off. I could come get you around one, if that works for you."

"Sounds good!" I gave Alex directions to the condo.

"Well, Van, I'll see you then."

I loved the way he said my name. There was a smile in it. "Bye, Alex." I smiled back.

I hung up the phone and looked around the living room. It was disgusting. Aside from dog proofing, I hadn't really cleaned since way before the wedding. Joe's fur gathered together like tumbleweeds across the floor and in corners. I picked them up by the handful instead of vacuuming. I shook out the couch cushions and kicked a pair of flip-flops under the couch.

Cleaning one thing made everything else look dirtier and once I got going, it was hard to stop. I stashed dirty dishes in the oven, and ran upstairs with armloads of clothes from the living room to shove under the bed and in the closet.

Joe followed close, sniffing everything I touched. Were I not in a hurry, it would have been adorable, but I got tired of having to wipe wet nose marks off every surface. "Joe! Stop it!" I yelled, waving my fist at him. He seemed to think I might have a treat waiting in my tightly closed hand because he jumped up, put his paws on my shoulders, and tackled me to the floor, trying to shove his nose into my fist. When he discovered that my hand was empty, he kept me pinned to the floor so he could give my face a good lick.

When he was done, I ran upstairs to fix my makeup, and I realized, while I was wiping smeared mascara from under my eyes, that the bathroom was disgusting. I grabbed a wad of toilet paper, ran it under the faucet, and used it to wipe up the toothpaste splatters on the mirror. Joe found a sock behind the bathroom door and collapsed on the floor with it in his mouth like he was settling down to give it a good chew. I gave him a stern look. He dropped it and rested his head on top of it, looking up at me. I took it away from him and shoved it in the cabinet under the bathroom sink. I finished wiping out the sink. It wasn't clean, but at least it didn't look dirty. I washed my face to start over with my makeup.

Alex rang the doorbell at twelve fifty-three. Joe started barking. He ran down the stairs and back up. I had mascara on my right eyelashes, but not on the left, so I made Alex wait. He gave me a full minute before he rang the doorbell again.

Running down the stairs, I realized that my socks didn't match. One was black and one was blue. Alex didn't seem like the type to think less of me for it, so I left my mismatched socks just the way they were.

When I opened the door, Alex was leaning in the door frame giving me a goofy smile that was all teeth. He was wearing a navy blue knit cap that made his eyes look even brighter. His jeans were pale blue, washed down to thin soft threads and spattered with bleach spots and ancient paint-stain freckles.

"Now, you sure are worth the wait," he said, his eyes crinkling at the sides. His smile was kind and earnest, and I swore I could feel the warmth radiating from it. Joe pushed his head under Alex's hand. "Hey, buddy!" Alex bent down to eye level with Joe and scratched him behind his ears. Joe's tail wagged at warp speed, hitting my legs at every pass.

"He loves you," I said. "I thought dogs hated the vet."

"Well, he has good taste." Alex winked at me. He was the only person I'd met who could make a wink look natural. "Get your shoes, cutie." He gestured to my feet.

I waited, but there was no comment about the socks. I slid into my Airwalks, wishing I'd thought to find sexier shoes, or at least ones that weren't ten years old and looking their age. Crouching down to tie my dirty laces, I noticed that Alex's work boots were worn and creased and covered with paint stains like his jeans.

"What were you painting?" I stood up.

"Huh?"

I pointed to his boots.

"Oh, all sorts of stuff," he said. "The office, my dad's tool shed, my deck. That"—he picked his foot up and turned it to the side—"that blue there? That's a bookshelf I painted for my grandma. Spilled the can all over the garage." He laughed. "I should get new boots, but these are comfortable, you know?"

"I think my sneakers are ten years old," I said, feeling better about my shoes.

"See, you get it. Nothing like broken-in shoes."

When we got out to the car, Alex opened the passenger door for me and Joe and then ran around and slid into the driver's seat. Joe sat between us, and licked the side of Alex's face from chin to ear.

"Thanks, bud," Alex said, laughing and wiping his face with the back of his hand. He rubbed Joe's head, leaving the fur on his head standing straight up like a mini-Mohawk.

We laughed about Joe's new punk hairstyle. I liked the sound of Alex's laugh. I liked the way it felt to sit with him and Joe on the bench seat of his truck, like a little family. I fought to keep my thoughts from getting too far ahead of the situation. We were just going to take the dog for a walk. It was entirely possible that this meant nothing beyond that. Years of lusting after Peter—thinking every pat on the back, or arm brush, or knowing look meant surely he liked me as more than just a friend—created a complete lack of faith in my ability to ever have anyone seriously fall for me. So even while I was soaking in every minute with Alex, I couldn't help but think that maybe he just felt bad for me, this pathetic woman who got drunk and bought a dog off the Internet. Maybe he saw me as a failure of a person and he was one of those missionary types who felt it necessary to step in and help. Maybe he was a dog zealot and didn't want to see Joe end up at the pound. He was, after all, a vet. He obviously cared about Joe's well-being. And after all the times I'd gotten my hopes up with Peter and been let down, I didn't think I had it in me to hope too much anymore. It was better to call it what it most likely was: a guy who cares about dogs, helping out someone who doesn't know what the hell she's doing.

"First things first," Alex said, when we got to the parking lot at the canal path, over by the playground. "You cannot keep walking him on that backward leash contraption you've got going there." He reached behind his car seat and pulled out a chain-link collar and a blue nylon leash. "My gift to you." We got out of the truck. He slipped the collar over Joe's head and hooked the leash on.

"You didn't have to do that," I said, embarrassed that I still hadn't gotten around to getting Joe a real collar.

"Not a problem. I had an extra."

He showed me how to hold the leash at my side, not giving Joe any slack, and we started walking.

"Do you have a dog?" I asked.

"Two," Alex said. "Rosie and Tinsel." He pulled out his wallet, flipped past a few business cards too fast for me to get a good look, and pointed to a picture of a chubby Golden Retriever and a small black and tan German Shepherd running in the grass. "Rosie's the Golden," he said. "Tinsel is probably a Shepherd like Joe. She's a little small, but she doesn't look like she's got any other breeds going on."

"Tinsel?"

"Yeah." Alex blushed. "Mindy named her. Someone abandoned her on our doorstep a few days after Christmas last year. She was really sick. She had parvo, and she almost didn't make it."

"Oh," I said, picturing him and Mindy in matching flannel pajamas waking up to find a puppy in a basket on their front porch. "Are you and Mindy together?" My voice got higher and squeakier with every word. "I didn't realize you lived—"

"No, no!" Alex said. "We're not together."

"Oh," I said, trying to keep a poker face, even though I was pretty sure I'd just shown all my cards.

"Someone abandoned Tinsel at the clinic. She was probably a holiday gift they couldn't handle. Mindy found her in a cardboard box when she was opening up for the day. She was going to call a rescue group to try to help find her a home, but then her fiancé said he might take Tinsel when she got better. But I took Tinsel home with me the first night, because I worried she wasn't going to make it, and then I couldn't give her up. She worked her way in." He smiled. "She was too tiny." He held his hands out to show me that she was only about a foot long. "I wore a sweatshirt for days and walked around with her in the pouch pocket to keep her warm, like a kangaroo."

"And she's okay now?" I said, feeling like the little clamp on my heart that was trying to keep me from getting my hopes up was starting to crack, because how could you not get your hopes up about a guy who would spend days walking around with a puppy named Tinsel in the pocket of his sweatshirt?

"She's on the small side," he said, "but she's perfectly healthy."

We reached the end of the playground and I tried to get Joe to turn around with me. He didn't want to move, and I ended up tripping over him. Alex caught me. His arms were solid. It didn't feel like there was any chance that he'd drop me. He helped me find my balance.

"I was just wondering," I said. "About Mindy. I didn't mean to pry." I rubbed the toe of my sneaker into the dirt, making a thick line. "I just—I mean, do you take all your clients to the park with their dogs?"

"No," he said, resting his hand on the small of my back. "I don't." He took Joe's leash from me. "Just you."

He smiled and then looked down quickly and gave Joe's leash a tug. "K nohe," he said, firmly. Joe walked to Alex's left side and sat down. "K nohe," Alex said again. He clicked out the side of his mouth. Joe stood, and they walked in unison. When Joe started to stray, Alex would give his leash a tug and say the command again. I wondered if he knew all the Slovak commands already, or if he learned them just for me.

They got to the end of the playground and turned perfectly together. It was freezing. As soon as I stopped walking, I started shivering. I shoved my hands in my coat pockets and watched Alex and Joe walking back toward me. I felt funny making eye contact when they were so far away. I looked at Alex and he looked at me and then we both looked away. I watched Joe. He watched Joe. I looked at Alex and he looked at me. We looked away again.

By the time they got back to me, Alex's face was beet red and there was no mistaking it. He gave Joe's leash back to me, and his hand lingered on mine for much longer than necessary.

"Thanks," I said, wrapping Joe's leash around my hand.

"He's been trained really well," Alex said. "You can tell someone worked with him a lot. And he's very eager to please. So, it's just a matter of teaching you how to work his commands."

"Are you saying I need training?"

Alex laughed and didn't say anything.

"I'll take that as a yes," I said.

"I didn't say a word," Alex said, giving my arm a playful swat.

We spent about an hour going over Joe's command sheet. Alex made sure I knew what each command meant, and how to make sure Joe adhered to good form. He was a good teacher. And so patient when I couldn't get the footwork down to keep Joe in heel position. We did it again and again, and he explained and reexplained without the slightest hint of frustration. I wasn't used to that kind of patience. Even my mom would have lost patience with me by the third or fourth time, but Alex just smiled and said, "Okay, now lead with your left." And when I'd get confused again and lead with the right, he'd just say, "No, the other left" or "Almost. You're so close."

"It's not that I don't know my right from my left," I said. "It's just that my brain thinks left, and then I think about what Joe's going to do, and then we start walking and my right foot moves instead of my left."

"I've got an idea," Alex said, jogging backward. "Stay there."

Joe tried to follow, but I held him back and made him sit by my side.

When Alex got about twenty feet away from me, he stopped and called out, "Okay, you walk toward me, and just let Joe do his thing. Don't think about Joe, just focus on me."

And it was that easy. I looked at Alex, and it wasn't awkward this time. I had permission to. I looked right in his eyes and he looked right in mine, and I imagined Alex and me drinking red wine in big globe glasses on a patio overlooking the Aegean Sea at sunset. Peter and Janie were nowhere to be found.

I made it all the way over to Alex without leading with the wrong foot or tripping over Joe, and after that, it was easy. We did it five or six more times, and Joe and I walked in perfect unison.

"You were just overthinking it," Alex said. "Sometimes, you need to let go to get everything to work." He knelt down next to Joe and rubbed the sides of his face. "You're such a good boy!" Alex said.

Joe licked Alex's chin and leaned against him. The fact that Joe was so at ease with him made me like Alex even more. I crouched down to pet Joe too. My hair fell in my eyes and Alex reached over and brushed it off my face with the tips of his fingers. He smiled. His face was very close to my face. He leaned in and I closed my eyes and waited for him to kiss me. The anticipation of feeling his lips on mine made my knees feel like they might stop working altogether. And then Joe knocked Alex over, pulled the hat right off Alex's head, and ran across the field, leash trailing behind him.

"Damnit, Joe!" I yelled. Joe obviously was not the stellar wingman I'd thought he was.

Alex ran after Joe, who ran in zigzags, swerving to fake Alex out. Finally, Alex got close enough to grab Joe's leash. Joe dropped the hat and jumped up to lick Alex's cheek.

They came running back to me. "It's impossible to stay mad at this guy, isn't it," Alex said, laughing. He shoved the hat in his jacket pocket.

We went back to working with Joe, but I couldn't stop thinking about our almost kiss.

By the time we called it quits, I could barely feel my fingers, or my toes, or my ass, for that matter, and my face was windburned, but I didn't want it to end. So when we got back in the truck, and Alex asked if it was okay if we stopped by his friend Louis's house on the way back so he could drop off a book, I was thrilled. Even if it was just a quick stop, it was an extension of our time together.

"Of course," I said.

Joe sat on the seat between us. His eyelids started drooping, but he'd sit up at attention again when we'd hit a bump or make a turn. Finally, he gave up fighting sleep, and flopped down on the bench seat, resting his head on Alex's thigh.

We stopped at a red light. "I see a lot of dogs," Alex said, scratching Joe's ear with one hand while he steered with the other, "but this one here is in a class by himself."

"It's a very happy accident," I said.

Alex smiled, and we had another quiet moment. I knew he was blushing, and I knew he knew I was blushing. It was the best kind of uncomfortable there is.

"Now, let me fill you in on Louis," Alex said, breaking the silence. The traffic light changed to green. Alex pulled his hand away from Joe and put it back on the steering wheel to make the turn. "Louis is a character. I guess that's the best way to put it." He looked over at me and smiled. He kept his eyes on me for just a little longer than I thought was okay for him to not be watching the road. "He's almost eighty, but he's quite the charmer."

"Really?" I'd assumed Louis was Alex's age, although I wasn't quite sure what Alex's age was. Thirty maybe? Thirty-five? Twenty-eight? I couldn't figure it out.

"Really. We'll only stop for a minute, but it deserves a warning. I swear, I take the man out to dinner, every waitress in the place is bringing us stuff. I go alone, I can't even get a refill on my coffee." He laughed. "The man has some mojo or something." He winked at me. "He's giving me lessons."

"Seriously?"

"No," he said with an impish grin.

"You had me worried for a minute!"

"That you wouldn't be able to resist me?"

"Sure. Something like that." I turned and looked out the window.

"Just for the record, I will be offended if you ask me to leave you with Louis." Alex didn't look over at me when he said it, and I think I saw his ear go pink.

"I'll try not to fall too hard." I picked at the seam on the side of my jeans. I didn't know where to put my hands, and everything I said embarrassed me after I said it.

"So—what else about Louis." Alex cleared his throat. "He's been married three times. His last wife, Gloria, she was the one.

"What happened?" I asked. "Did she die?"

"No. She ran off with the UPS guy."

"What?"

"She started ordering all this stuff off of one of those home shopping shows, so she got, um, familiar with the delivery guy."

"Oh my God!"

"Then one day I took him bowling, and when we came back, she was gone. There was a note, explaining—but she left all the stuff. Boxes and boxes of cheap jewelry and fake alligator purses. Tons of scarves. It was crazy." I noticed that his eyebrows moved a lot when he talked. "Louis had me get rid of all of it. Hauled it to Goodwill. Boxes and boxes. We thought that would do it, but it didn't make him feel any better. It's been months." He leaned his left elbow up against the door and sighed. "He just can't get over it."

"Yeah," I said, softly. "I can understand that."

"Three wives. And the one who left him was the first one he really loved." Alex sighed. "Poor guy. He got a taste of his own medicine. He knows it, too. I think that makes it harder. He's just been moping around. It's hard to get him to go out with me anymore."

We stopped at another light. Joe lifted his head and looked around, and then rested his head on Alex's leg again with a big sigh.

"Well, sure," I said. "I mean he's got to be so—" I trailed off. I couldn't think of how he would feel. "So how many times have you been married?" I laughed.

"Just once."

"Oh, God! I'm so sorry. I was joking. I didn't mean to—"

"Van, it's fine," he said and smiled. "I'm not hiding anything. It's good for you to know." He looked at me quickly and then back at the road. "Sarah Evans. She didn't take my name." He took a deep breath. "We were together in college. And then we got to the end of college and everything was changing. I think we got married to keep things the same. She moved down to Knoxville with me when I went to vet school. We gave it a try." He rolled his hands around the steering wheel. "If we hadn't gotten married, we would have drifted apart. You know, missed phone calls and postponed weekend visits. The way everyone's college love fades when you get out in the real world." He didn't sound upset. It was a story, not a tragedy.

"I'm sorry to hear that," I said, because he didn't seem like he had any more to say and I didn't know what the proper response was.

"It wasn't messy. We signed some papers and that was that. She stayed in Knoxville. She'd already found someone else. She said she didn't meet him until we were separated. You know, you wonder still. But either way, we wouldn't have worked."

I felt awful for bringing it up. I, of all people, knew what it was like to love someone who loved someone else. It wasn't something I ever wanted to talk about either. "I really didn't mean to—"

"Van, it's fine." He patted my leg again. "No worries. Okay?"

"Okay."

"You can't stay with the wrong person. I guess the trick is finding the right one to begin with. Right?" He glanced over at me really quickly and then looked back at the road. He pushed his hair out of his eyes and sighed. "Sarah and I don't talk anymore. It's weird, you go through that much"—he paused to think of the right word—"life with someone, and then you don't even exchange Christmas cards anymore. We're not on bad terms or anything. It's just, there's nothing else to say, I guess." He smiled. "I promise that's my only deep dark secret."

"Impressive. I've got at least twelve." I raised my eyebrows and gave him a silly smile. He laughed.

As we sat in silence, I looked out the window, watching the rows of perfect little tract houses with postage stamp lawns like something out of a documentary about the fifties—shrubs bundled up for winter in burlap and twine, white plastic sticks with red reflectors like lollipops at the end of every driveway.

The houses reminded me of the time I went to Levittown to meet my father. Every third house was exactly the same, with a green plastic awning here and a pair of concrete kissing Dutch kids there, to let you know that the people inside were not all made from the same blueprint.

I drove out to Long Island, marched up to his house, and rang the doorbell twice. No one answered. I consoled myself with the idea that I could have rung any doorbell and talked to any man, and it would have meant the same thing.

"Whatcha thinking about, Van?"

I looked over and his eyes were right there to meet mine.

"Just taking it all in."

"I didn't freak you out, did I?"

"Oh, no! I appreciate your honesty." My words echoed in my head. *I appreciate your honesty.* It sounded like I was reading aloud from a form letter.

"That's my house," Alex said, slowing down as he pointed to a raised ranch with brown shingles and black shutters. The hedges were a little overgrown and there was a Frisbee on the roof. At the end of the driveway stood a big wooden bear statue. He was wearing orange plastic sunglasses.

I smiled. It looked like the kind of house where you could put your feet on the coffee table.

We drove about a quarter of a mile, and turned in to a driveway in front of a yellow ranch.

"Well, here we are," Alex said. "On the way back, you'll have to tell me your life story, and at least ten of those deep dark secrets."

Joe woke up when we pulled into the driveway. His eyelids were still droopy, but he surveyed the scene, ears at attention, trying to make sense of where we were. As soon as Alex put the truck in park, a short man in a long white apron came out of the door next to the garage door. Louis was not what I expected. He looked like Jimmy Durante. He was a round little man, with thinning hair that might have been dyed black with shoe polish, and a nose like a sweet potato.

Alex leaned in to me and said, "Wait for it. The charmer part. It'll all make sense."

"Hey, Lou!" he yelled, as he opened his door.

"Oh, Alex the Great! Alex the Great!" Louis called back, waddling over to the truck.

Alex got out of the car, and Joe followed him, bounding over to Louis.

"Crap!" I yelled. I got out of the car and grabbed for Joe, but he darted away from me.

"He's fine," Alex said.

Joe circled Louis once and gave him a sharp bark. "All right, all righty," Louis said. He leaned over and patted his knees. Joe put his paws on Louis's knees and licked his chin before running off to smell the mailbox post. "See, we're good buddies already," Louis said, wiping his face as he stood up. "This must be Savannah."

I was amazed that he knew who I was. It meant that Alex had been talking about me. I wondered what the nature of the conversation was, if it was more on the side of "I'm taking this crazy girl to the park and then I'll stop by with that book you were waiting for," or if it was more of a "I really like this girl, I'm going to think of an excuse to come by with her so you can check her out."

"You didn't tell me she was so lovely." Louis talked to Alex, but waddled over to me and hugged me around the waist. He pulled away and kissed me on both cheeks. His cologne was dizzying. The hand he kept on my side was so big that it made my waist feel tiny. "I've heard great things about you," he said, and his breath smelled like cigarettes and peppermint. The parts of him didn't make sense, but the pieces all together were quite something.

"Come in! Come in!" Louis said, trying to corral Alex with his free arm.

"We need to get going," Alex said. "I just stopped by to give you that book you asked for." He did a half jog over to the truck.

"What do you mean, 'get going'? You say you'll come by, I bake! I just poured the honey on the baklava, and there's a pound cake in the oven. Stay! Stay!"

"Next time, Lou," Alex said, walking over to the truck.

"You can stay, right?" Louis asked me, nodding to prompt my answer.

Alex came back with a biography of Elizabeth Taylor. I raised my eyebrows at him. "Long story," he said.

"Now, we have coffee," Louis said. "Vannah wants to stay and have coffee. You stay."

"Are you sure it's okay, Van?" Alex asked. "This guy is great at putting words in your mouth. He's talented in that way." Alex winked at me.

"It's fine with me," I said. "As long as Joe isn't a problem."

"Problem?" Louis asked. "He's a gift! Look at him." He gestured toward Joe like a circus announcer presenting him to a crowd. "He's beautiful. Beautiful. Joey! I have biscuits in the cupboard!" Joe's ears perked up. He raced over to Louis and sat in front of him at full attention. I couldn't blame him. I'm sure Joe had no idea what a biscuit was, but Louis's enthusiasm was strangely compelling. "Come on, Joey," Louis said, and Joe followed us to the house.

Louis kept one arm around me, the other around Alex, until we got to the door. He pulled Alex down closer to him and said, "I love this kid. I just love him," and kissed him on the cheek.

Whenever I'd talked to my mom about a guy, she asked me if he came with "references." Her theory was that if a guy's friends thought a lot of him, and they seemed like nice people, it validated him more. Apparently, no one liked my father much. He didn't have any good references. Alex, on the other hand, had a very enthusiastic reference in Louis.

We went in through the garage. It felt like a real garage. Louis had a shiny black Lincoln Continental. But there were oil stains on the concrete and folded-up beach chairs hanging from the rafters. Diane's garages all had spotless floors and were just for storing cars. Lawn furniture had its own outbuilding.

When we got to the kitchen, just off the garage, the oven timer was beeping. Louis scurried over, and pulled the pound cake out of the oven, using the corner of his apron as an oven mitt. "Hot, hot, hot!" he yelped, dropping the loaf pan on top of the stove and shaking his hand out. Joe ran over to Louis and sniffed his hand. "Oh, you're a good boy," Louis said. "You worry about old Lou, huh?" He pulled a handful of biscuits out of a box in the cupboard. He broke off a piece and gave it Joe, and then shoved the rest of them in his pocket, effectively making him Joe's new favorite person.

The kitchen smelled like garlic and coffee and vanilla. It was warm. The walls were a creamy orange color, like those foamy marshmallow pumpkins that come out at Halloween. Alex looked at me and raised an eyebrow like he was asking a question. I tried to raise an eyebrow back at him, but they both went up. Worried that Alex might not get that I was okay with being there, I said, "Louis, thank you so much for inviting us for coffee."

"Sit!" Louis gestured to the kitchen table, which was under a huge fake crystal and gold chandelier. He'd set the table for coffee, and the baklava was arranged on a pretty flowered plate.

Alex and I sat at the table and waited for Louis. Well, I waited. Alex snuck a triangle of baklava off the plate as soon as Louis turned his back.

"I'm starving," he whispered, and popped the baklava into his mouth. I liked how at ease he was in Louis's house. I wondered how he and Louis knew each other, but Louis was busy pouring the coffee into a thermos pot at the other end of the kitchen, and Alex had his mouth full, so it didn't seem like the right time to ask.

I looked around the room. The kitchen–living room area was an assault on my eyes. The rooms shared a wall, and the change from kitchen paint to living room paint seemed to have been made arbitrarily—a crooked, hand-painted line from ceiling to floor where foamy orange met mint green. The line from brown kitchen tile to canary yellow shag carpet seemed more planned, and came right before the doorway to the hall, about three inches after the line on the wall, as if Louis had run out of orange paint.

I stared at the wall like it was a piece of postmodern art at MoMA.

"Vannah, you like it?" Louis came over with the coffee thermos. I tried to find something to say about it, as Louis gestured to the living room. I hadn't noticed the Pepto pink curtains. Luckily, most of Louis's questions didn't require answers.

"My first wife, she thought walls should be white, but Greta"—he sighed and gestured around the room—"Greta loved color."

I wondered if Greta was responsible for the couch. It was brown and bulgy, like a fat old man.

"Vannah," Louis said, sitting down, "you remind me of Greta. You have color."

"Thank you," I said. Alex laughed with his mouth full, and tried to hide it. He was already on his third piece of baklava.

"Takes me two days to make it, and you eat it in five minutes," Louis said, pretending to scold Alex, but it was obvious he was pleased. He poured each of us a cup of coffee, and passed me the cream and sugar.

The coffee was rich and dark. "This is amazing," I said.

"Chicory," Louis said, "and some vanilla. You scrape it off the beans. Not this stuff from a bottle."

"Louis is an excellent cook," Alex said. "He's giving me lessons." I pictured Alex and Louis in aprons, covered with flour, like a Laurel and Hardy routine.

"A man should know how to cook," Louis said, holding his index finger up. "None of this 'man's work' and 'woman's work.' A man should cook." He elbowed Alex. "Women think it's sexy."

Alex turned bright red.

Louis looked at me. "Right? Right."

I laughed. "He's right," I told Alex. "I personally speak for all women, and we do think it's sexy."

"What do I tell you?" Louis said to Alex. "You listen to old Louis. I know a thing or two."

"Or three?" Alex said.

Louis shrugged. "Eh, three is pushing it." He smiled at me and winked.

I loved being with them. I didn't feel judged. I didn't feel like I wasn't good enough. It didn't matter if I didn't say the right things, or that I spilled coffee on my jeans. Joe slept happily under the table, with his head resting on my foot. Alex and Louis joked around and told me stories and were elated when I laughed with them. Louis told me about how, when Alex was a kid, he used to try to save all the desiccated worms stretched out on his driveway on a hot day. He collected them in a cup and hosed water on them to "wake them up."

"I tell him, I say, 'You leave those worms overnight and in the morning they'll be fine.' " Louis laughed. "I didn't have the heart—I'd wait until he went home and then I'd dig a bunch of fresh worms to refill the cup."

"For the longest time," Alex said, "I was convinced worms could be reconstituted. Before I left for vet school, Louis pulled me aside to tell me about the worms. He wanted to make sure I knew."

"I didn't want him to fail Biology," Louis said.

"I already knew by then," Alex said.

"Eh." Louis winked at me. "I'm not so sure."

I told them about the time I got chased by a goose at Gedney Park and fell in the pond in my Easter dress. "Oh, my mom was so pissed. Like fullname pissed. 'Savannah Marie Leone! How could you?' " I said, copying her Long Island accent.

Alex snorted. "Oh, you know you're in trouble when they pull out the full name," he said.

"She made the dress herself and it was the first thing she'd ever tried to sew. It was hideous and crooked, but she was so proud of it, and she wanted to take Easter pictures. She went to the car to get the camera and came back to me looking like Swamp Thing. She didn't see it happen, and she totally didn't believe me. But that goose was mean. Hissing and everything." I shuddered. "My mom made me pose for the pictures anyway. I had duckweed in my hair, and I was covered in mud. But we had pictures of it. A whole roll of film of me posing by the pond holding a tulip."

We traded stories for hours. I gave them my best impression of Mr. Wright telling me about the pet weight limit. Alex showed me how he could bend his elbow back farther than anyone rightly should. Louis told us a joke about Dean Martin and the Dalai Lama that made absolutely no sense, but he had us laughing until tears ran down our faces anyway, because of the way he told it—many hand gestures and an absolutely awful Jerry Lewis impersonation.

We drank all the coffee and ate all the baklava, leaving only a sticky mess of honey and walnut bits on Louis's milk-glass platter. Louis showed me his stamp collection, and wedding pictures from all three of his marriages, while Alex did the dishes, and Joe licked biscuit crumbs off the kitchen floor. I felt like I belonged there, like there was nothing at all weird about hanging out in a kitchen with my dog's vet and his eighty-year-old friend.

When we were getting ready to leave, Louis noticed the pound cake sitting on the counter. He smacked his forehead and muttered something to himself in Italian.

"I think we're too full for pound cake now," Alex said.

"Tomorrow!" Louis said. "You come back tomorrow."

"Louis, I'm sure Van is busy," Alex said, sighing.

"No," Louis insisted. "You can come back, right?" He shuffled us to the door and gave me a hug good-bye. "I have an idea. I have something important."

"Uh-oh," Alex said, laughing.

"No! Good!" Louis said. "Good idea. Tomorrow. Promise?"

We made plans to come back for pound cake and whatever Louis had up his sleeve.

Joe bounded out the door as soon as we opened it, and ran laps in the front yard until Alex opened the truck and let him in.

"You speak Italian?" I asked, as we pulled out of the driveway.

"I speak Louis," Alex said, shrugging. "Sometimes there's a little Italian thrown in with his English. If you're around him enough, you just know what he's saying."

Joe was wide awake, after his leisurely nap on Louis's kitchen floor. He sat up and looked out the window, growling, soft and low, whenever he saw a pedestrian or a motorcycle. Alex and I giggled at him.

When we turned down my street, Alex said, "Look, I really appreciate the way you humored Louis. If you don't want to go back again tomorrow, just say the word. I mean, you thought you were getting a training lesson and the next thing you know you're having coffee with Louis for three hours. Don't feel like you have to go tomorrow too."

Suddenly, I felt silly. Like maybe I'd humored too much or was too accommodating or somehow made it so that Alex couldn't get on with his day. I mean, Alex had been trying to leave and I was the one who agreed to stay. And maybe I had overstayed my welcome. I started doubting everything. Maybe he hadn't tried to kiss me at the park. Oh, God, I thought, picturing myself kneeling in the grass with my eyes closed, waiting for him to kiss me, when maybe he was just reaching over to pick some fuzz out of Joe's fur or something. And maybe taking Joe to the park wasn't a date. Maybe he was just helping me out of pity. I couldn't trust my instincts anymore.

"It's fine," I said. "Either way, really. It's fine." I started playing back all the things I'd said. Everything I'd thought was witty suddenly seemed stupid and inappropriate. That story about the goose and the Easter dress, mimicking my mom's accent. When I said that I spoke for all women about cooking being sexy. Good Lord!

When we got to my condo, I collected Joe's new leash and collar from the backseat. "Thanks," I said, holding them up. "And thanks for helping us."

"Anytime," Alex said, but that's just something people say. He didn't have to mean it.

I said a weak good-bye and got Joe and myself out of the car and into the house before I could embarrass myself any further.

I settled down to try to get some work done. I checked for an e-mail from my client, but there wasn't one. I ran out to the mailbox to look for a check from my other client, but there wasn't one. There was, however, the most obscene credit card bill I'd ever gotten. In addition to the charges for all the dog stuff I'd bought for Joe, there was the actual charge for Joe. Then the wedding charges: the manicure, the hair and makeup, that ugly, ugly dress and the final fitting, those stupid sandals and the elbow-length gloves. Plus, there were my regular charges: groceries, gas, and late-night trips to Wegmans for nonessentials like ice cream, Marshmallow Fluff, and beer. The bill was more than eight thousand dollars. Even if my client did finally come out of hiding and pay up, I wasn't going to have the money to cover it. I'd just paid off my credit card debt from college, and here I was going under again at the worst possible time. I needed a new home. I needed a down payment and Realtor fees and moving expenses and good credit. And I needed a cushion, because I had no one to fall back on.

I tried to sit at my desk and do the little bit of work I had, but I couldn't focus. I felt clammy. I rolled a highlighter around on my desk with the palm of my hand, listening to the ridges in the cap clicking against the wood, and I tried to clear my head. I caught myself breathing too much, but I felt like I wasn't getting enough air. I wrung my hands. I ground my teeth. I got up and paced around. Joe got tired of following me, and collapsed on the floor with a big *harrumph.* I didn't know what to do with myself, and I needed a distraction, badly. In the absence of one, I started replaying the whole date with Alex in my head, trying to figure out if it was actually a date, or if I just misunderstood everything. He's been married before, I thought. Sarah Evans. And in my head, I saw Janie and Peter's wedding all over again, except Alex was the groom, and he wore a red flannel shirt with his charcoal gray tuxedo. I pictured the vows. I pictured the kiss. I felt like my heart would break all over again. And before I knew it, my phone was in my hand, and I was calling Peter.

"Hey," I said to his voice mail. I knew I'd get voice mail. I didn't even know if he had international service, or what was involved in international service. And even if his phone did work in Paris or Düsseldorf or wherever he was on this leg of his honeymoon, I doubted he'd pick up. "Just thought I'd check in and say hi. I was thinking about you and just wanted to . . . say hi. So I hope you're having a good honeymoon, and I guess I'll see you when you get back, or you can always call me, and maybe we can talk about—" I caught myself. I realized what I was doing. I was panicking about the real things in my real life and I was turning to Peter, like he was actually the cause and the solution. Like maybe he'd finish what he almost said in the carriage house and we'd have this happy ending and all of a sudden everything would be certain and I wouldn't be worried about stupid real stuff. And then all I could think about was Janie. The way her face crumples when she cries. Her top lip curls and her forehead wrinkles. Her shoulders shake and she sobs so quietly that you can barely hear it. "Say hi to Janie for me," I said, and hung up.

I stood there staring at my cell phone. The screen said the call had taken fifty-four seconds. In fifty-four seconds, I could have done damage. I could have told him I loved him. I could have told him that when he came to see me in the carriage house, I thought he was about to say that he loved me. What if I'd said something real, that couldn't be explained away, and Janie checked the message? What if she found Peter's phone on the dresser and saw that there was a call from me? What if she decided to check the message because she missed me and just wanted to hear the sound of my voice and how my day was going? What if I'd actually said, "I love you.

Leave Janie. Choose me." I wished I could go back to before Peter ever met Janie, when sometimes I just wanted to hear the sound of Janie's voice, and knowing how her day was going made me feel better.

I ran downstairs, grabbed my purse from the coffee table, and sat down on the couch. Joe jumped up and sat next to me. He pushed his nose into my purse while I tried to sift through old receipts and bent business cards. I pushed him away. He thought it was a game. He pawed at my hand and stuck his nose back in my purse, pulling out a granola-bar wrapper with his teeth. He jumped off the couch and proudly marched it around the living room. I took it away from him and went back to riffling through my purse. I was starting to panic. Joe ran upstairs and came back with his favorite rubber bone, jumped on the couch, and dropped it in my purse. "Stop it!" I yelled. He licked my cheek, completely unfazed. He took the bone back and settled down on the couch next to me to give it a good chew.

Finally, way in the bottom of my purse, folded up in quarters, I found Diane's check. I'd just thrown it in there, like it was a receipt for groceries or the paper wrapper from a drinking straw. I was so hurt by it that I hadn't wanted to acknowledge its importance. I wanted to pretend it was garbage, but the truth was that I needed it. I needed to pay my bills, I needed to find a new home, and I needed to accept Diane's terms. I needed to stay away from Peter.

I unfolded the check and smoothed it out against my leg. I cleaned the receipts and garbage out of my purse and put the check in my wallet.

Chapter Sixteen

The next morning, I went to the bank, first thing, before I even had coffee or showered. I threw on some sweats and my coat and drove over. I wanted to deposit the check in the ATM machine, so I wouldn't have to deal with anyone, but I knew that was a dumb idea. So, I stood in line, hands shaking, fighting back tears and losing the fight. When I got up to the teller, I handed her the check and my bank card.

"Checking?" she asked.

I nodded, pulling a crumpled-up tissue out of my coat pocket. I blew my nose, hoping she'd think I just had a cold. Maybe she wouldn't notice the tears.

I half expected her to push the red button that was probably right by her knee, like I'd seen on TV. Guards would come out and take me away for questioning. Because how the hell would someone like me, who had negative numbers next to her name, show up with a check for one hundred and seventy-five thousand dollars? How could they not demand an explanation? But she just slid the check back and asked me to endorse it, and kept her hands above the desk while she processed it. She handed me a receipt and asked me if there was anything else she could do for me. I shook my head and gave her a weak smile. I shoved the receipt in the back pocket of my jeans and walked out the door. And, with that, I had washed my hands of Peter.

I expected to be a wreck when I got back into the car. I expected to feel like I'd lost everything. Like no one loved me and no one ever would. I expected to cry more. But, instead, I felt relieved. I felt like I could finally move forward, and it was my decision to move forward this time, instead of the decision being made for me. Pete decided to pick Janie. Pete decided to marry her. And he decided to come see me on his wedding night. Diane decided to pay me off. My mother decided to keep me at arm's length at the end when she was sick. Those were all things that happened to me, but this was something I was choosing to do for myself. I finally felt like I had a little bit of control over something in my life. I felt like I had the freedom to move forward.

I got home and made myself a real breakfast, the kind of breakfast you eat when you're starting something—the first day of school or the first day on the job. I made eggs with cheese on toast, and started a pot of coffee. I made Joe a plate of eggs too, and we sat on the kitchen floor together and ate.

Joe slurped up his eggs with so much enthusiasm that he flung little bits of them everywhere. All over his fur, all over the floor, all over me.

"You're so gross!" I told him. He ignored me until he got every little last bit of egg off his plate.

The phone rang. I got up to answer it, leaving my empty plate for Joe.

"Hi, Van." It was Alex. "I was calling to see if you were still game for pound cake at Louis's house this afternoon."

"I'm still game," I said, smiling. Moving forward felt very good.

"So here's the thing," Alex said, when he picked me up later that afternoon. "I talked to Louis last night and I know what he's up to."

"What?"

"He made me promise that I'd let him tell you, so I will. But it's huge. And it could be a really good thing for you, but maybe it won't be. I don't want you to feel pressured about this. Don't give him an answer about it while we're there. And I won't let him do the thing where he just assumes you agree with him and that's that. I love Louis, but he can be really overwhelming and I don't want you to get overwhelmed. Okay?"

"Okay," I said. My mind was racing around trying to figure out what he could possibly be talking about. What was Louis up to? Why did it involve me?

When we got to Louis's house, he greeted us at the front door in a gray box-plaid three-piece suit with a bright red tie, and shiny black and tan shoes. His hair was slicked straight back.

Alex grabbed my arm, and when I looked up at him, he was pressing his lips together for dear life, trying not to laugh.

"Come in! Come in!" Louis said, waving us in, and planting kisses on our cheeks as we passed him.

"I feel underdressed," Alex said, pointing to the hole at the knee of his jeans.

"Eh," Louis said, waving Alex's comment away like it was inconsequential. "I have a business proposition for our Vannah here and I wanted to look like business."

Alex laughed. It was a kind laugh, like he and Louis were both in on the joke. He said, "Well, you do look like business."

Louis laughed along with Alex and reached up to give his cheek a good pinch.

Louis's ranch house was just a big rectangular box, and I could see from our spot at the front door that the kitchen table was set up for coffee, and the pound cake was sliced and arranged on a plate, but Louis had us sit down in the living room. Alex and I sat on the bulgy brown couch.

From the squeak of it, I could tell that it was vinyl, not leather, and I tried to sit as still as possible to avoid any embarrassing noises.

Louis sat in a red velvet wing chair across from us, his arms on the armrest and his feet resting on a small red footstool. He looked like a king on a throne. The canary yellow shag carpet had been vacuumed, haphazardly, leaving a weird pattern of vacuum trails around the room.

Louis took a deep breath, exhaled dramatically, and then did it again. "Okay," he said, looking at me. He gave me a warm smile and his eyes almost disappeared behind his chubby, wrinkled cheeks. "You and Joe should live here."

"Oh," I said, trying not to sound appalled. I couldn't imagine what had been going through Alex's head that he could possibly think that moving in with Louis would be a good thing for me. "Wow, I really don't know what to say." I took a deep breath and let it out. "You know, I uh, I need my space, and I'm home a lot, and I think that it might just be hard to live with—here with . . ."

"No, no!" Louis said. "Just you and Joe. Not me. I'm going to Florida."

"Louis's brother lives in Florida," Alex said, "and he's been talking about moving there forever now."

"I'll miss this guy," Louis said, pointing at Alex, "but winter is bad for my arthritis." He opened and closed his hands to show me that he was stiff. "You need a house. I need to move. Maybe it works?"

Alex cleared his throat and raised his eyebrows at Louis like he was trying to remind him not to push.

"All right, all righty," Louis said. "You don't answer now. You see the house!" He stood up and raised his arms in the air grandly. "Kitchen, you've seen it! Living room. This is the living room. Here, here," he said, waddling over to me. He grabbed my arm and dragged me out to the garage to show me that there was a keypad to open the garage so I could walk Joe without bringing a key. "Very clever," he said. "They think of everything these days." He shook his head in reverence to the brilliant minds at work engineering garage door openers, and gave me a big smile. "You like?"

"It's convenient," I said, trying not to give Louis too much to twist into an answer, like Alex warned. But I did like it. I mean, I didn't like the canary carpet or the orange and green walls, but I liked the idea of buying a house that I knew wasn't going to fall apart around me. I liked the idea of having a real home with a fenced-in yard and a garage door keypad. I liked the way Louis had said "our Vannah." I liked the way that this home felt like a real home, and I hoped I could change the carpet and the paint and still keep that feeling.

When we got back to the kitchen, Alex was leaning in the door frame between the kitchen and the hallway eating a piece of pound cake, cupping one hand under the other to keep from spilling crumbs. He was so tall and lanky. His head was only a few inches away from the top of the door frame. The way his straw-colored hair flopped around his face and his shirt and jeans hung from his body, he looked kind of like a scarecrow—a ridiculously hot scarecrow. He caught me staring at him and winked.

"Now, let me show you the bathroom." Louis clasped his hand to his face in a way that even he seemed to know was dramatic. "You will feel like a queen in this bathroom."

When I got to the doorway, Alex grabbed my sleeve, spilling crumbs, and whispered, "I'll help you paint." His breath was warm on my ear.

"Phew," I said. I loved that he was committing to a future painting date. He wanted to see me again. He wanted to paint with me. And he wanted me to know that he wanted to.

"I'd better get this." Alex pointed to the crumbs on the tile.

"Okay." I patted his arm as I walked past him.

The bathroom was very bright. The linen closet and shower doors were mirrored and the mirror over the sink went from the counter all the way to the ceiling. The rest of the bathroom was done up in a complicated 1970s Greek Revival pattern of blue and white tile.

"This room, this is Gloria. The perfect mix of color and white," Louis said, and I noticed that his eyelashes were wet.

He reached over to me and grabbed my hand. He looked at me in the mirror over the sink, instead of looking me in the face.

"Don't you break this boy's heart, Vannah," he said. "I deserved it. This boy—oh, this is a good boy. This is a good man."

I watched my face flush in the mirror.

"I don't think it's my heart to break," I said to Louis, still watching my cheeks.

He pulled my hand up with both of his hands and held it flat, with the palm facing up.

"It's here," he said, peering into my hand like I was holding a baby chick. "Maybe you don't see it yet, but it's right here."

I looked at him, and our eyes met. He smiled for a minute and then started laughing.

"All right," he said, dropping my hand and wiping tears from his eyes. "All right. That was too much. Even for me, that was too much!" He waved his hands in the air and laughed like a little boy.

The bedroom was surprisingly tame. The carpet was Kelly green but the walls were white and the bedspread and curtains were pale blue.

There was a small guest room across the hallway with sailboat wallpaper, a red shag rug, and a twin bed with a red, white, and blue quilt. The curtain tiebacks were red plastic anchors.

"Makes a nice sewing room," Louis said.

"I don't sew," I said. "I mean, I don't know how."

"Alex knows."

"Really?"

"Oh, yes! For school. He had to practice when he was home on breaks." Louis did an exaggerated pantomime of pushing a needle through fabric.

"Practice?" I asked.

"I practiced my stitching," Alex called from the hallway, walking in to us. "I had to practice doing stitches."

"He and Gloria used to sit in here and stitch away," Louis said.

"She made quilts," Alex said. "I sewed up banana peels. It was over Christmas break one year. It's not like it was a regular thing."

Louis stared into the room like he could still see them there sewing. His eyes got misty again.

"Okay, we should see the library," he said, taking a deep breath to collect himself.

"Oh, this is cool," Alex said.

The library was the bedroom at the end of the hall.

Louis opened the door and said, "Ta-da!"

The room was crowded with tall bookcases that looked handmade, slightly uneven and painted brown with thick, drippy paint. Each shelf was crammed to maximum capacity with magazines. There were sections devoted to *Popular Mechanics*, *National Geographic*, *TV Guide*, and several smaller sections for different hobbies like fishing and cigars, all labeled with blue plastic tape. There wasn't a single book, just magazines from ceiling to floor.

There was a big tan saggy leather chair in the center of the room next to an end table stacked with coasters and scarred with drink rings.

"So, what do you think?" Louis said. "You want the house, I'll throw in the magazines." He was beaming. "It's a good deal."

"I'm sure Van likes the house, Louis," Alex said, saving me from having to answer, "but we're going to have to give her some time to think about it."

"Yes, yes, we will. Patience," Louis said, holding his index finger up as if he were telling himself.

After we ate the cake down to the crumbs, Louis slid an envelope across the table to me. "You like the house, this is the deal." He winked.

I started to open the seal on the envelope.

"No, no, no!" Louis said, reaching across the table to get me to stop. "You open it later. I'll get embarrassed."

I folded the envelope over and slipped it in the back pocket of my jeans.

Alex poured me another cup of coffee and passed the milk, and I realized that the way I'd been feeling the day before wasn't in my head. I really did belong.

Chapter Seventeen

I had such a good time chatting with Louis and Alex that I almost forgot about the envelope, but as soon as we pulled out of the driveway, Alex said, "Go ahead, open it."

I wriggled around in the seat trying to reach into my back pocket.

"What do you know about this?" I asked.

"What do you mean?" Alex asked, in mock surprise. "Just open it."

The stitching on my jeans scratched my fingers as I pulled the envelope out. I opened it and pulled out a scrap of paper with 40K written on it in pencil.

"Are you serious?" I asked.

"Not me, it's Louis," Alex said, shaking his head.

"What is he thinking?" I asked, and then realized it probably sounded rude. "I mean, does he know the house is worth more than twice that?"

"He knows," Alex said. His eyes were crinkling up at the corners, and he was pursing his mouth up in a small smile. He kept his eyes on the road.

"But why?"

"The way he sees it—he bought the house for twenty thousand, so he's doubled his money."

"But what about inflation? When did he buy the house?"

"Midfifties?"

"So it cost like what, ten, fifteen cents for a loaf of bread? I mean, he didn't really double his money, right?"

"Louis. This is just the way he is. Don't feel like you have to buy it. Think about it. Okay?" He patted my thigh, and I let myself think that maybe it wasn't so casual.

"Is there more to think about? It's a house for forty thousand."

"Well, there's that."

"Joe would have a yard. The room with all the bookshelves would make a good office."

"Speaking of a good office, you're self-employed, right?"

"How did you know that?" Of all the things we'd talked about, I was pretty sure my job hadn't come up.

"I read your file," he said, softly.

"My file?"

"The paperwork you filled out when you brought Joe in."

"You've been researching me."

"Yes." He flinched dramatically, like it was paining him to admit it, or he was bracing for the aftermath.

"No fair. When do I get paperwork on you?"

"Ms. Leone, do you ever answer questions about yourself?"

"Dr. Brandt, I'm a grant writer."

"A grant writer?"

"Yes."

"What is a grant writer?" he asked in his best reporter voice.

"I write grants." I smiled and played along, giving him my best interview answers.

"Well, yeah, but how does that work, smarty-pants?"

"I get paid to research and write proposals for organizations."

"So people pay you to write requests for money."

"Basically."

"How did you get into that?"

"One of my professors did a lot of grant work on the side. She hooked me up with some people. It was supposed to be until I found a real job, but then it took off."

"That's awesome," Alex said, losing the reporter voice.

"Actually, I'd love to pick your brain a bit."

"Pick away."

"I'm working on a proposal for the expansion of an equine rehab facility in North Carolina. I could use your help with some of the medical terms. It's like they speak a different language. I have to look up everything they say."

"I have some time now, if you want me to translate."

"Really?"

"Absolutely." He flashed me his killer smile.

He looked back at the road. I slid Louis's slip of paper back in the envelope.

"So who is Louis?" I asked.

Alex gave me a mock blank look. "You just—the guy in the suit?"

"No, I mean who is he to you? How do you know him?"

"Had me worried there a second," Alex said, laughing.

"You knew what I meant."

"Yeah, I did," he confessed. "Louis was my grandfather's best friend. And he raised my dad." He said it like that was the end of the story.

"How did that happen?" I asked, leaning my head against the car seat.

"They were buddies in Korea, and they made a pact that if one of them didn't make it back, the other one would take care of things . . ." Alex trailed off as he made a left into traffic.

"So, your grandfather died in the war?"

"No, they both made it back. They bought houses on the same street and everything." He laughed. "They were quite a pair, from what my grandmother said. Always pulling pranks on each other. Two years later, my grandfather died in a car accident, and Louis told my grandmother the pact still stood. He helped with bills, fixed stuff around the house." Alex kept his eyes on the road. "He acted like my dad was his own kid. My dad even wanted me to call Louis 'Grandpa,' but Louis wouldn't have it. Said it didn't honor the right person. So he's just Louis."

"It must be really nice to have a Louis," I said, smoothing the envelope out against my thigh.

"Everyone should be lucky enough to have a Louis," Alex said.

Joe barked at us when we opened the front door. He was used to me coming in through the garage, and being alone. The fur around his face was disheveled and his eyes were barely open.

"Looks like we woke you up, Mr. Joe." Alex bent down and scratched behind Joe's ear.

"So, Joe's a German Shepherd, right?" I asked.

"Right."

"But why does he have long fur like that?"

"It's a long stock coat." Alex ran his fingers through Joe's fur. "Some people call it a plush coat. It's like some people have blue eyes, and some have brown. Genetics." When he stood up, he made my living room look smaller. He was so tall that he was out of scale with my furniture, like putting a He-Man action figure in a dollhouse.

He stood so close to me and all of a sudden, I got nervous. Really nervous. This guy liked me. This amazing, sweet, kind, funny guy liked me. The benefit of being in love with someone who was with someone else was that I never had to honestly face him with all those feelings. They were hidden and secret and protected. But Alex liked me, and it was okay for me to like him back. I didn't know what do with myself. I didn't know how to act. I felt like my knees were going to quit on me. "I can go get that grant," I mumbled, backing away from Alex. I started walking up the stairs. He followed and Joe stayed downstairs so he could go back to napping on the couch.

I looked back over my shoulder at Alex on my way up the stairs. He flashed me his big crooked smile.

"It's kind of messy." I tried to picture the state of my office. I couldn't remember how I'd left it, but I knew it wasn't good.

"I don't care."

"I might." I shrugged my shoulders up toward my ears.

"Don't." Alex put his hand on my waist and gave it a squeeze.

I tried not to think about my back fat. After he pulled his hand back I sucked in my stomach so if he did it again I'd be ready.

He followed me up to the door. I peeked in and did a quick scan of the room. It wasn't too bad. The paper shredder was overflowing, gum wrappers were piled up on my desk in mounds like raked leaves, and there were three coffee cups by the monitor, but the carpet was fairly clean and most of my paperwork piles were neatly stacked.

"Wow," Alex said, walking in behind me.

"I know, it's a mess." I hoped he wasn't one of those people who was obsessed with order.

"No. This." Alex pointed to the whiteboard that covered the wall next to my desk. "What is it?"

"I diagram my grants."

He gave me a blank look.

"See, I take all the requirements for the grant and put them up on the board." I walked over and pointed at the board. "Then when I do research and fill things in, I can check off what I've covered." I felt like a spokesmodel showing him the points I'd already covered.

Alex came over and stood next to me, very close. He tipped his head to the side and wrinkled up his forehead. He was really trying to figure it out, not just being polite. No one else ever understood my work, or even tried to. Peter, Janie, and Diane all acted like I was practically unemployed just because I worked flexible hours and often in my pajamas. It was nice to be taken seriously for a change.

I looked at him, and he looked back at me. I thought maybe he would kiss me, but then his face turned red and he moved over to read the next column on the board.

"It's probably really boring." I walked over to the desk, gathered up the pile of gum wrappers closest to the keyboard, and shooed them into the trash can.

"Not at all," Alex said, putting his hand on my shoulder to pull me back to the board. I loved the way his hand felt on my back. I loved the way he smelled like laundry detergent. My daydreams about Peter always involved us having these extravagant lives, but standing in my office with Alex and talking about work was suddenly the most romantic thing I could imagine. He was interested in me. He respected me. It was far more romantic than the Mediterranean Sea at sunset. It was real.

Alex grabbed an orange marker and put a star next to the rehab exerciser. "There's an exerciser that's closer to a treadmill."

He was standing really close again. I took a deep breath. I couldn't believe this was happening. This tall, handsome scarecrow was standing in my office, marking up my board.

"It doesn't cost as much as other exercisers." Alex kept the marker on the star. His brow furrowed when he was concentrating. It was really sexy. "So if they went with that, the extra money could go to the trailer." He drew a line over to the line that read *Transport Trailer–No Money* and made another star.

"Thank you," I said, looking up at him, nodding my head like I'd actually been paying attention instead of wondering if he was ever going to kiss me. "This is great."

"So are you," he said, looking into my eyes. He laughed and covered his face with his hand. "I'm sorry, that was really lame, huh?"

I realized that he was nervous too, and it made me like him even more. "Works for me," I said, quietly.

We stared at each other for a minute, and then Alex leaned in and kissed me. He put his hand on my neck just under my chin. We stumbled, lips locked, until my back was against the wall. His lips were soft and there was the slightest scratch of his stubble against my cheek. All that stupid movie talk of fireworks or stars in your eyes or falling head over heels—that kiss made me get it. I felt it in every inch of my body. He pulled away and looked at me.

"Wow," he said.

"Yeah," I said, feeling like my head might never be able to form cognitive thoughts ever again, and I was completely okay with that.

Alex's eyes widened. "Oh, crap!" he said, pointing behind me.

I turned around and realized that we'd erased half my board with my back.

"I'm so sorry!" he said. "I didn't mean to mess up your board."

"As long as you're not sorry you kissed me," I said. My cheeks flushed.

"Not the least little bit," he said, brushing my hair out of my face. "But is your work okay?"

"It's fine. I have copies of what was up there." I grabbed a packet off my desk and handed it to him. "The list of definitions I need to look up is on the last page."

"I'll write them in for you," he said, flipping through the pages.

"Thank you. That'll save me so much time."

"My pleasure." He rolled the report into a tube and shoved it in his back pocket. He slid his hands into his front pockets and rolled forward on his feet. "Since you'll have some free time now, do you think I could take you out to dinner tomorrow?"

"I think you could," I said, smiling.

Before he left, he wrapped his arms around me again, and we stood in the doorway kissing until Joe barked at us.

As soon as Alex left, I ransacked my closet. I had no nice clothes. I had no reason to have nice clothes. The ones that were presentable when I was in college were either worn out, too tight, or a fun combination of both. I found the black Betsey Johnson dress I got at the outlet mall with my mom. I didn't want to try it on. Maybe it was too *come and get it.* It was probably too small. It still had the tags on. It reminded me too much of her.

"It was made for you, lady," she'd said when I came out of the dressing room. It was a black jersey knit that hung low and loose off my shoulders and was tight in all the right places.

"I don't have anywhere to wear it, Mom." I tugged at the sleeves to see how far down the shoulders could go before it got dangerous.

She grabbed for the price tag.

"It's on sale," she said. "And everyone should have a dress that makes them feel like this." She picked a piece of lint off of my breast and flicked it away from us. "You make a place to wear something like this."

I pulled skirts off hangers and let shirts slip to the floor as I thumbed through them. But nothing was right, so I slipped the dress over my head. I slid my arms into the sleeves as I walked into the bathroom and the dress fell into place. It fit perfectly. I studied myself in the mirror from all angles, piling my hair up on my head while I checked out the back. I sucked my cheeks and pouted. Joe dropped his chew toy on the floor and watched me.

I wished I could call my mom to tell her I finally had a reason to wear the dress.

Chapter Eighteen

The next night, at five minutes to six, Joe growled and ran over to my bedroom window. I followed, wearing two different shoes, because I couldn't decide which ones worked better.

I peeked out the window and saw Alex's pickup truck sitting at the end of my driveway. I kicked off the low-heeled shoe in favor of the higher one with the patent leather bow. When I couldn't find the mate, I decided that the bow was too precious and the plain ones would work better anyway.

But after all of that, he still hadn't rung the doorbell. I worried he might be having second thoughts.

I checked out the window. The truck was still there.

I ran into the bathroom, gargled some mouthwash, and touched up my lip gloss. When I looked in the mirror, I felt pretty. I'd forgotten that I was pretty. I was so used to wearing ratty jeans and messy ponytails that I had forgotten how good it felt to look good.

I ran down the stairs and peeked out the window. The truck was pulling up the driveway.

At exactly six, the doorbell rang.

Joe tore over to the door and sat in front of it, barking.

I opened the door, and he ran out and jumped on Alex.

"I'm sorry!" I said, trying to grab Joe's collar and pull him back inside.

When I leaned over, the neck of my dress fell forward, flashing my bra. I hugged my free arm up to my shoulder to cover myself. If Alex saw, he did a good job of pretending he didn't.

"No problem." He reached into his sports jacket and pulled out a rawhide bone. "Okay?" he asked, waving it at me.

"Yeah."

"Here you go, buddy." Alex held the bone out.

Joe took it gently between his teeth and jumped up on the couch.

"Some men bring flowers. You bring rawhide," I said, laughing. "I guess you've figured out that the way to my heart is through my dog, huh?"

"Yup," Alex said, smiling. "And this is for you." He handed me a rolled-up tube of paper. "I wrote all the definitions in. Let me know if you can't read my handwriting."

"Thank you!" The writing on the first page was strange and square, like an architect's—like maybe he worked extra hard to make it clear for me.

I stepped back into the house to let him in. As soon as I closed the door, he wrapped his arms around me.

"I'm so glad we're doing this," he said.

He seemed so comfortable hugging me. Did it mean as much to him as it did to me? Maybe he was one of those people who hugged everyone. I hoped he couldn't feel my heart pounding against my chest.

He breathed in deeply, as if he was smelling my hair. I hoped it smelled good. I'd washed my hair, but I didn't have any flowery shampoo, just the stuff that was on Shopper's Club special at Wegmans.

Alex stepped away from me and held my hands. "You look amazing," he said.

"Thanks." I remembered seeing this thing on PBS about smiling. We have like a million different types of fake smiles, but only one true, involuntary smile. The way Alex made me smile was totally involuntary. My cheeks hurt.

The light blue shirt he had on under his sports jacket was worn down to white threads at the very tips of the collar. His pants were charcoal gray. The crease was still sharp and they looked brand-new. He had a tie wadded up in his jacket pocket. I reached over and pulled it out. It was pale yellow with maroon and blue paisley patterned across in diagonal lines. I held it up to him.

"I don't know how to tie a tie," he said. "I thought maybe you would."

"Yeah," I said. "Well, not so well. But it's worth a try."

He buttoned the top two buttons of his collar and held his arms out to the sides like a paper doll.

I flipped his collar up, slipped my arms around his neck, and passed the tie from one hand to the other to pull the ends to the front. I milked it. I liked the feel of his hair against my hands. I liked my face so close to his that I could feel his breath on my nose.

I twisted the tie around itself and pulled the knot up toward his neck. The last time I'd tied a tie was for Peter. I lingered, taking longer to stay close to him too, but my hands hadn't had the same nervous shake, and my fingers hadn't fumbled as much.

"Thanks," he said.

I ran my hand down his tie to smooth it out. Alex put his hand over mine. He leaned forward and kissed me. I kept my eyes closed for an extra second when he pulled away. The insides of my eyelids glowed warm orange. When I opened my eyes, everything still looked warm.

He threaded his fingers into mine and gave my hand a tug. We smiled at each other, big goofy grins.

"We have reservations," he said, softly.

"Do we?" I said, raising my eyebrows. I stepped away from him to grab my purse and coat.

He blushed. "Leonardi's. Six fifteen." He took my coat and held it out for me to slip into.

"I've never been." I buttoned up my coat and pulled my gloves out of the pocket. I didn't put them on, in case Alex wanted to hold my hand in the car.

"Louis recommended it."

We said good-bye to Joe, who was so busy chewing on his rawhide bone that he barely noticed we were leaving.

Alex opened the passenger door, and closed it gently after I got in. I worried that it might not be closed all the way. I always slammed my car door shut.

He slid onto the seat next to me. When he turned the car on, country music was blasting. Something about a Whirlpool washer and dryer. I couldn't tell if it was a commercial or a song. Alex reached for the knob on the radio and turned it down.

"I'm guessing you're not a country fan," he said.

"How'd you know?" I asked, still with the big smile. It wouldn't go away.

"Your accent is the opposite of country."

"I don't have an accent." I laughed. "You have an accent."

"Oh, really," he said, in mock annoyance. "Missy, you say *coffee* like there's a *w* in it."

"There isn't?" I stuck my tongue out at him.

He looked over at me, then back at the road. "Don't stick out your tongue unless you intend to use it."

"What, are you in high school?" I pushed at his shoulder lightly.

He smiled at me and I could see the crinkles around his eyes in the yellow streetlight.

"Are you going to stop short and try to cop a feel?" I blurted out, surprising myself.

Alex laughed. When we got to the stop sign at the end of the road, he hit the brakes a little hard and reached his arm across me.

"You make me feel like I'm still in high school," he said, grabbing my shoulder and giving it a squeeze.

"Is that a good thing?" My mind raced through tubes of Clearasil, bad hair, and sneers from the head cheerleader when she found out about my secret crush on her boyfriend.

"It's a good thing," he said softly and chewed his bottom lip.

Chapter Nineteen

When we got to the restaurant, Alex dropped me off at the door and parked the truck. I stood in the lobby waiting for him. Two blue-haired ladies with handbags and shoulder pads sat in the corner. Twinkle lights from a fake ficus tree reflected in the polished wood walls.

"Gladys," a woman with a huge gold pleather purse said, loudly, to the woman sitting next to her on the bench, "did you see the Brandt boy drive up?" She was leaning in to Gladys like she was telling a secret.

"The Brandt boy?" Gladys said, leaning back, equally loud.

"Yes. The blue truck." She fished through her purse and pulled out a lipstick.

"He drove up but he didn't come in?" Gladys started rummaging through her purse too.

"I think this one is his date." The woman smeared hot-pink lipstick around her mouth.

"Which one?" Gladys raised her chin and gestured at the woman to wipe the corner of her lip.

"This one," the woman said, pointing at me. I was the only other person in the lobby.

I looked away and pretended I couldn't hear them. There was an enormous gumball machine in the corner of the lobby, even though I couldn't imagine they had a big market for gumballs.

"Oh," Gladys said, like it had six syllables. She looked back at the other woman. "She's the spitting image of Mary Alice."

"She's prettier than Mary Alice."

"Mary Alice is a gorgeous girl."

"I'm not saying she isn't gorgeous, I'm saying—"

Alex's ex-wife's name was Sarah. Who was Mary Alice?

Alex opened the door and stepped into the lobby. He hooked his arm into his side and offered me his elbow. I smiled and took his arm, trying to keep my worries to myself.

"Shall we?" he said.

"Oh, Alex," Gladys said, waving the tips of her fingers at him. "How are you?"

"Mrs. Liberatella, Mrs. Goldfarb!" Alex said, turning us toward them. "You look terrific."

"We were just talking about you," Gladys said. "Weren't we, Ruth?"

"Yes," Ruth said, reaching in her mouth with her index finger to scrub off any lipstick that might have made it to her teeth.

"Good things, I hope."

"Oh, you!" Gladys winked at him, showing off her shiny blue eye shadow.

"This is Savannah Leone."

I put my hand out to shake theirs. Ruth shook my hand back. Gladys used my hand to pull herself up so she could hug me. She was shaky on her feet. She smelled like lavender and her body was soft like jelly around her bones.

She put her hand on my face. "It's nice to meet you, dear."

"Nice to meet you."

"We have a table waiting," Alex said, excusing us.

"Enjoy!" one of the ladies yelled after us. I turned around and they were both waving.

A waiter in a white shirt and a black bow tie seated us at a small round table in the corner. He pulled a long lighter out of his apron pocket and used it to light a candle in a squat red votive cup at the center of the table. He grabbed my napkin, snapped it out with one hand, and draped it across my lap. Alex grabbed his and put it in his lap before the waiter could get to it.

"Something to drink?" the waiter said. His slick hair glimmered in the candlelight. He opened the wine list in front of Alex.

"Do you have a favorite?" Alex asked.

"Red?" I laughed. "I really don't know my wines."

"Me either," Alex said.

"I'll leave you with a moment to decide," the waiter said, rushing off.

Alex slid the wine list between us so we could both look at it. The restaurant was dark and the writing on the wine list was light and curly. I had to lean in close to read it. Alex ran his finger down to one in the middle of the red list.

"This look okay?" he asked, pointing to a cabernet.

"Fine," I said, but kept leaning in to him.

"Okay then," Alex said, keeping his finger on the page. "We just have to hope he comes back now."

"Hey, who's Mary Alice?" I felt bold in the dark with him.

"Mary Alice?"

"Before you came in, I overheard Mrs. Liberatella talking about her. She said she was gorgeous."

"I think she's beautiful," Alex said, smiling. "But she's my mom. Maybe I'm biased."

"Ah," I said, hoping my relief wasn't too obvious. "What's she like?"

"She's fun. She's—" He opened his palm out to me like he was trying to find the right word to wave in my direction. "She's not like other moms."

"Does she wear a cape and fight crime?"

"Exactly," Alex deadpanned. "She shoots webs from her wrists and swings from buildings. No flying. That I know of."

If I were doling out points, he would have gotten a bunch for playing along with me.

"My mom was pretty young when she had me," Alex said. "She and my dad met in high school. They're best friends. It's really cool. They've been married for a really long time, but they still have fun together, you know?"

It made me feel so sad for my mom, raising me by herself. She met my dad in high school too, but after he bailed she never really found anyone else. Diane was the closest thing to a best friend she had. I just wish she hadn't had to do everything alone like that.

"What's going on in there?" Alex said, reaching across the table. He placed his index finger on my forehead. When he took it away, I could still feel the pressure of his fingertip between my eyes.

"Are you ready to order?" The waiter came over to our table, saving me from answering. I was relieved. I loved Alex's interest. I loved that he was so easy to talk to. But I couldn't continue talking about moms and keep it together. And I didn't want to cry on our first real date.

"We'll have a bottle of the cabernet, and I'll have the eggplant parm," Alex said, handing his menu to the waiter. He looked back at me and I ordered the fusilli with tomato and basil.

I loved that Alex didn't know about the wine, or that he was supposed to let me order first; it made me feel more at ease. Peter knew all these things—all these weird rules and strange manners—and it always made me feel like there was something I was missing or forgetting. With Alex, it felt like if we missed something, it probably didn't really matter to begin with.

Alex grabbed a breadstick out of the basket, took a bite, and then waved his half-eaten breadstick at me. "So where are you from?"

I grabbed a breadstick to wave back at him. "Downstate." I took a bite of it and crumbs spilled down the front of my dress.

"Where downstate?"

"Outside of the city." I knew what was coming. It was the normal flow of conversation. I'd avoided it with talk of Joe and Louis and housing issues before, but here it was: Where are you from? Do you go home often? Do your parents still live there? Normal questions, and I hated that I didn't have normal answers. Alex laughed. "Could you be more specific?"

"About fifty miles north." I hated saying Westchester. The response was always the same. "Oh," and then a second once-over, to see if they could pick out the fact that obviously I must have come from money to be from Westchester County. And then I could either explain that not everyone from Westchester was a yuppie snob, or just let them think that I was.

"Are you in the witness protection program?"

"Westchester." I tried to discreetly knock crumbs off my boob, but in the end I had to just go for it.

"How'd you end up here?" Alex grabbed another breadstick and spread butter on it with his dinner knife.

"School. And then I just stayed." I knew I should give him more, but I just wanted to change the subject and go back to talking about superheroes and how neither of us knew anything about wine.

Alex balanced his knife in the tines of his fork. "Does your family still live in Westchester?"

"No." I grabbed another breadstick and broke it into bite-size pieces over my bread plate so I wouldn't get crumbs on my boobs again.

Alex laughed. "You really don't like to volunteer information, do you?"

"No." I tried to laugh it off, but it sounded forced. I realized I should just tell him. He was honest with me about his ex-wife. I didn't like talking about my mom's death, but it had to come up sometime. Eventually. I looked down at my bread plate, tracing my finger along the curve of the edge. "My mom died three years ago," I confessed. I didn't think saying those words would ever get easier. I felt my throat tighten up. I took a deep breath and tried to keep myself from getting messy.

Alex reached across the table and grabbed my hand. "I'm so sorry."

"It's okay."

"That's got to be really hard, Van." He didn't stop holding my hand even though he had to hold his arm up and reach around the candle to get to it. He couldn't have been comfortable.

"It was breast cancer—why she died. I don't remember my dad. I was two when he left." I hated feeling like such a sad sack, so I added, "But I do have Joe."

"You don't have to try to make me feel better about it."

"I always feel like I have to," I said. "It makes people uncomfortable." I realized I was holding a piece of breadstick like a cigarette. I put it down on my plate. "Thank you for not telling me you know how it is because your grandma died or some aunt you only sort of knew."

"Do you get that a lot?"

"Yeah."

"Oh, man." He shook his head and pressed his fingertips to his forehead. "That's terrible."

"People mean well, I know—it just makes it worse. Like I feel more alone because nobody gets it." This wasn't date conversation. Date conversation was "Oh, my life is wonderful, and I'm so popular, and my phone always rings, and everyone wants me at all of their parties." Instead, I was saying, "I'm a big lonely mess and no one loves me except my dog," but the thing was, Alex didn't seem to mind. He wasn't trying to change the subject. He wasn't trying to move on to more pleasant topics like the weather or whatever sport was in season. He wanted to know about me, even when it wasn't all happy and pretty.

"Well, I won't try to say I get it, but I respect it." He squeezed my hand and let go.

"Thank you."

"So what was your favorite thing about her?" he asked.

I thought about it for a minute, but all I could say was, "Everything." I thought I was going to lose it. I looked up at the ceiling. It was acoustic tile, which totally didn't go with how fancy the restaurant was trying to be. "I think she actually could fly," I said, trying my damnedest not to cry. "Not too into capes, though. Tall boots, no capes."

Alex got it. "So, does the cape help with the flying, or is it just for show?" he said, pulling me out of the hole.

"I think—" I took a deep breath to collect myself. "I think it's like how stores hook streamers up to fans so you can see the airflow."

"Interesting," Alex said, tapping my foot with his under the table. The way his face softened when he listened, and the way he looked at me so intently, made me feel like I was the only person in the world who mattered to him at that moment.

"Sometimes I think I remember my dad," I said, "but then I'll see some Italian guy on TV, and I'll realize that he was the guy I was picturing as my dad. My mom didn't keep any pictures of him."

"Did you ever try to find him?" Alex asked.

"Once, but he wasn't home, and I wimped out." I shook my head. "It doesn't matter. It's not like he ever tried to find me or anything."

"That's too bad," Alex said. "He's missing out."

"Thanks," I said.

Alex hadn't poured the wine yet, so I did. I didn't know what else to say and it gave me something to do with my hands.

Alex puckered up after his first sip.

"Not a wine person?"

"I'm really more partial to beer." He gave me an apologetic smile.

"We didn't have to order wine."

"Louis always tells me you drink beer after you mow the lawn. You drink wine with dinner. He called tonight to remind me."

"Seriously?" I liked that Louis knew about our date.

"That's Louis for you."

The waiter brought our food. With my first two bites, I managed to flick tomato sauce on myself and splatter the table.

"Italian food is always messy!" Alex said, laughing as I blotted my dress with the napkin.

I cut my fusilli into tiny pieces to make it easier, but I ended up getting frustrated and just drinking wine. Alex never had another glass, and I finished the bottle by myself. If he noticed, he was too polite to mention it.

Alex told me he was an only child too, but his cousin Ollie came to live with them for a few years while his aunt got her act together, so it was sort of like having a sibling. Kind of like Janie and me. Ollie lived in Santa Fe now, had long blond dreadlocks, and worked for a guy who made guitars by hand. They still sent handwritten letters to each other, because Ollie didn't have a phone or a computer. He was obsessed with living off the land.

We talked about everything from making mud pies when we were kids to that awful feeling you get when you first get to college, right after your mom leaves and you realize you're on your own.

Alex told me he was an Aries, but he didn't believe in astrology. He and his mom climbed all forty-six of the Adirondack High Peaks over the summers from junior high through high school. Ollie was with them for twenty-three peaks. His dad preferred to go fishing instead of climbing, and they'd come back from their hikes to fresh trout cooking in a cast-iron pan over the campfire. They slept in tents, in sleeping bags right on the ground, and he couldn't believe I'd never been camping. His first crush was on a girl named Suzie from his kindergarten class, but he got over it when she wiped a booger on his arm. And he had a teddy bear named Rusty that he slept with until he was ten.

When he talked, all I wanted to do was listen. I wanted to soak up everything he'd tell me, and I was sure it wasn't just the wine talking. I felt like I'd already known him for a really long time. I'd never felt like that before about anyone, not even Peter.

Alex slipped the waiter his credit card before he even brought the bill over. He got up before me and pulled my chair out as I stood up. He offered me his arm as we walked to the door. I wonder if Louis had coached him, or he could tell that the wine had gone to my head.

"Wait here," he said, in the lobby. "I'll get the car."

"It's not raining," I said. "I won't melt."

"You might freeze."

"I'll risk it." I took my hand off of his arm and fished for his hand.

He opened the door for me. We were quiet walking to his truck. It was a comfortable silence.

He tilted his head up to the sky, pursed his lips, and blew puffs of air into the cold. My heels clicked loudly on the pavement. The air was crisp and there was a ring around the moon.

"It's going to snow," I said, using my free hand to point to the moon. "There's a ring."

"Oh, yeah," Alex said. "It's about time. We haven't had anything stick for more than a day or two yet. It's December already."

I was proud of myself for knowing about the moon. I'd read it somewhere. Maybe it made me seem woodsy and rugged. I pictured us in front of a cabin wearing matching flannel shirts and knit caps like Paul Bunyan, chopping wood in the snow.

"You haven't gotten your tree yet either, right?" Alex slowed down his pace and looked at me.

I shook my head. I hadn't ever gotten my own Christmas tree. My mom and I used to get a little one from the parking lot of the pink brick church in Mount Kisco. But the past two years by myself, I'd just tried to forget Christmas even happened. I got grocery store sushi, rented a bunch of Brat Pack movies, and holed up in my condo until it was over. This year I was planning to get a stocking for Joe, but I hadn't even considered getting a tree.

"I was going to go to the Public Market to get one on Sunday." Alex swung my hand back and forth. "Do you want to come?"

"Yeah," I said. "I'd like that." The hand he wasn't holding was getting cold, so I shoved it in my coat pocket.

"I can fit both trees in the back of the truck."

Both trees. My tree and Alex's tree. I let my head spin through shopping trips for ornaments, eggnog and bourbon, and listening to Bing Crosby while we decorated my very own Christmas tree.

"We've got to get there early, before all the good ones are taken. You know how the Public Market is."

Alex opened the door for me when we got to the truck. I hopped up onto the seat. He pushed my dress against my leg before he closed the door so it wouldn't get stuck.

"I've never been to the Public Market," I said. The car wasn't any warmer than the outside. Alex got in and wasn't making a move to hold hands again, so I pulled my gloves out of my coat pocket and slipped them on.

"Well, the Public Market here isn't going to compare with New York City or anything, but it's pretty cool." Alex turned the heat way up and fiddled with the air vents.

"It opens at five, but I won't make you get up that early." He held the back of his hand to one of the middle vents to test the temperature. "I'm guessing you're not a morning person."

"See, you say I don't volunteer info, but you already know everything about me."

"I just figured if I worked at home, I'd probably sleep in." He felt the air vent again, nodded his head in approval, and angled it in my direction.

The warm air started thawing out my cheeks. It smelled like pine needles mulling on an old steam heater, or at least what I imagined that would smell like.

Alex told me a funny story about how his dad used to take him to the market when he was a kid and he'd feed kettle corn to the live chickens at the poultry stand when no one was looking. He told me that he'd wanted to be a vet since he knew what a vet was, and that when he was six he had a guinea pig named Mrs. Frisby, after the book his mom used to read him. I watched him while he drove and talked and I realized that I wanted to know absolutely everything about him.

When we got back to my place, he left the truck running and started to get out.

"If you're coming in, you should probably turn that off," I said. It was the wine talking. I never would have had the courage otherwise.

Alex turned the truck off. "I didn't want to assume anything."

"It's only eight thirty. Come in for a drink."

"Looks like someone waited up for us." Alex pointed to the living room window. Joe's nose was pressed up against it, fogging up the glass.

"He's strict about my curfew," I said, fishing my keys out of my purse. It took a while to dig through the receipts and gum wrappers to find them. I dropped coins. Alex leaned over to pick them up.

"Not bad," I said, laughing.

"Huh?"

"I was enjoying the view." I found my keys and held them up.

"Are you drunk?" Alex laughed and dropped the coins in my purse.

"Getting there." I was really feeling it. I managed to get the key in the door on the first try. "You left me to tackle that wine by myself." I turned the knob and leaned against the door to open it. "You have to catch up."

Joe raced out to see us, panting and sniffing our clothes.

I kicked my shoes off in the foyer, dropped my purse on the floor, and threw my coat over the side of the couch. The excuse of being drunk made it easy to be bold. I grabbed the lapels of Alex's coat, pulled him close, and kissed him. He kissed back, running his hand down the side of my neck. "I should get you that drink," I said, with my lips still pressed to his. I felt his head nod.

"Have a seat," I said. "I'll be right back."

His eyes were almost closed, like someone had just woken him up.

I had half a bottle of Stoli and about a third of a bottle of Wild Turkey. I looked in the fridge for something to mix it with, but the orange juice carton had only a sip left, and the milk was questionable. Miraculously, the ice tray was full.

"Bourbon or vodka?" I yelled into the living room.

"I don't guess you've got a beer."

"Sorry!"

"Vodka," he said, like it was a question.

I poured vodka into two tumblers, plunked in the ice, and topped it off with a few squeezes from the plastic lime I found in the butter tray.

Alex was sitting forward on the couch, one hand on his knee, the other scratching Joe's head. Alex looked uncomfortable, like he was trying to be on his best behavior.

I handed him his drink and sat down next to him, pulling my legs up under me. Joe jumped up on the couch and sat between us.

"Off!"

Joe jumped off the couch, slinking over to the other side of the coffee table. He collapsed on the floor and sighed.

Alex laughed. "He's so dramatic!"

"He's used to getting what he wants."

"Must be nice." Alex made a face when he took the first sip of his drink. I worried the lime juice was bad, but when I tried it, it tasted fine.

We sat there, sipping our drinks quietly. The sound of the ice cubes clinking was deafening.

"So," Alex said, "this place is nice. Too bad about the dog policy."

"Yeah. Thanks. But, I'll be just as happy to go. The people next door are crazy." I stretched my legs out. When I pulled them back up on the couch, I let my knee touch his thigh.

"Really?" He didn't move his leg away.

"They have this little yippy dog, and the walls are thin, and I can hear them having sex all the–" I realized what I'd said. Everything surged. My cheeks got hot.

Alex's face was red. He took another sip of his drink. He was almost done.

"I'll get you another one," I said, taking his glass from him, the tips of my fingers brushing his. I took my time in the kitchen, waiting for my face to cool down and my pulse to go back to normal. I moved slowly, cracking the ice cube tray, and trying to jostle the cubes out of place by shaking the tray instead of picking them out with my fingernails.

When I got back to the living room, Joe had stolen my seat.

"I'm going to put him upstairs," I said. "He's not used to sharing the couch."

I was about to put Joe in the bedroom, but I thought maybe there was a chance I didn't want to. Did I? Was this what people did on real dates, when they were grown-ups and free to date and didn't have to sneak men into their dorm room after it was too late for Peter to stop over? Is this how sex happened for everyone else?

I scrambled to grab socks and underwear scattered around the room, threw them in the closet, and pushed the doors shut. I pulled one of the blankets off the bed and dragged it into my office. Joe followed me, but when he caught on that I was going to leave him in my office, he pushed his head between the door and the frame.

"Back."

He didn't budge.

"Buddy, please. Back." He slipped his head back, his eyes big and sad. "Thank you, buddy. I love you." I closed the door carefully.

Alex's glass was just ice when I got back. He stood up and kissed me before I could sit down. He pushed his hands into my hair and pulled it gently to tilt my head up to his. His lips were soft. Out of the corner of my eye, I could see our reflection in the window, a sliver where the shade was crooked and didn't cover the glass. The light was bright, the night was dark, and our reflection was clear and bold: his hair falling into my hair, his hands running down to the small of my back, pulling my body against his. I couldn't stop watching. This is what it looks like to be wanted, I thought.

I started with his tie. He pushed my dress off my shoulders, dangerously low. I fumbled with his shirt buttons, taking forever to unbutton them, missing one and doubling back. I wriggled out of my stockings on the staircase. His undershirt came off at the top of the staircase, pants in the hall, followed by socks. He pulled my dress over my head in the doorway of the bedroom. "I'll race you," he whispered, and we ran and jumped on the bed. I hit my head on his elbow. "All right?" he asked.

I rolled over on him and held his wrists against my pillow. "I'm fine. How are you?" I said playfully, like we were just having a polite conversation. I took my bra off and held it out to the side for a minute before I let it drop to the floor.

"Fine," he said, playing along. "So things are good?"

"Things are good," I said, casually. I leaned in and kissed his neck.

"Things are definitely good." His voice broke when I brushed my lips against his ear.

I pressed my cheek to his chest. I could feel every rib. His skin was damp and smelled like soap.

"Are you okay?" he asked.

"Yeah." I smiled and my cheek pressed into him harder. He ran his finger along my mouth. I bit it lightly.

"Is this okay?" He slid his hand along the band of my underwear like he was asking to take them off.

"I should probably get something."

"Yeah."

I leaned off the bed and fumbled through my nightstand, scraping through pens and old remotes until I felt the rough foil edges of a condom packet. I climbed back up on the bed. Reaching for his hand in the dark, I pressed the packet into his palm. I listened to him wriggle out of his boxers and tear open the packet.

"I want you to know," he whispered, "this is a big deal for me."

"Me too," I whispered back.

He threaded his fingers between mine and held my hand the whole time.

When I woke up, it was still dark, barely light outside. I was alone, naked, twisted around the sheet. I rolled to the other side of the bed and looked around the room. The condom packet, ripped in half, was on the floor next to my bra, but Alex's underwear was gone. My nose tingled and my eyes started to sting. Then I heard the toilet flush. The faucet ran. Water splashed. Was he washing his face? Was he trying to sneak out? I sat up, but I couldn't see his pants in the hall. The bathroom door creaked when it opened. I dropped my head back to the pillow and pulled the sheet up to cover my face.

The floor shook when he walked into the bedroom. The bed dipped down when he sat next to me and my legs slid toward his. He brushed my hair out of my face. I tilted my head and yawned like he'd just woken me. He kissed my temple and then my forehead.

"I have to go to work."

"It's night."

"It's five."

"It's night." I grabbed his arm and tried to pull him back to bed with me.

"I have volunteer hours at the ASPCA and then two surgeries back at the office. And I think I need to catch a nap in between." He laughed. "Someone kept me up late."

"Who, me?" I mouthed and pointed to myself.

"Yeah, you, beautiful." He pulled the blankets over me and smoothed my hair against my shoulder. "Go back to sleep. I'll call you later, okay?"

"Yeah."

He kissed me long and soft and slow.

He let Joe out of the office on his way downstairs. I heard Joe follow him to the door and then race upstairs to reclaim his spot on the bed. He dug at the blankets and then plopped down next to me, sighing again. I lay there and replayed the night in my head. Joe started snoring. I shoved him, but he didn't stop. I turned on the TV to drown it out, and fell asleep thinking about Alex.

Chapter Twenty

The phone rang. Joe barked and then started pawing at me. I looked at the clock. It was only eight AM. I rolled over and grabbed the phone, assuming it was Alex.

"Hey you, how's it going at the pound?" I asked. The TV was still on and there was an infomercial playing.

"I'm at JFK." It was Peter.

"Oh." I reached around in the blankets to find the remote and turned the TV off.

"Why would I be at the pound?" Peter's voice was hoarse.

"I'm sleeping." I ran my hand over Joe's forehead. I'd forgotten that Peter could still call–that he was actually going to come back. I cashed that check and in my mind that was the end of Peter, as if cashing the check completely erased the fact that I'd called him or that I even knew him to begin with.

"I left you three messages last night," he said.

"I didn't check," I said. I wanted to hang up the phone. I wanted him to just fade away. I wanted it to be over. But I still wasn't over the fact that the sound of his voice always made me melt.

"I need you."

I froze. Had the damage already been done? Was what I said to his voice mail more incriminating than I thought? Could I really turn him down? After all this time, could I really tell him I didn't need him back?

"I need a favor," he said. He sounded tired.

"Are you kidding me?" *I need you* and *I need a favor* are two very different things. "Bye, Pete."

I rolled over to hang up the phone, but I hesitated. Peter yelled, "Jane thinks you're throwing her a party," loud enough for me to hear with the phone halfway to the receiver.

"What?" I pulled the phone back up to my ear.

"Jane thinks you're throwing us a welcome-home party."

"Why?" I asked. Was this one of those traditional maid-of-honor duties I didn't know about—like making that stupid rehearsal bouquet out of a paper plate and bows from the wedding shower gifts? Deciding I was done with Peter when he was in Europe was one thing, but I hadn't thought things through. Was I done with Janie too?

"I don't know," he said. "She's got it in her head that you've got something planned." Peter could never stand still when he talked on the phone. I always thought it was cute, but now the idea of him walking in little circles in the airport lounge annoyed me.

"Who put it in her head? And when have I ever thrown anyone a party, anyway? Why would she just think I was going to do this?" The closest I'd ever come to throwing a party was ordering pizza on my mom's birthday.

"She's kind of going through postwedding letdown." He talked slowly. "I thought this might cheer her up. You know, to have one more thing to look forward to."

"So you're a letdown," I said. It came out so easily.

"Wow." He took a deep breath loud enough for me to hear.

"Me. No coffee. Eight AM. Don't expect nice." I wanted to know if he'd gotten my voice mail message yet, but I wasn't going to ask.

"Eight's not that early. What were you doing last night?" He laughed.

I didn't want to tell him. It wasn't like in college when I lied to Pete about other guys just in case I still had a shot with him. I finally had something that was mine, and it was good, and it had nothing to do with him or Janie or Diane. I wanted to hold it close, with a tight fist. I worried that if I told him about Alex it would jinx things. "I was working late," I said. "I have a deadline."

"So can you do this?"

"Are you kidding me?"

"Come on, Van," he whined. The Pete I knew would have given up already.

Part of me liked having this kind of power over him, but the rest of me hated that he'd go to all extremes to make Janie happy, without even caring how I felt. He used to care how I felt. He used to know exactly how I like my coffee and that I hate crying in front of people or talking before eleven AM and that the sight of Jell-O makes me cringe. But since he and Janie got together, it felt like every day he took another step away from me, and now, he felt like a stranger.

"When are you getting back to Rochester?" I asked.

"Man, you're a great maid of honor," he said. His voice was flat. "You don't even know when we're getting back?"

"Man, you're a great groom. You don't even know you're supposed to spend your wedding night with your bride." I knew I was being nasty and I just didn't care.

"Van, I– I need us . . . I need–"

"Have you ever thought about what I need?" I couldn't believe I'd actually said it. Something opened up in my chest like a rubber band stretching to the breaking point. All of a sudden, I felt like I could breathe deeper. "Have you ever thought about it even once, Pete?"

"Van, I– I can't have this conversation now, Van." His voice was low and strained, like he was talking through clenched teeth.

"Whatever." I missed the old Peter. The one who would call just to tell me how his day went–before he had someone else to tell. That Peter had dinner with me every Friday night and we talked about real things and he was an amazing, supportive friend. This Peter was just my friend's husband. I wanted this Peter to disappear.

"We've got a long layover here, so Sunday morning would work best. Please, Van." I pictured him with his eyes all squinted up, pacing circles around a row of chairs.

"Sunday? I'm supposed to throw a party for you on Sunday?" I looked at the clock. "It's Saturday already." I thought about just hanging up and turning the ringer off. "I have plans."

"Just call my parents. They'll invite everyone."

"For what?"

"Brunch." He said it like it was easy.

"Brunch? Here?" I said it so loudly that Joe woke up and lifted his head. I patted his pillow and he put his head back down. "Pete, I have plans!"

"You can change them, can't you?"

I thought about walking hand in hand with Alex, checking Christmas trees for bald spots, drinking hot cider from a stand, and breathing plumes of body heat into the brisk air.

"I don't want to," I said, and considered just slamming the phone down. Everyone could show up for the party, but if I just wasn't there, they couldn't do anything about it.

"Come on! You're her best friend!"

"So that means I'm supposed to drop everything?"

"Yeah, Van, it does. That's exactly what it means."

I wanted to scream at him, but then I thought about Janie at my mom's funeral. I pictured her so clearly in my head in that long black dress with her little black ballet flats. I thought she was going to be a mess, and it would be my job to put her back together again, like always. But she was just there for me. She barely even cried. She got me out of bed and dressed and to the service when I didn't even think I could move. She had a never-ending stockpile of clean tissues in her purse, and continually swapped them out for my crumpled, snot-filled ones. She held my hand the whole day, her cold little fingers tapping against mine to calm me when I started sobbing.

She made sure I ate. She didn't leave my side once. I don't even think she peed the entire day. I leaned against her with all of my weight and she didn't budge one bit. She loved my mom too, but she stayed strong to take care of me, and now I couldn't even drop one little date to take care of her. Not to mention the fact that I called her husband on her honeymoon.

"Even if I did change my plans, I don't know how to throw brunch." If I was going to cave, at least I could make him work for it.

"Go get some bagels and make a lot of coffee." His voice softened, but still sounded annoyed.

"Where the hell do you think I'm going to get bagels?"

"Smith's makes good bagels."

"They're upstate bagels. I might as well get a bag of Wonder bread and cut circles in the middle." I still had the remote in my hand. I turned the TV back on and put it on mute.

"Jane likes that place. We go there all the time."

"Well, Janie isn't expecting her parents, is she? I can't serve Diane upstate bagels. I'll never hear the end of it." Just the thought of Diane made me squirm. "If they're coming, I'm not doing this, Pete. Not with upstate bagels."

The infomercial on the television was for some skin care system. There were split-screen pictures of people with horrible acne and then perfectly clear skin. The after pictures looked like completely new people. I wished I could peel all my skin off and be a completely new person—one who didn't know Pete or Janie or Diane anymore. A person who was free to move on without any complications or guilt.

"Of course Diane's coming. She's Jane's mom."

"You really think they'll come on such short notice?"

"They drove up yesterday. They're staying at Woodcliff."

"Diane and Charles drove up yesterday for a party at my place that I didn't even know about? God, Pete! Really!"

"I know, Van. I know." His voice was soft and deflated. "Please. I owe you."

"Yeah, you do."

"Thank you."

Joe cuddled up closer to me, resting his head on my chest. He let out a big sigh.

"You're so dramatic," Pete said, but his voice was lighter. It wasn't a dig.

"That wasn't me. It was Joe."

"Oh." I could hear the hurt in his voice, and I liked it. "Who's Joe?"

"Oh, you don't know him," I said. "You've been gone awhile."

"I should go," Peter said, quickly. "Janie should be coming back from duty free any minute." He took a loud, deep breath. "So we're good?"

"I'll see you tomorrow."

"Bye." He was waiting for me to hang up first.

"Hey, Pete?"

"Yeah?"

"Why didn't you warn me about this before you left?"

"I didn't know about it. You know how she is."

"Yeah. Bye." I hung up the phone. Joe started pawing at me to take him out.

After Joe and I got back inside, I tried to go back to sleep. I kicked my boots off and climbed into bed. Joe jumped onto the bed next to me and dug at the covers for a minute before lying down. His paws left wet marks on the sheets. I closed my eyes. Joe wriggled around, trying to get comfortable. I put my arm around him to try to get him to calm down. His ribs, rippling under layers of fur and skin, raised and lowered my arm with each breath. When he did settle back to sleep, it was with his nose pressed up against my cheek, like warm wet leather. One of his nostrils was channeling his breath right into my ear.

"All right, buddy. This isn't working."

I got up. I thought he'd come with me, but he flopped over into the spot I just left and nosed his head onto my pillow. He yawned and stretched his front legs out until his feet shook.

"You're such a boy," I said, as I walked out of the room. Joe was already snoring.

Chapter Twenty-one

I went downstairs, started a pot of coffee, and sat down at the table to sort through a pile of junk mail. The list of phone numbers Janie gave me before the wedding was at the bottom of the mail pile. I picked up the phone to call Peter's mom, Scotty, but I didn't dial. I didn't want to. I put the phone down. I'll sort the mail and then I'll call, I told myself, but then I got wrapped up in an L.L.Bean catalog addressed to Rocco Leonard or Current Resident. I was also the Current Resident recipient of Rocco's extensive list of lingerie catalogs. It was way too early in the morning to look at fake breasts trapped in fishnet, like unfortunate victims of the tuna industry, so I stuck with L.L.Bean, flipping through pages of monogrammed travel kits and lambskin slippers.

I imagined Alex and me sitting in Adirondack chairs, looking out at the Maine coast in matching fleece jackets, cozying up in front of a campfire under a red wool blanket, Joe stretched out across our feet. I inserted us into every picture, and even let myself flag flannel shirts he might like by folding down the corners of the pages. In the men's section, there was a picture of a model who looked like Peter, with dark hair and a square jaw. He was standing on a dock wearing a blazer, khakis, and boat shoes, smiling that big fake catalog smile, with a woman who looked like her clothes never wrinkled and her hair never frizzed.

I turned the page on them and looked at fireplace accessories, trying to think about Alex and woodsmoke and Christmas trees instead. I could just go with Alex. I could just ignore them. I didn't have to do this. I could move on and leave them to pick up the pieces for once.

The phone rang. I let it go to voice mail, but my heart did this awful *thunk, thunk, thud* thing until the phone beeped to tell me I had a new message. I called in to check it.

"Hi, Van!" It was Janie. "I miss you so much! Our flight got delayed, but we're boarding soon. Just wanted to say hi. Can't wait to see you and show you all the pictures. And so many magnets! Nat would be proud, but I feel bad for your fridge." She laughed. "Okay, I think we're boarding now. Love you! Bye!"

Janie and Diane and my mom and I had this running joke where we bought each other hideous tourist magnets whenever we went anyplace that had a gift shop. Janie and Diane brought back magnets from glamorous places like the Eiffel Tower and London Bridge when Charles took them with him on business trips. And we'd bring them magnets from rest stops or the aquarium in Norwalk. The goal was to find the tackiest magnet ever. When my mom and I stopped at South of the Border on a road trip one summer, we totally won. Diane and Janie had a five-inch-wide fluorescent pink sombrero on their fridge until Charles said he was sick of looking at it and it had to go. Then the sombrero took hitchhiking trips, secretly stuck to the side of a car or slipped in someone's purse when she wasn't looking. Eventually, it disappeared. No one was quite sure who had it last. We hadn't done the magnet thing in years. Even before my mom died, it just kind of faded away. I wondered why Janie was starting it again. Maybe she missed my mom too. Maybe she missed the way things were.

I deleted all three messages from Peter without giving him a chance to say more than, "Hi Van," "Hey, listen, I—," and "It's me. Call me ba—"

There was one more message.

"Savannah, hi. It's Scotty Clarke." She spoke briskly, like she had better things to do than leave me a message. "Just wanted to give a call with the tally for tomorrow morning. We have eighteen yeses and five maybes, not including Janie, Pete, and you. See you at eleven."

My pulse quickened. Even Scotty knew about the party before me. I took a gulp of coffee. It was too hot. I swallowed and it burned the back of my throat, making my eyes tear up.

I'd done a good job of avoiding the Clarkes throughout the wedding festivities. It wasn't hard. It's not like they were tracking me down to catch up. I'd seen them periodically over the years, always in passing. The only time I'd ever spent any real time with them was the night Peter took me to have dinner at their house after midterms, freshman year.

I'd spent hours trying to find something to wear. I had gotten the base layer down—a black tank top and a long khaki skirt. But none of my sweaters looked right. They stretched too tightly across my boobs. I pulled a blue button-down shirt out of my closet, and was about to try it on, when the buzzer rang. I ran downstairs to open the door. Peter came in with a rush of cold air. I shivered.

"Hello," he said, rubbing his hand up and down my arm to try to warm me. His hands were freezing, but I didn't care. It was the first time he'd touched me.

"Hello."

"You look great."

I laughed. "I'm not done getting dressed. Come up for a sec?"

"Sure," he said, raising his eyebrows at me.

"Don't get your hopes up." I raised my eyebrows back at him. "None of this is coming off." I waved my hand up toward my head and then pointed down to my toes like I was showing off a prize on a game show.

I walked up the stairs in front of him with an extra swagger in my step. I knew he was watching me. I resisted the urge to look back at him.

When we got to my room, he walked around and looked at everything.

"No roommate?" he said, pointing at the empty bed across from mine.

"Technically, I have a roommate." I pulled the blue shirt on and buttoned it. "She stayed here the first night and cried hysterically the whole time."

"Wow."

"Yeah. Her parents live like twenty minutes away," I said, "so she stays there mostly, and she brought most of her stuff back home. She studies here between classes sometimes." I pointed to her desk.

Peter walked over and opened the top drawer. A lone pencil rolled forward. "You must be lonely."

"Oh, it's okay." I smiled bravely. "I practically have my own room. As a freshman. It's pretty cool." In truth, I was horribly lonely. All the other girls on my floor went to dinner with their roommates, switched outfits, shared shoes. Even the roommates who were terribly mismatched at least had someone to venture out with until they met other people. "So, how does this look?"

Peter stood back from me and put his hand on his chin like he was considering a painting. He swirled his index finger in a circle. I spun around for him.

"What else you got?"

"I don't look that bad, do I?"

"You look great. I just want to know what my options are."

"Oh, I see." I laughed and unbuttoned my shirt slowly, staring him down. I couldn't believe that this was my life. That this was what it was like to be in college. That someone this unbelievably hot was in my dorm room helping me pick out an outfit and taking me to meet his parents.

"And see you in that tank top again." He bit his bottom lip and raised his eyebrows. I threw my shirt at him. He caught it. "You're a handful, aren't you?" He was staring at my breasts when he said it, but he wasn't referring to them. When his eyes met mine, he smiled. Then his eyes got wide and his face turned red. "Trouble," he mumbled. "I mean, you're trouble."

"Ah." I smiled.

"I'm going to look at your CDs." His face was still red.

"I'll put this on." I grabbed my black cotton cardigan.

I watched him as I buttoned up. He thumbed through my beards—U2, Dar Williams, Pete Yorn, Radiohead, the skinny guy who played at the coffeehouse in Mount Kisco—the CD collection I had carefully crafted to look hip, alternative, and off the beaten path. The Boston tapes my mom made me were tucked away in my underwear drawer.

"How's this?" I turned around again.

Peter leaned on my desk and crossed his arms. "Looking good."

"Not too much?"

"Too much?"

"It's a little tight."

"In all the right places."

"I'm going to meet your parents?" I put my hands on my hips and pretended I was scolding him.

"You look great," Peter said. He flashed his perfect smile and, for a moment, I felt like I was perfect too.

Peter clicked his car open before we got to it. "It's open," he said, and climbed in. "It's my dad's old one. I can't wait to get my new one when I graduate."

The dashboard lights were bright and blue, and even though the car was a hand-me-down, it was newer and nicer than anything my mom had ever driven.

"So what should I call your parents?" I asked.

"Mom and Dad," Peter said, laughing.

"Seriously." I shoved his arm.

He looked over at me with his eyes open really wide, smirking. "Van, I'm driving here. We could have an accident."

"Shut up," I said, laughing.

"You shut up!" Peter shoved my shoulder gently.

"Peter, you're driving."

"Yeah, so?"

"So, we could have an accident." I tried to deadpan it, but I got the giggles.

"Shut. Up." He was laughing too.

"No, you shut up. What do I call your parents?"

"Do you want me to shut up, or do you want me to tell you?"

"Oh my God!" I was laughing so hard my eyes were tearing. "Just tell me!"

"I'd go with Mr. and Mrs. Clarke. It's the safe bet. My friend Drew calls my mom Scotty, but he's known her since before he could talk."

"Why does he call her Scotty?" I wiped my eyes, and tried to catch my breath.

"That's her name."

"Really?"

"Actually, it's Scottsdale."

"Scottsdale, like Arizona?"

"Scottsdale, as in Scottsdale Home Materials." He said it proudly, like I should be impressed.

It didn't ring any bells. I shook my head.

"Insulation mostly. Not the pink brand, the yellow kind."

"I don't know a lot about insulation. It's not my forte," I said, smiling.

"Ephram Scottsdale was my great-grandfather. He had two girls, so there wasn't anyone to carry on the family name."

"So your grandmother named your mom Scottsdale?"

"Yeah."

"No offense, but that's awful." I'd always thought Savannah was too weighty a name, but Scottsdale was so much worse.

"Yeah. Scotty isn't bad, though."

"So she's the end of it, right? I mean, she's the last one to carry on the family name."

"Eh, I think I'm expected to."

"Scottsdale Clarke, Junior." I made a face.

"Guess I'd better hope for boys," he said.

"So they can have the same name as their grandmother?"

"Well, her middle name is June. I wouldn't keep that." He talked about having kids with the same level of comfort that he might talk about a movie he planned to see. He seemed so easy with his picture of his future. I couldn't even think past getting out of the car in his parents' driveway. At the time, I was in awe of his certainty. Now, I think it had more to do with the fact that he was never allowed to make any choices. Being certain of your future is easy when there's only one path out in front of you, and it's well lit and clearly marked.

The Clarkes' house was smaller than Diane's, but it was still huge. Diane would have called it a McMansion, and turned her nose up at the newness of it. Diane loved to point out the signs of new money, even though she hadn't had money before she married Charles. I found it amusing that Diane lived in a respectably old house, while Scotty Clarke lived in a new one. Scottsdale Home Materials had been around since Peter's great-grandfather. Diane's marriage to Charles was only a few months older than Janie.

Mr. Clarke opened the door before we even got close enough to ring the bell. He was holding a full martini glass complete with an olive on a blue glass pick. When Diane drank martinis at home, she just used a tumbler and plunked some olives in to hang out together at the bottom of the glass.

"Well, what do we have here," Mr. Clarke said, giving me the once-over. His eyes rested on my cleavage, and stayed there even as he shook my hand.

"Nice to meet you, Mr. Clarke," I said, trying to make eye contact and failing.

"This is Van, Dad," Peter said, patting his dad on the shoulder as he walked past him into the house.

"You're not Peter's roommate, are you?" Mr. Clarke said, still standing in the doorway, so I was stuck out on the front step.

Peter yelled, "Mom, we're here!" and walked away from the door. I couldn't see him anymore.

"No. He's in my—we're in a class together." I shifted my weight, hoping if I looked uncomfortable, he'd invite me into the house, and I could find Peter.

"I was going to say, Peter lucked out on the roommate lottery." Mr. Clarke took a sip of his martini, and finally looked up at my face. "Well, come on in!" he said like I'd been the one holding things up. "Can I get you a drink?"

"I'm fine," I said.

He turned sideways in the doorway to let me past, his smile growing wider than his mustache.

Peter was standing in the entryway holding two glasses of iced tea with lemon wedges and long spoons. "Come meet Mom," he said.

"Let me talk to her first," Mr. Clarke said, rushing past Peter.

"Did I do something wrong?" I asked.

"I don't know. Did you say anything political?"

"No."

"I'm sure it's fine." Peter handed me one of the glasses.

Scotty Clarke walked into the entryway. She was a small woman with very straight, very blond hair, and impossibly skinny hips. When Peter introduced me, she said, "Nice to meet you, Van," in a soft, flat voice, and offered me her cold, limp hand. Peter smiled at me encouragingly. "I put the hors d'oeuvres in the living room." She smoothed her apron against her skirt. It was a crisp white half apron, and completely spotless, as if she wore an apron over her apron while she cooked. "I'll be in shortly."

The living room had a cathedral ceiling and too many windows with too many window treatments—blinds and curtains and valences on every one. Even though there was a fire in the fireplace, the living room didn't smell like woodsmoke. Stargazer lilies, perfectly arranged in big vases, sat on the mantel and the table behind the couch. Their cloying, plastic smell crowded the room. I wanted to sit in one of the chairs, away from the flowers, but Peter sat on the couch and put a coaster on the coffee table for me, so I sat down next to him. The flowers made my eyes tear.

Assorted flaky dough puffs in different shapes with different, unidentifiable fillings were arranged on a big white platter on the coffee table. Peter held a napkin under his chin and popped one in his mouth. I did the same. I think it was spinach and cheese, but all I could taste was lilies.

Peter hooked his index finger with mine and gave a tug. When I looked up and smiled at him, his pupils dilated. I read in *Cosmo* once that men's pupils dilate when they like what they see. I tugged back on his finger.

Mr. Clarke came in with a full martini glass. His footsteps were heavy and loud, even on the rug. Peter unhooked his finger from mine and rested his hand on his leg. I left my hand on the cushion next to me, in case his finger was coming back.

Mr. Clarke sat down in one of the armchairs across from us. "Sure you don't want a drink, Van? Peter's driving."

"Um, no, thanks." My voice was stuck behind throat scum. I coughed softly to clear it. "Thank you, though."

"So Petey, when do we get to meet this Dan fellow?"

Dan was Peter's roommate. They hadn't been expecting me.

"I'm sure you'll meet him sooner or later," Peter said, reaching for another puff.

Mr. Clarke laughed. "Sounds like you're not eager to force the issue." He pulled one of the olives off of his pick with his teeth and chewed it loudly. I wondered if he was new money like Diane.

"Dan's kind of a dick," Peter said.

Mr. Clarke laughed harder and his whole body shook. I thought a piece of his olive must have gone down the wrong way, because it turned into a laugh-hack combination, and his face went bright red. "That's my boy. He knows an asshole when he sees one, Van. I tell you, he's going to be a great litigator."

Once he settled down and went back to his drink, he said, "So, where'd you come from, Van?" The way he kept saying my name felt like he was either making fun of me or trying to sell me something.

"Van's from Westchester, Dad," Peter said, before I could say anything.

Mr. Clarke eased back in his chair and pulled his ankle up to rest on the opposite knee. "Whereabouts?"

"Chappaqua," I said.

He raised his eyebrows. "I do business in White Plains sometimes. Hell of a drive." He smiled, and his teeth were big and white under the dark fringe of his mustache.

"Yeah, it's a long one."

"I can't decide if it's more of a hassle to fly or just suck it up and get in the car. Have you figured it out, Van?"

"Six of one, half a dozen of the other," I said, relaxing a little. Flying instead of taking a six-hour drive wasn't in my vocabulary.

Mr. Clarke chuckled. "Yes. Exactly."

"What did I miss?" Scotty came in, sans apron, holding a glass of white wine. She sat down on the very edge of the other armchair.

"Van was just telling us she's from Chappaqua."

"How funny!" Scotty swirled the wine around in her glass. "My cousin lives in Chappaqua. Bronwyn Childs. Do you know her?" Her nose was very thin and very straight, and didn't move at all when she talked.

"The name sounds familiar." It didn't, but for all I knew, she could have been one of Diane's friends.

"Oh, Bronwyn spends all her time playing tennis. She makes it sound like that's all anyone in Westchester does." She laughed, so I did too. "Do you play?"

"A little." I'd hit balls around the court with Janie when Diane let me go to the club with them, but I didn't even understand how it was scored.

"Bronwyn plays at the Saw Mill Club."

"I play at Whippoorwill," I said, quickly. It spilled out of my mouth so easily, but once I said it, I was so conscious of the implications, and where I fell short. "I did, I mean. When I was home."

"You're a long way from home now, aren't you? It must be hard to leave your family like that."

"Yes," I said, softly, "I am."

"See, Scot," Mr. Clarke said, "some birds let their chicks out from under their wing." His martini glass was empty.

Mr. Clarke and Peter laughed. Scotty sat back in her chair a little farther, and stared into her wineglass. I focused on keeping my expression pleasantly neutral, like the mannequins at Neiman Marcus. When Peter and Mr. Clarke went on to talk about clients at the firm and which classes Peter should take, Scotty looked at me and rolled her eyes at them. I smiled at her and she smiled back.

"Why don't we sit down to dinner," she said. She took Mr. Clarke's glass from him as she walked past.

Dinner was Cornish hens in some sort of wine sauce. I didn't know how I was supposed to approach it, and none of the Clarkes gave any clues. Mr. Clarke and Peter were so busy talking that they barely picked at their hens, and Scotty spent her time cutting her asparagus into tiny, tiny pieces. That explained the hips at least. She didn't look at me or make any effort to start a conversation. I pulled the loose meat at the legs off with my fork, and then went to work on my asparagus like Scotty.

"So what line of work is your old man in?" Mr. Clarke cut his asparagus in half with the side of his fork.

"I don't know," I blurted out without thinking.

"What?"

"My dad left when I was little," I said, softly. "I don't know what he does for a living."

"What about your mother?"

I tried to brainstorm a way to recover, but came up empty. "She's a housekeeper," I said, finally, wishing I had the nerve to say she was the head of a Fortune 500, or ran her own PR firm.

All three of them stared at me. They must have thought I flat-out lied about the country club. I mean, obviously I wasn't a member of the Whippoorwill Club on my single mother's housekeeper salary.

"The family she worked for—I was best friends with their daughter and . . ." I thought maybe I could explain my bent truth without actually explaining it, but I stopped talking because it wasn't helping. Mr. Clarke started mauling his Cornish hen, and Scotty stared at Peter, pressing her lips together so hard they turned white.

Peter hooked fingers with me under the table. I looked over at him, but he didn't look at me. "That must have been hard," he said, staring back at Scotty.

No one said anything for a really long time. Scotty went back to cutting her food, dabbing her mouth with her napkin periodically, as if she'd actually eaten something. Mr. Clarke downed the rest of his drink and started some chatter with Peter about plans for renovating the law library at the firm. Peter didn't say much, adding only "ah," "okay," or "I see" every so often. I avoided looking at anyone by swirling a small piece of asparagus around in the sauce on my plate, making little circles and stars that disappeared quickly. I felt like I'd gone from being a guest to a ghost in a few simple words. It was painfully obvious that I didn't belong there.

Finally, Scotty pulled her napkin off of her lap, folded it, and placed it at the side of her plate. "You'll have to excuse me," she said softly, smiling weakly, with her eyes lowered. "I have a terrible headache." She pushed her chair back without making a noise and left the room quickly.

Mr. Clarke smiled at me. "You'll have to excuse her. She gets these all the time." He pushed his chair out. "I'm going to get more potatoes."

Peter said, "'Scuse me for a sec, Van," and followed his dad into the kitchen.

I heard snippets of conversation—the first parts of the sentences but not the ends, or the ends but not the beginnings.

"Come on, Dad—"

There was a big window behind Mr. Clarke's chair. It was dark out, and the curtains weren't drawn, so I could see my own reflection clearly. My sweater was too tight.

"What you do at your dorm is your business—but this—it's upsetting your mother."

I buttoned my sweater all the way up to the top button at my neck.

"–amazing–really smart."

"Bring her back when she wins the Nobel Prize."

Mr. Clarke came back out with another martini, but no potatoes.

"Hey, Vannie," he said, "sure I can't offer you a drink?"

"I'm sure," I said softly, looking at his plate. He'd eaten his hen down to its tiny pigeon bones.

Peter came out red-faced. He picked at his hen with his fork, but didn't eat anything.

"So, Van," Mr. Clarke said, "as in automobile?"

"Dad."

"I'm taking an interest in your guest, Peter." His eyes narrowed. "The origin of a name is acceptable conversation in polite company." He looked at me, and smiled like a game show host.

"Savannah," I said. My voice was barely there.

"Well, that's a pretty name, Savannah." Mr. Clarke wiped his mouth on his napkin and leaned back in his chair.

Peter turned to me. "Is it okay if we go?" His voice was shaking.

Mr. Clarke made a big production of saying good-bye to me. "Well, Miss Savannah," he said, shaking my hand and then holding it, "don't be a stranger." His palms were sweaty. Peter was halfway out the door before Mr. Clarke set me free.

In the car, Peter made himself busy fiddling with the CD player and the stack of CDs he had in the console.

"I'm really sorry," I said. "I hadn't meant to–"

"Van, don't–" He sounded so angry. I wanted to open my car door and tuck and roll myself into a ditch.

"No, I mean I wasn't lying. I did, we did play tennis, sort of, and Janie–but I shouldn't have, I shouldn't . . . I know what it implied, Pete, and I'm sorry."

"Fuck 'em," Peter said. He ran his hand through his hair and sighed. "They're fucking snobs. It's embarrassing."

He drove me right up to the door of my dorm. "I'm really sorry," he said, kissing me on the cheek.

We didn't talk all weekend and I worried we never would again. I spent the weekend moping in my dorm room, listening to my Boston mix tape, rewinding to listen to "My Destination" over and over again, getting choked up, because I'd honestly felt that my destination was right by Peter's side.

On Monday, Peter bought me coffee after class and we went for a walk again like nothing had happened. We didn't make it all the way to the park, though. Once it got too cold for our walks, he started taking me to dinner on Fridays instead of going home. He stopped talking about the car he was going to get when he graduated, and he avoided all mention of his parents. I waited for something more to happen between us, but it never did.

I deleted Scotty's message, sat down at the table with my third cup of coffee, and went back to thumbing through the L.L.Bean catalog. The back cover had information on Christmas tree orders. Since I wasn't going to get to go tree shopping with Alex, I called and ordered one, a blue spruce, six feet tall. The phone associate's name was Susan. I know it was her job, but she sounded like she was honestly happy to be talking with me. I wanted to tell her everything—how I was supposed to be drinking hot cider and feeding chickens with Mr. Perfect tomorrow instead of throwing a horrible party for my best friend and the man I'd been stupidly in love with for almost seven years. I wanted to tell her how hurt I was, and how much I missed my mom, and how tired I was of being the stage manager for *The Janie Show* and how I worried that made me a bad friend and a bad person. Instead, I ordered a stand, two dozen globe ornaments, aluminum icicles, six strands of white twinkle lights, a headband with reindeer antlers for Joe, a red wool blanket, and a men's flannel shirt in mariner plaid. Then I called and left Alex a message to tell him I couldn't go Christmas tree shopping with him. I said I had a stomach bug. It was easier than explaining.

Chapter Twenty-two

I knew I was supposed to be getting ready for the party, washing all my dishes and preordering bagels, but I just didn't want to. First I needed more coffee; then I thought I should shower. By the time I showered and got dressed, it was almost time for lunch, and everyone knows you're not supposed to shop hungry, so I shared a turkey sandwich with Joe and flipped through the channels while we ate. I got hooked on a PBS mystery and kept watching long after we'd eaten the sandwich down to the crumbs and moved on to ice cream. I didn't want to miss the end of Miss Marple to go get streamers and preorder bagels for a party I didn't want to have, celebrating something I didn't feel like celebrating, so I left it all to the very last minute.

I ended up at Walmart at three AM. The huge parking lot was completely empty except for a row of cars toward the back and someone sitting in his car in the far corner.

I grabbed a cart and wandered through the party goods section for at least a half an hour, trying to find decorations that didn't make me want to go home and stick my head in the oven. One paper plate set spelled out *Happily Ever After* in swirly letters on pale pink hearts and had matching *Once Upon a Time* streamers. The Blessed Union set had doves and was scattered with roses like chicken pox.

I briefly considered going with a dinosaur set from the kids' section, but then I noticed the discounted Thanksgiving decorations at the end of the aisle. Since the wedding had been at Thanksgiving, I figured I could get away with half-priced pilgrims and giant crepe-paper turkeys. I got the fancy plastic champagne glasses—the ones where the bottoms don't fall off—to assuage my guilt.

I grabbed three packages of frozen bagels, and was happily surprised to learn that Walmart was stocked with smoked salmon.

Walmart was almost empty, and there was something hypnotic about walking around under the fluorescent lights staring at produce.

Peter and Janie were probably expecting mimosas, but it was too late to go get champagne. They would have to settle for spumante with a screw cap, and maybe some wine coolers. I grabbed a few cartons of OJ and some cans of frozen limeade concentrate, with thoughts of making punch. I dumped a mesh bag of Key limes into the cart. I figured if I threw a few lime slices in with the punch, people might not realize it was juice from a can. Diane and Scotty would never serve juice from a can.

I had a choice between a real live checker and an automated checkout system. The checker gave me a big smile that revealed a full mouth of braces. She was young, but way too old for braces. She had stringy hair and thick oversize glasses. She looked like she wanted to make conversation. I flashed her a quick smile and went with the automated checkout, but then the damn turkeys wouldn't scan. I tried three times before the machine started beeping. I tried to just leave the turkeys and cut my losses, but the checker came running over. Her name tag bobbed up and down on her breast even after she stopped running. It was one of the temporary tags, and her name, Tanya, was scribbled in blue ink across it in bubbly letters. If she'd had an *i* in her name, I was sure it would have been dotted with a heart.

"Ooh, what do we have here," Tanya squealed. Her vowels were hard and sharp. She picked up the paper turkey and ran the bar code under the scanner. It beeped again. "Stocking up for next year, huh?" She waved the turkey at the scanner furiously, and it beeped back at her with the same intensity. "Aren't you a smart shopper?" She had alternating pink and green rubber bands in her braces.

"Thanks," I said, wondering why it didn't seem odd to her that I was in Walmart at almost four AM buying paper turkeys. What were other people buying in the middle of the night?

"I always buy holiday stuff on sale," Tanya said. She wasn't even trying to get it to go through; she was just leaning up against the machine. "But then when the holiday comes around, I can't even find it." She sighed, and rested her hand over her heart like it was a major crisis. "You know, they have those bins." She gestured over to one of the aisles. "Those Rubbermaid bins. They have orange and black for Halloween, and red and green for Christmas." She hit a button on the machine and tried waving the turkey under the sensor again. "I don't know if they have one for Thanksgiving, but maybe you could get an extra Halloween one. Or use a green top from Christmas with an orange bin from Halloween."

"Yeah," I said. I was ready to just leave it all and run for the door, but then the turkey finally registered. The automated voice asked for the next item.

"Anything else?" Tanya asked, holding her hand out.

I was going to tell her I could do it myself, but it was quicker to comply, so I handed her the first package of bagels.

"Oh, these are good," she said, looking at the label before she scanned them.

I pulled my credit card out while she finished scanning, and had it ready to go before the automated voice even asked for it.

"Well, it looks like I'm all set here," I said. "Thank you."

I grabbed my bags and made a beeline for the door.

When I got to the car, I was embarrassed. Tanya was just trying to be nice. We were two lonely people in Walmart at four in the morning. At least she was capable of making polite conversation. I thought about going back in to get some butter or something. I could go straight for Tanya's register, and make small talk and ask her if Rubbermaid made storage containers in Easter colors. But I had to go home and clean for the party, and I just didn't have it in me.

Chapter Twenty-three

After bringing the decorations into the condo and taking Joe out to pee, I was down to six hours and fifteen minutes. I wasted at least fifteen minutes staring at myself in the mirror, transfixed by the clogged pores on my nose.

Six hours even.

I started collecting dishes so I could run the dishwasher. There was a small army of coffee mugs in my office, and not one, but five, water glasses on my nightstand, with varied levels of water in them. I hoped Alex hadn't noticed. The water had dust and dog hair scum floating on top in all but the most recent glass. I dumped all the water into one, and stacked them up. Then I realized that the dishwasher was already full. I started it, and made a plan to hide some in the recycling bin in the garage if I couldn't get them all done in time.

My next round was garbage. Joe followed me while I made the rounds, getting underfoot and trying to sniff everything I picked up. I wished I could train him to clean up for me. When I emptied the bathroom trash can, which was overflowing with used tissues and cotton balls, the tissues kept the shape of the can from being jammed in so tightly. There were seven crumpled tissues under my pillow and several more on the floor next to the bed. And throughout my tour of garbage, I picked up dog hair by the handful. I had a full bag by the time I got back to the kitchen. Alex had left so early in the morning that it was still dark out. I told myself he couldn't have noticed any of it.

Joe ran into the living room and jumped on the couch. He stuck his head in between the slats of the blinds. His tail stopped wagging and he growled, long and low.

I jumped up on the couch next to him and looked out. Peter was sitting in his Beamer in the driveway. I hadn't even heard the car pull up. I pulled the elastic out of my hair and worked on twisting my hair up in a bun, trying to smooth it down. I ran my index fingers under my eyes to try to wipe away the oily puddles of melted eyeliner that had probably collected. I knew it was useless.

I grabbed my jacket.

"Back," I said to Joe. He backed away from the door and sat down. "Zustan." I held my hand out to tell him to stay and closed the door quickly behind me.

Peter was sitting in the driver's seat. I could see him clearly in the spotlight from over the garage. He looked down when he saw me coming, and didn't look up even when I opened the door and climbed in.

"Is that a dog in there?" he asked, before I could say anything.

"You spying on me?"

"You really need to close your blinds," he said. His voice was tired and snotty, like when I used to make jokes while he was trying to study.

"So perverts like you can't sit out here and get a peep show?"

"You didn't take your clothes off," he said. "I wouldn't have watched that."

"Thank you, Pete. Thank you so much." I spit the words out like sour lemon pits.

"That's not what I meant. I—"

"Shove it," I said. I knew he hadn't meant it that way, but it felt good to be mad at him and let him know it.

He lowered his head and looked up at me, trying to make eye contact. I didn't let him.

He looked down at his hands, still on the steering wheel. "Invite me in," he said. "It's cold out here."

"I don't care." I pulled a piece of Juicy Fruit out of its usual resting place in his console, unwrapped it, and shoved it in my mouth. It was stale and brittle, and it took a few rounds of chewing to come together.

"Come on. You're cold too," he said, rolling his hands up into fists and flexing his fingers out again.

"I can go in anytime I want to."

"Fine," he said, turning the key in the ignition.

"Where are you taking me?" I asked. There was a part of me that still wanted him to just whisk me away. We could drive to the airport and take the first plane out—who cared where it was going. I wanted that part of me to shrivel up and die, but it didn't seem like it ever would. I was so disappointed in myself.

"Nowhere. I just don't want to freeze." He turned the dials on the air vents to blow hot air in his direction. Then he reached over and turned the center one to blow on me.

"It's a waste of gas," I said.

"I don't care," he said, banging the sides of his hands on the steering wheel. His voice was even snottier than before.

"What the fuck is wrong with you?" I asked, and then cringed at how harsh it sounded.

"What?"

"What are you doing here, Pete?"

His cell phone rang. It was the *Mission Impossible* theme song.

"Cute," I said.

He stared at me in a dead panic.

"You'd better pick up," I said, crossing my arms and raising my eyebrows.

He didn't make a move. The phone stopped ringing, but just as he put it back in his cup holder, it started again.

"I won't say anything," I said, holding my left hand up like I was taking an oath. "The more time you take to pick up, the more freaked out she's going to be."

He flipped the phone open and held it up to his ear.

"Hi, Baby Jane," he said, plastering on a smile that was as fake as his sweet voice.

I sat there silently wishing that cars came equipped with vomit bags.

"No, our Wegmans didn't have any."

"Right. Well, they only had the other brand, and I know you don't like the other—"

"Exactly. I'm at the University Ave. Wegmans."

He stared at me while he talked, like he was expecting me to scream out, *Janie! He's in my driveway!*

"Yes," he said. "If it's not here, I'll try the Marketplace Wegmans and then I'm coming home."

He stopped looking at me.

"That's what I meant. If they don't have it there, I'll look for a CVS or a Walmart or something. That's what I meant."

He turned away from me. "I love you, too," he said into the phone.

Just as he flipped it closed, I yelled, "Hi, Janie!"

He jumped and turned back to me.

"Why did you do that?"

"Your phone was already off."

"But why did you do that?"

"Why are you here?" I said, not sure I really wanted to hear the answer.

"I don't like how we left things," he said, softening.

"Do you even remember how we left things?" I asked, rubbing my hands together in front of the heater. "You were trashed."

"I remember."

"Well, what am I supposed to say here?" I asked. "What do you want from me?"

He just stared at me in silence. Then he leaned over and kissed me. I let myself be kissed for a split second. I let myself feel what it was like to be kissed by him after all this time. It was almost like I thought it would be. His lips were soft, his breath was sweet, and my heart did a drumroll.

I tried to pull away, but Peter was holding the back of my head with his hand. I pursed my lips together. He kissed me harder.

"Come on, Van," he whispered. "This is what you want, isn't it? This is why you called me, right?"

He went in to kiss me again.

"No," I said. I tried to push him off of me, but he kept pulling me in to him. My hand slipped and I hit him hard in the stomach.

He recoiled into his own seat, holding himself and resting his head on the steering wheel.

I didn't apologize. I hadn't meant to do it, but I wasn't sorry.

"What the fuck?" he said.

"You know what the fuck!"

"I didn't think it was going to be like this," he said.

"Like what?"

"Like running around like crazy to buy Preparation H for her puffy 'airplane eyes.'" He turned his head toward me, still resting on the steering wheel.

His eyes were wet.

"You're not running around like crazy, Pete. You're sitting in my driveway."

He didn't say anything. He turned his head and rested his cheek on the wheel so he could look at me.

And then it dawned on me.

"This isn't about you having feelings for me, is it?" I looked down at my knees, trying not to explode. "This is about married life not being as perfect as you thought." I felt around for the handle of the door so I could be assured of an easy escape. The metal was smooth and cold. "This isn't about me. It's about you."

"Van—"

"No!" I yelled. "No. I'm not everyone's pawn. I am not your pawn." I couldn't look at him. I stared at the garage door, holding on to the door handle so tightly that the tips of my fingers started to go numb.

"I don't know what you're—"

"I'm not your pawn. Not yours or Diane's or Janie's."

"Van, calm down." He put his hand on my shoulder, but I slapped it away.

"You forget that I am a person," I said. "Well . . . well, when you leave the room, surprise! When you leave the room, my life keeps going."

"Come on!" He reached for me again, but stopped before he got close enough to touch me.

"No, you come on! You drive away, and I'll be stuck here with the fact that my best friend's husband just kissed me." I found the spot on the garage door where I hit it with my bumper last June. "And who am I going to call to talk it through? No one. No one. Because Janie is my goddamned best friend, and you're a close second. My mom is dead," I said, feeling my bottom lip start to shake, "and it's not like I'm going to call Diane about this."

"Aw, Van." He started to put his arms out to hug me, but pulled them back in when I looked at him.

"The thing is, Pete. The thing is that it's always been like that."

Joe was still watching us from the window, his big black snout poking through the blinds. I wanted to be done with this. I wanted to go back inside and sit on the couch with Joe and pretend Peter didn't even exist.

"Van," he said, pawing at my shoulder like he was grasping at straws. "I love you."

I had dreamed of him saying *I love you* for years, and now, it just made me mad.

"Well, goddamnit, Pete, I loved you, too, but I never used it as an excuse to stop being your friend."

I pulled the door handle and freed myself from the car.

"Wait," Peter said, before I could slam the door behind me.

I looked back at him. "Why?" I asked, but I didn't give him time to answer. I pushed the door closed until it clicked shut. I watched my shadow on the garage door as I walked past Peter's headlights so I wouldn't have to watch him watching me.

Joe ran out into the front yard when I opened the door. He ran around in a circle and then followed me into the house.

"We're not going to wallow," I said to Joe. He ran back to the window. I followed and peeked out. Peter was still sitting in his car in the driveway. Maybe he was still trying to figure out why. Maybe he was trying to think of the perfect thing to say to make me want to run away with him. Maybe he was just steeling himself for the next leg of his hunt for hemorrhoid cream. Whatever it was, I didn't care. I wanted it all to be over. I wanted to call Alex and drink cider and wear flannel and wake up with him.

This is it, I told myself. I will throw this party and then I'm done. Then I'll move on and have my own life. I stepped away from the window and dusted the coffee table with my sleeve.

Finally, we heard Peter's car back down the driveway. Joe jumped up on the couch to watch, letting out a long, low growl. The headlights lit up his face and he barked sharply, with authority, as if he were saying, "Yeah, you better go."

Chapter Twenty-four

I was down to four hours and forty-five minutes. I took out the vacuum to clean the crumbs and dog hair off the carpet, but as soon as I turned it on, Joe started to make a whiny sound in the back of his throat that grew into a sharp, high bark. He pushed himself between me and the vacuum cleaner and started biting at the wheels.

I yelled "phooey" at him a million times over, but he kept going. He growled and barked and bared his teeth at the vacuum in between bites. If he'd freaked like that when I first got him, I probably would have left the condo and never come back.

While I felt safe knowing that Joe was driven to be my personal protector, it wasn't helping me clean. I closed Joe in the bedroom. He yelped and whined, and I felt awful about it, but I had no choice. I was running out of time. I had to go back to vacuuming.

A few minutes later, the doorbell rang. Joe barked from up in the bathroom. I peeked out through the view hole to see Gail's husband, Mitch, standing there, hair crazy, in a green-and-maroon-striped bathrobe. I took a deep breath and opened the door.

"It's six thirty in the morning, Savannah," Mitch said through his teeth. His robe was too short, and I couldn't stop staring at his knobby white knees. "On a Sunday."

"Oh," I said. "I hadn't thought about it." I wasn't trying to be snotty; I really hadn't thought about it. Waiting for a decent hour to vacuum didn't fit into my preparation plan for zero hour. "I'm sorry, I have these people coming and I–"

Mitch's face was very red. "You can't do this. You cannot do this!" His fists were tightly clenched. His breath was steaming from his mouth. "We're trying to sleep, and that beast you have is keeping me awake."

"Oh, like that rat of yours doesn't yip all day long while I'm working."

"Make him stop!" He waved his hands at me like a conductor trying to make an orchestra stop playing. "And stop vacuuming. Normal people do not make this kind of noise at six AM."

"Well, the next time you and Gail are going at it, I'll stop by to remind you what kind of noises normal people make, Mitch."

"Get rid of him!" He was screaming. "Mr. Wright told you to get rid of him."

"I have three weeks left. We'll be gone before that," I said, hoping it was true.

"Thank God!" he yelled.

I slammed the door and watched him out the peephole. His robe blew open when he got to the end of the stoop. He had the flattest ass I had ever seen, and it was so white the streetlight almost made it glow.

An hour before the party, I pulled the bagels out of the freezer, smacked each one on the counter until they split, and stuck both halves on the oven rack. I shoved the bags way down in the garbage can, even though I knew I wasn't going to fool anyone.

When the bagels started browning, I turned the oven off but left them in to stay warm.

At forty-five minutes before the party, I realized I needed to shower. I ran upstairs full speed, tripped, and got rug burn on my knee. Joe had been passed out at the bottom of the stairs but ran to me when I fell, still in a confused sleepy haze. He tripped over my leg and landed on my stomach.

At thirty minutes before the party, I jumped in the shower, squirted shower gel everywhere, and turned around under the water a few times. There were still suds on me when I dried off. Joe licked at the bubbles on my calves while I gobbed mascara on my lashes and tried to dry my hair at the same time. I ended up with mascara in my hair, and for once was happy for hair the color of ink.

I should have had an outfit, a brunch outfit. Something suity, but not too formal. Maybe something pastel, or black crepe with white piping. I should have had shoes that matched perfectly. And I should have curled my hair with a curling iron and made sure it bounced.

But I barely even had clean clothes, and I didn't have time to dry my hair all the way. So I pulled my least-coffee-stained jeans out of the bottom of the closet, and found the only clean shirt left in the whole place. I knotted my hair up around a rubber band high on my head and tried to make it look like I was going for wet and disheveled.

I ran downstairs and fussed with odds and ends like corralling pens, paper clips, and twist ties into the junk drawer and using my sleeve to sweep dust off the bookcase. I hated waiting on everyone to show up. I just wanted to get this whole thing over with as quickly as possible.

At fifteen minutes before the party, the doorbell rang. Joe barked and ran for the door. I looked through the peephole and saw Peter and Janie.

They stood on the front step like they were posing for a picture. Peter had his arm around Janie's waist. She leaned in to him, with her hand placed gracefully over his heart. Peter looked smug. There was no trace of the desperation from our meeting in the driveway. He'd already fallen back into the perfect-husband role.

I sucked air in through my teeth and let it hiss out slowly. Joe jumped up and licked my chin. I opened the door, and he flew out at them.

Before I could even put on a big fake smile and pretend to be happy to see them, Joe jumped up on Janie and she screamed.

Peter yelled, "Down boy, down boy," over and over.

I watched them trying to make sense of Joe for a moment, before calling him back in.

"Joe! Ku mne!" He came running over to me. "Sadni." He sat. I scratched his head. "Good boy! Hodny." I was showing off the Slovak commands. I liked that Peter and Janie didn't know this about me.

"Va-an!" Janie whined. "What is that?" She was in a mood. I could see it on her face, by her furrowed brow and the intensity in her eyes. Sometimes she'd just get like that. Nothing anyone did would be good enough, and everything got on her nerves. Even when we were kids, some mornings she'd just wake up crabby and there was nothing anyone could do about it. Diane called her "Janie the Terrible" when she got like that. I hadn't slept all night, and I didn't want to be throwing this party to begin with. I was in no mood for her mood, and I was way too tired to worry if that made me a horrible friend.

"This is Joe. My dog."

Peter smirked. I think he realized that the Joe I mentioned on the phone was not my hot new boyfriend.

"Your dog?" Janie said, leaning in to give me a hug and a kiss on the cheek, but keeping as much distance from Joe as possible. "You don't have a dog."

"I do now." I hugged her back. She smelled like spring flowers and new leather. The black and silver purse hanging from her shoulder might have cost more than my car, and despite her bad-mood face, she looked gorgeous.

"But you're not a dog person," she insisted.

"Yes, I am. I just never had a dog." I scratched Joe's head and said, "Okay," so he could get up. "Diane wouldn't let me."

"Oh," Janie said. "I'm sure if you'd wanted a dog, Mom would have let you."

"I did–"

"Let's go in and talk about what's left to set up," Peter said, raising his eyebrows, giving me a warning look.

I wished he hadn't interrupted. I was feeling combative. I knew I was really more angry at Peter than Janie, but I was itching for an excuse to escalate everything to the point of storming out and leaving them stranded.

"Did you get bagels?" Peter asked.

"Yeah, they're in the oven warming up," I said, picking at a hangnail so I didn't have to look at him.

"Okay," Peter said. "Let's get the cream cheese out and start making coffee." We did have to get the cream cheese out and make coffee, but the fact that he was telling me what to do in my own home made me even angrier. But since I couldn't say, "How dare you come to my house and tell me you love me because you don't feel like buying hemorrhoid cream?" I choked it down and started a pot of coffee, feeling like a smoking volcano.

Janie just stood there and watched us. I don't think she knew how to help.

I grabbed two small bowls and a spoon and handed them to Pete. He scooped the cream cheese into the bowls. I poured OJ into my plastic Kool-Aid pitcher.

Pete and I worked like a well-oiled machine, peeling the salmon off the cardboard and arranging it on plates. He avoided making eye contact. I did the same.

Janie stood in the doorway and tried to avoid Joe. She held her hands up at her sides like she was wading into cold water.

"Okay," Pete said, wiping cream cheese off his hand with a dish towel I knew wasn't clean. "I think we're ready for the bagels."

I pointed to the oven. He opened the door, and grabbed for one, tapping it with his index finger first to make sure it wouldn't burn his hand. He pulled out one of the halves and held it up. He tapped it with his finger again, then he knocked it on the stove top.

"Van, these are rocks!"

"No!" I grabbed the half bagel from him and curled my finger into the hole. It felt like a hunk of concrete on a hot day.

"The party's ruined!" Janie rested her forehead on her fingertips and took deep breaths.

When we were kids, if we argued, my mother would step in to settle it by telling me I was wrong. "Now, Van, you be a good sport and tell Janie you're sorry," she'd say, bustling around nervously, rounding up tissues for Janie's ever-dripping nose. I was so tired of being a good sport. Get through this and move on, I said to myself in my head like a mantra.

Janie let out a little sob like a hiccup and I tried to remember if I even had tissues. Joe went over to her and leaned up against her.

"Geez!" She sidestepped away from him, but he leaned in again. "Go! Get away from me!" She tried to wave him away with her hand. "Van, get him off me."

I took a deep breath. "Joe, ku mne," I called. Joe came over and leaned against me. I ran my hand along his side. "He was trying to comfort you."

"No he's not. He's a dog, Van."

"So?"

"So, he's not comforting me."

"Well, he's trying, Janie." I wanted to say that we were all trying. I wanted to say that it was her own damn fault if she wasn't happy with it, but I thought about how she'd feel if she'd known I was one of the stops on her husband's quest for Preparation H. It made it easier to hold my tongue.

"He got fur all over me," Janie said, picking black hairs off her cream-colored skirt.

I felt Pete's eyes on me. When I finally looked at him, he raised his eyebrows and shrugged. It was infuriating.

"Why don't you two go get bagels?" I said. They'd been in my kitchen for less than ten minutes and already I desperately needed a breather.

Janie sniffed. It was her way of saying, "What do you mean, I have to go get food for my own party?"

"It'll give you a chance to make a big entrance," I said.

"Oh, that sounds like a good idea," Pete said, walking over to Janie and putting his arm around her. "Doesn't it, Jane? Everyone will be here and we'll make our grand entrance."

Janie sighed. "Fine."

As they walked back to the door, Pete looked over his shoulder and had the nerve to wink at me. He closed the door behind them. I threw the bagel at the door as soon as it clicked shut. I felt ridiculous as soon as I did it, but Joe grabbed it when it fell and jumped on the couch to gnaw on it like I'd just intended to give him a treat.

Chapter Twenty-five

I went for the bottle of Stoli I kept under the kitchen sink. I thought about the limeade and OJ I'd bought, but drank straight from the bottle to save time.

I took a swig and then the phone rang.

"Hello?"

"Hi, Van!" It was Alex.

Joe dropped his bagel and sat up to look out the window. I ran over and jumped up next to him. A black Town Car was pulling into the driveway.

"Hello?" Alex said.

"Um, hi." With my free hand, I dropped Joe's bagel behind the couch and brushed crumbs into the crack between the cushions.

Charles got out of the car and started walking around to the passenger side.

"Not feeling so hot, huh?" Alex said.

Charles opened the passenger door and Diane slipped a black pump out onto the asphalt.

"Yeah," I said. "I'm sorry, I can't talk right now." I took a big swig out of the bottle.

Diane was out of the car and smoothing out her suit.

"I can call back later. I just wanted to see if you needed anything. Is there anything I can get you? Ginger ale? Crackers?"

Diane and Charles were walking up the path. Diane looked up at the condo. She clearly saw us—Joe and I peeking out of the window—and curled her lips into a slow, cool smile.

"Van?"

"Oh, no. I don't need anything. I wouldn't want you to catch it." I faked a cough, and I felt horribly guilty about it. He was being so nice. "I should go. But thanks for calling. I'll talk to you soon," I said, quickly, desperate to finish the conversation before Diane and Charles got to the door. I hung up as soon as Alex said good-bye, and dropped the phone on the couch.

I ran over to the door to get it before they rang the doorbell and Joe started barking.

When I opened the door, Joe ran out to greet them.

"Savannah, you get this thing away from me," Diane said calmly through her smile. I'd been so nervous about how Diane would react to me when she arrived. She'd paid me to stay away from Peter and here I was throwing him a party. I should have known she'd just play it cool.

"Joe, ku mne."

Joe ran back over to me and sat down.

Diane and Charles walked in, slipped out of their coats, and handed them to me. I still had the bottle of Stoli in my hand. I grabbed the coats with my other arm and threw them over the side of the couch.

Diane pursed her lips.

"Once everyone comes, I'll take all the coats upstairs," I said.

"Shouldn't you have a paper bag over that?" Diane gestured to the bottle.

Had it been just Diane and me, I would have said something like "Tip your head back. I'll pour," but not with Charles around. He always looked like he was about to pull a pair of white leather gloves out of his pocket and smack me across the face. So I just said, "I thought you might want screwdrivers."

"Charles?" Diane asked.

"Please," he mumbled to Diane. Charles never spoke directly to me if he could help it. I wasn't even hired help. I was the extension of hired help.

Diane followed me into the kitchen. Joe followed too, walking next to Diane and licking her hand.

"Oh! Oh!" Diane looked at her hand like it might turn black and fall off. "Tell me about this beast you have here."

"He's not a beast." I grabbed the OJ out of the fridge.

"He looks feral." Diane held her hand out, limp at the wrist, to keep it from touching her clothes.

"He's from Slovakia," I said, dropping three ice cubes in each glass. "He's from working lines."

"So he's a working-class dog?" she said, raising an eyebrow.

I poured a glass of vodka and splashed enough OJ into it to change the color. I handed her the glass, but she looked at her hand.

"I have to wash up."

"Upstairs," I said. "It's the only door that's open."

Diane's heels clicked across the linoleum until she got to the carpet. Joe followed her and I heard her say, "You leave me alone," before shutting the bathroom door.

I gave her drink to Charles. He was standing in front of the couch, staring at it like he couldn't decide if it was safe to sit on.

"Here," I said. "It's mostly vodka." I'd known Charles pretty much my entire life, and I'd never felt comfortable around him. Actually, I didn't think Janie or Diane did either. He was grouchy and humorless. And even when he was being fairly pleasant, I was always waiting for the other shoe to drop. Charles angry was not a pretty sight, and it was hard to predict what might set him off. Usually, when he left a room, I'd realize I'd been holding my breath.

"Good girl," he said, without looking at me.

"It's not going to bite you," I said, pointing at the couch.

He pulled a cigarette out of a silver case in the inside pocket of his sports coat. "Ashtray."

"I don't really smoke," I said.

"I do." He looked away from me. He pulled out a lighter. It was slim and silver like a fancy pen. He lit his cigarette and blew smoke at my couch cushions.

I went back to the kitchen and got an old coffee mug. I plunked it down on the coffee table. "Ashtray," I said. I was flirting with the idea of saying more, thinking that maybe a Charles temper flare might cut the party short, but the doorbell rang.

Joe came charging down the stairs, barking. The hair on his back stood up, and as he barked, he bared his teeth. Charles stepped back. He looked paler than usual, and the hand he held the cigarette with was shaking.

I told Joe to bark, "Štekat'! Štekat'!" but held my hands out and waved them up and down like I was trying to get him to calm down.

Charles was actually sweating. "Aren't you going to answer the door?" he asked, his voice in a higher register.

Peter's aunt Agnes pushed her way in as soon as I opened the door. She wore a big red church hat and a purple coat that made her look as wide as she was tall.

"Hi, Vannie, remember me?" she said, in her singsongy voice. "Peter's favorite aunt." I was scared she might try to pinch my cheeks.

Joe walked right up to her and sat down at her feet.

"Oh! You precious baby!" she squealed, and bent down. He licked her face. She cupped her hands under his jaw. "Oh, you're just a lover, aren't you! Oh, yes you are, ohyesyouare!"

"Oh, Aunt Agnes. Joe sure does love you," I said with a big smile. For once, I was happy to see her.

Charles scowled and mashed his cigarette into the coffee mug.

"Now, this is for you, Van, dear," Agnes said, pushing the handle of a shiny red gift bag into my hands. It was heavy. "It's just a little something for our gracious hostess." She looked at Charles. "How's it going, Charlie?

I don't know if you remember me. We met last year at the engagement brunch. I barely saw you at all at the wedding."

Charles grunted a hello and sat down on the couch. He sank in until his knees almost touched his chest.

"Let's get this in the kitchen now," Agnes said, patting the bottom of the bag. She put her arm around my waist and hustled me into the kitchen. "I was so sorry we didn't get to talk at the wedding."

"Me too," I said, feeling guilty about avoiding her at the wedding. Right now, chatting with Agnes was a comfort.

She opened cabinets until she found the right one, and pulled out two glasses. "I always liked you, Van. You're good to my Peter."

I was still holding the red bag. Agnes reached in it and pulled out a bottle of Maker's Mark. Then she grabbed ice out of the freezer in two fistfuls and plunked them in the glasses. She opened the fridge and pulled out a carton of milk. She sniffed it before pouring, filled each glass to about half, and gestured for me to pour bourbon.

I splashed a few fingers into each glass and looked up for her approval. She smiled and raised an eyebrow. I poured a little more in her glass.

"Perfect!"

She lifted her glass and held it up. I did the same.

"To Pete," she said.

"Yeah," I said, and clinked my glass against hers.

"So, does Pete know that Joe is a dog yet?" Agnes took a sip of her drink and looked up at me. The sparkle in her eyes seemed magnified by the crow's-feet that framed them. I knew Peter called her constantly, but I couldn't believe he'd told her that. It was a new level of weird, even for Peter and Agnes.

"Did you do it on purpose, or was it just convenient?" she asked.

"He told you about Joe?" I took a big gulp of my drink. I didn't think I'd be able to get away with acting like I didn't know what she was talking about. The milk cut down on the burn of the bourbon, but I could still feel it.

"Sweetheart, that boy is leaking all over the place right now. I don't know what to do with him!" She took a healthy swig of her drink. "He thinks he's being sly, telling me you picked up a boyfriend like it's nothing. But you know how he is." She looked me straight in the eyes like she was signaling to me that there was more meaning to her words. Her eyes were the same gray-blue as Peter's. "He's very protective of you."

"I— It just happened," I said, disarmed by her candor, and her Maker's Mark. It was the first time I'd ever admitted to something involving Peter. I'd always kept all the pieces jumbled up and hidden, but I'd just shown Agnes a corner piece. One piece would click into the next and then the whole picture would be there for all to see.

"Oh, sweetie, after all this time, it was bound to," Agnes said, patting my arm.

I wasn't completely sure what she meant, or if we were even having the same conversation. I took another gulp of my drink. My stomach was warm and getting warmer.

"Now what can I do to help, Van?" Agnes asked.

"Um, there's nothing that can be done. That's the problem."

"Well, surely there's something."

I didn't know what she wanted me to say. I didn't know what my options were. Was she going to be my evil ally and bust up their marriage? Was she going to smack Pete upside the head until he chose me? Did I even want that anymore?

"Oh, see Van, here. You don't have your main dish out yet. I can help you with that."

My face blushed so fast and so hard I thought I could feel the blood vessels in my cheeks bursting. Luckily, Agnes was oblivious, bustling around the table, moving plates, tearing a piece of salmon off and tasting it.

"Oh, oh yeah," I said. I could tell I was talking too loudly, but I couldn't seem to turn down my volume. "My main dish." I opened the refrigerator door like I actually had something in there.

"I saw that casserole in there. It looks great. I didn't know you were such a cook!" Agnes reached past me for the milk and started making herself another drink.

"Casserole." I saw the stockpot full of Joe's food on the top shelf. "Oh, yeah."

I pulled the pot out of the fridge, took the plastic wrap off the top, and wadded it into a ball. The condensation from the wrap dripped down the leg of my jeans.

Agnes found a baking dish out in the cabinet and spooned Joe's food into it. She preheated the oven.

"Have a drink with me while we let that heat up."

Before I knew it, there was another glass of Maker's Mark and milk in my hand.

Diane walked into the kitchen, her heels clicking sharply on the linoleum.

"Your dog is terrorizing my husband, Van," she said. "Maybe you should put him away."

"Charles?" I asked. "I think it would be better if you put him away. I'm scared he might bite."

Agnes giggled into her drink and winked at me. Diane huffed out a big sigh, turned on her toe, and walked out of the kitchen.

"You burnt the toast," she snapped, as she left the room.

I had no idea what she meant.

It wasn't until the smoke detector went off a few minutes later that it registered. Joe tore into the kitchen, barking.

I opened the oven door and got a mouthful of charred-bagel smoke. I grabbed one of the bagels to pull it out. It burnt the palm of my hand, but I couldn't think. I couldn't let go of it.

Agnes came running over with a dish towel, grabbed the bagel out of my hand, and threw it in the sink. I could see a red ring forming on my palm. My eyes filled with tears.

"Oh, you poor child," she said, smoothing my hair, and tucking a piece behind my ear. "I'm so sorry. I didn't mean to ruin the bagels like that. I didn't know they were in there." She handed me her drink. "Take this, sweetie. It will help."

Chapter Twenty-six

The smoke detector was still blaring, the oven was still on, and the bagels were still smoking. Agnes was putting a plastic grocery bag full of ice in my hand when all of a sudden, Alex came running into the kitchen, holding a Christmas tree in one hand and a Wegmans bag in the other. Joe ran over to him, barking and wagging his tail. He tried to take the tree from Alex like it was another present for him.

The tree was small, but perfect. And Alex was perfect, standing there in his gray wool jacket. The gust of air he brought in with him was cool and it felt good. I wanted him to just pick me up and carry me out of the party like my knight in shining armor. I wanted to be done with the party and the drama and everything else and just move on.

"Are you okay?" he said, resting the base of the tree on the floor.

I nodded. My hand was pulsing and my head was spinning.

Agnes opened the kitchen window and fanned the towel at the smoke detector until it stopped beeping. Joe tried to bite the towel as she waved it.

"What is this?" Alex said. "I thought you were sick." He held up the grocery bag. "I brought you soup." He shook the tree a little. "You said you were sick."

"I'm sorry," I said, quietly.

Agnes squeezed past us to get to the oven. "I'm Peter's aunt, Agnes," she said over her shoulder as she used a towel to push the bagels into the garbage.

"Who's Peter?" Alex asked.

"Well, this is under control here," Agnes said, shoving the garbage pail back under the sink. "I am going to check on the rest of your guests. I hear more people." She winked at me and scooted out of the room.

"What are you doing here?" I asked Alex.

"You hung up so quick. I was worried."

"About me?"

"Stop being coy," he said.

"I'm not coy. I'm drunk," I said. Tears started dripping down my face. "I'm so drunk." I buried my head into his chest. He stiffened.

"Look," he said, pulling away from me, "if you didn't want to go to the market with me you should have just said so."

"But, I did," I said. "I wanted to. It's just really complicated, Alex." I couldn't bring myself to look up at him. I wasn't sure I could hold it together if I did. I took the ice off my hand and stared at the red ring on my palm. It was so red it almost glowed.

"So, explain," he said. "I'll listen."

I wanted to explain. I wanted to tell him that this was the last little bit of my old life following me, that it was almost over and then things would be simple. But I heard heels clicking on the kitchen floor again, followed by dog nails.

"Savannah Leone," Diane called as she walked over to us, "don't you want to check in on your guests?" She pulled a cigarette out of her clutch and lit it off the stove.

"It's not a good time," I said to Alex.

"What am I supposed to do then?" Alex said. "Sit around waiting for it to be a good time? I don't understand what's going on here, Van. I thought— I trusted you."

I thought about him, in my bed, holding my hand. I thought about how badly I wanted things to work with him. And I knew I couldn't let Diane get in the middle of it.

She was just standing there, leaning against the counter, puffing away on her cigarette, watching us. She had ways of making a mess of everything and I didn't want her to mess this up too.

"I didn't ask you to come," I said to Alex. My head was swimming, and I was panicking. I just needed him to leave. "I didn't ask you to bring me a tree. I can't talk about this right now. It's complicated."

Alex picked up the tree. "I'll make things a little more simple for you," he said, and walked out of the kitchen. His big heavy shoes made the floor shake as he walked past me.

"Alex! Wait!" I said, but he didn't even turn around.

I was going to follow him. I should have followed him, but I didn't want Diane to see me beg for Alex to forgive me. I didn't want Diane to know anything about Alex. I wished taking Diane's payoff had freed me from caring what she thought about me, but it hadn't. I didn't want her to see how alone I really was.

Diane coughed lightly. "Can we talk about your guests now?" she said. "There are ten people— Look at me, Van."

I looked up, staring at the middle of her forehead so I didn't have to look her in the eye. My palm throbbed like a drumbeat. I could almost hear it.

"That's better." She gave me a smug smile. "There are at least ten people standing out there in their coats with nothing to drink. And Janie will be here any minute. You need to hustle."

"You need to hustle," I said. The words bunched up in my throat for a second before I spit them out. I stared at her shoes. They were black leather with a flash of red on the inside of the heel. I hadn't seen them before. There was a time when I'd known every shoe in Diane's closet by heart. But she'd had plenty of time to take plenty of shopping trips without me.

"Van." Diane used her warning voice. She looked at me and tapped ashes from her cigarette into the sink.

I took a deep breath to try to calm myself, but then I realized that I didn't want to calm down. I'd just let Alex walk out. He probably felt hurt and confused and vulnerable, the way I would have if I were in his shoes. I knew how bad that felt, but then I made him feel that way. And then I just let him walk out.

"Goddamnit, Diane!" I yelled, loud enough to make the chatter in the other room stop completely. "I'm sick of this. I am sick of all this scrambling around to protect Janie's feelings. And I'm sick of no one protecting mine. That," I gestured to the door, "that was important to me. He was important to me, and I let him walk out because you're upset that I haven't greeted my guests? What else can you take away from me, Diane?"

"Don't make a scene," Diane hissed.

"You made the scene," I said, waving my finger in her face. "You made the scene." I stormed out of the kitchen into the garage and slammed the door behind me.

I couldn't drive. Even if I weren't completely wasted, there were six or seven cars in the driveway blocking mine.

I walked back into the kitchen, trying my best to hold my head high.

Diane was leaning against the counter. She took a drag from her cigarette. Even with all the chatter coming from the other room, I swore I could hear the paper burn. "Well, that was quite a spectacle," she said, blowing smoke in my direction.

"Fuck you, Diane." It came out so easily. There'd been so many times I'd wanted to say it before, but the words just got tangled up in a lump in my throat.

"Excuse me?" she said, picking a piece of dog hair off her skirt with her fingernails.

"I said, fuck you, Diane." I said it loud and slow like she was hard of hearing. The chatter in the living room quieted again. "And you heard me the first time." I couldn't get my voice to lower. "Why do you have to fuck up everything?" I was right in her face, yelling, and I couldn't stop. "I don't have that much, Diane. I don't have that much to begin with, and you just take it like it's yours. Like you own everything. You don't own me, goddamnit." I didn't realize I was crying until I felt a tear drip down my chin. I wiped it away with my good hand. "You don't own me, Diane." I wasn't yelling anymore, and I could hear in my own voice how drunk I was. "You don't own me," I said, one more time just to hear my words. They slid together like syrup and melted butter on a plate of pancakes.

Diane threw the end of her cigarette into the sink, still burning, and lit another one. Her hands were shaking.

The milk and Maker's Mark was curdling in my stomach. I ran out of the kitchen, tripping twice on the way up the stairs to the bathroom.

I leaned my arms on the toilet seat and puked. My stomach burned, and I couldn't focus my eyes. I rested my head on the side of the toilet, but I hadn't cleaned under the rim well enough, and the sour, musty smell got me going all over again.

When I was done, I leaned back against the bathtub and closed my eyes. I heard footsteps and paws and then the bathroom door opened. Joe ran in and licked my cheek.

"Someone was worried about you," Agnes said.

I hugged Joe around the neck and listened to him pant, changing my breath so my ribs pushed against his when we breathed out.

"Are you okay, Vannie?" Agnes grabbed my towel off the rack and ran the end under the faucet. She hiked up her slacks and knelt down next to me, groaning a little as her knees hit the floor. "Don't get old, Van," she said. "It's no barrel of monkeys, I tell you." She flopped over and shimmied herself closer to the bathtub so she could lean against it.

I pictured the yellow barrel of plastic monkeys Janie and I used to play with and Agnes in her big red hat with one arm curled like a handle and the other hooked, waiting to grab on to the next monkey.

"I'm so drunk, Agnes," I said, letting her wipe my face with a towel. The terry cloth was rough and she rubbed hard. She rinsed the towel under the bathtub faucet and patted her leg. I leaned my head into her lap. Her thigh was like a well-stuffed pillow. Joe leaned his head on her other knee.

"I ruined everything," I said.

"It's your party; you'll cry if you want to." She smoothed my hair out of my face.

"It's Janie's party."

"It wasn't fair of them to do this to you." She scratched Joe's ears.

I thought about Alex, standing there in the kitchen like a deer in the high beams. "I love him, I think. Or I would have."

"Peter's not good enough for you," she said. "He's my nephew, and I love him, but the boy's got to get his act together. He can't go stringing—"

"Not Peter." I shook my head, and it made her pants swish against their lining. "Alex."

"Oh. Well, he was a looker. I'll give you that." She laughed and fanned herself with her hand. Her whole body shook. It was dizzying, watching her face disappear and reappear behind her waving hand. I closed my eyes. I felt like all the life had been sucked out of me and flushed down the toilet. I thought for a minute that I would fall asleep right there on the bathroom floor in Agnes's lap, but then she said, "What say we get out of here and get you something to eat?"

She pushed Joe and me off of her lap and began the production of hoisting herself back up to standing, leaning on the bathtub, then reaching across to the sink. "I'm sure if we put our heads together we can figure out a way to get that boy back." She reached her hand out to help me up, grabbing my elbow to avoid my burned hand. I knew she couldn't take my weight, so I had to manage getting up with one hand and the little strength I had left.

Chapter Twenty-seven

Agnes led me downstairs with such authority that no one questioned her. I kept my fingers wrapped tightly around Joe's collar and my eyes down, focusing on all the feet in my living room. Brown Rockports, black wingtips, gray orthopedics straining against their laces. Then there were Peter's boat shoes and Jane's Kate Spades right at the doorway. I looked up. Peter was holding two large paper bags. Janie was clutching her purse with both hands.

"Where are you going?" Janie asked.

"We're just going to run out for a bit, love," Agnes said.

Janie let out a long guttural sigh. "You're leaving?"

I was about to tell her that I didn't even want to throw this stupid party in the first place, and that this party had ruined the one little foothold I had in having my own life, but Agnes pushed me past them out the door before I could get a word in. She shooed Joe out behind me, and saved me from doing something I'd probably regret later, like telling Peter where he could shove those upstate bagels.

"We'll be back in just a bit," Agnes said in a bright, chirpy voice like everything was wonderful.

I heard Janie say, "Classic," and then Peter said, "Let it go, Jane." Then they shut the door to my home and went to eat their bagels and celebrate their wonderful marriage, while I stood out in the cold with a burnt hand and a broken heart. "Classic," I said to Joe. He leaned up against my leg while we waited for Agnes to dig her car keys out of her purse.

She found them and clicked the key fob to unlock the car. Then she helped me into her shiny black Cadillac and shut the door behind me, trapping in the thick smell of new car and fake apple pie. There was a lace bag filled with potpourri chips and trimmed with fake rosebuds hanging from the rearview mirror. The smell was suffocating. The seat leather was stiff and it creaked when I shifted my weight. I wondered if anyone else had ever sat in it.

She bustled around to the back of the car, opened the trunk, and then the back door. She spread a brown fuzzy blanket that smelled like dryer sheets over the backseat and said, "Okay, Joey."

Joe jumped up on the seat. He sat in the middle, panting hard and looking pleased with himself.

Agnes closed the trunk with a good slam and climbed in the car. She pushed a button on the door and her seat moved up so close to the steering wheel that it touched her belly. "Much better," she said, starting the car.

Agnes hit the gas pedal hard enough to make my head smack against the headrest. Joe lost his balance and decided to lie down.

"So what are you in the mood for, Van?" She paused at the stop sign at the end of my road and then gunned it to get out into traffic, oblivious to the brakes squealing around her. "We can grab an early lunch. Chinese? Mexican? Italian? There's this Greek place right around the corner. Have you been? The souvlaki is too, too good. They don't skimp on the onions."

Onions and fake apple pie and new leather seats and fabric softener and Agnes and her Maker's Mark and lavender perfume. My insides felt fuzzy and dizzy and raw. I leaned my head over and pressed my face against the window. I'm not going to puke in Agnes's new car, I thought, concentrating on the cold glass against my cheek. I'm not going to puke in Agnes's car. "Right around the corner sounds good," I said.

We left Joe in the car with the windows cracked open. Agnes got us a table while I ran to the bathroom, trying to be discreet and failing miserably. I almost ran into a waitress carrying a tray full of rice pudding in metal dishes. We looked at each other in horror before going our separate ways.

The chips in the tiles of the bathroom floor were filled in with dirt and toilet paper lint. It smelled like stale cigarettes and the smoke detector hung from the wall on a wire. I stared at the toilet for a minute. I felt hollow and empty. My stomach groaned, but nothing came up. I flushed the toilet anyway, and was thankful I didn't have to put my face too close.

I ran my burnt hand under cold water. It stung, and I wanted to cry, hard and loud. I wanted to throw that kind of tantrum kids throw when they fall off their bike and skin their elbow and their mom is all out of Spider-Man Band-Aids. I wanted to scream and cry and have someone carry me home and tuck me in bed and press the back of a cool smooth hand to my forehead and kiss my cheek and tell me it was all going to be okay.

Instead of pitching a fit, I dried my hands and checked for messy mascara in the mirror. My eyes were droopy and tired and made me think of my mom after chemo. I tried to ignore the rest of my face. I couldn't bear the picture as a whole. I did a quick wipe under my eyes with my index fingers and made a silent promise to myself to stop drinking, or at least take a breather for a while. Diane and my mom always joked that a little bourbon fixed everything, and a lot made you forget there was ever anything to fix. Their prescription clearly didn't work for me.

"I ordered you tea," Agnes said when I got to the table. "I asked for chamomile, but this was all they had." She fingered the Lipton tag hanging out of a little metal teapot.

"Thank you," I said, sitting down across the booth from her. I scooted over, past a rip in the red vinyl seat, and leaned up against the wall. Maybe,

I thought, I'd already thrown my tantrum, back at the house, and I guess Agnes was taking care of me, but it wasn't the same. She wasn't my mom.

"I don't get out to the west side very often. And none of my ladies are into *ethnic* food." She whispered like it was some sort of scandal. She emptied two packets of sugar into my teacup, poured, stirred, and slid it over to me. "The sugar will rehydrate you."

I took a sip and burned my tongue. The cup was small and the tea was syrupy.

Before I could even pull a menu out from behind the sugar dish, our waitress brought food to the table. She put a souvlaki plate in front of Agnes, and a bowl of chicken soup and a plate of French fries in front of me.

"Hangover food," Agnes explained. "It's just what you need."

I wasn't hungover, I was still drunk, but I just said, "Thank you."

The soup burnt my already tea-burnt tongue. My hand was still throbbing. I wrapped my palm around my water glass and took a long drink. The water tasted like chlorine. I thought about Joe, by himself in the car, and wished I'd just sucked it up and hid in my bedroom. We could have locked the door, climbed into bed, and watched TV until everyone left. We could have called the cops on the party and let them clear it up. I pictured Diane yelling at Rochester's finest.

"What are you grinning about, lady?" Agnes was cutting her souvlaki and pita bread into uniform squares. She pulled her napkin up from her lap to wipe her mouth after every bite. "Thinking about that tall blond cowboy of yours?"

The second she said it, I pictured Alex's face. He was standing there with that Christmas tree and he looked so horribly sad. I didn't turn out to be the person he'd hoped I'd be. I knew that disappointment. I didn't want to be that disappointment. "Oh, God, Agnes. What am I going to do?"

"It's not that bad."

"He left."

"Maybe he just needed to cool off."

"It's too early for cooling off."

"He'll come back."

"Why would he?"

"Sweetie, if you don't know why, you can't expect anyone else to." She shoveled another forkful of souvlaki into her mouth. "Eat up, dear. It'll help."

The next time the waitress came by, Agnes borrowed a pen and scribbled her phone number on a Sweet'N Low packet. "You'll have to keep me apprised of the situation, lady," she said, smiling, as she slid the packet across the table to me.

Chapter Twenty-eight

By the time Agnes polished off her souvlaki, at least four cups of coffee, a shot of Sambuca, and a bowl of rice pudding with raisins, we were sure the party had cleared out.

She dropped Joe and me off in the empty driveway. "Call me if you need anything," she said, squeezing my shoulder. "This too shall pass, sweetie."

She waited until we unlocked the door to drive away. As I closed the door behind us, I heard tires squeal.

I was expecting a big mess: an overturned lamp or two, some crushed blue plastic cups spilling cheap keg beer into the carpet, like the remnants of a frat party.

I knew they hadn't turned brunch into a kegger after I left, but they'd trashed my weekend. It was disappointing to find the place spotless. I wanted proof that they were destructive, soul-sucking people who made a mess and left it behind for me to clean up.

Joe sniffed around the living room for a minute and then darted upstairs, barking.

A woman screamed. It was the exact same scream Janie let out when Harold Winston the Third dropped a frog down the back of her bathing suit at the club.

I stood at the bottom of the stairs for a minute, listening to Joe barking and Janie yelling, "Get away! Get away!" I grabbed on to the banister and leaned back a little and then forward, using the momentum to haul myself up the stairs. My headache raged in full force.

Joe sat on the floor in front of my closet, barking. He looked over when I walked in the room, and then went right back to barking at the closet.

There was Janie, crouched in the closet in the middle of a pile of my dirty clothes, crying.

"Jane?"

"Van!" Her mascara pooled under her eyes like a raccoon's mask. She looked like shit. In all the time I'd spent with her, I'd never seen her look anything less than adorable. "Make him stop. He won't stop!"

"Joe! Dost'."

Joe stopped immediately. He licked my hand, and ran over to the bed to lie down. He let out a big sigh as he settled into the blankets.

"Oh, God," Janie said. "I thought he was going to kill me."

Joe flopped over on his side and closed his eyes.

"What are you doing in my closet?"

"Why did you leave?"

"Janie."

"This was for me. You were supposed to be throwing us a party, but you just ruined the bagels and left." She fell from squatting and sat down in a pile of darks.

"Are you sorting my laundry?" She always did weird things like that when she was upset. Once, when Diane and Charles had a big blowout fight, my mom and I came home from the grocery store to find that Janie had arranged every book on our bookshelves in alphabetical order and color-coded all the take-out menus in the junk drawer.

"You just left!" she said, as if that made sitting in my closet and sorting my laundry the only reasonable option left to her.

"You're sorting my laundry because I left?" I walked over and offered her my hand. "Come on."

She didn't take it. She used her heels to push herself back farther, under the few old shirts I had hanging.

"All your clothes are dirty," she said, sobbing. "Why don't you have clean clothes?"

"Janie! Get out of my closet," I said, sighing. It felt too much like the fights we had when we were kids. We'd both get mad, but then Janie would fall apart. Putting her back together always took precedence over resolution. Here she was, married to Peter, mucking up my life with her party, but she was the one who needed consoling? If anyone had the right to fall apart, it was me.

She didn't say anything. She just sat there sniffling.

"You know what? Stay there," I said, walking out of the room and leaving her in my closet. "I'm going to go make coffee. If you want to talk, I'll be downstairs."

Someone had washed out all the glasses and mugs by hand, and laid them out upside down on a dish towel on the counter next to the sink. There was a plate of the new bagels on the counter. They were stacked neatly under plastic wrap pulled tightly. The coffeepot was sparkling, scrubbed clean of the rings that usually lined it. I started a pot. Then I noticed the turkeys.

All the paper turkeys were lined up on the kitchen table, watching me with their creepy printed red eyes. I had never been a fan of birds. The orange and brown streamers I hung up were folded in small piles next to them. I turned the turkeys around, because for some reason a row of turkey butts didn't bother me as much as a row of turkey faces.

I grabbed a mug and switched it with the coffeepot, poured the coffee that was in the pot into the mug, and waited for the drip to finish filling it.

Joe stared at me longingly and licked his lips. I realized he hadn't really eaten since I got back from Walmart. I liberated a plain bagel from the plastic wrap and handed it to him, and he ran over to the couch to tear into it.

Janie came padding into the kitchen in her stocking feet, carrying her shoes. Joe dropped his bagel and ran over to her. She raised one of her shoes up like she was going to hit him with it, so I called him over to me. He sat down on my feet.

She'd cleaned up her face so that her raccoon eyes were smoky and smudged like a *Cosmo* cover girl's. Her nose was blushed red, but no longer dripping with snot. She looked like a fairy-tale character, a waif in need of rescuing. All she needed was a tear in her skirt and a strategically placed smudge of dirt on her cheek to be the perfect damsel in distress.

She put her shoes down on a chair at the kitchen table, and sat down on the other chair.

"You've been weird through the whole wedding," she said.

"No, I haven't," I said. I was shocked that she'd noticed. I thought I'd done a decent job of phoning it in and keeping up that happy bridesmaid/cheerleader front. I'd honestly given it everything I could have.

"Things have been weird with us for a really long time." She flexed her fingers out and inspected her manicure. She was playing it cool, but I could see her eyes tearing up. "Why can't you just be happy for me?"

Oh my God, I thought, it's so much more complicated than that. I should have chosen my words more carefully, but instead, I blurted out, "Maybe it's not all about you all the time, okay?"

Immediately, the tears went from a trickle to a deluge. I'd always thought if a chipmunk could cry, it would sound like Janie sobbing.

"I can't believe this," she said through a waterfall of tears. "You're supposed to be my best friend." She put her head in her hands. "You ruined my party and now you're yelling at me."

I resisted the urge to go over and hug her and apologize and reset everything back to square one again. But I wasn't even yelling. I hadn't yelled at all. And I was so tired of her blowing everything out of proportion all the time.

"You know what?" I said. My voice was low and shaky and quiet. It surprised me. "You know, you're supposed to be my best friend too." I took her shoes off the chair and put them on the floor. I sat down on the wrong side of the turkeys. They were staring at me again. I tried my best to ignore them. "You've never acted like it."

"What are you talking about? I made you my maid of honor! I– You're my best friend. You've always been my best friend."

"I have always been your best friend." I didn't want to look at her, but I made myself. I looked her square in the eyes and said, "But you've never been mine."

"I don't understand." She shook her head like a little kid trying to avoid a spoonful of peas.

"Have you ever been in a crowded room, like the DMV or something, and looked around and realized that every single one of those people there has a life? They have a whole complete life that has nothing to do with you. Jobs, bills, family, pets."

"What are you talking about?" She was too distracted to keep crying.

"See, you don't know what I'm talking about," I said, and pointed my finger at her. "You don't know what I'm talking about because you can't get over the idea that someone else matters. People other than you get to have a life."

"Van! I don't–"

"I get to have a life that matters." I looked at her. Part of me felt awful for yelling, the other part of me was done with feeling awful all the time. "I get to have a life that doesn't involve you."

"Oh, really, Van? Really?" she said. She pulled her eyebrows in to meet each other and the wrinkle they made above her nose was not cute. She looked like a different person. "Let me get this straight, Van." She smacked her hand down on the table.

I was fascinated.

"So, when you convinced me to have boys to my sweet sixteen, because it would be 'fun' and 'cool'"–she was using finger quotes–"and then you spent the whole night making out with Leo Birnbaum, that was you being my best friend."

"Janie, I–" I started to feel bad and then yanked it back to angry. "Do you remember *my* 'sweet sixteen,' Jane?" I used finger quotes right back at her. "Do you?"

"Yes," she said. She wasn't apologetic, and I wanted her to be.

"We had pizza in the carriage house and watched *Sixteen Candles*. I wasn't a princess. I didn't have a four-piece band. I didn't have a special dance with my father," I said, choking up. I looked up at the ceiling to try to get my tears to reabsorb, but it didn't work, so I ended up using the edge of my sleeve.

"You had me! I spent the whole night with you. Remember?" She looked right at me. She was walking straight into the conflict, head-on.

"It's not like you had anything else to do," I said.

"Yes, I did," she said. "Michelle Macmillan was having a sleepover, and you weren't invited, and it was your birthday, and I chose you." Her eyebrows softened. "And we had fun, remember? We wore our matching pajamas and slept on the floor and talked all night about how much Michael Schoeffling looked like Matt Dillon. And Mom and Nat got drunk and started singing 'Scandal' really loud."

I did remember. I could still see them, in the back of my head somewhere, standing on the couch, singing at us. My mom was singing "The Warrior" into Diane's hand like she was holding a microphone, and Diane was spilling bourbon on our couch.

"I planned my birthday party for us. They brought out a cake with both our names, and I had a crown for you too, and the band played 'Sixteen Candles.' But then no one could find you. You just weren't there. You were off with some boy." She looked away from me. She spread her left hand out in front of her and twisted her engagement ring around her finger. "And then you left my wedding, and God knows where you were. Today, you leave my party, and Mom said that was all about some guy too. And then you're saying that you were always my friend, and I was never yours. But I was there, Savannah. And you weren't." She didn't whine it or cry it. She just said it.

"It was hard for me to be there. You stole my mother," I said. And then

I realized that if we were really having it out, we needed to get all of it. "And you stole Peter."

"He's still your friend, Van. It's not like you can't have your weirdo dinners with him anymore. It's not like he's gone."

It must have been splattered all over my face, because then she just looked at me and said, "Oh."

We didn't talk for a really long time. I watched Joe sleeping on the floor. He was chasing rabbits again.

Janie played with one of the turkeys. She made tiny tears in the tissue paper tail with her fingernails. The whole turkey moved. The head bobbed like it was trying to talk to me.

"Stop it," I said, reaching across the table to knock her hand away.

"I'm sorry," she said. "I didn't know you were saving them."

"I'm not. Stop making it move." I shuddered.

"I forgot about your bird thing," she said, laughing. "Freak." One by one, she took the turkeys and put them on the floor so I wouldn't have to look at them.

"Takes one to know one," I said, smiling. "Takes one to know one" had been our favorite comeback for all of fourth grade.

"Do you still love him?" she asked, after she put the last turkey on the floor, her smile suddenly gone.

"Peter?"

She nodded. The makings of a teardrop collected in the corner of her eye.

"You know," I said, "I don't think so." It was a relief to say it, and to know that it was true. Even though I was alone, I was done lusting after someone else's husband. I was done chasing someone who didn't know how to love me back. I started crying. It felt clean, like I was washing out toxins or stale feelings or something.

Janie got up and put her arms around me, resting her chin on my shoulder. One of her tears ran down my neck.

"Are we going to be okay?" she asked.

I sat there for a minute and cried with her. Her arms were so skinny, but they were strong. She held me tightly. I thought about how many times I had hugged Janie and told her everything was going to be okay—all the nights she snuck over to the carriage house when Diane and Charles were fighting. My mom and I would sandwich her on the couch and hug hard.

It felt so nice to be hugged back, so I let things hang there for a minute before saying, "Diane gave me a hundred and seventy-five thousand dollars to leave you and Pete alone." I didn't want to keep secrets between us anymore.

She stiffened, and then stood up.

"You are so full of shit." She picked up her shoes and slipped into them, putting each foot down with a click.

"I'm not, Jane."

"I thought we could be grown-ups," she said.

"When have you ever been a grown-up?"

"What the hell is that supposed to mean?"

"It means that everyone has always taken care of everything for you. My mom. Your mom. Peter. Me." I knew I was being too mean. I knew I was going too far, but I couldn't stop myself. "It must be nice to be able to call Mommy and Daddy every time something goes wrong in your life—to have them there to pay off anyone who might ever get in your way."

She picked up one of the turkeys, threw it at me, and walked out. Joe got up and tried to follow her, but she slammed the door too fast.

It was the truth about how I'd been feeling. It was the anger and the resentment that had been building up for a long time, but saying it out loud to Janie made me feel awful and ugly. I watched her for a while, standing at the end of the driveway, yelling into her cell phone. I didn't understand how it was possible to love someone so much and still be so hurt by them, to feel like they'd taken something from you, encroached on the life you could have had.

In my head there was this other Van, whose mother had waited tables to put herself through school. That Van grew up in an attic apartment in Mount Vernon, with those old-style heaters that smell like melting crayons.

The floors creaked and the bathroom faucet leaked, but the rent was cheap and they were happy. Her mom graduated and became an art teacher and had summers free and they went on road trips and lived like gypsies for two months every year, visiting places like Maine and Nova Scotia, singing along to Boston in the car, and eating in crazy little dive restaurants along the way. That Van went to the U of R and met Peter, and he never met Janie, and they had this sweet, simple wedding and lived happily ever after.

Of course, that Van probably had to drop out of school when her mom got cancer. That Van was probably drowning in medical bills and funeral costs. And maybe Peter wouldn't have done such a great job of being her rock. He was kind of a wimp when it really came down to it. And that Van wouldn't have Joe.

I stopped watching Janie out the window and went up to bed. Joe followed me and curled up next to me, nuzzling up to my neck. I buried my head in his fur and cried.

Chapter Twenty-nine

Peter didn't ring the doorbell. I guess I forgot to lock the door after Janie when she stormed out, and he let himself in. Joe growled long and low when Peter walked into the room.

"That is a big dog," he said. His voice sounded shaky.

"Technically," I said, "he's still a puppy."

Peter walked toward me slowly, like he was preparing himself to turn tail and run if he needed to. He eased himself down to sit on the end of my bed. Joe sat up next to me and stared at him.

"I don't want you on my bed," I said, pulling myself up to sitting.

Peter stood up quickly. He looked around and held his hands up in front of him like he didn't know what to do with them.

"Janie's waiting in the car." He reached down and grabbed the corner of my comforter and played with the frayed ends. "Diane really did it. Didn't she?"

"Yeah."

"I tried to tell Janie, but she just—you know how she is. She doesn't see what she doesn't want to."

"Then you better be careful, Pete. Don't take advantage of that."

He sat down on the end of the bed again. He looked defeated. I didn't make him get up.

"I know," he said, looking into his palms.

"Well, if you know, you have no excuse."

He sat at my feet like he was about to read me a bedtime story.

"Who's the guy?" He looked at my face, but he didn't look me in the eye.

"Alex."

"Who is he?"

"Joe's vet."

"That explains the clothes," Pete sneered. "Diane said he looked like a lumberjack."

"Hey, watch it," I said, sharply. "You are two commands away from getting your balls ripped off," I said, pointing at Joe. "Remember that."

His eyes widened and he stared at me for so long. I tried to think of something to say to break the silence, but I couldn't. He looked like he might not say anything again. Joe lost interest and flopped down on the bed with a big sigh.

Finally, I said, "I fucked it all up anyway."

"You'll get him back."

"You don't know that. I lied to him about the party. I told him I was sick."

"Why?"

"Because, I didn't want him to know about all of this. I didn't want him to know about you, or Diane's payoff money—all the chaos. I wanted a chance to start over. And I thought it would be easier to just put him on hold until today was over and you and Jane would start your new life and I could move on with mine."

"So tell him that," Peter said. He looked as uncomfortable as I felt.

"What kind of guy would let you go just because you told a little white lie?"

"What kind of guy would let me go because I don't have good breeding and a trust fund?"

"Van."

"Well, I came into some money recently, so the joke's on you." I tried to laugh like it was all wordplay, but we both knew it wasn't.

"How long was he going to be around anyway, Van?"

"What are you talking about?"

"You've never kept a guy around for more than a month, maybe two. No sense crying over spilled milk." He had his lawyer face on. His jaw was set.

"I'm sure it'll be easier the next time around, since I'm not in love with you anymore."

He looked at me for a long time. I stopped looking back. He leaned in and put his hand on my cheek. It was so thin and cold.

"I'm sorry," he said.

I pushed his hand away from my face, but kept holding it. His eyes were shiny.

"I know," I said.

"I wish I were"—he looked around like he was searching for the right word—"stronger." He rubbed his palm over the back of my hand.

I grabbed his fingers and we looked at each other. He had tears running down his cheeks, and his eyes were red. I felt like it was the first time I was really seeing Peter. In my head, he had always been the larger-than-life movie star guy who rescued me from total embarrassment on my first day of school. That image of him was so ingrained in my mind that I'd failed to notice that he was a real person, that he was imperfect like me and everyone else. He wasn't a hero. He was a coward. He didn't have the courage to stand up for himself or for what he wanted in life and it made him hurt the people he loved. I felt an overwhelming sadness for the time I'd wasted on him, for the commitment Janie had made to him, and for him, because it couldn't feel good to have failed yourself, your wife, and your friend. I desperately wanted him to be better than he was and come through for himself and for Janie.

"Your wife's in the car," I said. I was crying too.

He nodded, and looked away, dropping my hand.

"Bye, Van," he said, standing up.

"Bye."

He started to walk away, but then turned back to me. "Van, make sure this vet guy knows how you feel."

"If I'd told you, would it have made any difference?"

"Probably not," he said, turning away from me again.

"You knew anyway."

"I did." His back slumped and he looked at the floor. "I'm sorry." He took a deep breath. "Bye, Van."

"Take care of her, Pete."

"Yeah." He dragged his feet on the carpet as he walked out.

Joe started to follow him, but I called him back. He lay down next to me and rested his head on my chest. I wiped my eyes on my sleeve and watched Joe's eyes close into little slits, and then I fell asleep too.

Chapter Thirty

When I woke up about an hour later, Joe was still asleep, snoring away with his head just under my chin. His eyes were squeezed shut and his brow was furrowed. He whimpered softly, and let out high-pitched little woofs.

I lay there, thinking about Peter saying I should let Alex know how I felt. I wondered if this time it might actually make a difference. The portable phone was on the bed by my foot, but I didn't want to move. I stared at it, thinking that if I could make it move with my brainpower, I'd call Alex. Of course, it didn't budge. I kicked it with my foot, and it slid out of my reach.

"Hey Joey," I said softly.

He kept his head down, but his ears twitched when I talked.

"Hey Joey, get the phone for me."

He opened his eyes, pushed his nose into mine, and licked my face.

"Maybe it wasn't meant to be," I said, messing up the fur on the top of his head. I hated the way my voice sounded when I said it. I didn't believe in "meant to be." I believed in doing things, in fixing things, in changing things. I used to, at least, when I had my mom to back me up. I hadn't realized how much it had helped to have someone to tell me how amazing I was. Even though I knew she was completely biased; sometimes, when she said it, I actually believed her.

I kicked the comforter up with my foot until the phone slid close enough for me to reach. I needed a pep talk. I needed someone to back me up. I pulled the Sweet'N Low packet with Agnes's number out of my pocket. It seemed kind of strange to me that I actually wanted to talk to Aunt Agony, but I did. She hadn't turned out to be who I'd thought she was.

She answered on the first ring.

"Agnes Clarke speaking." She spoke clearly, overenunciating every consonant.

"Hi, Agnes. It's Van."

"Van, honey, are you feeling any better?" she asked, sweetly. It was comforting to have someone be so concerned for me.

"You're not going to believe what happened." I told Agnes about finding Janie in my closet and about Diane and the money, Janie in the driveway, and Peter in my bedroom.

"Oh, lady," she said, her breath rushing against the receiver as she talked, "they've put too much on you. It wasn't fair." She sighed. "Did you call your lumberjack?"

"He's a vet. Diane told Pete he was a lumberjack. Why does everyone think that?"

"Well," Agnes said, like she was considering it very carefully. "He was carrying a tree."

"True," I said, laughing.

"Call him."

"I don't think he wants to talk to me."

"Call him, lady. And call me back to tell me about it when you're done." She hung up before I could argue with her.

I stared at the buttons on my phone until the line clicked over to a dial tone. I thought about not calling him and just letting the whole thing fade away. It was one night, a walk with Joe, a few games of Go Fish, and some coffee cake at Louis's house. I'd had other little flings. It didn't have to mean anything. I could get another vet. I could buy a different house. I could probably even find another date if I tried hard enough. Maybe I could roll bandages at the Red Cross or spoon out mashed potatoes at a soup kitchen. Maybe I'd meet someone new and it would completely change my life.

But in all the years I'd known Peter, I'd never felt like there was anyone better. Alex was, and that was worth putting myself out there, even though I was nervous. I dialed his number, pressing the buttons on the phone with shaky fingers. I could feel my heartbeat in my ears while I waited for Alex to pick up; it thumped louder with every ring. By the fourth ring, I was a big ball of nerves. I was about to hang up, when I heard his voice.

"Hey." It was his cell phone, so he must have known it was me before he picked up. And he still picked up.

I heard dogs barking in the background. "Are you at work?" I rubbed Joe's nose and watched his eyes close up into little lines.

"Home."

"Hey, so you got a tree." I tried to act casual, like nothing had happened, but I could tell my voice sounded forced.

"Yeah, I did," he said. I could tell he wasn't smiling.

"Do you need help setting it up?"

"My dad's coming over tomorrow."

"Oh. Well, I could maybe–"

"Van, look–"

"Alex, I'm really sorry. What happened is– I'm really sorry. I should have just told you the truth." I stopped petting Joe. He opened his eyes and nudged my hand.

"I don't think I can do this," he said, softly.

"Didn't we have a good time the other night?" My voice was high and squeaky. I felt pathetic. Joe licked my hand until I started petting him again.

He took a deep breath. “I’m sorry. I’m just not– I’m just not ready for this. I’ve been down this road before and I can’t do it again.”

I wanted to tell him I wasn’t a road, but I didn’t say anything. I just listened to the sound of my breath making static in the phone.

He sighed. “Hey, your hand’s okay, right? Did you bandage it?”

My hand was naked, raw, and red. “I took care of it.”

“Good. I’ve gotta go. You take care, Van.”

He hung up before I could say anything else.

Chapter Thirty-one

When Agnes found out that I was in the market for a house, she insisted on taking me to look at properties. "It'll get your mind off your lumberjack."

We spent the better part of Tuesday visiting a string of houses in her neighborhood and out of my price range. All the magazine-perfect Berber carpeting and fussy window treatments made me long for Louis's house with the mismatched paint and ugly shag. Even if I could afford one of the places we saw, none of them were houses I would ever feel comfortable in. They were "no feet on the furniture, no dogs in the living room" kinds of houses.

"Do you want me to call a different Realtor?" Agnes said when we got in her car after we saw the last house on the list. "I can set up something for tomorrow."

"You know what? I have a property I'm going to check on first," I said, trying to sound official, hoping Louis would still sell to me. It wasn't a pretty house, but I could easily afford it, and it felt like a home. Although,

I worried that the homey feeling was more about Louis and Alex than it was about the house.

"Well, call me if you want a second set of eyes," she said.

"I will."

"Looks like Santa came early," she said, when we pulled into the driveway.

A Christmas tree bound up like an umbrella leaned in the doorway next to two big brown cardboard boxes. For a minute I thought it was some kind of elaborate present from Alex, and my heart jumped. Then I remembered where it came from. "It's just my order from L.L.Bean," I said.

"Well, phooey," Agnes said, "I was hoping it was from Alex."

"You and me both."

Agnes beeped three times as she drove off. Joe had his nose pressed against the living room window. When I opened the door, he darted outside and ran circles around the front yard. He peed on Gail and Mitch's side of the yard before I could stop him, bounding back at me, lifting his legs high like he'd done something to be proud of. He sniffed the tree. It must have looked like a big stick to him. Joe bit at the trunk and tried to lift it up, but it was too heavy. I picked it up from the middle and started to drag it in.

I put the tree down in the middle of the living room, dropping needles everywhere, and went back for the boxes. Then I sat down on the floor and unpacked all of it, the stand, the glass globe ornaments, aluminum icicles, white twinkle lights, the headband with reindeer antlers for Joe, the green plaid shirt for Alex, and the red wool blanket. I wrapped the blanket around me and slid the antlers over Joe's head. I put Alex's shirt in the coat closet so I wouldn't have to look at it. Joe ran around like a drunk, shaking his head, trying to get the antlers off.

I resisted the urge to hit up Agnes's bottle of Maker's Mark and put the water on for tea instead. I ran out to my car and dug out the Chipmunks' Christmas CD my mom got me as a joke one year. I blasted it on the stereo and sang along. Joe chewed on his antlers while I set up the tree.

I missed our old ornaments—the pinecones with glitter glue, the Smurfs figurines we hung on the branches by tying silver string to the ends of their little white hats. They were probably still in the green cardboard box in the crawl space at the carriage house.

Diane had a decorator come to "style" the tree in the main house with silver ribbon and Limoges ornaments all in the same color scheme, but I always liked our tree better. Every year we added to our ornament collection, sitting at the kitchen counter with mugs of hot chocolate, jars of library paste, and tempera paint. One year we made a superlong paper chain out of strips of newspaper and magazines, another year we stuffed plain glass balls with mementos from the year: movie ticket stubs, my mother's very last car payment bill run through a paper shredder, a broken necklace, blue and green pebbles from the bottom of our unsuccessful fish tank, complete with a tiny plastic fish. We'd stay up all night eating candy canes, making a mess of the kitchen, while Christmas movies played in the background. The carriage house smelled like pine needles and cinnamon. Janie was never invited. She was probably off doing the holiday party circuit with her parents anyway. So, it was just my mom and me. It was our family.

The last year, I think she was hiding how sick she was. We made origami penguins. They were simple and subdued. No glue. No mess to clean up. Less than an hour in, she kissed my cheek and said, "Well, kiddo, I think I'd better hit the hay." It was only nine thirty. I guess I should have suspected something.

When I was done putting all my L.L.Bean ornaments on the tree, I sat down at the kitchen table and made two penguins out of newsprint. I hung them on the tree with dental floss, facing each other, like they were having a conversation.

Chapter Thirty-two

The next day, I went to see Louis. I couldn't remember exactly how to get to his house and had to drive around a few of the neighborhoods off of the main road before I found the right one. I almost lost my nerve. Maybe it was a sign that I couldn't find Louis's house; it was a stupid idea. But just as I was about to give up and go home, I realized I was finally on the right street.

When I found Louis's house, I parked in the driveway and walked up to the front door. Halfway up the path, I thought about leaving. I stood there for a moment, debating if I should stay or go. Before I could come to a decision, Louis tapped on the window and waved at me. He opened the door.

"What a lovely surprise, Vannah!" he said, grabbing my arm as soon as I got close enough. "Come in! Come in!"

"I hope I'm not bothering you," I said.

"Bother?" Louis shook his head. "No, no!" He closed the door behind me. "Sit. I'll put coffee on."

I sat down at the kitchen table, trying to work up my nerve to ask him about the house. Or say something about Alex.

Louis poured water in the percolator and said, "Sfogliatelle? You like?"

"I don't know," I said. "I've never—"

"Eh, what's not to like?" Louis said, putting a plate of flaky pastries on the table.

"Really," I said, "you don't have to go to any trouble."

"What trouble?" Louis said, waving his hand in front of his face. "It's not trouble to have friends. It is a gift."

"I worried maybe you'd be upset with me," I said. I looked down at the kitchen table. It was old and nicked. Mug marks and water rings, scratches and indents. It had history.

"That's between you and Alex," Louis said, handing me a cup of coffee and sitting down. "I don't get involved. You and me. We good. You and Alex, you work it out."

"I don't know if we will," I said.

He smiled and pushed the plate of pastries closer to me. "Eat! It fixes everything, no?"

Even though it didn't fix everything, the sfogliatelle was amazing. It had a flaky shell and the filling was creamy with a hint of orange.

"You're an amazing cook," I said.

"My mother," Louis said, crossing himself, "God rest her soul, was an amazing cook. Me, I try. My father say a man doesn't belong in the kitchen, but my mother—she was a saint, that woman—she say a man belongs where his heart is. I love to bake. So I bake."

Louis took a bite of his sfogliatelle, and watched me as he chewed, like he was considering something. He washed it down with a sip of coffee and said, "That boy, he got hurt. Very hurt." Louis held his hand up in front of his mouth. "Ah, I say too much. Too much. It is not my place."

"I didn't mean to hurt him," I said.

"No, not you. Her," Louis said. He sighed. "Here I go. Not my place. This is not my place." He leaned his elbow on the table. "So, you tell me, Vannah. Do you like this house? To be a home for you and Joe?"

"I would really like that," I said, "if the offer still stands."

"Of course. Of course it stands! What is it going to do, sit?" Louis laughed.

I laughed too, because it was funny how funny Louis found his own jokes.

We talked about the details. Louis said he would put his furniture in storage and stay with a friend so I could move in before I got into more trouble with the homeowners' association.

"It's better to move to Florida in the summer," he said, "when the snowbirds fly home."

"I don't want to inconvenience you," I said.

"It's fine! Fine! I have some more time with my friends before I move. I have to take the time I have, right? Some of them might not be here the next time I come back for a visit."

Louis got quiet for a minute. Then he said, "You know, that boy, his wife, Sarah." Louis said her name and mock-spit after he said it. "He was a good husband. She was not a good wife. Maybe I shouldn't talk, because I was not always a prince to my wives, but that man, he was a prince. He trusted her and she bent that trust." He picked up another piece of sfogliatelle and was about to take a bite, but then he kept talking instead. "The day they sign the divorce papers, she's out with another man." He grabbed my arm. "Already. Poor Alex. He's still in Tennessee. I fly down to be with him. We go get a nice meal. I say, 'Your life starts again. We celebrate!' But then we see her, with this fancy man, in a suit and a shiny watch." Louis shook his head. "You could tell it was not their first date." He sighed. "She always worked late. Alex says he's a fool." Louis held his finger up. "I tell him it is never foolish to fall in love. But I see him change. He moves back here. He works and works and takes care of old Louis. He's not living." Louis looked into his empty coffee cup. "Then he meets you, and I see the old Alex. The prince." Louis looked me right in the eyes and smiled. "You, don't give up on him." He patted my hand.

He finally took a bite of his pastry. "Plus, her, I never like," he said, with his mouth full. "You, I like."

He got up to pour us more coffee. "Oh," he said, shaking his head, "I said too much. I always say too much!"

When I got home, I called Alex. "Just thought I'd say hi," I said to his voice mail. I stayed up, lying on the couch with Joe, reading a book from the library on how the canine mind works, hoping that my phone would ring.

Maybe he's in surgery, I thought. I'll just read until nine and then I'll do something else. Maybe he's pulling a late shift. I'll just read one more chapter.

I thought of every excuse to stay up later, way past the point when any reasonable person would return a phone call, because I didn't want to give up the hope that he would call. But at three AM, when I finished the book and he still hadn't called, I shuffled upstairs to brush my teeth and go to bed, tucking the phone next to my pillow, just in case.

Chapter Thirty-three

On Christmas Eve, Agnes took me to dinner at this fancy place I'd never heard of, out by Lake Ontario. The walls were draped with evergreen boughs and white lights, and we had a view of the lake from our table. Agnes ordered king crab legs and a bottle of pinot grigio for us. I was careful to leave my wineglass alone, and went through three glasses of water before the waiter came to our table with the mountain of crab.

I tried to say no when she asked me to dinner. I wasn't comfortable with the idea of going out on Christmas Eve with someone else's aunt. I'd come to terms with my role in family holidays since I didn't have a family. I made a practice of staying out of sight and acting busy so no one felt compelled to offer any invitations they didn't really want to offer. But it seemed like Agnes actually wanted to invite me to dinner. When I offered up my usual vague plans, she said, "Please, Van. I already have to spend Christmas Day with my pompous ass of a brother and his anorexic Stepford wife. Give me an excuse to bail on Christmas Eve." After we made plans and hung up, I realized that the anorexic Stepford wife and pompous ass were Peter's parents.

Since my mom died, most of the conversations I had with people felt like a race to put my foot in my mouth. My voice always sounded fake and my mouth dried out. When I was done talking, I'd play what I said in my head over and over again like a videotape with tracking problems, replaying every dumb thing I said. But Agnes and I sat at the table wearing plastic bibs with melted butter running up to our elbows, and I didn't care how I looked or if I said the wrong thing.

"Oh, you're a mess, lady," Agnes said, leaning on her elbow and waving her tiny crab pick at me.

"Oh, you are too, lady," I said, waving my crab pick back at her.

We laughed hard, and the glasses on the table clinked together like they were laughing with us.

"Would you and your mother care for dessert?" the waiter said when he took my plate full of salt water and crab shells away from me.

Agnes winked at me. "Oh, I'm not her mother," she said. "I'm her younger sister."

The waiter looked back and forth between us until we burst into giggles.

"You had me going there," he said, playing along for the sake of his tip.

"We're friends," Agnes said, patting his arm. "And we care for dessert."

Chapter Thirty-four

Joe and I spent Christmas Day on the couch watching Ralphie, the Griswolds, and the Cary Grant version of *The Bishop's Wife.*

"*It's a Wonderful Life*, my ass," I said to Joe. "Jimmy Stewart has nothing on Cary Grant."

My mother and I used to debate this every year, neither of us willing to budge an inch. Joe cocked his head from side to side while I talked, but offered no opinion. I hadn't rented *It's a Wonderful Life* and I regretted it. I wanted to lie on the couch with my eyes closed, listening to it, so I could pretend my mom was sitting in the chair next to me getting teary at the end and mouthing all her favorite lines.

I scanned the channels for Jimmy after I finished watching the movies I rented, but I couldn't find him on any channel. I ended up watching *A Christmas Story* again, with commercials, even though I'd just watched it without. Joe sprawled out on his side on the floor. I slid off the couch onto the floor next to him and curled up against his chest. He kicked me a few times before settling back to sleep with his paw over my arm. I closed my eyes and listened to him snore until I fell asleep too.

When I woke up, I realized Diane hadn't called to wish my voice mail a merry Christmas, the way she had the years before. I wouldn't have picked up anyway. My heart would have pounded long after the phone stopped ringing, and I would have spent the rest of the night arguing with her in my head. The fact that she didn't call made me feel panicky in a different way.

I picked up the phone and dialed the carriage house. It was the first time I'd called there since my mom died. The answering machine picked up. "Hi," my mom's voice said. "This is Natalie." There was a pause. "And Van," I chimed in. I think I was all of sixteen the last time we changed the message. "We can't come to the phone," she said. "You know what to do," I added, in my best TV announcer voice. There was an extra beat before the beep, and I could hear us stifling giggles in the background. I hung up and called back to listen to the message. I called six or seven times. The last time I called, Diane picked up.

"Hello?" she said.

I didn't say anything.

"Van?"

I hung up the phone. A few minutes later my phone rang, but I let it go to voice mail.

I went back to watching TV with Joe. I channel-surfed until I found Jimmy Stewart, then I curled up on the couch, closed my eyes, and pretended I was back at the carriage house with my mom.

Chapter Thirty-five

Four days after Christmas, Peter called and begged me to meet him at the bar down the road from me. He was drunk, and when I told him I didn't feel like going out, he slurred, "No, no, no, you have to, Van." Eventually I agreed to meet him, because it was easier than arguing.

I thought about sending a cab so I wouldn't have to deal with him, but I didn't know the name of the bar. Peter hadn't said the name of the bar when he called; he just said he was at the bar with the big blue anchor.

It was just down the road from my condo. Even though I drove past it all the time, I'd never looked at the sign to see what it was called, although I'd never understood why it had an enormous anchor out front when the only nearby body of water was the algae-filled pond at the entrance of the condo development.

When I got to the bar, Peter was sitting on a stool at a counter against the window. He looked completely out of place. He was holding an empty glass close to his chest, staring longingly at a full drink on the counter. His hair was sticking up, like it was trying to run away from his face. The green neon Heineken sign in the window cast deep shadows in the pockets under his eyes and the wrinkles in his brow.

I stood in front of him outside the window and stared, but he didn't notice. Finally, I tapped on the window. All at once, he was animated, like someone had just wound him up and let him go. He slammed the empty glass down on the counter and waved madly, gesturing for me to come in.

When I opened the door, he smiled, showing his teeth and the lines he was starting to get around his mouth. "I took the liberty of ordering you a drink," he said, like he'd been rehearsing it in his head while he waited for me. He slurred even more than on the phone. He took his cashmere coat off the stool next to him and slid the full drink over to me. It was the color of weak tea and swam in the condensation that surrounded it, leaving a trail like a slug on the sticky counter. He put his coat up on the bar, but it fell to the floor immediately. He didn't even notice.

"No, thanks," I said, pushing the drink back to him. I picked up his coat and hung it on a hook on the wall next to a grease-stained blue uniform jacket. The bar was empty except for the bartender and two guys in the corner playing darts. I sat down next to Peter.

He picked up the drink and took a sip. "Did you want a T and T? I think there's a bottle of Tanqueray behind the bar. They didn't have real bourbon. Well, crap and Jack." He gulped down half the glass and shook his head. He stood up and waved at the bartender. "Hey, hey, do you have any real gin back there?" He lurched over to the bar. "Not that crap in the well. I'm keeping my eye on you."

I was certain that between the bartender and the two men playing darts in the corner, Peter was going to leave with a black eye. I went over to collect him, but as I got closer, I realized that the bartender was amused.

"I mean, it's not like I expect you to have Kensington," Peter said, shaking his head, "but something that isn't crap would be nice."

The bartender pulled a green bottle off the shelf behind him and held it out to Peter by the neck, holding it up with his forearm, like it was a bottle of fine wine. "Will this suffice?" I got the impression that they'd spent a few hours together perfecting their repartee.

"That will suffice." Peter got stuck on the *f*'s in *suffice.*

The bartender laughed.

"I'm fine, Pete," I said. "I don't want a drink."

"You don't want a drink?" He held his arms up on either side, making a giant *W* out of himself. "But you're Van." He grabbed my arm and pulled me close, making me trip over my own feet. "You're Van. Have a drink!"

"No, thanks." I pulled his hand off of my arm and put it down by his side, patting it to tell him to keep it there.

"'No, thanks,' she says." Peter leaned in to the bartender to conspire. "'No, thanks.' What am I supposed to do with that?"

"I don't know, bud," the bartender said absentmindedly, slapping Peter on the shoulder.

"What say we buy these boys another round? And I'll have a T and T." Peter patted at his chest and then the back of his pants. "Where's my wallet? I'm not wearing my coat?"

"I've got his credit card over here," the bartender said to me, pointing to the register.

"Can you close him out after that round?" I asked.

He nodded, handing Peter a drink that was heavy on ice.

"He's a nice guy," Peter said to me in a loud whisper. "I told him he should dress better."

I grabbed his arm and dragged him back to the counter by the window.

"Have some." He pushed his drink into my hand. It was almost empty already.

"What is this? Why are you here?" I asked, putting his drink down on the counter.

"What is this?" He picked up the drink again, held it up, and tipped the glass back until an ice cube fell into his mouth. He slurped at it. "What's you not having a drink? What's that?" He cracked the ice to bits with his molars like Joe with a biscuit.

"I'm your DD."

"You?" He poked my shoulder. "I'm the one who carries you home."

"Your scrawny ass is too weak to carry me home," I said, waving his hand away.

"I was speaking—" He hiccupped. "I was speaking figuratively."

"Your figurative ass is weak too."

"Don't be mean. Don't." He poured more ice in his mouth. A few of the cubes fell from either side of his mouth. He brushed them off his pants, and looked into his glass like he couldn't figure out where the ice came from to begin with.

"Let's get you home," I said.

"Not yet," Peter said, crunching another ice cube.

He sat there for a moment, his brow furrowed, like he was concentrating hard. Then he looked at me and said, "I suppose you're wondering why I asked you here." He gestured around the room, and the movement appeared to make him dizzy. I was starting to worry that my ass was too weak to drag him home. He gripped the edge of the bar and his knuckles turned white. "I asked you here so I could tell you to stop fucking with me."

"How am I fucking with you?"

"I'm trying, Van. I'm trying so hard." He leaned his elbow on the bar and rubbed his head into his hand hard, leaving red marks on his forehead. "And then I hear it all day. On Christmas. Van this, Van that. I'm helping Van house hunt, and we went out to dinner and she's so funny."

"Agnes?"

"Yes, Agnes! What do you think I'm talking about?" He clenched his teeth. "You don't even like Agnes."

"Not true."

"You used to call her Aunt Agony."

"That was different," I said.

The bartender dropped off Peter's credit card and the slip.

"How? How was it different?" Peter said.

"I was different." I handed Peter his card and grabbed the slip. His tab was almost seventy bucks. I added up the tip and signed his name as a squiggle.

"You're just fucking with me."

"I like Agnes. She's my— We're friends."

"Bullshit, Van." He picked up his glass. "Bull"—he took a sip and swallowed—"shit." He slammed the glass down on the counter so hard that I was surprised it didn't break.

"Let's get you home. We can talk about this tomorrow."

"No! Nooooo!"

"Janie's going to be worried about you."

"She went to her parents' house on Saturday. I said I had to work on a brief, so I wouldn't have to see Diane." He laughed like he'd just told a joke.

"Nice."

"Diane's not nice."

"You got me there." I got his jacket from the hook, fished his keys out of the pocket, and dropped them in mine. "Come on."

He stood up and put his arms back like he wanted me to put his coat on for him. I threw it over his shoulder and slapped him on the back.

"You can't stay here, and you can't drive." I dangled his keys in front of him. "Get in my car or call a cab." I started walking, but he didn't follow me. "Or walk."

He fumbled with his jacket, reaching in to pull his shirtsleeve back to his wrist. By the time I got to my car, he was running to catch up.

I brought Peter home with me. I wasn't really comfortable with the idea, but I knew he shouldn't be alone when he was so wasted.

"You have a Christmas tree!" he said, when I got him in the house. He tripped on the carpet and fell to his knees.

Joe must have been sleeping upstairs, but the thud woke him up. He came barreling down the stairs, barking. He jumped down from the landing, clearing the rest of the steps, and pushed Peter over, pinning him to the floor.

I worried for a minute that Joe might attack him, but he put his paws on Peter's shoulders and licked his face with furious conviction.

Peter sputtered and shook his head back and forth trying to get Joe off him, but it only served to get Joe more wound up. Peter squealed, closed his eyes, and pressed his lips tightly shut. I thought he was panicking until he opened his mouth and let out a full, loud belly laugh. "Ah! Ah!" Peter panted, rubbing his hands on either side of Joe's neck. Joe jumped off him and pulled a green rubber ring toy from under the coffee table. Peter grabbed for it and Joe pulled back and dragged Peter onto his belly and halfway across the living room.

I'd never seen Pete like this. His shirt was riding up to his armpits and he was getting rug burn on his belly, but he didn't care. His face was shiny with tears and slobber. I laughed along.

I got a blanket out of the closet and left it on the couch for him. He was so busy playing with Joe that he didn't even notice when I got up to go to bed. I left the Christmas tree lights on for Peter, because he'd seemed so excited about the tree. I watched them play for a few minutes from the top of the stairs. I had to admit that it was kind of nice to have another person in the house.

Chapter Thirty-six

When I got up the next morning to take Joe out, Peter was lying on his back on the couch with one foot on the floor. He was in his undershirt, his dress shirt wadded up under his head like a pillow and his jacket draped over him. He hugged the blanket I'd left him like a teddy bear. He was breathing through his mouth in a combination of snoring and sputtering.

I ran Joe out to pee and when I came back Pete was still asleep. I started a pot of coffee and fed Joe, trying to be quiet about it, which, of course, made every *clink*, *clank*, and *clunk* sound ten times louder than it was. But Pete kept snoring away.

I poured two mugs of coffee and got some sugar out for Pete's. Joe ran into the living room and a second later, Pete yelled, "Good God!" and Joe came running back to me, wagging his tail.

When I brought our coffee into the living room, Pete was sitting up, wiping his face; a piece of rice from Joe's breakfast stuck to his forehead.

"Hey, sleepyhead," I said, handing him a cup of coffee as he sat up. "Should I bang some pots?"

"Aspirin?"

I ran upstairs to the bathroom and brought the aspirin bottle down. I shook it like a rattle in front of Peter's head before I handed it to him.

He squinted up his eyes. "Damnit, Van."

"Damnit, Pete. What the hell are you getting so drunk for, anyway? This isn't like you."

"No, it's like you."

"Shut up." I sat down next to him and shoved his shoulder.

He looked at me for a long time, like he was trying to read my face. Finally, he said, "When I left, after the party, I really thought I could just walk away, you know? I thought I could just move on without you. But I can't. There are all these little things that happen in my day and I think, Oh, I've got to remember to tell Van. And then I'm miserable for the rest of the day, knowing that I can't tell you. Everything makes me think about you and I don't know how to not have you there." He put his head in his hands and made a noise that was half yawn, half yelp. "I was so set on coming over here and reaming you out for all the Agnes crap, but I didn't know what to say or how to say it. I thought I'd have a drink and then I'd come over, but the more I drank, the less any of it made sense. Any of it." He looked me in the eyes, and I could feel the pull of it, like he was trying to make me understand that he was saying more than he was free to say. "Why can't it just be like it was? Remember? We were always together. It was so"—he ran his hands through his hair and breathed in like it hurt—"uncomplicated."

"I don't think it was ever uncomplicated," I said, rubbing his shoulder.

"I felt comfortable with you. I don't feel comfortable with anyone anymore."

"That's because you're weird," I said, smiling. "You wear boat shoes and listen to bad music."

"Come on, Van," he said, "I'm trying to have a real conversation with you."

"But see, that's the thing. It wasn't real. We didn't have real conversations. We skirted the issue. We avoided the uncomfortable." I pulled my legs up and hugged them to my chest. "I don't think my feelings for you were ever just friendly. And you knew that, but we never talked about it."

He rested his head on the back of the couch and closed his eyes.

"I guess I'm not who you wanted me to be either," I said, "and I'm sorry. Maybe as much as it wasn't fair for you to know about my feelings and pretend you didn't, it wasn't fair of me to have those feelings and pretend I was just being your friend."

"So we both suck," Peter said.

"Basically," I said, smiling. For that little moment, we were back to normal. We sat there for a while. I didn't want to say anything. I just wanted to sit there with him, because in that moment, he felt like my good old friend Peter. I watched him breathe through his mouth, his chest rising and collapsing under his bright white undershirt.

He turned his head toward me and opened his eyes. His eyelashes were wet. "So what do we do? Are we done?"

"Maybe we all need to take a break for a while. You have a marriage to jump-start. Those things take time."

"You know," he said, sniffing, "aside from everything else, you always were my best friend." He wiped his eye with the back of his hand. The wet streak it left dripped a little before he wiped it on his shirt.

"You need to be Janie's best friend now," I said. My chest ached and my throat was tight. "And she needs to be yours. And I don't know where that leaves me, but that's the way it has to be, Pete."

I covered my face with my hands. Peter grabbed my arms and pulled me in to his chest. I hugged him and my tears soaked his undershirt.

"At the very least, I liked it better when I could pretend it was uncomplicated," he said, leaning his chin on my head.

"The good old days." I sat up and wiped my face with my hand.

"Look at us, carrying on like a couple of girls," he said, pushing me.

"Speak for yourself." I pushed back and sniffled, trying to keep my nose from dripping. "It's going to be okay, Pete. We just need some time to figure out what *okay* means."

"But you promise we're not done," Peter said.

"We're not done," I said. "We will figure out how to be friends. I promise."

"Swear?" he asked. He held up his pinkie.

I hooked mine into it. "Swear," I said.

Chapter Thirty-seven

I got Peter situated on the couch with a cup of coffee and a bowl of Cap'n Crunch.

"Don't feed Joe," I said. "No matter how cute he looks. He's had breakfast." I felt shy around him, like we were strangers again, getting to know each other on new terms.

He put his feet up on the coffee table and balanced the bowl between his knees. His toe was poking through a hole in his black socks.

There's something you can't do at home, I thought. All of it—the Cap'n Crunch, eating in the living room, feet on the furniture—would make Janie crazy. I went upstairs to take a shower, but before I even got to the landing, I could hear Joe crunching cereal.

"I know what you did," I yelled down the stairs.

"He likes it."

"No more!"

I grabbed clothes to change into in the bathroom, so I wouldn't risk being seen running down the hall in a towel. It was weird showering with someone else in my house. I was careful not to sing or take too long. I cringed when the shampoo bottle let out a loud, flatulent sound as I squeezed shampoo into my hand. I forgot to turn the fan on when I got in, and when I got out, the room was filled with steam. I wiped the condensation off of the mirror and tried to put my makeup on before it clouded up again. When I was done, I gave the mirror one last swipe to get a good look. My face looked sweaty, and my mascara was thick and threatening to drip.

My jeans stuck to my thighs and took forever to pull up. My bra straps twisted and pulled at my skin. Usually, I showered with the bathroom door open, and walked around naked until I was dry. Joe was the only one around to see, and he was naked all the time.

Peter knocked on the door.

"I'll be right out," I yelled, trying to pull my shirt over my damp belly.

"Van? It's Joe. He—"

I opened the door.

Peter stood there in his undershirt. Joe wasn't with him. There was a small streak of blood down the side of his shirt.

"What did you do to him?" I said, not thinking about what I was saying. It was highly unlikely that Peter bit Joe.

I pushed past him and ran down the stairs. My hair soaked my shirt. My bare feet thumped hard on the stairs.

"Joe! Joey!" I yelled.

Joe was lying on his side on the floor, panting. There was blood dripping out of his mouth onto the carpet. I knelt next to him and ran my hand along his side. He was shaking.

"I don't know what happened," Peter said. All the color had drained from his face and he was shaking too. "We were playing with that ring toy and he was fine. And then he got really slow. He wasn't pulling back. And he gave me this look. He was just staring at me. Then his eyes rolled back in his head and he fell and he started shaking. I think he bit his tongue. That's where the blood is coming from, I think."

Peter wrinkled up his forehead and ran his hand through his hair. "I didn't know what to do, so I just tried to hold him down." He shoved his hands in his pockets and rocked back and forth on his heels. "I really hope I didn't make it worse."

"I have to take him to the vet," I said. I was surprised by how calm I was. Everything felt like it was happening very slowly, like maybe it wasn't really happening at all. It couldn't be. Joe was my hero. He was my "jump over burning bales of hay, save me when I fall in a well" dog. This couldn't be real.

"That guy, right?" Peter said. "The one from the other day."

"I guess so. I don't know anyone else."

Joe let out a hacking, coughing sound. He licked at his teeth.

"Can you come with me?" I asked. I was sure bringing Peter wasn't going to win me any points with Alex, but I didn't want to be alone. I didn't want to do any of this alone.

"Of course," Peter said, like there was no question about it.

Peter stayed with Joe while I got ready to go. He put his head down next to Joe's head and stroked the fur behind Joe's ears.

I slipped on my shoes without bothering to tie them. It took me way too long to find my keys. This is why people are organized, I thought. Emergencies happen and you just have to go, and you need to know where your keys are. I felt the panic start to creep in. My throat tightened. I took a deep breath, and covered my face with my hands. I knew I didn't have the luxury of falling to pieces.

I finally found my keys on the floor of my bedroom. They must have fallen out of the pocket of my jeans when I took them off the night before.

Peter and I tried to coax Joe into standing, but his legs wobbled. He kept making that horrible coughing sound. I tried not to let my mind wander to all the awful things that could have caused this. Peter scooped Joe up in his arms and carried him to my car, and I ran in front of them to get the door open. Peter was careful to make sure he didn't bump Joe's head as he set him down gently on the backseat.

Peter drove. I sat in the backseat with Joe's head in my lap. Joe sat up as we pulled out of the garage, but then he lay back down again. His big brown eyes were glassy and he had that bewildered look he gets when he first wakes up from a nap. Usually he snapped out of it after a few minutes, but he wasn't snapping out of this. He was in a daze. When we pulled alongside a motorcycle at a red light, he didn't even growl.

Peter parked right in front of the clinic. We helped Joe climb out of the car, but then Peter picked him up again to carry him in.

"Oh, Joey!" Mindy yelped the second we walked in the door. "What happened?" She ran around the desk and rushed over to Joe.

"He just started shaking," Peter said. He was straining under the weight of Joe, but he didn't put him down. "His eyes rolled back. It was awful." I was so thankful he was there, that he could explain what happened, and that I didn't have to do this alone.

"Poor baby!" Mindy said, petting Joe's head. She ushered us into an empty exam room.

Peter put Joe down on the exam table, and I crouched down so I could look him in the eyes. His ears perked up and he licked my chin and whined.

"Alex is finishing up with a patient," Mindy said. "He'll be done in a few minutes. I'll tell him it's an emergency."

"Thanks," I said. I felt my heart race when she said Alex's name, but I didn't have it in me to worry about what he might think. I just wanted him to fix my dog.

Mindy slid the door closed carefully. Peter came over and stood next to me and kept his hands out like he was making sure Joe wouldn't fall off the table.

"I'm so glad you're here," I said to Peter, my voice wavering.

He put his hand on my shoulder. "That's what friends do, right?" he said.

The door slid open and Alex walked in. Peter pulled his hand off my shoulder.

Alex's jaw was set and he kept his eyes on Joe's chart. "Tell me what happened," he said, leaning against the counter. I wanted to go over and hug him and cry it out and tell him what happened and beg him to make it all better, but he was acting like he didn't even know me.

"He was playing," I said, "and then he just started shaking." I thought of the way Alex held my hand and pinned it to the bed. We were so far from that now. I couldn't even look at him anymore. I focused my attention on Joe. Joe's brown eyes. Joe's big black nose. Joe's fuzzy ears. I needed Joe to be okay.

"Can you be more specific?" Alex said, writing in Joe's chart. I wondered if he was really writing anything, or if he was just trying to avoid looking at me as much as I was trying to avoid looking at him.

"I don't— I wasn't there," I said.

"I was," Peter said. He and Alex stood there, staring at each other until Peter offered his hand and said, "Peter Clarke."

Alex raised his eyebrows slightly. He grunted, shook Peter's hand, and pulled away to look at Joe's file again. "Can you tell me what happened?"

Peter explained the chain of events thoroughly, like he was being deposed, using words like *convulse* and *nonresponsive*. He even admitted to feeding Joe some Cap'n Crunch.

I held Joe's paw in my hand, smoothing down the tufts of fur between his toes.

Alex came over and ran his hand along Joe's side, feeling his belly. I placed Joe's paw on the table gently and moved away to give Alex some space. He pulled the penlight out of his pocket and looked in Joe's eyes and ears. Joe barely resisted when Alex pried his mouth open to examine.

"He keeps hacking and then licking his mouth," I said.

Peter sat in the chair in the corner of the room. He met my eyes and gave me a reassuring smile every time I looked at him.

"He bit his tongue badly," Alex said, pointing to the side of Joe's mouth. "He probably has blood and extra saliva running down his throat." He went back to the counter and wrote more notes in Joe's chart.

"So what it sounds like," Alex said, leaning against the counter, "is that he had a seizure." He looked at me and then Peter. "I'd like to keep him overnight to run some tests. Sometimes dogs just get seizures. It's just the way they're wired. Sometimes there's an underlying cause, and I want to make sure we rule that out. We don't want to miss a bigger problem, if there is one." He was using a kinder voice now. "So we'll admit him and cover our bases," he said. "Is that okay with you?"

"Of course," I said.

"I'll get Mindy to take him back and prep him for testing. We'll call you if anything changes," Alex said.

If anything changes, like if he dies or he has a brain tumor, I thought. Alex must have seen the look of horror on my face because he looked me right in the eyes and said, "We'll take good care of him, Van. I promise." He grabbed Joe's chart and left the room.

I held Joe's face on either side and pressed my forehead in to his. "You be okay," I said. "You just have to be, Joe."

Mindy came in and she and Peter helped Joe off the table. He was standing better. His legs were more stable. "Do you think you can walk for me, Joey?" she said.

"I can carry him," Peter said. He lifted Joe up, knees buckling under his weight.

I kissed Joe on the nose. "Bye, buddy," I said, praying it was not the last time I was going to see him.

Peter followed Mindy into the back room. I went out to the car, sat in the passenger seat, and cried. A few minutes later, Peter got in the car. He leaned over and wrapped his arms around me. "He's going to be okay," he said.

"What am I going to do if he isn't?" I said. "I'm buying a house for him! My whole day is about when he needs to eat and when I need to walk him. He's always happy to see me. He's always there when I need him. He's my family. What am I going to do without him?"

"He's going to be fine." Peter brushed my hair out of my face and wiped the tears off my cheeks. "Buck up, soldier," he said, imitating his father.

Peter dropped me off at home and then ran to Wegmans and the video store. The condo was quiet. Before Joe, it was just me and I'd been used to it, but now it was so much worse. I got myself a glass of water and turned around expecting to see Joe right behind me. I walked into the living room and turned on the television, but he wasn't there to jump up on the couch next to me. So even though I felt kind of weird about hanging out with Peter, I was relieved when he came back with a quart of mint chocolate chip for me, a quart of French vanilla for him, and a stack of old Jackie Chan movies.

"Jackie Chan. Really?" I said.

"Jackie Chan is the kung fu master," Peter said, gravely. "Trust me, it'll take your mind off things."

So we sat on the couch and watched Jackie Chan kick the crap out of bad guys, and we played cards and talked smack, and it did take my mind off of things.

Two movies in, we heard the *Mission: Impossible* theme song coming from his phone. Peter picked up. "Hey, sweets," he said, walking out to the garage to take the call.

I paused the movie for him. But then I kept trying to make sense of Peter's muffled words, even though I knew I shouldn't listen in. I couldn't stand just sitting there, trying to figure out if he was talking about me, holding my cards, with Jackie Chan in midkick. I turned the movie on again and collected the cards to shuffle so we could start over. He came back about ten minutes later.

"Oh, this scene kicks so much ass," he said, pointing to the television as he walked into the living room. "What did I tell you? The kung fu master!" He sat next to me on the couch and put his feet on the coffee table.

I wanted to know if he'd told Janie he was with me, but he didn't say anything about the phone call, so I didn't ask. I just dealt the next round of cards.

I think Peter could see it on my face whenever I started to think about Joe, and he did the best he could to distract me with stupid jokes or more food. We ate ice cream, and ordered pizza and wings and stayed up late, and it wasn't awkward the way I worried it might be. We'd been friends all these years and it just fell back into place. Only, it was better, because I wasn't pining over him. I wasn't worried about how I looked or if I said something stupid. He was just my friend Pete and he was kind of a dork, but he was there when I needed him.

Chapter Thirty-eight

The phone woke me up. I was on the couch, covered in the blanket from my bed. I didn't remember falling asleep on the couch. Peter must have gotten the blanket for me. He was asleep on the floor next to me, wrapped in the blanket he'd slept in the night before. I jumped over him and ran to the phone.

"Savannah?" It was Mindy. I recognized her voice.

"How is he?"

"He's doing much better. He's a little groggy, but he's such a sweetheart. He's been giving kisses to anyone who comes close enough," Mindy said. "We can have you come pick him up at ten this morning, if that works for you."

"Do you have the results?"

"Well, I'll have to let Alex go over them with you. I'm sorry."

I told her I'd be there at ten. Peter was sitting up rubbing his eyes. "Is he okay?" he asked.

"I don't know. He's feeling better, but I don't know about the test results."

"Can we pick him up today?"

"Ten o'clock. But don't feel like you have to come. You have work and Janie, and I don't want to—" I started to panic at the idea of sitting in that exam room by myself waiting for Alex, waiting for the results, but I didn't want to overstep my bounds.

"Van, we're going to be friends, right? This is what friends do. I'm off work until Monday, and Janie is at Diane's until Diane decides to release her again. So, I'm here. We'll go get Joe."

He was really coming through. He was putting all our other stuff aside and he was being the person I needed him to be. I was proud of him. And if he could do that for me now, I hoped he could do that for Janie for the rest of their lives, the way he promised in his vows. I made my own vow to hold him to it.

We made coffee and Peter had cereal, but I couldn't eat. I was way too worried about the test results. I poured milk in my coffee and studied the blooms of white that came up from the bottom of the cup, while Peter crunched away happily. I wondered how Janie felt about having to listen to someone eat cereal that loud for the rest of her life.

Chapter Thirty-nine

Mindy was on the phone when we got to the office. She waved to us when we walked in the door.

Peter and I sat on a bench in the corner and waited. I felt like I was going to be sick. What if Joe had cancer? What if he had only a few weeks to live? I could not stand to think of losing him. I knew he wasn't going to live forever, but he was supposed to live a long, healthy life full of long walks and treats and naps on the floor. I wasn't supposed to lose him now. He was still a puppy.

Peter nudged me and pointed to a picture of a humiliated Dalmatian in a Christmas sweater on the wall across from us. He raised his eyebrows.

Mindy hung up the phone. "Hi, Van," she said. "Why don't you go on back and wait in room two. Alex will be with you in a sec."

There was only one chair in the exam room.

"Go ahead," Peter said.

I sat down. He leaned against the wall in the corner of the room looking at a model of a cat's urinary tract. He poked at a clear plastic orb that was supposed to be the bladder, and the whole model fell apart. He was scrambling to put it back together when Alex walked in the room.

"I'll go get Joe for you in a minute," Alex said, eying Peter, who was trying desperately to reconnect the plastic urethra to the bladder.

"What's Joe's typical diet like?" Alex asked. He looked softer today. The crease between his eyebrows wasn't as sharp as it had been yesterday. His jaw wasn't as tight. I worried maybe it meant he had bad news for me. Maybe he felt too bad about what he had to tell me to stay mad.

Peter dropped the plastic cat bladder. He picked it up and put it on the counter with the other fake cat parts and pushed them to the back of the counter. He slid his hands in his pockets. "Sorry," he said.

"I feed Joe chicken, rice, and carrots, mostly," I said. "I cook for him. He came with a recipe. I think that's what he's been eating all along. Sometimes he eats other stuff, like pancakes and eggs. But I never give him chocolate or onions or grapes. Nothing on the ASPCA list." I was trying to stay calm, but my hands were shaking and I had a lump in my throat that hurt like hell. "Is he okay? He doesn't have a brain tumor, does he?"

Alex smiled. "No, he doesn't have a brain tumor. And I think he's going to be just fine."

I felt my eyes well up. I took a deep breath and tried to calm myself. "Is he going to keep having seizures?"

"Probably not," Alex said. "He has a thiamine deficiency. He's not getting adequate amounts of B_1 in his diet. The imbalance is what caused the seizure. We gave him some thiamine shots while he was here, and if we can get him back on track, he shouldn't have any more seizures."

"So, this is my fault," I said, putting my hands over my face. "I thought I was doing a good thing by cooking for him. He came with a recipe and—"

"He's going to be just fine," Alex said. "Please don't beat yourself up about this. The diet issues probably started before you had him and now we can fix them. I want you to start feeding him regular dog food, plus supplements. I'll write down the name of the brand I recommend." Alex scribbled something in his chart. "I'm going to put him on antibiotics for two weeks for his tongue. There's a puncture wound where he bit it. It's not infected now, but we want to keep it that way."

He clicked his pen and stuck it in the breast pocket of his lab coat. Then he reached for the cat model, snapped the pieces together, and put it back on the stand. "It's a little tricky," he said to Peter.

Alex looked at me for a second. I thought maybe he might say something about us. Maybe he'd consider giving me another chance.

"Thank you, Alex," I said.

He looked away and cleared his throat. "I'll go get Joe. Mindy will have your prescription up front. Unless his tongue gets infected, or he has another seizure, we don't need to see you until his vaccine boosters this spring." He grabbed Joe's file and walked out the door to the back room.

He didn't need to see me until spring. And he probably didn't even want to see me then.

A few seconds later, we heard the frantic scratching of dog nails on the linoleum floor. Joe came tearing into the exam room with Alex behind him, holding onto a skinny blue cord leash. When Joe saw me, he leapt across the room, put his front paws up on my lap, and licked my face. His mouth was open and he almost looked like he was smiling. "Oh, buddy," I said, and threw my arms around his neck. He put his paws up on my shoulders and tried to climb in my lap. His tail was wagging so hard that it shook both of us. All I could see was a mass of black fur. I was afraid he'd knock me over, so I pushed him off me and bent down to give him another hug. "I missed you," I told him.

When I looked up, Alex was gone and Peter was holding the other end of the leash. "He just handed it to me and left," Peter said.

"You know," I said, "for a minute there, I thought maybe—"

"I know." Peter wrapped his arms around me. "I'm so sorry. I am so sorry, Van."

I wiped my eyes with my sleeve. "But my dog is okay, right? That's the important part." I slapped Peter's back. "Buck up, soldier."

He laughed. "Fuck 'em. Right?"

I gave him a weak smile, grabbed Joe's leash, and we went out to the lobby.

"All better there, Joey?" Mindy leaned over her desk and handed Joe a biscuit. "I bet you were a perfect angel."

An older woman with a big gray Poodle came in. Joe strained at the end of his leash to try to get to the dog. The poodle's legs were shaking, and she hid behind her owner. I held Joe firmly at my side.

"Hi, Kim," Mindy said. "You can go on into exam room one. Dr. Brandt will be with you shortly."

Joe whined as the Poodle walked away from him.

"Did Alex explain the medication?" she said, reaching for Joe's chart. I noticed that she called him Dr. Brandt to the Poodle lady, but Alex when she talked to me.

"Sort of," I said, fumbling through my purse for my credit card, dropping Joe's leash in the process. Joe ran to the other side of the waiting room and jumped up on the bench so he could look out the window.

"Let me go get Joe's prescription." She went into the back room.

Peter put his arm around my shoulder, leaned his head to mine, and whispered, "I'm going to run to the men's room."

"Can it wait?"

"No."

"It's down the hall to the right."

He squeezed my arm before he let go.

"Van, is that your boyfriend?" Mindy asked, returning from the back room with a big green pill bottle just as Peter was leaving. Her voice sounded pinched.

"No, Peter's just a friend," I said. "He's actually married to my friend Jane."

"That's sweet of him to be here with you," she said, carefully. It looked like she was putting pieces together in her head. I wondered how much she knew.

She rattled the pill bottle. "Okay, so, you need to give Joe two of these twice a day. Do you know how?"

I shook my head no.

"Okay, let me see." She looked at the label again. "It's okay to give these with food, so just wrap them up in a piece of cheese. You know those American slices? The ones in the wrapper?"

"Yeah."

"Mush it around the pill like Play-Doh. That's what I do. He should just take it, no problem." She handed the bottle over to me. "If he doesn't, give me a call and I'll talk you through it." She winked at me, and then we locked eyes for a minute. "Don't worry. It'll work out." She tapped her finger to the side of her little button nose. "I have a sense about these things."

"Thanks," I said, rolling the bottle between my hands. I wasn't sure she was still talking about the pills.

"It's nice to have sun," she said, filling the silence as she ran my credit card. "I'm always much happier when it's sunny."

"I can't picture you not happy," I blurted out.

"Well, thank you, Savannah!" She beamed, showing off her perfect pearl teeth. She held the credit card slip up to the corner of the exam receipt and grabbed her stapler. "That's so nice of you to say—"

We heard a rolling noise and then a slam, one of the pocket doors in the exam room being pushed into its pocket. Hard.

"If I wanted your opinion, I'd ask for it!" Alex yelled.

Mindy froze, stapler in one hand, receipt in the other. We listened to footsteps in the hallway. Peter came walking into the lobby, head slumped low, face red.

"What did you do?" I grabbed for Joe's leash.

"We should go."

Mindy finally clicked the stapler. She handed me the receipt. "You have a good day, now. Okay?" She forced a smile and tapped her finger on the side of her nose again. "Bye, Joey!"

Chapter Forty

"What did you do?" I slammed the car door too loud and the sound of it echoed in my head. "Did you take a fucking dump in the hallway, Peter?"

"Don't be vulgar," Peter said.

"Vulgar?" My hands were shaking too hard to get the key in the ignition. I stopped trying, and smacked the steering wheel. "Well, did you? Because I don't understand how going to the bathroom ends with Alex yelling at you."

Joe wasn't fazed by the yelling, but he was pushing at Peter to win back the front seat.

"Van, I was trying—"

"You know what? You know—shut up." I felt bad yelling at him after he'd been trying so hard over the past two days, but he'd definitely crossed the line and I was angry. I made another attempt with the key and got it in the ignition this time. I backed out of the parking space and slammed on the brakes before I put the car in drive. Joe's feet slid on the console and he fell. I shifted into park and put my head down on the steering wheel. "I think I need you to drive." I pulled up the emergency brake and got out of the car. Joe jumped out behind me and followed me to the passenger's side. I opened the back door for him, and I got in the car again, praying that Alex wasn't sitting in the back room watching.

Peter got behind the wheel. I pressed the side of my face against the glass and rested my hand on my forehead, covering my eyes. I pulled my face away for a minute and looked at the smudge my makeup left against the window: translucent beige, textured by pores. I tried to put my face back in the makeup outline exactly.

Peter got us back to the main road, but I could tell he didn't know which way to go. He didn't signal, and he let a few cars pass when he could have easily turned in front of them. He drummed on the steering wheel and looked around for a minute, finally choosing to turn right.

He found his way back to the highway. Joe pushed his snout through the space between my seat and the door, and pressed his nose against my hand. Peter fiddled with the radio.

"What did he say?" I asked.

"He said it's too much." Peter let out a sigh, heavy with disappointment, like Alex had just broken up with him. "He's divorced."

"I know." I picked at the ragged cuticle on my index finger. "What did you say?"

"That the whole mess was all about Diane, and Janie, and me, and you told him you were sick to protect him from all of it. I told him that Diane's a tornado of drama, but she doesn't live here or anything. I mean, if you wanted, you could probably never see her again. And Jane and I will keep our distance."

My stomach wobbled, the way it does when you put your toes to the edge of a cliff and look down. If I wanted, I could probably never see Diane again. I pictured myself spreading my arms out wide and jumping.

"I'm so sorry, Van." He brushed his knuckles against my arm carefully. "I made it worse."

"Fuck 'em. He doesn't know what he's missing, right?" I asked, trying to convince myself that it was Alex's loss more than mine. I was failing miserably.

Peter pulled into the parking lot of the bar with the big blue anchor, and parked my car next to his. I made Joe stay in the car while I got out to get in the driver's seat.

Peter met me around the back of the car and hugged me hard. "I'm so sorry." He held me tight and whispered in my ear. "You know I was trying to help, right?"

I nodded and smiled, hooking my finger into his as I walked away. We stayed connected until our arms couldn't reach and our hands fell apart.

The slam of his car door was loud and hollow. I got back in my car, threw it in drive, and peeled out of the parking lot, so I could leave before I was left.

Chapter Forty-one

We stopped at Wegmans to pick up the dog food Alex recommended. I left Joe in the car with the window rolled down just a little. He jumped onto the driver's seat and watched me walk away with his wet nose pressed through the opening. I can't believe I almost lost him too, I thought, and felt my throat tighten up. I tried to push the thought of it out of my head, while I rushed through Wegmans to the dog food aisle. I found the food Alex recommended. Newman's Own Organic Chicken and Rice kibble. It had carrots and everything—like what we'd been eating only in dog-food form. I wondered what I was going to eat now. I wished Paul Newman made human kibble too. I couldn't bring myself to cook just for me, but I liked cooking for us. Sometimes it was easier to take care of Joe than it was to take care of myself.

When we got home, it was just after noon. I opened the fridge and thought about making lunch, but there was nothing to eat. I fished a pickle out of its jar, wrapped the end of it in a paper towel, and went upstairs to work. I sat at my desk and slurped on the pickle while I waited for my computer to boot up. Joe put his front paws in my lap and tried to get a bite.

"You don't like pickles. We've been through this." I held it out so he could smell it. He sniffed and then blew air out of his nose like he couldn't get the smell out fast enough. "Told you." My voice was thin and hollow. "Told you, Joe," I said again. I have no one else to talk to, I thought. This is it. I have no one. Alex won't talk to me. Peter's gone home to try to figure out how to be a husband, and I am talking to my dog.

I tried to work on the grant, but I couldn't focus. After a couple of hours of trying to work, I gave up. I was staring more than I was writing and I needed to give it a rest.

I shut down my computer and went downstairs to scrub Joe's bloodstains off the carpet. I looked under the sink for carpet cleaner, but all I found was Agnes's bottle of Maker's Mark and half a pack of scrubby sponges that I'm pretty sure were there when I moved in.

I pulled the cork out of the Maker's Mark, and with my nose up to the bottle, I took a deep breath. My nostrils burned and my mouth watered. I poured a few fingers into a tumbler and then leaned over the sink and swirled it around, watching the golden brown waves hit the sides of the glass.

Joe smacked his water bowl with his paw. It spun a little, teetering before it hit the floor with a metallic crack. I dumped my glass in the sink and bent down to grab Joe's bowl. He licked my face and wagged his tail, elated that I got what he was trying to tell me. I filled his water bowl and set it down, and while he lapped it up, I turned the bottle over and emptied it down the drain. It disappeared in a few big glugs. I squirted dish soap in the sink and ran the faucet until the smell disappeared and all I could smell was fake lemon.

The carpet cleaner wasn't in the bathroom or the garage. I looked in the coat closet and saw the flannel shirt I bought Alex for Christmas on the top shelf. I took it down and ran my hand over it. It was so soft. When I bought it, I'd pictured Alex wearing it for years, until it was threadbare. I'd pictured being there with him to watch it wear over time. I imagined throwing it on to sleep in when he went away and I missed him. I wasn't sure what to do with it. Throw it away? Donate it? Leave it in the coat closet and get upset every time I came across it? For the first time I'd really let myself dream about having a life with someone other than Peter. I hugged the shirt to my chest. I wasn't ready to just let Alex go without a fight.

Joe got excited when he saw me grab my shoes. I sat on the couch to put them on, and he jumped up next to me and pushed his head under my arm, licking my face and whining. I didn't have the heart to tell him he couldn't come.

Joe rode shotgun. I opened the window a little bit for him, even though it was freezing. He pushed his nose into the crack between the window and the door frame and sniffed hard. His big fluffy tail wagged back and forth, hitting the emergency brake.

I wasn't sure what I was going to say. I started speeches in my head. "Alex, I think you got the wrong impression of me" or "Please give me another chance. I don't usually lie about being sick so I can throw parties at my house."

I still didn't have anything by the time I turned down Alex's street. My hands started shaking when we pulled into his driveway. Maybe he's not home, I thought. My heart and my stomach and all of my blood pulsed together like the beat of one of those huge tribal drums that drummers beat hard with the heels of their hands. If I'd been alone, I would have lost my nerve, but Joe sat in the passenger's seat and wagged his tail expectantly, smacking it against the door, like he just knew we were about to do something exciting. He'd be thrilled to see me when I got back in the car, no matter what happened.

I left Joe on the front seat with all the windows open, and walked up to Alex's house. Then I realized that I'd just seen him at the office a few hours ago. He's not even home, I thought. I'll leave the shirt on the doorstep. I'll call and leave a message to explain it. Down at my side, I crossed and uncrossed my fingers three times like Janie and I always did for luck when we were kids.

Alex opened the door before I could ring the doorbell. Joe barked from the car. I told myself he'd just think Joe and I were running errands. We'd gone to the park. We were on our way home from PetSmart. There was no way it would be immediately obvious to him that I brought my dog along for moral support.

"Van." I couldn't read his face. He didn't even say hi. Just Van.

"Hi," I said, giving him a weak smile. "You're here. I figured you'd still be at work."

"It's New Year's Eve," he said. "Half day."

I nodded. I'd totally forgotten it was New Year's.

He looked at his feet and ran his hand through his hair. It fell back into his face one pale strand at a time. "I can't do this, Van. It's too—"

"Alex, just—"

"Complicated. It's too complicated." He grabbed at his hair with both hands, holding it in a ponytail. The shorter strands slipped out and flopped in his face. He shifted his weight back and forth from one foot to the other. "I can't." He let go of his hair and reached for the door.

He'd almost closed the door completely when I blurted out, "What a load of horse shit!"

He opened the door and stared at me. "Excuse me?"

"I'm sorry, but it's horse shit. Everything is complicated. Paying bills, buying houses. Groceries are fucking complicated. Nothing is easy." My voice was shaky. "Where do you get off thinking it's going to be easy? Because let me tell you—let me tell you, it isn't. It's hard and it's complicated and sometimes it really, really sucks. But sometimes it doesn't." I looked right in his eyes and didn't worry about trying to read his reaction. "You're no walk in the park either, but I think you're worth it. And I'm worth it. But if you can't see that—if you want to live in some fucking bubble—I can't change that."

He stared at me and didn't say anything, and it felt like I was standing there for hours, even though it couldn't have been more than a whole minute.

"Here." I handed him the shirt. "I'm not going to stand around and wait for you to say something." I walked back to my car, watching my feet carefully so I wouldn't trip. I thought I heard footsteps behind me, but when I sneaked a peek over my shoulder, Alex was still in the doorway, holding the shirt and watching me like he didn't know what had hit him.

When I got in the car, Joe tried to climb in my lap and beeped the horn with his shoulder. I wanted to crawl in a hole. I pushed Joe back over to his seat, cranked up the radio, and backed out of the driveway fast, thanking the heavens for not hitting Alex's mailbox.

"Oh, God, Joe! 'You're fucking complicated. I'm fucking complicated. I'm worth it. Here's a shirt.' Brilliant."

Joe was already back to his studied attempt to sniff in as much outside air as possible. I gave his tail a tug. He turned to face me and pressed his cold nose against my cheek.

When we got home I asked Joe if he wanted ice cream. His ears perked up and he ran over to the fridge. "I've trained you well, Grasshopper," I said, scratching behind his ear with one hand and grabbing the carton of French vanilla with the other. Joe shuffled backward and sideways on our way to the couch, keeping his eyes on the ice cream.

I only gave Joe one spoonful for every four or five of mine so he'd still have room for his kibble. I barely even tasted the ice cream. I just spooned it into my mouth and tried as hard as I could not to replay the scene at Alex's house in my head. It was impossible. I couldn't stop thinking about the look on his face. His eyes were wide, his forehead wrinkled. Was it shock? Was it disgust? Was he embarrassed for me? I was embarrassed for me. I'd put myself out there, as far out there as I could go, and he just stood there and let me walk away alone.

I ate until my stomach hurt and the carton was empty. I put the empty carton on the floor for Joe to lick and flopped over the couch. I hugged my knees up to my chest and Joe jumped on me and pawed at my legs like he was trying to unfold me again. When I wouldn't budge, he jumped off the couch and ran upstairs. He came back a moment later, jumped on the couch, and dropped his red rubber bone, his favorite toy, on my head, like he was trying to be funny.

I made Joe a party hat out of newspaper and a rubber band, like my mom used to do. Joe ran around the room shaking his head, trying to get the hat off. When he finally did, he jumped up on the couch with it and ripped it to shreds. We stayed up to watch the ball drop on TV. At least I have my dog, I thought, giving him a big hug as the crowd of people in Times Square shouted, "Happy New Year!" and threw confetti.

Chapter Forty-two

A few days later, when I was coming back to the condo with empty boxes I'd snagged from the liquor store, Janie's little silver Audi was parked in my driveway. Janie sat in the driver's seat, wearing enormous black Jackie O sunglasses, drinking her usual frozen caramel macchiato through a straw.

I pulled up next to her. She grabbed another macchiato out of the cup holder and held it up to show me.

I flashed her a little smile and hit the garage door opener. I parked in the garage, got out of the car, and waved her in.

She jumped out of the car and did a quick jog into the garage.

"I talked to Mom when I was home after Christmas," she said, handing me the other frozen coffee. She pushed her sunglasses up on her head.

She was wearing black leather gloves, but my hands were bare and already cold. I handed it back to her.

"Can you carry this in?" I asked. "I have to grab some boxes." I wasn't ready to just dive right into it.

"Sure," she said.

I felt so clumsy, trying to stack boxes to get as many as possible in the house in one trip. Even without looking, I could feel her standing there watching me.

"Well, I'm sorry," she said finally, gulping down some more of her drink. "She told me about the check."

"She did?" I kicked the back door of the car closed and gestured to Jane to open the door to the kitchen for me.

"Peter made me ask her." She balanced her drink in the crook of her arm while she opened the door.

"Really?" I pulled the boxes through the door and dumped them on the kitchen floor.

"She said it was money she'd been saving for you, over the years. So you'd have a nest egg. She said it was a nice thing. But then I asked her if maybe the timing of her giving it to you was a little too convenient. Like maybe even though she'd meant it as something nice, she used it to let you think– Oh, Van, I'm so sorry." She handed me my drink. Her eyes were wet. "I asked her and she just got quiet. Then she asked me if I liked the hotel she picked for us in Naples. And you know her. That's the closest she's ever going to come to admitting she did something wrong." She kept taking sips though the straw. "I hate to think– She shouldn't have done that."

"It's okay," I said. "I mean, if you think about it, it's a really stupid thing to complain about. Damnit, Diane gave me a huge check."

"Don't!" she said. "Don't play it off like it's okay. It's not okay for her to treat you like that."

"What am I going to do about it?"

"Well, don't stay away from us," Janie said, "for starters." She pulled her gloves off with her teeth and dropped them on the counter.

"I already spent a lot of the money." I felt like a little kid who couldn't manage to save her allowance.

"Van, you deserve that money. You earned it. And regardless of how she used it, she wanted you to have it. I can't think–I know it couldn't have been easy." She looked at her shoes. She had a salt stain on her left shoe, and she rubbed it up against the back of her left leg. "I've thought about it a lot. I mean, your mom got paid to take care of us." She stopped looking at her shoes and looked at me. "You didn't."

"It's not like I was taking care of anything. My mom did all the work."

"You took care of me." As soon as she said it, tears as big as marbles rolled down her face.

"No, I didn't."

"Yes, you did. You made me brave. You made it okay to be me. To quit ballet. To be a Girl Scout. To wear a bikini. To go to Brown. To study art history."

"You did those things," I said.

"But I never would have. I never would have deviated from the Grand Driscoll Plan." She laughed. "Dad didn't want me selling Thin Mints. He wanted me dancing in some ballet troupe at Harvard." She wrapped her arms around me and rested her chin on my shoulder. "I need you. I can't dance for shit."

She was so unnatural when she cursed. I laughed and hugged her back.

"You're family," she said.

We stepped back from each other, but she held on to my arms.

"I'm not having Easter dinner with Diane or anything," I said.

"Okay," she said, laughing. "I'm not either." She started working on her shoe again. "Hey, where's your dog?"

"He's spending the day at the new house with Louis, the guy I'm buying the house from, so I can get some work done."

"Pete said you were buying a house!" She leaned up against the kitchen counter and crossed her legs

I was curious as to whether or not Pete told her about his drunken night and our trips to the vet, but I wasn't going worry about it. That was between him and Janie and I didn't need to get in the middle of it.

"That's fantastic," she said. "What's the house like?"

"It's going to need a lot of work. It's kind of ugly," I said, cringing at the thought of showing Janie the sewing room with the anchors everywhere and the orange and green wall. "I'm going to have to paint and maybe get new kitchen cabinets eventually."

"That's so grown-up." She wrinkled her nose at me and smiled her little-kid smile. "You're a big old grown-up, Van." She reached out and poked me in the ribs.

"You and Pete bought a house," I said. "It's no different."

"Pete's dad bought it for us," she said. "We didn't even pick it out. It just appeared."

"Your mom basically bought my house for me."

"No, she didn't." She waved the idea away with her hand. "This is big, Vannie. You have your own house." She stood up from the counter and walked into the living room. "Can I help you pack?"

"Have you ever packed anything?" I asked. "Do you even know how to pack?"

"Teach me," she said, shaking her head and smiling.

"Freak." I stuck my tongue out at her and went to grab a box.

"So what are you taking?" She leaned back on her heel and surveyed the living room.

"What do you mean?"

"What's coming with you?"

I hadn't thought about not taking everything. I guess it didn't make a lot of sense to take my makeshift furniture. It wasn't worth hauling my cinder-block-and-plank bookshelves to the new house. It probably wasn't worth taking the blue-and-white-checked couch either. I bought it at a yard sale years ago, and it sagged so badly that if you sat right in the middle, your knees ended up pressed to your chest. But I didn't know what I'd do without the couch, and I had way too many books to leave the bookshelf behind.

"I guess it's all coming," I said. "I don't have any other furniture yet."

"Yes, you do," Janie said, smirking.

"I do?"

"You have a whole carriage house full." Her smile got wide and toothy.

"I couldn't."

"You could." She swatted my arm. "And you should, Van. It's your stuff."

"It's mostly my mom's stuff."

"Well, it's more yours than it is my mom's. You should have Nat's stuff."

I thought about the coffee table my mom and I made together. She painted white hearts on my cheeks and then we couldn't wash them off. I spent the rest of the weekend with cold cream smeared all over my face. By the time we got all the paint off, my cheeks were bright red.

I wanted that coffee table, and I wanted the couch that had pizza sauce stains on every side of every cushion, and I wanted our collection of romance novels.

But I didn't want to see Diane. I didn't want to have to ask her for it.

Janie must have read my face, because she said, "We'll go get it together." She reached out and hugged me. "We'll be a united front. She'll have to behave." She laughed. "Or at least we'll have each other if she doesn't."

Chapter Forty-three

Louis volunteered to take Joe, and I rented a truck for the trip. Janie showed up bright and early with a travel mug of coffee in one hand and a blue leather Marc Jacobs weekend bag in the other. She was overly chipper for six AM on a Saturday, and I was about ready to shove her in the back of the truck, until she went out to her car and came back with a second travel mug full of coffee for me.

"Did you think I was going to ride in that truck with you if you didn't have coffee?" she said, shaking her head. "I'm not crazy."

The seats in the rental truck were too hard and too slippery, and the shocks were shot. I kept waiting for Janie to complain, but she didn't. She just held on tight to the handle on the door and fiddled with the heater. The heater dial was broken, so it only had two settings, full blast and off. Full blast was like being in an airplane hangar with the jets on. We turned it on periodically to warm up the cab, so we could talk in between blasts.

"This was all they had left," I said. I didn't mention that I'd never driven anything so big before, and I was terrified any time I had to back up or turn. I didn't think Janie needed to lose confidence in my abilities while she was stuck in a rickety death trap with me.

"It's okay," she said. "It's part of the adventure."

"Who are you, and what have you done with Janie?"

"Who are you, and what have you done with Van?" she said, laughing. "You're driving a truck. Seriously."

It started to snow just before we hit Syracuse. I turned the wipers on and they squeaked loud enough to make my teeth itch.

"From bad to worse," Janie said, gleefully. Her stainless steel coffee mug was rattling in the cup holder.

"What's with you?" I said. "You're wearing jeans. You're not complaining about the truck. You didn't wipe the seat down with antibacterial wipes before you sat down."

"I'm on a road trip with my best friend," she said, smiling. "I've never done this kind of stuff." She held on to her coffee mug to steady it and the rattling stopped.

"You've driven back and forth from Chappaqua a gazillion times," I said.

"But alone, or with Peter, not with you. Peter never wants to stop at dive diners or weird souvenir shops, and I'm always scared to when I'm by myself. I used to watch you and Nat pack up her old Rabbit with beach chairs and the cooler and laundry baskets full of clothes instead of suitcases, and I always wished I could go with you. You came back with the best stories and those weird magnets. When we went on vacation, I was stuck in boring hotels and boring museums. We had excursions. You and Nat had adventures."

She picked up her coffee mug and took a sip just as we hit a pothole. Half the coffee spilled in her lap.

"You've been christened," I said, handing her the roll of paper towels I'd tucked next to the driver's seat. My mom and I never left home without a roll of paper towels in the car. "You're officially a road warrior."

Janie laughed and mopped up the mess. She didn't say a word about her ruined shirt or her wet jeans.

When we got to Syracuse, I took I-81 to Route 17 instead of staying on the interstate, so we could have lunch at the diner in Roscoe and drive through the Catskills, and it would feel like more of a road trip.

Chapter Forty-four

I was fine for most of the drive. Janie told me about the gondola ride in Venice and visiting the Ponte Vecchio in Florence. I confessed to her that I'd bought Joe by accident, and we laughed so hard we could barely breathe. These were the best parts of the old Janie—the way we were when we were kids—but we were building something new.

When we merged onto the Saw Mill River Parkway, I felt my heart beat in my stomach and I started to sweat, even though we hadn't turned the heat on in ages.

"You look green, Van," Janie said. "Are you getting carsick?"

"I think I'm getting Diane-sick."

"Me too, a little," she said.

"Really?"

"Don't act so surprised. You know how she is. And you haven't been around her much since—since Nat." She shook her head. "She hasn't handled it well. She's like the same, but more so, if that makes any sense."

It made perfect sense. My mother was Diane's balance. Without her, it was hard to know where Diane was coming from.

"How are you supposed to handle it well?" I asked, thinking about all the times I drank too much, or cried so hard my eyes were swollen shut the next morning.

"I don't know," Janie said. "Maybe you're supposed to go to one of those groups where you sit in a circle and talk about your feelings."

"Ha," I said. "I can see Diane sitting there, smoking like a fiend, telling everyone they should just get over it, and for God's sake get a decent haircut!"

Janie laughed. "I can totally picture it," she said. "Some woman is crying because her husband left her, and Mom would tell her he left because she isn't fooling anyone with those knockoff designer shoes."

We were so busy laughing at the idea of Diane in group therapy that we breezed through town and made it to the Driscolls' house without any major panic attacks or breakdowns. But when we drove up the driveway and parked the truck in front of the carriage house, my stomach started doing jumping jacks.

"What if she's in there?" I asked.

"It'll be fine," Janie said, but she didn't sound confident.

"I don't want to see her." I looked out the window, searching for signs of her.

"Do you want me to go in first?"

"No! If you go in alone, you're leaving me out here, and if I'm out here alone, she could come out here and you won't—"

"This is silly," Janie said. "She's not the boogeyman." But she wasn't in any hurry to get out of the truck either. She stayed in her seat, staring out the front window until I got out of the truck.

The snow on the stairs wasn't shoveled, and there were footprints going up the stairs. Triangles with tiny circles following behind, punctuating each step. A set of triangles pointed up and a set pointed back down. Diane was probably gone. But she could have been in the carriage house when it snowed, left, and come back.

I got my key out and ready to go. I could picture her having the locks changed, so I'd have to go pound on the door to the main house; but thankfully, when I slid my key into the lock and turned it, it clicked open.

I pushed the door open. The air felt thick, like the weight of Diane's stale cigarette smoke could push us back out the door. Janie made a face.

The bathroom door was closed, and there was a sliver of light leaking out the bottom of the door. The shower was running.

"She's here," I said.

"Mom?" Janie said.

"Shhh!"

"Van, it's not like we can get all this furniture out of here before she gets out of the shower. And she knows we're coming anyway."

"Why is she showering here?" I asked.

"I don't know," Janie said.

"She's your mother."

"That doesn't mean I understand even the slightest bit of anything she does." Janie ran her hand along the back of the couch. "Your mom is the only one who ever did."

There were half-drunk glasses of bourbon doing service as ashtrays, and empty Camel boxes and magazines everywhere.

I walked into my mom's room. The bed was slept in. There was another bourbon-glass ashtray on the nightstand. I ran my hand over the indent in the bed and smoothed out the sheets. The pillowcase was spotted with mascara stains like a watercolor. Wads of tissues nested next to the pillow.

"Oh my God!" Janie yelled from the kitchen. "Look what's on the fridge."

I ran into the kitchen. Janie was holding up the fluorescent pink sombrero magnet. "I wondered where that ended up," she said.

We heard the water shut off. Janie stiffened.

"It'll be a while," I said. "She's got to know we're here. And she's not coming out until she's done her hair." Still, I was nervous. I mean, she was going to come out eventually. And what then? Would we fight? Would we cry? Would we have it all out? Would she tell me I couldn't take my mom's stuff after all? Would she ask for her money back?

We heard the loud whir of my mother's old hair dryer. We stood in the kitchen and watched the bathroom door, like we were waiting for a bear to come out of a cave. Janie got herself a glass of water and sipped it slowly. "It's silly that we're so nervous," she said. "What's she going to do, anyway? We're adults. We can handle this." She wasn't very convincing.

Janie opened the junk drawer and we sorted through all the twist ties, expired coupons, plastic army men, and cereal box prizes that had been thrown in there over the years.

We were laughing over a coupon for Smurf-Berry Crunch that expired in 1985 when Diane came out of the bathroom wearing a beige silk robe. Every hair on her head was in its proper place and she had a full face of makeup on.

"Get me a drink, Van, will you?" she said, like nothing had ever happened.

I looked at Janie. Her eyes were wide. She raised her eyebrows at me. I shook my head and went to pour Diane a bourbon.

Diane sat down on the couch and pulled a cigarette and lighter from her stash under the coffee table.

"Could you at least open a window or something?" Janie said.

"It's winter," Diane said, lighting up.

"Secondhand smoke kills, Mom."

"So does old age," Diane said, flatly, "but people don't quit having birthdays."

Janie rolled her eyes and opened the window.

"There's a pizza in the fridge," Diane said. "And I've got a stack of movies. John Cusack this time."

She pointed to a stack of DVDs by the television. *Better Off Dead*, *Say Anything . . .*, *The Journey of Natty Gann*, *True Colors*, and *Grosse Pointe Blank*.

My mom used to order the pizza and pick the movies. We hadn't had a movie night since my mom went to the hospital for the last time. We'd all crowded around my mom's hospital bed in those sticky pink vinyl chairs and watched a John Hughes marathon on TBS. She couldn't eat solid foods anymore, but she had Janie go down to the hospital cafeteria to get pizza for the rest of us. "So it's more authentic," she said. There was nothing authentic about our last movie night. She had tubes going in and out of her from every angle. Her breathing sounded like Darth Vader's.

I wondered if Diane's insistence on us having a movie night again was her way of trying to erase the last one. I thought maybe I needed to do that too. So we sat down and had a movie night like everything was fine. Janie seemed to be resigned to going along with it too.

We made it through the early Cusacks, but Janie fell asleep on the couch right in the middle of *True Colors*, sometime around when John Cusack chokes James Spader. I went into my old bedroom and got my comforter for her. She didn't even move when I draped it over her, like always. Janie was always the first one to fall asleep when she and Diane came over to watch movies.

"You've always been good at looking out for her," Diane said, patting the seat next to her.

I sat down. She lit a cigarette for me.

"I only ever smoke with you," I said, taking it from her. I leaned back on the couch and put my feet on the coffee table.

"As much as Nat was a good influence on Janie, I was an awful influence on you, huh?" she said, laughing.

"No, not at all," I said, sarcastically, shaking my head. I smiled at her.

We sat there, our heads resting on the back of the couch, trying to blow smoke rings. Diane could make perfect Os, but I never could. We didn't talk for a long time, and we didn't look at each other. It was like we were testing the waters, figuring out if it could be okay to be together in the same space again.

"I miss her so much," Diane said, finally. "I didn't even know you could miss a person this much."

"I know," I said. My tears welled up fast and dripped from the corners of my eyes into my hair.

Diane sniffed. "Right here," she said, "with you and Nat and Janie, this was my world." She flicked her cigarette into a watery bourbon glass on the coffee table and picked up her current drink. "I never fit in Charles's world the right way. Those women at the club, judging, picking apart every little thing. I didn't fit there. I still don't. With Nat, I fit."

I remembered Diane, lying on my mom's hospital bed, my mom cradled in her arms. My mom was so small. She was just bones and skin as fragile as wet tissue paper, but she looked so peaceful.

I'd just left the room for a minute. After days of sitting with my mom, holding her hand, letting Diane and Janie bring me food, taking sponge baths in the sink in the hospital room, I'd gone for a walk with Janie. I needed some air. And when we came back, my mom was gone. I hated Diane so much for that. For being the one who held her. For being the one who spent those last moments with her. But maybe my mom was waiting for me to leave. Maybe she didn't want to do that to me, to die on my watch. Maybe she was protecting me. Maybe Diane was too.

I looked over at Diane. She looked harder than she used to. Her jaw was tight. Her eyes were sad. I wondered if she'd laughed, really laughed, since my mother died.

The two of them used to get going and they'd be red-faced, tears streaming down their faces. You couldn't understand a word they were saying, but you got the feeling they could still understand each other. It was one of my favorite sounds. I loved lying in bed, listening to them out in the living room, laughing.

"Nat was so strong, leaving your father, going out on her own," Diane said, taking a sip of her drink. "I married Charles because I thought I had to. My parents couldn't afford for me to finish college. I wasn't going to get to go back, and I didn't feel like there was anything out there for me. Charles showed up at the club and he was older and ready to get married. His parents hated me, but once I got pregnant, it was all said and done and they just had to get over it." She swirled her glass around in her hand, watching the bourbon make a whirlpool.

"You're strong," I said. "My mom always said you were a force to be reckoned with." I felt like we were talking like two adults, like it was the first time we ever had.

"I made the best of what I had to work with, maybe," Diane said. "But I always wondered who I could have been if I'd had the courage to do it on my own like Nat. She was a far better person than I could ever be."

She used the sleeve of her robe to wipe her eyes. I hadn't realized she'd been crying.

"That's why I saved that money for you," she said. "A few stocks, some savings bonds. A little here, and a little there, so Charles wouldn't notice."

"Why did you tell me it was life insurance money?"

"I didn't want you to feel like you owed me anything, and I wasn't sure you'd take it if I told you the truth," she said. "I didn't want you to be like me. I wanted you to finish school. I wanted you to find someone you love. I didn't want you to feel trapped, because you grew up here, around money, and maybe you'd think it was easier to just marry someone who could take care of you." She looked over at me. Her cheeks were wet. "I didn't want to see that fire and independence die. That part of you is all Nat, and I've already lost enough of her."

"Thank you, Diane," I said, choking back tears. "Thank you."

She wiped her cheeks and took a deep breath. "Even though I saved that money for you for the right reasons, maybe I didn't give it to you at the right time. I can see why you might be mad and maybe you should be." She sniffed.

It was the closest thing to an apology I'd ever heard Diane give to anyone.

"You gave me my picture back," I said. "I thought you were done with me."

She looked at me, mouth open. "I found it in my purse and thought you'd get a kick out of it. It wasn't—" She took a deep breath. "I am not now, nor will I ever be, done with you, Savannah Leone. I told Nat I'd take care of you, so you're stuck with me, and there's not a damn thing you can do about it."

I smiled.

She drank the last dregs of her drink. "Go to bed," she said, suddenly composed again. "I called movers to load up the truck for you. They'll be here at eight." She got up, poured herself another bourbon, walked into my mom's room, and closed the door.

I got up and went to bed in my old bedroom for the very last time. I lay there in my old flannel sheets and wished I could hear my mom and Diane laughing in the living room.

Chapter Forty-five

Diane was gone before we woke up. She'd managed to leave without waking Janie. She'd even left us a plate of bagels and a note: *Headed out for the day. Have a safe trip. D. P.S.: Thought you might need a reminder of what a real bagel tastes like.*

I studied the note while Janie was in the shower. I went into my mom's bedroom and sat on the bed, smoothing out the wrinkles in the pillowcase. For a moment I thought, I can't take this away from her. Diane was using this place like her own secret clubhouse. Maybe she needed it.

I pulled my mom's quilt over my lap. It was the quilt I hid under when I was scared of lightning, that helped make a fort in the living room, that my mom bought with her first month's paycheck. I realized that I couldn't let Diane take this from me. And I knew she didn't want to.

I took the quilt. I left the sheets. I wadded them up and left them in the clothes hamper. I took the bed. I thought maybe I'd put it in the room with all the anchors.

I took the nightstand. In the top drawer, there was a diary, pink and shiny with a little gold lock, like a child's. There were pill bottles and letters, a few empty paper cups, receipts, slips of paper, and a copy of *Tuesdays with Morrie* that I'm sure Diane bought for her. I shoved a throw pillow in the drawer to keep everything from moving around. I didn't want to go through my mother's nightstand too carefully. It didn't seem right. Maybe someday, with a bottle of wine and some Joni Mitchell, and incense burning like it was a ritual, but I couldn't go through it like it was just packing.

I went into the kitchen and pulled out the glasses and dishes I wanted to take, leaving them on the counter to give Janie something to do. She wrapped them in newspaper and packed them while I went through my mom's closet. I heard something break in the kitchen while I was sorting through sweaters, but I didn't feel like checking on what it was. None of our dishes ever matched anyway, and if it was something important, like one of the set of the Dr. Seuss juice glasses we had to eat gobs of jelly for months to collect, I didn't want to know about it.

I took the bigger, bulkier sweaters that would fit me, and left the smaller ones that would fit Diane. I don't know why. I couldn't imagine leaving the house in one of my mother's sweaters, trying to recognize her scent hiding deep in the fibers, or worse, realizing it had been washed away completely, and I couldn't picture Diane wearing a cotton roll-neck sweater from The Gap, but I felt like I needed to divvy them up between us.

I slipped my mom's Boston records into the bottom of the box and piled sweaters over them so Janie wouldn't see. She and Diane always made fun of my mom and me for listening to Boston. I folded the tops of the sweater box in on itself to close it.

"This one is done," I said, taking it out into the living room and putting it in the pile with the rest of the things I was taking.

"It's weird that she didn't say good-bye," Janie said.

"I feel bad taking everything from her," I said.

"It's your stuff," she said, shoving some extra newspaper in the box with the glasses. She wrote *Fragile* on the side with one of my old scented markers. "Don't feel bad. If she had a problem with it, she wouldn't have hired guys to help us move this stuff."

Janie moved on to the bookshelves. I grabbed an empty box and went into the bathroom. I left the towels, except for the big ratty beach ones. I took the shower curtain with the purple embroidered fish and orange bubbles. I left the bath mat; I couldn't remember it ever being ours anyway.

I'd taken almost everything from my room a little bit at a time over the years, so there wasn't much left. I took the posters off the walls. The blue poster putty was dried out and it cracked off, leaving oily spots on the walls. I threw out the poster of a dolphin jumping over a rainbow into the ocean and the *Hang in There* kitty. I kept my U2 poster and the one of Basquiat and Andy Warhol in boxing gloves and shiny shorts, even though I knew I'd never hang them up again. I rolled them up and wrapped a hair elastic around them.

I packed the record player and the answering machine. I pulled the box of Christmas ornaments out of the crawl space. When Janie wasn't looking, I snuck the sombrero magnet into her purse.

Janie finished packing the romance novels. We left the magazines in the baskets under the coffee table. Later, the movers took the coffee table and the couch, and the baskets were all that was left in the living room.

It looked so small. My mom and I had lived in this space with just three rooms and a bathroom, and it had never felt small until now.

When the movers had loaded up everything, Janie came over and hugged me. "It'll never be the same again," she said.

"It already wasn't," I said.

"What do you think Mom will do with it?" she said.

"Meditation room," I said, laughing. I could picture Diane in a black leotard and high heels, sitting cross-legged on a pillow with her eyes closed, a drink in one hand and a cigarette in the other.

"Yoga studio," Janie said.

"What did she call it when my mom took that yoga class that time?" I asked.

"I believe she said it was 'new age hippie communist bullshit,'" Janie said, laughing.

"How is yoga communist?"

"Who knows," Janie said. "She just says things. They don't always make sense." She stepped out into the middle of the room. "You know what I would do here?"

"What?"

"I'd leave it just like this so I could come up here and do cartwheels." She raised her arms and her right leg and jumped into a lopsided cartwheel.

I joined her. We did clumsy cartwheels until our wrists hurt and we were laughing so hard we couldn't get up again.

We lay on the floor next to each other and stared up at the skylights. I remembered lying on the rug, coloring with Janie when we were kids. She always stayed in the lines, and I never did.

Janie kicked me lightly on the side of my leg. I looked at her. She said, "Don't you ever, ever stay away from me." She looked over at me. "No matter what, okay? If someone makes you an offer, I'll double it." She was laughing and crying at the same time.

"This could work out well for me," I said, kicking her back.

"I need you," she said.

"I know. Me too."

"You need you, too?" she asked, leaning her head on my shoulder.

"Yes," I said. "Desperately." I leaned my head on top of her head. "And you."

We lay there for a while longer without saying anything. I was soaking it all in, and I think she was too. I was trying to memorize the way the light looked on the floor, and the way the rug felt against my arms.

Janie got up and said she had to get something at the main house, but I think she was just trying to give me a little room to say my good-byes.

I closed my eyes and tried to imagine that my mom was there too, but she just felt farther away. I thought about what Diane said about fire and independence. And I thought about all the nights my mom and I stayed up late with mugs of hot chocolate, blasting Boston and playing board games, all the inside jokes and the crazy craft days, and crawling into bed with her when there was a bad thunderstorm; none of that was here. It happened here, but it was gone. All I could do was take her stuff and the things she taught me and the things I remembered about her, and try to do my best with them. I'd lost Alex, but I had a life to go home to. It was small, and it was simple, but it was a start. I had my freelance work and my new house. I had Peter and Janie, and Agnes, and Louis, and, of course, I had Joe. My mom would have been happy for me. I think she would have been proud of the way I was finally learning to carry on without her. And she would have loved Joe.

I got up and walked around the carriage house apartment, running my hand along the bookcase, and looking out the window of my bedroom one last time.

I went into the kitchen and washed Diane's glasses out by hand with lots of soap, rinsing all the cigarettes into the garbage disposal. I lined up the glasses upside down on a dish towel on the counter next to the sink.

I went into my mom's closet and stepped up on the shoe rack to reach the back of the very top shelf. I pulled down the carton of cigarettes my mom kept in secret so Diane would never run out in a crisis. I grabbed the auxiliary bourbon from behind the dishwasher detergent under the kitchen sink. I left the bottle and the cigarettes next to the glasses on the counter.

I found my purse and got my keys out. Using another key, I pried the ring apart so I could get the carriage house key off. It was my first key; all the other keys on the ring had come after. I knew Diane would let me keep it, but I was ready to leave it behind. I placed it on the counter with the rest of my offering.

There were probably more things I could have packed up, but I was done. I closed the door without doing a final scan of things and went to find Janie.

Chapter Forty-six

Janie wanted to drive back, and against my better judgment, I let her. She ground the gears and drove ten miles under the speed limit for the entire trip, but she was so excited to be driving a truck that I didn't have the heart to tell her to pull over so we could switch.

I watched for frozen waterfalls striping the layers of rock on either side of the highway. Sometimes they ran directly down the grooves the dynamite left when they'd blasted to make the road.

There was a deer trail running alongside the highway. I watched it run up and down the hills we drove past until it disappeared into some shrubs.

We were about an hour and a half late getting back to the condo. Peter and Agnes were already there, ready to help load the rest of my things in the truck so we could take everything over to the new house.

Well, Peter was ready to help. Agnes said she was there to supervise, which for the most part involved telling us to be careful ten times in a row and saying, "Lift with your legs, dear," any time anyone picked up something that looked even remotely heavy. Still, it was nice to have her there.

I thought when we got to my new house there would be a few papers to sign and then we'd start moving in, but the four of us walked into a crowd of strangers standing in my new living room. Louis had turned it into an event, inviting the whole neighborhood.

"Vannah!" Louis yelled when he saw us kicking off our shoes to add to the collection at the front door. "Welcome home!" He gave me a big hug and a kiss on both cheeks. "Who are your friends?"

I introduced him to Janie, Peter, and Agnes, and he hugged all three of them, one at a time. None of them knew what to make of him. Peter smirked, Janie stared at him wide-eyed, and Agnes fanned herself with her gloves.

"Come in! Come in! Eat!" Louis shooed us into the kitchen. His furniture was already packed up and moved out, so he'd laid out a full spread, buffet-style, in big foil trays on the kitchen counter. There were three different pasta dishes, lunch meat, rolls, and a huge bowl of roasted red peppers in oil.

"Where's Joe?" I asked.

"Oh, he's in the yard," Louis said, smiling. "That is a dog who loves his yard."

I went out through the garage and opened the door to the backyard. Joe was sitting in front of the toolshed, wagging his tail. His big pink tongue was hanging out of his mouth and his head was cocked to the side. I had planned to just let him in since I wasn't wearing shoes, but I was so happy to see him that I ran out into the yard in my socks. He barked when he saw me, ran over at full speed, and knocked me on my ass. His whole body was wagging. He put his paws on my shoulders and licked my face until I was drenched. "I missed you, buddy!" I said, laughing and wiping my face with my sleeve.

When I looked up, Alex was walking out from behind the toolshed with a rake in one hand and a Frisbee in the other. "It was on the roof." He gestured to the toolshed with the rake. He looked down at his boots and back at me. "Hi," he said. Joe bounded over to Alex, grabbed the Frisbee from his hand, and ran to the far corner of the yard to chew it.

"Hi," I said.

Alex leaned the rake against the house, offered me his hand, and helped me up.

He kept holding my hand. "I'm sorry," he said. He took a deep breath and talked slowly. "I don't want to live in a fucking bubble, and I know you're worth it, and I'm sorry. And all of that sounded a lot better when I said it to myself on the way over." He let go of my hand. "My ex-wife swore she didn't, but really she left me for this other guy. And until it happened, I was oblivious. She hid it and I didn't go looking. It wasn't the cause, it was the symptom, I know, but it hurt. Badly." He sighed. "I felt like I was in the dark with you, and it scared me. I should have just talked to you about it. I just didn't think I could do this again, but that's not fair because you're not her. You're amazing, and beautiful, and I can't stop thinking about you, and I realized, I can't not do this. I can't walk away from you, because honestly, from the first time I met you—" He paused and looked at me. His eyes were wide and his eyebrows made round arches. "I mean, I've never met anyone like you, Van."

"You mean that in a good way, right?" I asked, smiling.

His face softened and his voice got quiet. "In a very good way," he said.

I slid my arms around his neck and kissed him hard.

He wrapped his arms around my waist and picked me up so my feet weren't touching the pavement. "You're not wearing shoes," he said.

"My feet are freezing," I said, laughing.

Alex swung me around and carried me inside with my feet dangling just above the ground. Joe followed behind us.

Janie was standing in the kitchen next to Louis, who was spooning more food onto a paper plate than she probably ate in a week.

"You need to eat! There's no meat on these bones! Peppers, do you like peppers?" he asked her, stopping with the spoon in midair when he saw

Alex carrying me into the kitchen. "Oh, this is what I like to see!" His eyes filled with tears. "The people I love are in love," he said to Janie, handing her the plate.

Alex put me down and Louis hugged both of us at the same time. "You make an old man happy," Louis said, putting his hand over his heart.

After everyone ate, Louis and I signed the papers for the house. When we were done, Louis threw his hands up in the air. "That is that!" he said. Everyone clapped. A few of the women were crying. A tall man, about Louis's age, wearing a tweed cap, shoved his fingers in his mouth and whistled.

Louis went into the cupboard and pulled out a jar that looked like it was filled with water. He strained for a minute before the lid twisted open and then poured it into tiny cordial glasses. He handed them out to me, Alex, and the bewildered attorney. It smelled like old socks.

"Grappa," Louis said. "Puts hair on your chest."

"Louis's cousin makes it," Alex said, squeezing my hand.

"To Vannah!" Louis raised his tiny glass toward us. "The glasses, I leave to you. May you use them in good health."

We clinked our glasses together. Some of the grappa spilled on my finger and got in a crack at the cuticle. It stung like all hell. I sucked on my finger while Louis drank. Alex dumped his into the sink while Louis was busy pouring for the rest of his guests.

Alex and Peter somehow got into a discussion about local animal husbandry laws. And once Peter got going on anything legal there was no stopping him. I gave Alex a sympathetic smile and did the rounds to meet my new neighbors. Mr. and Mrs. Whitehall lived across the street. They had nine children who were all grown up. Mrs. McCairn was a widow who had dressed in all black for twenty-nine years. Mr. Hewn had an eye patch like a pirate. Ms. Murphy preferred to be called Lenore and called Louis "Louie." And Mr. and Mrs. Caldwell wore matching Buffalo Bills jogging suits with bright white sneakers.

They stayed for hours. They ate and drank and asked questions that made me blush and said things like, "We're so happy our Alex has found such a nice girl." They moved on to coffee and crumb cake, requested decaf, and stirred in Sweet'N Low packets Louis must have nabbed from a restaurant.

And then the house was mine. They filed out one by one, leaving sloppy kisses on my cheek and slapping Louis on the back.

When Peter and Janie left, Janie said, "I'll come over tomorrow and help you unpack." She looked at Alex and then back at me. "But not too early, I promise."

Agnes and Louis were the last to go. Somehow he'd talked her into giving him a ride to Alex's house, where he was staying until he moved to Florida.

"Ah, bella!" Louis put both hands on my cheeks. "You be happy here." It was a royal decree. He patted my shoulders and walked out the door like he'd made it so.

Agnes hugged me good-bye. "That Louis is something," she whispered breathlessly in my ear.

Alex shut the door behind them and grinned.

"Hey," he said. "I got something for you."

"Is it a pony? I've always wanted a pony."

"Yes," Alex said, nodding his head and grinning. "It's a pony. You're totally zoned for ponies here, I think."

"I'm sure you can always ask Peter about it," I said.

Alex laughed. "He sure can talk," he said, "but he and Janie are really nice."

"They're amazing," I said. "They're good friends."

Alex went out to the garage and came back with a paint can and two brushes. "I know how you feel about orange, so I thought we could change things up." He pulled a Swiss Army knife out of his pocket and pried the can open.

"Close your eyes," he said, waiting to pick up the lid so I couldn't see the color.

I closed my eyes and put my hands over my face.

I heard a soft swish.

"Okay."

Alex had painted the outline of a heart on the wall in a beautiful deep red.

"It's beautiful," I said. I gave him a little jab in his ribs. "Is this how you get the ladies, going around painting hearts on their walls? Did Louis tell you to do that?"

"Nope," Alex said, laughing, "I thought of it all myself." He filled in the heart with more paint. "Do you really like it?"

I wrapped my arms around his waist. "I love it."

"Really? You can tell me if you don't."

"I never would have picked it, but it's perfect. I would have picked white or something. Eggshell," I said, thinking about my blue wall disaster. "But that's so boring."

"It screamed you."

"Really?"

"Yeah. I was at Home Depot and the paint chip was just screaming and waving around. Savannah! Savannah!" Alex waved his hands around in my face.

"You're such a goofball," I said, smiling. "Eh, I'll keep you anyway."

"You better." He slipped his hand into my back pocket.

"So, I'm not very good at painting," I said, thinking of the messy bright blue wall in my condo.

"Well, that, my friend, is about to change." He handed me the paintbrush.

"Now?"

"It's easier to paint without furniture everywhere. We can move your stuff in later."

I ran out to the moving truck to get the record player and my mom's old records.

"Oh, this is a great album," Alex said, slipping *Don't Look Back* out of its sleeve as I cleared a space on the kitchen counter for the record player. "I love Boston."

"Me too," I said.

We put the record on. I hadn't listened to it in years, but I still knew every skip and pop in the vinyl.

Joe stole Alex's paintbrush and dripped paint all over the kitchen floor. We wiped it up, but we left a single paint paw print in the corner for posterity. And we laughed and painted and listened to Boston until the whole kitchen was a beautiful red.

Acknowledgments

To my wonderful agent, Rebecca Strauss, thank you for all your hard work, your wisdom, tenacity, patience, and fantastic sense of humor. Thank you for making my dream come true. And a huge thank-you, also, to Ian Polonsky, and everyone at McIntosh and Otis.

To my editor, Erika Imranyi, thank you for your fierce dedication to this book, every step of the way. Thank you to Brian Tart, Ava Kavyani, Christine Ball, and the fantastic team at Dutton for giving Van and Joe such a wonderful home. And thanks to Monica Benalcazar for designing a jacket that captures the essence of *Stay* so perfectly.

To my long-suffering writing group in all its incarnations: Joan Pedzich, Melanie Krebs, Jennifer DeVille, Keith Pedzich, Liz Valentine, Darby Knox, Erica Curtis, and Eric Brown. I don't have big enough words to thank you. You are my favorite writers.

Thanks to Neil Gordon for being awesome way beyond the need for exclamation points. To Corinne Bowen, thank you for being my fellow fiction writer in the "cubicle" next door. Your words and kindness amaze me.

To Michele Christiano, thank you for all of your support and sage advice.

Thank you to my kind and patient friends who sat down with a huge stack of rumpled papers and gave me constructive and critical feedback: Dash Hedgeman, Mindae Kadous, Rachel Chaffee, Kim Janczak, and Emily Brown. To Kristin Dezen, Brian Herzlinger, Bryan Hoerauf, Jen Bloom, Vince, MMC, and MOD, thank you for your support and your belief in me and my book. Thank you to Ben Fountain, for being so kind and generous.

To my beautiful and inspiring Ladies: Sarah Playtis (the best messy friend a girl could ask for), Julie Smith (thanks for letting me use the whole half!), Brenda Kirkwood, Lisa Malin, and Rainbow Heinrichs, thank you. Van and Janie wouldn't have such a deep and durable friendship if it weren't for you.

Thanks to Form Collective: J, Xtian, Chris, and Joe for the amazing Web work, and also for being so collective, and having great form. To Writers & Books, for making Rochester such a rich place to be a reader and writer. To Chris Sutton at Wergo, Inc., for keeping me strong and constantly reminding me of my successes. To Armanda and everyone at Made You Look, for providing such a wonderful oasis in the middle of Rochester. To Nick Tebrake, and everyone at The Kittle House. And to Dog Holiday, Eastridge Veterinary Hospital, Animal Emergency Services, Cornell Companion Animal Hospital, Wooftown Doggie Daycare, and the German Shepherd playgroup for keeping my good buddies happy, healthy, and active.

Thank you to The Greenists: Melissa, Mickey, NPW, A Free Man, Noelle, Made By Rachel, The Modern Gal, Stefanie, Dianne, Dingo, and especially Courtney Craig. To David Quilty at The Good Human for being my blogging guru, and to Vera Sweeny at I'm Not Obsessed for introducing me to the wonderful world of blogging. And thank you to all of my blog, Facebook, and Twitter friends for cheering me on along the way.

Sarah Freligh, thank you for starting it all with two little words, and giving me such a solid set of fiction tools. To Bill Waddell, for all the help, encouragement, and root beer. To Sarah, Bill, Mary Anne Donovan,

Jonathan Rich, James Lohrey, and MJ Iuppa, thank you for being such supportive, inspiring teachers and for continuing to include me in the community of creative people at St. John Fisher College. To Jack Hrkach, Barbara Anger, and Susannah Berryman, at Ithaca College, for teaching me how to create a character. To Marty Heresniak, for taking such an interest in how I learn. Thank you to Bea Matz, Beverly Lewis, and John Cuk. To Bira Rabushka, for creating an environment where creativity and kindness mattered above all else, and to all my teachers from NWCA, especially Ray Girardin, Jan Callner, Joan Thundhorst, Bobbie Bramson, Christine Kluge, Roger Baumann, Alysa Haas, and, of course, the incredible Joe Tomasini—thank you for being my village.

Thank you to the Larkins: Doug, Terry, Jacob, Amanda, Jason, Jackson, Emma, and especially Michele, for your endless encouragement and for letting me plaster the Larkin name on a book full of bad words.

Most important, Jeremy, thank you for your unwavering support, limitless love and patience, and for being even better than the man of my dreams. You made this all possible. And, special thanks to Ez, Stella, and, of course, my trusty dog, Argo.

About the Author

Allie Larkin lives in Rochester, New York, with her husband, their two German Shepherds, Argo and Stella, and a three-legged cat. She is the cofounder of TheGreenists.com, a site dedicated to helping readers take simple steps toward going green. *Stay* is her first novel.